WHEN SHE TEMPTS

A DARK MAFIA ROMANCE

GABRIELLE SANDS

THE FALLEN

THE FALLEN SERIES

When She Unravels

The story of Valentina & Damiano

Available Now

When She Tempts

The story of Martina & Giorgio

Available Now

When She Falls

The story of Gemma & Ras

Coming Summer 2023

To Charlotte Brontë, for giving us Jane Eyre and thus inspiring countless authors to lock up moody alphas with feisty heroines in remote castles.

CHAPTER 1

GIORGIO

THE SUN IS ALREADY low in the sky when my plane lands in Ibiza, but the scorching temperature hasn't begun its descent. Everyone at the airport appears to be barely awake. Given how things normally run here, it's somewhat surprising they don't just close the airport during siesta and tell everyone to go home and nap, but then again, if there's one thing Ibiza loves more than maintaining its reputation for being a worry-free paradise, it's money.

I meet De Rossi's driver in the arrivals lounge, and he takes me to the car. He's competent, clearly trained in defensive driving, but I'd prefer to be the one behind the wheel. I don't like being at anyone's mercy, let alone someone I've just met.

He eyes me in the rearview mirror when he thinks I'm not looking, but I notice it in my periphery. I notice *everything*. It's one of the skills that have kept me alive all these years.

Sometimes I still can't believe I'm thirty-three. It feels odd, like I'm living on borrowed time. I always thought I'd die young. I guess that's a pretty strange thing to think as a kid, but when you see boys only a few years older than you dying on the news every day, certain expectations are set.

In Secondigliano, the district of Naples where I was born and raised, optimism is a myth. The populace lives in collective apathy, knowing that each day brings the possibility of death, drug busts, or yet another tragic overdose of some twelve-year-old whose parents were both high on meth. Secondigliano is where most dreams die before they're born. If you're unlucky enough to have even a shred of ambition, there's only one path.

Become a man of the Camorra *sistema*.

I drag my hand over my trimmed beard. My cynicism is showing. I should probably try to keep it in check given the task at hand and its implications. It's not every day that everything you've ever wanted falls into your lap. I could at least attempt to enjoy it.

Like most men, I'm a single-minded creature, and there's been one thing that's kept me going through the years.

This one damn thing that I'd give up everything for.

Justice for my mother.

I've spent over a decade trying to figure out how I can get it without throwing everything into chaos, so I was surprised when De Rossi called me last night and unknowingly gave me the final piece of the puzzle.

A favor in exchange for keeping his sister, Martina, safe while he makes his bid to become the next don of the Casalesi clan.

A favor I know exactly how I'm going to redeem. De Rossi isn't going to like what I ask for, but his fatal flaw is that he's a man of his word. If I do my part, he'll do his.

Martina De Rossi might not know it yet, but she's about to acquire a shadow. I'm going to be watching her every move. Not one hair on her head will be harmed while she's with me, because I won't give De Rossi a single excuse to break our deal.

We pull into the driveway of the Spanish villa I visited less than two weeks ago, and through the windshield, I spot two guards flanking the front door, as well as a sniper pacing on the roof. Looks like De Rossi finally implemented the security measures I told him to put in place.

About fucking time.

If he'd done it sooner, he could have avoided that breach last week.

Tension creeps into my shoulders at the thought of what happened. Lazaro, the ex-husband of De Rossi's new wife, broke into the house and took Martina hostage. As if that girl hadn't been through enough already. This had been the second time Lazaro managed to get his hands on Martina, the first one being a few weeks prior during a trip she took to New York.

That's the kind of shit that's not going to happen on my watch.

I get out of the car and make my way to the door.

"Tell De Rossi that Napoletano is here to see him," I say to one of the uniformed guards.

The man eyes me through his sunglasses as he brings a walkie talkie to his mouth. A few moments later, he receives the go ahead and leads me inside.

We pass through the empty living area and take a turn down the hallway that leads to De Rossi's office. The house is strangely quiet. Where is his wife? She seems like the type who'd grill me before I leave with Martina to make sure the girl's in good hands—not that I need or give a crap about her approval. De Rossi asked me to do this for him because he knows I'm the best. I've been the Casalesi's security expert ever since Sal, the current don, brought me on over a decade ago—a move he'll deeply regret if things go my way.

A voice filters through the door, and the guard waves me in.

"Napoletano, have a seat," De Rossi says.

I sink into the leather chair across from him and take in the state of the office. It's a mess. There are papers everywhere, a few drawers pulled open, and two empty whiskey tumblers sit on the coffee table at my side.

It looks like things were sorted through and discarded in a rush. De Rossi's probably putting his affairs here in order before he leaves.

Despite the chaos around him, the man himself is composed. He and his sister have lived the past decade exiled in Ibiza, but by blood, they're Casalesi royalty. Before Sal murdered De Rossi's father, he was one of the most powerful dons the clan has ever had, and their grandfather is credited with leading the Casalesi to victory against the Nuova Camorra Organizzata back in the seventies. Despite Sal's best efforts, the De Rossi name is still muttered quietly over nightcaps with respect and admiration.

The same can't be said for my own name. De Rossi and I might buy our suits from the same tailor, but some days when I see myself in the mirror, I can't shake off the feeling that I'm wearing a costume. I still have the threadbare striped sweater I used to wear during the winters of my adolescence stuffed somewhere in the back of my closet. Before I got sucked into the vacuum of the *sistema*, I was a nobody. I suppose I'm a somebody now, yet no amount of achievements will wipe the subtle stink of lowborn blood off my lapel.

De Rossi pins me with a serious look and drags a hand over his silk tie.

"You dismissed the household staff?" I ask.

He nods. "Told them to leave while they can. A few hours ago, we received our first cocaine shipment from the Americans. We'll be in breach of Sal's contract with his suppliers —" he glimpses at his watch "—twenty-five hours from now, when we fail to pick up their weekly drop. As soon as word gets back to Sal, he'll catch onto what's happening."

Cut off Sal's drugs, then cut off the flow of money from Ibiza. It's a move that'll cause deep ripples in clan business and put the don's power into question.

It's a move that'll start a war.

Do I think Damiano is going to be the best don we've ever had? No. But he'll be far better than Sal.

Not to say that I was thinking of the clan's best interests when I agreed to support him. He's simply the most likely candidate to get the position, and I've grown tired of seeing Sal on his throne.

The wait's been long, and my patience isn't infinite.

Sal will pay for what he did to my mother, and then my wait will finally end.

"Vale and I will be leaving Ibiza tomorrow," De Rossi continues. "Some meetings are already lined up."

At the first sign of weakness, some of Sal's allies will turn on him. Our don isn't well liked by anyone with half a brain between their ears. Still, that leaves more than a few idiots who'll stay loyal, and unfortunately, they control a lot of manpower.

"The wife's coming with you?"

"She wouldn't have it any other way. While she's with me, I need to trust you'll keep my sister safe."

I hold back a sardonic laugh that threatens to spill past my lips. "You don't need to worry about Martina," I say, when what I really want to tell him is *I'm not you, stronzo.*

The fact that he's failed so badly at protecting her is embarrassing.

I mean, the situation in New York was unfortunate and perhaps hard to preempt, but what happened in his own home? An inexcusable shitshow.

It was pure negligence on Damiano's part. He was too wrapped up with his wife and his scheming to follow my instructions with appropriate diligence.

Why was Martina even allowed out of the house? Given the situation, she should have been confined to her room.

Annoyance pulses in my temple.

This island's made him too relaxed. He's forgotten how made men keep their women safe.

I haven't, though.

"How did Martina take the news about coming with me?"

De Rossi lets out an exhale that suggests she didn't take it well. "She's hard to read at the moment. The latest attack has left her in a bad place mentally."

I furrow my brows. "Explain."

"She's...not really there. I thought the wedding might cheer her up, but she just, I don't know, *existed* through it. She put on a smile when the situation demanded it, talked when spoken to, ate when food was served. She went through the motions, but that's it."

The girl nearly got killed in her own home, and De Rossi thought a party would make it all better? *Cazzo*, despite what he thinks of himself, he's definitely not winning brother of the year.

"Have you tried talking to her about what happened?" I ask.

His eyes narrow. "Of course we've tried talking to her. I've tried, Vale's tried, even Ras. One-word answers are all we get as soon as the topic comes up. I wish Lazaro was alive so that I could kill him a second time."

It was his wife who killed Lazaro, but I decide not to rub it in.

"What about having a doctor see her?"

"A shrink? I already offered. She refused."

"Who's in charge here, you or her?"

De Rossi huffs. "What do you want me to do? Put a gun to her head? She's not a mark. She's my sister. I can't force her to talk to someone if she doesn't want to talk."

"The change of scenery will be good for her."

"I hope so." He looks up at the ceiling and exhales a long breath. "I know she never stopped feeling guilty about what happened to her friend, Imogen. I've told her it's not her fault a million times, but I haven't been able to get through to her. Vale told me she thought Mari was starting to let go of it, but then Lazaro appeared again and dragged her right back down to that dark place."

No fucking shit. Martina got away from Lazaro in New York, but her friend wasn't so lucky. Survivor's guilt can destroy someone from the inside out if it's not properly dealt with.

I clench my jaw. This is a problem. How bad is she? I can protect Martina from external threats, but unless I handcuff myself to her, I'm not going to be able to keep her safe from herself. I have to know she's not going to slit her wrists as soon as I leave her alone.

An unpleasant sensation spreads through my chest at that thought. I don't know the girl, but she seems like a nice kid. The idea of her being so down on herself... It's not right. I've got to get her to snap out of it. Do something to get her spirits up.

Plus, she needs someone to take control of her situation, since she's clearly incapable of getting out of it herself. And by someone, I mean me.

After all, Damiano needs to focus on the task at hand—outsmarting Sal and his cronies—which means the quicker I can take Martina off his mind, the better.

"Are you going to tell me where you're taking her?" he asks.

"Better not. The less people know, the better." My gaze slides to the hidden camera placed on the bookshelf just above De Rossi's shoulder.

He notices what I'm looking at and makes an incredulous sound. "How are you able to spot it so quickly?"

"I know what to look for. Tell me that's not connected to the Internet."

"Local network only, just like you said."

"Good. Martina will be somewhere safe, and I'll be keeping a close eye on her."

De Rossi rises, grabs two clean glasses off a shelf, and pours us a finger of whiskey each. "I'm not sure being around you won't just worsen her mood," he jokes, handing me the drink. "Maybe practice smiling before you meet her. She's not used to your sour face."

"She'll be fine if she's managed to live with yours."

He lets out a low chuckle and tips his glass at me. "To change. The only constant in our world."

"To change."

I throw back my whiskey and check the time. "We should be leaving soon."

De Rossi stands. "I'll go get her."

Leaving the office after him, I make my way back to the living room and stop in front of the sliding doors that lead out to the pool.

The sight of it triggers a memory of the girl.

Yes, *a girl.*

Although when I saw Martina by the pool the last time I came around, that wasn't the first descriptive word that came to mind.

I place my forearm against the glass and press my forehead into it.

She was lying there in a yellow bikini that barely contained her curves, and before I realized who she was, my cock stirred at the image of me peeling it off her with my teeth. Then Damiano reintroduced us, and I pushed that image far out of my head. The first time we met, she was a gangly thirteen-year-old with braces and a pair of prescription glasses that made her look like a bug, so I latched onto that memory instead.

Still, one would have to be blind not to appreciate that she's bloomed into something quite spectacular since then.

Silky blonde hair, petite frame, and curves that any man would be lucky to handle. Her expression was all shy innocence, but that body was pure sin. If she wasn't only eighteen and wasn't De Rossi's sister, things could have gone very differently for us, but I'm not one to linger on things that could have been.

Any second now, Martina will become my ward.

And that's all she'll ever be.

I push off the glass and drop my arm to my side. Turning away from the pool, I take a seat in one of the armchairs and check my watch again. They're taking their damned time.

My attention snags on a book on the coffee table. I've seen that cover before.

It's the pocket-sized special edition of *Jane Eyre* that Martina was reading by the pool that day.

I like Brontë. Reading is one of the ways I pass my time when I'm not out doing Sal's bidding. I pick up the book, flip through the pages, and nearly smile when I find the line: *"I am not an angel, and I will not be one till I die."*

Last time, De Rossi left us on our own for a few minutes. Martina was bashful and shy around me—qualities I've never valued in women before, but in her, they struck me as endearing. A strange weightlessness crept inside my chest while I stood beside her, and when I noticed it, I immediately set out to crush that feeling by any means necessary. In general, I dislike things that throw me off. So I said those words to her, inspired by the book in her hands, and meaning them as an honest warning. She blushed a deep red in response, the color making her even prettier.

When I left that day, I convinced myself whatever that episode was, it wasn't going to be repeated. Women came and went in my life like the winter season. The first glimpse of snow is always exciting, but by the time it's late February, you're sick of the cold and ready for something new.

Martina, though... That girl is summer, through and through.

A door opens. Voices float from upstairs into the living room.

My gaze drifts to the side of the staircase, and a moment later, two sun-kissed legs begin descending the steps.

Fuck.

My fingers tighten on the book, the hard edges of the cover digging into my palm.

An inexplicable urge grips me—*take the book.*

Just before Martina's face comes into view, I give into it and slip the book inside the inner pocket of my jacket.

CHAPTER 2

MARTINA

LAST NIGHT I dreamt I was flying. A vast green valley unfurled dozens of meters below me, and on the horizon was a great, brown mountain with a snowy peak. I had a premonition that there was something special on the other side of that summit, but no matter how far I flew, the mountain never got any closer. Eventually, I started to fall. Just before I crashed face-first into the ground, I woke up.

Now, when I close my eyes, that mountain is there before me.

Then, I hear my brother's voice calling, and it's gone.

"Mari, Napole— I mean, Giorgio is here."

I sit up on my bed and glance over my shoulder at my brother standing in the doorway. His expression is carefully guarded, but I know him well enough to see past the mask. He might be Damiano De Rossi to the rest of the world, but to me, he's just Dem, and right now, he's worried.

Worried about me.

I force a small smile. "Okay. I'll be right down."

"I'll help you with your bags," he says, stepping inside and looking around the room. "Where's Vale?"

"Bathroom."

My sister-in-law's spent all day helping me pack. She's far more stressed than I am about the fact that no one but Giorgio has any idea where he's taking me.

She asked me what I wanted to bring, and when I told her it didn't really matter, her face fell. Maybe I should feel guilty for making her worry, but I didn't feel anything.

Even now, there's nothing. Not a pang of anxiety. Not a whisper of sadness. Not even a small hint of apprehension. I'm leaving my home to go to an unknown place with a stranger while my brother wages a war against the most powerful man in the clan, and I feel...

Nothing.

My brother sits down on the bed beside me and wraps an arm around my shoulders, tugging me into his side. "We won't be apart for long, all right?"

He can't know that, but I nod anyway. "Yeah."

"It might be good for you to get some space from this place."

I drag my gaze around my predominantly pink room. It feels like the inside of a Pepto-Bismol bottle. Pink chair, pink duvet, pink carpet. Even pink walls.

This room screams easy target.

That's what I am.

Grabbing my phone off the nightstand, I slide out from under Dem's arm and go to grab my small purse. "We shouldn't keep him waiting."

My brother watches me, his shoulders slightly slumped. He's always been there for me, but recently, it's like I've forgotten how to talk to him. He often asks me how I feel, and the question stumps me.

I don't know. *I don't know.*

My bare feet press into the woven runner as we go down the steps. Behind me, Dem is carrying my two big suitcases, while Vale trails him with my backpack. They've refused to let me carry anything, as if they think I'll break under even the smallest bit of weight.

And yes, I do feel fragile, but I've survived more in the last two months than what most people do in a lifetime. I don't want to worry my brother, so I pull my shoulders back and lift my head a little higher.

I just have to keep at it.

One day at a time.

That's as far as I allow myself to think.

When I reach the final step, my gaze lands on the man waiting for me in the center of the room.

Giorgio Girardi.

My steps slow. When our eyes meet, the all-encompassing numbness recedes for a brief moment, and an electric charge runs down my spine.

He's so vivid...like a splatter of color against a grayscale canvas.

It must be my hormones. I already know there's something about this man that taps right into my pituitary gland.

Until I saw him two weeks ago, I was convinced I was asexual. One look at him was enough for me to realize I'm *definitely* not.

While my friends at school went through their boy-crazy phase, I watched from the sidelines, unable to muster up a single crush. Yes, some of my classmates were objectively good-looking, but I've known most of them for years. There was nothing intriguing about them. Nothing that made me want to know them in ways a simple friendship wouldn't allow.

But when I saw Giorgio, I felt something very different.

He was masculinity personified. Tall, fit, classically attractive. The kind of dark Italian man luxury brands hired to be the face of their expensive cologne. His brown, nearly black hair fell in smooth waves over his head. I had no idea if he spent any time making it look like that, or if he just woke up looking perfect.

I was *very* intrigued by him. For days after his last visit, my mind was filled with ideas I've never thought about before.

Like how his big hands would feel on my thighs, or how his lips would fit against mine.

And most importantly, how he'd look with his shirt off.

He has a broad chest, and I'd bet my bank account balance that if I peeled open his dress shirt, I'd find a set of perfect abs.

I realize I'm staring when he says my name and extends a hand. "Martina."

The sound of my name on his lips sends heat spreading through my chest. I drag my eyes to his face and take the offered hand. "Hi."

"How are you?" he asks in accented English. I guess my brother must have told him at some point that my Italian isn't that great. I can understand just fine, but my vocabulary is basic. Dem and I moved to Ibiza when I was just a little kid, and I've done all of my schooling here in Spanish and English.

"Fine, thank you."

"Are you ready to leave?"

If I'm being honest, no. My brother broke the news that he was sending me away less than twenty-four hours ago, and in my current state, I'm a bit slow on the uptake. My brain's not processing things the way it normally would. Despite my fascination with Giorgio, when Dem told me I'd be living with him for the foreseeable future, I didn't feel a thing.

Now, with him right in front of me...

I swallow. "Yes."

"She's as ready as she can be, given she doesn't know where you're taking her," Vale pipes in from somewhere behind me. A second later, I feel her palm press against the center of my back.

My sister-in-law is formidable. Vale was dealt a rough hand by her family when they forced her to marry Lazaro, a man who can only be described as a psychopath, but she was strong enough to run away from him and rescue me in the process. She came to Ibiza with nothing, and through sheer stubbornness, she managed to convince my brother to give her a job. The rest is history. I glance at Dem, only to see his eyes sparkle with proud fondness as he watches his new wife.

Vale's taller than me by a few inches, but she still has to crane her neck to meet Giorgio's eyes. "Are you going to treat her well?"

Something that looks like mild amusement passes over his expression. "I was wondering when it was coming."

"What?"

"The interview. Strange to do it after I already got the job, don't you think?"

Vale tosses her hair over her shoulder and gives him a glare. "My husband trusts you, so you have that going for you, but that doesn't mean I'm not worried. You didn't answer the question."

"Rest assured, Martina will be well cared for."

The serious way he says it makes a pit appear in my stomach. What does that mean? How is Giorgio going to care for me? I've spent zero time pondering what living with him is going to be like, but my immediate assumption is that I'm not going to see much of him. He has his own life, his own responsibilities. He'll probably lock me up someplace far from civilization and check in every few days, right?

Giorgio and Dem step aside to exchange a few words, and Vale watches them suspiciously for a few seconds before turning back to me. Her frown softens. "Mari, I'm sorry you have to leave. I wish Dem wasn't insisting on it, but I understand why he thinks it's necessary. He won't be able to handle it if anything happens to you again."

Or maybe my brother has finally realized what a liability I am. I got Imogen killed, and I nearly did the same to Vale, the woman he loves.

"Don't be sorry. You didn't do anything wrong."

Her lips tremble before she clamps them into a tight line. "Neither did you."

But I did. In fact, it seems I can't do anything right.

"Maybe I should go with you," she whispers, her fingers tightening around my shoulders. "I don't want to leave Dem, but—"

"You have to stay with him," I interrupt. "He needs you."

Dem's been scarce on the details of his plan to take over as don, but everyone knows what he has to do in order to ensure the transition of power is done according to the all-important Casalesi custom. He'll have to kill the current don by strangling him with his bare hands. It's how our father lost his power.

I wish he could just have one of his men do it for him, but I know that's not an option. If anyone other than Dem does the killing, the clan won't recognize his claim—a recipe for chaos.

Dem's killed people before, but I've never gotten the sense he enjoys doing it. With Sal, though? I wouldn't be surprised if he was looking forward to it. Sal is the reason we lost our parents. Dem also said Sal was the one who set Lazaro on Imogen and me. I guess the don thought that if he managed to capture me, my brother would be his lapdog. That didn't happen. In fact, the New York fiasco is what finally pushed Dem into this war. He's going to make Sal pay dearly for all the ways he's wronged us.

While vengeance might soothe my brother's soul, it rings hollow to me.

No amount of vengeance will bring Imogen back.

Vale pulls me into her and wraps her arms around me. "When you return, everything will be better."

"Yeah."

The other conversation in the room stops, and Vale lets go of me hesitantly.

"It's time to go," Dem says.

Outside, while Giorgio and the driver load up the car, we go through another round of goodbyes. My brother holds me tightly and kisses my hair, whispering assurances to me, then Vale does the same again.

The low buzz of their words wraps around me, and then it's suddenly gone, and I'm being helped inside the car. The door slams shut. Through the window, Dem and Vale wave at me, and I lift my hand and press my palm against the glass.

This might be the last time I see them.

I shudder and wrap my arms around me as I force myself not to engage with that thought. My mental walls rise back up. Out of the corner of my eye, I see Giorgio shooting me a wary look. He's probably wondering what's wrong with me. In a not-too-distant past, I would have been mortified, but now it's just another bullet point on a long list of things that don't matter.

We pass through the gate, and they disappear out of sight.

An unpleasant itch starts to build beneath my skin, so I reach inside my purse and take out my phone. Today began just like any other, with me scrolling through my feeds for a good two hours before I summoned up the strength to crawl out of bed. There's nothing new for me to check or read, but I pull up Facebook anyway.

Graduation pictures, someone's new dog, an ad for a bikini.

My finger hovers above it. It's cute. If I was at home, I would be putting in my credit card details already, but I don't even know the address of where we're going. Regretfully, I scroll past.

The next picture makes me pause again.

It's posted by Señora Bouras. Imogen's mom.

It's a picture of Imogen when she was a kid and the caption talks about how deeply she's missed by her parents.

A tight sensation appears in my throat. They never got to say a proper goodbye. The story Dem told Señora Bouras was that Imogen died in an unprovoked attack, and that her body couldn't be recovered. Señora Bouras didn't believe him. I stood on the other side of the door to my brother's office and eavesdropped on the call. He kept telling her she needed to let it go. He told her over and over until she must have hung up on him.

I don't know what happened afterwards, but somehow, she allowed us to come to the funeral. There was an empty casket. While Dem was talking to someone, she took me around a corner where no one could see us and shoved me against a wall. Angry tears streamed out of her eyes. She told me it was all my fault that her daughter's gone.

I didn't say a word. There was nothing to argue.

I scroll past the long wall of condolences, knowing better than to leave one of my own. She won't want to see it.

Instead, I pull up my messages and tap on Imogen's icon.

I'm leaving my home, Imogen. I don't know when I'll be back, and maybe that's for the best. The farther I am from people I love, the better, especially now. Dem is working on something dangerous that will make his enemies swarm around him like flies, and I'm his weakness. If I fall into the wrong hands, I'll ruin everything. I'm not good under pressure. I don't know what to do, how to act. I lose my head. I miss you.

Flipping my phone facedown on my lap, I press my temple against the window. I started sending Imogen messages a few days after I came back to Ibiza. I'm not crazy. I know they're just going into the digital void, but they make me feel better. Sometimes, when my mind starts playing tricks on me at night, they're the only thing that helps.

On the other side of the window, the sky is nearly dark. I can make out a few stars and a half-moon. Its edge is sharp and precise, and for some reason, the sight of it makes me shiver.

"You're cold."

I startle, whipping my head around in the direction of the voice.

God, I swear I forgot Giorgio is in the car with me.

His piercing blue eyes are trained on my bare thighs.

An unexpected bout of heat travels up my neck before it dawns on me he's looking at my goosebumps.

I drag a self-conscious palm over them. "I'm fine."

His jaw ticks, and then he shrugs off his suit jacket and hands it to me. "Put this on."

My fingers curl around the expensive fabric. It's still warm from him. I lift my gaze to his and exhale a shuddery breath. "Okay."

He watches me as I put the jacket over my shoulders. I wish he wouldn't, because the moment his scent reaches my nostrils, my thighs clench. Musk, leather, and something else I can't quite name.

"Turn the AC off," he commands the driver.

"Thank you," I say quietly and reach for my phone again.

In my periphery, I see him adjust the cufflinks of his crisp white dress shirt, and something catches my eye. He's got two tattoos peeking out from the insides of his wrists.

I think the one on the right is the crest of Casal di Principe. Dem has one of those too, only his is higher up his arm. All of the made men in the clan get them after their initiation.

The other, though... It looks like a different crest.

Giorgio's movements halt, and I realize he's noticed me staring.

He unbuttons his left cuff, folds it over, and drags his thumb over the tattoo. "Do you know what this is?"

I shake my head.

"Do you know my nickname?"

"Napoletano." It's what Dem calls him. "Why do they call you that?"

"I used to be part of a different clan based in north Naples— the Secondigliano Alliance," Giorgio says. "Sal traded for me and made me a Casalesi when I was around eighteen or so. The clan wanted my expertise."

I sink my teeth into the right corner of my bottom lip. "I didn't know that was a thing. Trading people."

"It's rare," he says, tugging his sleeve back into place, and doing up the cufflinks. "But it happens on occasion."

"And the Alliance just let you go?" I ask after a moment.

"The dons made a deal."

Sal must have given up something big if Giorgio's expertise was that valuable to him. Why else would the other clan give him up? And speaking of his expertise, the only thing Dem told me about what Giorgio does is that he's some kind of security expert.

I eye the man sitting beside me. "You hide things, right? That's your job?"

"Sometimes I need to find them first," he says, his gaze fixed on the back of our driver's head. "But yes, I've been entrusted with many of the clan's things over the years."

"So I'm just another thing for you to hide," I conclude.

"You're in good company. Priceless art, ancient artifacts, enough solid gold to fill a walk-in safe..." Slowly, he turns his head and pins me with his gaze. "Every object under my protection is of immense value, Martina."

Having his attention on me is like being under a spotlight. Suddenly, the car feels too small. It shrinks even further when he leans over and adjusts his jacket, tugging on the lapel to make it engulf me even more. "And you might just be the most valuable of them all."

CHAPTER 3

GIORGIO

THE GIRL'S glued to her phone.

She clutches it in her hand as she climbs out of the car, the wind on the tarmac whipping her long blonde locks across her face.

I ignore the weird tug inside my chest at the sight of her wrapped up in my jacket. It's so big on her that it nearly reaches her knees. She rubs the tip of her nose with the back of her hand and looks toward the private plane we're about to board.

She's less curious than I would have expected. Not a single question about where we're going or what we're going to do when we get there. All she seems to care about is swiping and typing on that damned screen. Once we get on the plane, I'll need to take her phone away so that I can encrypt it. If she uses it when we land, her signal might give our location away.

I grab her backpack out of the trunk, tell the driver to load the suitcases onto the plane, and round the vehicle.

"Come on. I want to be far from here when the storm hits."

"The storm?"

"Didn't you see the forecast?"

"No, I didn't check," she says with a frown.

We greet the pilot as we board, and I lead her to a seat before taking the one opposite. The plane's engine comes to life, its hum filling the air. Once we land, I'm going to erase the plane records so that no one can track where we landed, but the pilot could be a concern. He's one of De Rossi's guys —clean record, seven years on the job, well paid. He checks out on paper, but I told De Rossi to put a set of eyes on him. If Sal gets it into his head to go after Martina, he'll try to get information out of someone on the staff.

It's a good thing I don't have many staff members to worry about at the castello. Just three civilians, and only one of them has some knowledge of the things I'm involved in. The others suspect but are smart enough to pretend like they don't. When it comes to working for a man of the *sistema*, ignorance truly is bliss.

Martina peers at the sky through the small window, a line appearing between her brows. Just then, thunder booms in the far distance, and her face grows pale.

She doesn't like storms.

Or maybe she just doesn't like flying through them. Who does?

"Pilot said we're going in the opposite direction," I tell her. "It's only a ninety-minute flight."

She pulls her full bottom lip into her mouth and nods without looking at me.

I wait. Is she not going to ask where we're going?

Her silence sends frustration burning through me.

"Seat belt," I snap as the plane begins to move.

Her gaze comes to my face for a split second before she does as she's told. Her obedience should please me, but I don't like that it reeks of indifference. I get the sense she just doesn't care what happens to her.

My elbow lands on the armrest, and I press my closed fist against my lips. On the other side of the glass, everything blurs, and as we lift off, Ibiza grows smaller and smaller beneath us.

Tucking her legs under her, she adjusts my jacket around her shoulders and pushes a few strands of golden hair out of her eyes. Her expression is somber, the corners of her lips pointing down.

If someone was to paint her, they'd title the piece *Melancholy*.

I'm not the kind of man who makes a habit of talking about feelings, but I also don't make a point of avoiding those conversations when they're necessary.

And right now? It's fucking necessary.

I lean forward, placing my elbows on my knees. "What's going on with you?"

She gives me a sideways glance. "Nothing."

"You're a bad liar."

"I'll add it to the list." Her voice is flat.

"What list?"

"All of the things I'm bad at."

Cazzo. She says it in this resigned kind of way that makes discomfort prickle at the back of my neck. "You keep a list?"

"Sure."

"Strange hobby. What are your other interests?"

Her expression doesn't crack. She tucks a strand of hair behind her ear and answers without looking at me. "I like to shop."

"What else?"

She lifts up her phone. "This."

I narrow my eyes. No fucking shit. "I hope you like nature."

That earns me a cautious glance. "Why?"

"A lot of it where we're going. Have you ever been to Umbria?"

"No. I haven't seen anything in Italy besides Casal di Principe and Naples, and that was so long ago I barely remember it."

De Rossi kept her away from Italy all these years because he didn't want her anywhere near Sal, but even if Sal discovers Martina is with me, he'll never know where I'm taking her.

"We're going to an old castello about forty minutes from Perugia."

Perugia is the capital of the Umbria region, and I bought the castello over a decade ago. It's under a false name, so no one knows that I own it.

Martina taps her index finger against the armrest. "Just you and me?"

"No. There are three servants there. A maid, a cook, and a groundskeeper. It's a small staff for a place as big as the castello, but we'll only be using the first two floors."

She nods and turns back to the window.

A noise of frustration threatens to escape me, but I hold it down. I am *not* used to being the talkative one. In fact, one of my hobbies is letting silence linger and seeing how long it takes for people to become visibly uncomfortable. It's a surprisingly amusing pastime.

But this silence? Nothing amusing about it. It spreads through the recycled air of the plane and leaves a sour taste at the back of my mouth.

When she starts scrolling through her phone again, my patience can't take it anymore. I unbuckle my seat belt, reach over, and snatch it out of her hand. "No phones."

Her hazel eyes go round, and she drops one of her feet to the ground. "What?"

My gaze skates up her shapely calf before I can stop myself. "You heard me. No phones."

"Why?"

"Phones can be tracked. I can't have you giving our location away."

Her eyes dip to my own phone lying on the table.

"Mine's encrypted," I explain.

"So encrypt mine."

I turn her device off. "You'll benefit from less screen time."

There. That's the line that finally gets me the response I want. She purses her lips, and for the first time since I picked her up, something sparks inside her gaze.

"That's ridiculous. What am I supposed to do with my time?"

"Reading, cooking, going on walks. There's plenty of other things to do at the castello besides filling your head with nonsense. Humanity existed for a long time before it invented screens and somehow managed to entertain itself just fine."

"They also had a life expectancy of like forty because they probably died of boredom. Just because that's how people used to do it, doesn't mean it was better."

Ah. So she's got some spunk when she's not so absorbed with being miserable. Nature and some fresh air is going to do her a lot of good.

"My house, my rules," I say with a shrug, my tone firm.

Her fingers tighten on the armrests, and panic flits across her face. "I need my phone."

"No. You don't."

She shakes her head. "You don't understand. It helps me."

"Helps you with what?"

Her gaze falls to the ground before hesitantly crawling back up to me. "A lot of things. It helps me get to sleep."

Yeah, right. Staring at a glowing screen is definitely not helping her with that. "I don't think so. In fact, it probably does the opposite."

"Please, Giorgio." Her voice cracks.

My gaze narrows at that pitiful sound, and something squirms inside my chest.

Why is she so upset about it? It's just a fucking phone.

But her eyes are turning liquid as she waits for my response...and that's when it dawns on me.

This thing is her fucking crutch. She probably spends her entire day on it, numbing her mind to the real world.

She's addicted, and I just took away her fix. What's going to happen when she's left alone with just her thoughts?

Fuck, this is worse than I thought. How did De Rossi allow her to get this bad? And that wife of his? She's the reason Lazaro came to Ibiza, so the least she could have fucking done was make fixing Martina her priority.

Martina wipes under her eyes, preemptively catching her tears before they track down her cheeks, and stares at me.

Cracking my neck, I look out the window. I don't like how her teary eyes make me feel. Just then, a thought occurs to me. This phone might be the only thing she cares about at the moment, and she wants it back.

Why not use that drive? Why not give her a distraction? Something to keep her busy for a few days so that she doesn't just spend them spiraling in bed...

My gaze drops to the device in my hand.

"I'll encrypt it for you," I say, slipping the phone inside my pocket. "Afterwards, you can have it back."

She heaves a sigh of relief and adjusts her position, crossing her legs. "Thank you. How long will that take?"

"However long it takes for you to find it."

Her relief disappears in a blink, and her mouth slackens. "What do you mean?"

"You heard me. I'll encrypt the phone tomorrow and hide it somewhere in the castello. If you want it back, you'll need to find it yourself."

There's a drawn-out pause while she absorbs my words.

Her other foot drops to the floor, and she shrugs off my jacket. "You're sending me on a scavenger hunt for my phone? I'm eighteen—nearly nineteen, actually. Given your age, I understand that I probably seem very young, but I can assure you, I grew out of scavenger hunts at least a decade ago."

I choke on a laugh.

Given my age?

Little Martina De Rossi is talking back to me.

"How old do you think I am?" I ask, cocking an amused brow.

Her eyes narrow, her outrage palpable. "To be honest, I don't really care. I just want my phone back."

"Then you're going to have to play along," I say with a shrug. "Shouldn't be that hard."

"This is stupid," she mutters, shaking her head. "Did my brother put you up to this?"

"Why would he?"

"He always complains about me being on my phone too much."

Ah, so De Rossi did notice. Not that he gets any credit for it. He hasn't done anything about it.

"Only people your age think it's a problem," she adds, giving me a cross look.

My jaw muscles tighten at her repeated dig. Am I really that ancient in her eyes? Thirty-three isn't that old.

Then I catch myself. *Why do you care if she thinks you're old?*

Irritation crawls up my spine. Enough of this.

Uncrossing my legs, I plant my elbows on my knees and lean forward. "This isn't a negotiation."

She blanches.

"You want it back, you find it."

Her lips tighten into a resigned line. "Are there any rules?"

I cock my head to the side. "It'll be inside the castello." After a moment, I add, "And don't let me catch you looking for it. If I see you're getting close, I'll move it to a new spot."

"You want me to sneak around behind your back?"

"Call it whatever you want. These are my rules," I say even as my heart pounds out a guilty beat.

She's young. She's De Rossi's sister. She's already a big enough problem as is.

And yet we left Ibiza less than an hour ago, and I've already discovered I can't seem to keep my eyes off her fucking legs.

Better keep her occupied and out of my damned sight.

CHAPTER 4

MARTINA

WE LAND on a tiny grass airstrip somewhere in Italy. There's no airport—only a hangar, fields, and a few homes in the far distance, their windows flickering with orange light.

It's been an hour since Giorgio confiscated my phone and my opinion of him has rapidly soured. He might be handsome, but he's a jerk.

I'm raging.

Seriously, what's his problem?

"I think you might benefit from less screen time." Who asked him for his opinion?

While the plane taxis down the runway, he takes out his phone and starts typing out a text, rubbing salt in the wound.

My fists clench.

I get the distinctive feeling Giorgio's decided to make me his problem, and I don't like it one bit. All I want is to be left alone. Where is the man I met by the pool who told me how bad he is, and how I should stay away? I thought I'd be living with *that* version of him.

This version? He cares too much. Of course, I'm not saying he cares about *me*. He doesn't even know me. But Dem probably told him to keep a close eye on me or something along those lines, and Giorgio's clearly taken the task to heart.

My desperation to get my phone back is making me nearly feral. I'll get it back tomorrow. I *have* to. The way I rely on that device should make me pause, but honestly, I don't care enough to examine it. The itch has already returned, and I know it'll just get worse. I need to be able to message Imogen. It's how I stay sane.

I drag my hands over my face. No way I'm doing any of the other "activities" Giorgio proposed. They all sound exhausting. Really, just thinking about them makes me feel tired.

The plane rolls to a stop. Both Giorgio and I rise at the same time, and the space between our seats is so small that his sleeve brushes against my arm. He drops his heavy gaze to my face. "A half-hour drive, and we'll be there."

I curl my fist around his jacket and hand it to him. "I don't need this anymore."

He scans my body with a lazy flick of his eyes, then pushes the jacket back to me. "Yes, you do. It's cold out here at night."

"I said, I'm..."

He doesn't listen, he just rounds the seat and moves toward the exit of the plane.

Angry fire licks up my insides. My teeth clench. I'm not sure what's worse: feeling nothing the way I did this morning, or feeling like I want to strangle him in his sleep.

A car waits for us, the driver a gray-haired man with a potbelly and a thick mustache. His name is Tommaso, and he greets Giorgio with a two-handed handshake and me with a warm smile.

"Welcome back," he says to Giorgio. "Sophia is going to be so happy to see you. She's missed you a lot, Giorgio."

My brows pinch together. *Who's Sophia?* I thought he said it was just us and three members of staff.

A ghost of a smile passes over Giorgio's lips. "I'm looking forward to seeing her too."

Maybe it's the maid, and everyone knows he's sleeping with her.

Irritation scratches at my throat. Yep. I'd bet anything Sophia is the maid, and she has the extra duty of keeping his bed warm. Given we're talking about Giorgio, I doubt she sees it as anything other than a benefit.

The wind plasters his white shirt to his muscular back while he talks to Tommaso, and even as annoyed as I am, the urge to check him out is impossible to resist. This man is built like a taller version of Michelangelo's *David*. So many ridges and valleys.

I sniff. Sophia is a lucky girl.

We get into the car, Giorgio taking the driver's seat, Tommaso on his right, and me in the back. The road is only two lanes, and we don't pass a single car on the journey. It's too dark to make out much on the sides of the road, but I get the impression of a lot of fields and trees.

I've never been to Umbria, but I know it's foodie heaven. In the forests of the region, truffles grow under the soil, and people forage for them using sniffing dogs. I used to get excited about things like that in the past, but my interest in cooking has dwindled ever since New York. I had a few bursts of inspiration in the beginning when Vale came to live with us, but after Lazaro's latest attack, even those have stopped.

It is what it is.

I glance at Giorgio. He's speaking quietly to Tommaso in Italian, and I can't really make out what he's saying from the back, but I swear I hear him say Sophia again.

Rolling my eyes, I look away.

The car turns onto a narrow dirt road that disappears inside dense woodland, and when the trees around us part again, I get my first glimpse at the castello.

The sight of it steals air out of my lungs.

It stands on a hill, the moon illuminating a tall medieval tower and a three-story building that's surrounded by pines and lush oak trees. On the horizon behind it are layers upon layers of hills that protrude from the ground like enormous spines before melting into the night sky.

I roll down the window and suck in cool, woodsy air. Giorgio was right, it is chilly out here, but I keep his jacket folded across my lap. Not because I'm stubborn, but because I don't want to get used to the smell of his cologne.

This crush of mine needs to die. At least it's just physical. His personality can use a lot of work.

Sliding my hands under my thighs, I peer out the window just as we pull into a large courtyard. A motion-activated light flickers on.

There's a lot to take in, but then Giorgio sees me yawn, and no matter how I protest, he insists on taking me inside.

"You need to rest," he says gruffly, leading me through the enormous front door with his palm wrapped around my elbow. "You'll have plenty of time to look around tomorrow."

We pass through a large entry hall illuminated by a few wall sconces, before going up a spiral staircase made of creaky old wood. Giorgio walks past two doors before stopping in front of the third. As he turns the handle, he looks at me. "This is your room."

The bedroom is large, far larger than the one I have back in Ibiza, but the furnishings make the space feel cozy. There's a four-poster bed with a sheer canopy, a sitting area by the window, and a stone fireplace with a painting of the castello hanging above it.

It feels like I've been transported back in time.

"How old is this place?"

"Couple hundred years," Giorgio says. "It's been renovated many times, the last time was about thirty years ago. Most of the furniture is antique."

I run my fingertips over the embroidered bedcover before I sit down on its edge. The mattress sinks slightly below me.

Giorgio points to the right. "Bathroom is through that door. The door beside it is the closet."

"What about that one?" I ask, nodding at a third door on the other side of the room.

"That leads to my bedroom."

A nervous laugh spills past my lips. "Is that a joke?"

"No."

My eyes widen at the same time as something warm curls inside my belly. "Why are we staying in connected rooms?" Doesn't that seem slightly...inappropriate? This is a big place. He didn't choose to put me in this room because of space constraints.

The way he purses his lips tells me he thinks I'm making a big deal out of nothing. "It's for your safety. In case anything happens, I'll be close enough to intervene right away."

"What could happen?" Does he honestly think someone would break into this room and kidnap me?

"Anything."

"Why don't you just give me a gun or something as insurance?"

"Do you even know how to use a gun?"

"Well, no," I say, bristling.

"Then it's either me sleeping next door to you, or a camera in your room." His voice lowers. "Which do you prefer?"

A hot film of outrage and embarrassment sticks to my skin. "What are you going to do? Watch me while I sleep?"

"If that's what I need to do to keep you safe."

"What if I told you I sleep naked?"

A flash of surprise passes over Giorgio's face, and then his eyes narrow. He drags his assessing gaze over my body, like he's trying to imagine exactly what I might look like beneath my clothes.

My muscles freeze. All blood inside my body rushes to my face. *Why* did I say that? By the time his gaze makes it back up to meet mine, I'm sure I'm bright crimson.

He drags his tongue over his upper teeth and slides his hands into the pockets of his slacks. "All jobs have their challenges."

I deflate.

"And their perks."

I'm sorry, *what?*

I must have misheard him. There's no way Giorgio just implied watching me sleeping naked would be a perk.

Before I can attempt to read his expression, he turns away from me and takes a few steps toward the door to his room. "I take my promise to your brother very seriously, Martina. It may take a few days, but you'll get used to being here."

"Uh-huh." I drag my palms over my cheeks. *Pull it together.*

"Me being next door is a simple safety precaution, nothing more," he says, his voice all cool professionalism.

I swallow, still flustered. "A safety precaution against who exactly?"

When he turns back to me, his eyes soften the tiniest little bit, and it finally clicks.

He doesn't need to say it. The answer is in his gaze.

He thinks I might hurt myself.

A wave of unpleasant shivers runs down my back, and I dig my nails into my palms.

The backs of my eyes prick, but I won't let him see me cry. "Anything else?"

"No. Get some rest. You'll meet the rest of the staff tomorrow at breakfast."

"Fine."

When the lock of the door clicks behind him, I sink to the floor and press my palms against my eyes.

Don't cry. Do NOT cry. One day at a time.

But without my phone, there's no outlet for the muck swirling inside. There's nothing to get me through the night.

I drop my palms on the floor and glance around. Everything is unfamiliar, and shadows flicker in the corners of the room. A chill drifts over my arms even though all the windows are closed. Straining my ears, I try to hear Giorgio on the other side of the wall, but besides a dull footstep or two, there's nothing.

It's a small relief. The last thing I want to hear tonight is him reuniting with Sophia.

Eventually, I get myself off the hardwood floor and drag myself to the bathroom. At the sink, I splash some water on my face and wipe off the little makeup I have on with a wet towel. That's as much as I have the strength to do tonight. My four-step skin care routine will have to wait for a better day.

I slip on my pajamas, crawl into bed, and flick off the lights.

The castello is silent.

Sleeping in an unfamiliar bed is like pulling on a random glove and hoping it fits. I move my body until I find a comfortable position and drag the duvet up to my chin, inhaling the scent of clean laundry. Did Sophia make my bed this morning?

An image of a slim, beautiful, dark-haired woman in a sexy maid uniform appears inside my head.

Ugh. *Stop it.* I have enough things to torture myself with already.

I push the image away and let my body relax into the mattress.

Then I hear the floor creak.

The sound makes me sit up. It's close, like it's coming from somewhere inside my room, and I glance around, my eyes adjusted to the darkness by now.

Everything is still except for the shadows. They flit across the walls, swaying and twisting, and the longer I stare at them, the more I start to see.

Wolves chasing through the woods after a small, bleating sheep. An old house with a door that swings on its hinges until someone jerks it shut. A girl on her knees, crying with her back to me, until she whips her head around and shows me her face—a bullet between her brows.

I suck in a breath and squeeze my eyes shut.

Imogen.

An icy hand wraps around my heart. She didn't want to go to New York. I made her come, and then I told the men who took us who she was because I was too dumb to keep my mouth shut. Things could have gone differently if I was just a little bit smarter.

Or a little bit braver.

And when Lazaro came for the second time, I could have tried to fight him off instead of waiting for Vale to save me once again. His hand was by my mouth. Why didn't I bite him? Why didn't I do anything but cry like a pathetic loser?

A sob catches in my throat, and I clamp my hand over my mouth. I don't want Giorgio to hear me. I don't want him to come storming in here and burden me with his worried eyes.

Out of habit, I reach under my pillow, looking for my phone, but it's not there. There's nothing to calm me, nothing to distract me from my thoughts.

Pulling up the duvet all the way to my nose, I tell myself to go to sleep, even as the room keeps creaking and shadows dance around me.

CHAPTER 5

MARTINA

SOMEONE IS SCRATCHING at the wall.

My consciousness latches right onto the sound, as if it's bait at the end of a fishing line, and I'm pulled awake.

My eyes fly open. The room is filled with bright sunlight.

The realization that I made it through the night sends relief rushing through me. God, I wasn't sure I'd make it. I had to force myself to breathe through bouts of terror and overwhelming guilt. I don't know what time it was when I finally managed to fall asleep, but it must have been late. I don't feel well rested.

The bed makes a low creak as I climb out of it. The view out the window didn't impress me last night when everything was mostly shrouded with darkness, but now it makes me gasp. On the other side of the glass, stretching over the hills, is a dense, majestic forest.

More scratching pulls my attention back to the room. What *is* that? I thought it might have been a remnant of a dream, but I'm awake now.

I follow the sound. It's coming from the other side of Giorgio's door.

Shifting my weight between my feet, I consider what I should do. The sound is strange, definitely worthy of an investigation, but to investigate it, I have to go into Giorgio's room.

The shiny door handle taunts me.

If anything, our conversation last night established his clear lack of respect for my privacy. These sleeping arrangements are outrageous. And that comment about the camera?

I glance down at my silk pajamas. Black shorts and a loose tank top. I've never slept naked in my entire life.

Does he, though?

I clear my throat. Well, if he doesn't care about my privacy, why should I care for his?

My palm curls around the door handle. If he really didn't want me coming in, he'd keep the door locked.

And yet the handle moves with ease. I tug the door open.

"Agh!"

Before I can see into the room, something heavy crashes into me, knocking me to the floor. I land hard on my butt, and pain shoots up my spine. It takes half a second for my brain to realize there's a big dog drooling over me.

"Who are you?" I ask, my heart racing with fear and surprise.

The animal ignores the question and proceeds to sniff me.

I let him or her do its thing, because the last thing I want is to get my fingers bit off. I love animals, but Dem and I have never had any pets, and I don't have a lot of experience dealing with them.

The dog is wearing a black leather collar with a metal tag. As it stretches its neck to sniff my hair, I catch a glimpse of the name scratched into the metal.

Sophia.

An incredulous laugh escapes me. Oh my God, *this* is who's been missing Giorgio?

A dog.

A freaking *dog* instead of the sexy maid I've been imagining.

My mood lightens.

"Hello, Sophia," I say as she finally steps off me. She's got short, chocolate-colored fur sprinkled with some white spots, big brown eyes, and floppy ears. I sit up and carefully pet her on the head. She seems to like it, because when I stop, she bumps me with her wet nose as if to indicate she wants me to keep going.

I oblige, taking the opportunity to peer inside Giorgio's room. At first glance, it appears to be empty. Did he leave for the day?

Giving Sophia one last rub, I get back on my feet. What are the chances he stashed my phone somewhere in his bedroom? We got in late last night, and he may have been too tired to hide it elsewhere.

My teeth sink into my bottom lip. I shouldn't let this opportunity go because who knows how hard he's going to make this silly scavenger hunt for me? Better nip it right in the bud if I can.

I step inside his room.

Heavy velvet curtains block most of the sunlight, except for one long beam of light that stretches from the window to the bed.

His bed.

I swallow, my eyes skating over a pool of messy satin sheets and a misshapen pillow. Giorgio seems like someone who'd make his bed, he's always so put together... If I had to imagine his room, I don't think I would have imagined this.

The space feels lived in. A tie is slung over the back of a chair standing in one of the corners, and a crumpled shirt lies on the seat. A bottle of cologne sits on an impressive looking armoire. I resist the urge to check the label.

By the bed, there's a tall stack of books, suggestive of a nighttime reading habit. I walk over to it and get down on my haunches to read the spines. Biographies of Alexander the Great and Napoleon, a history of World War Two... Definitely not what I'd call light reading.

I'm halfway through the description of a book titled *The Secret War* when I realize what I'm doing.

Quickly, I put the book down and step away from the bed.

Why is it that a room can be just a room, but when it belongs to a man you find attractive, it becomes endlessly fascinating?

I groan and shake off that thought. I came here for a reason, damn it.

My phone.

Where could he have stashed it?

Looking around, I zero in on the nightstands. There are two, one on each side of the bed, and when I reach for the one closest to me, Sophia trots over and emits a low growl.

I glance at her. "Hey, come on. After that rubdown, you can let me get away with this one thing. Sit."

Hesitantly, she follows the command and cocks her head to the side. I've never felt judged by a dog, but I sure do now.

Inside the nightstand's drawer, I find only one thing, and it's not my phone.

It's a gun.

A ball of ice solidifies inside my belly.

I've seen plenty of guns in my life—my brother rarely leaves home without one tucked at his waist—but sleeping right beside one in a castello no one is supposed to know about?

Talk about paranoid.

I press that drawer shut and round the bed to get to the other nightstand, but before I reach it, a door swings open.

Giorgio emerges in a puff of steam.

Freshly showered.

Hair dripping.

A white towel wrapped around his trim waist.

He freezes in place.

My jaw drops.

I can't help but let my gaze ping pong across every inch of his exposed skin.

His body is a work of art made of smooth, lean muscle, including a prominent V that disappears behind his towel. Dark tattoos cover his upper arms and torso, giving him an unexpected edge. Who knew that's what he's been hiding beneath his tailored suits?

And those abs I was so curious about? Yeah, I'm counting eight.

A pulse appears between my legs and extends all the way down to my toes. When did this room turn into a sauna? I'm burning up. I don't even know what I'm doing. I should probably stop staring at him, shouldn't I? Oh, crap. *Stop it, Mari. RIGHT NOW!*

My eyes shoot up to his face. "What are you doing!"

A single brow arches up. "What am *I* doing?"

"Where are your clothes?" I choke out, my voice rising to a mildly hysterical note.

His gaze narrows and then he prowls over to me, crossing the distance between us with three sure steps.

He stops. *Way. Too. Close.*

I eye his right nipple. "Wha—"

He takes my chin with two of his fingers and turns my head as if I'm a plastic doll. "Where are you?"

When he makes my eyes land on a large mirror, I swallow. Our reflection is almost comical. Compared to my small frame, Giorgio looks enormous. "Your room."

He lowers his head, bringing his lips closer to my ear. "Ah, so you're not suffering a sudden bout of confusion," he says, his voice low. "Good. Now, *why* are you in my room?"

I take a few shallow breaths as I notice the shape of his flexed biceps in the mirror. He warned me, didn't he? He told me he didn't want to see me looking for my phone. I can't let him know that's why I was here.

"The dog was scratching at the door. I didn't know where the sound was coming from."

A beat passes.

"The door wasn't locked," I add.

His hold on my chin disappears. "I didn't expect you to come barging in."

Our gazes clash. "I didn't barge in," I protest. "I just opened the door to see what was going on, and then Sophia jumped at me. You could have warned me you had a dog, you know. She toppled me over," I say, pressing my palm against my sore tailbone to strengthen my point. "I'm probably going to have a bruise tomorrow."

"A bruise?"

"Yes."

"How bad is it?" He has the decency to look mildly concerned.

"I have no idea." My heart pounds inside my ears as I turn my back to the mirror and lift up the hem of my shirt at the same time as I tug my shorts a few inches down. "All I know is that it hurt a lot."

His eyes move to the stretch of skin just above my butt that I've presented for examination, and the muscles on his body visibly tighten. His abs become even more defined. His jaw ticks.

"There's nothing there," he mutters.

"Of course you wouldn't see anything from that far away," I say, my voice taking on a defensive note.

His chest rises and falls with a deep, slow breath. I expect him to drop it, but he doesn't.

Instead, he steps around me and lowers down on his haunches, bringing my tailbone to his eye level.

His towel rises up his thigh, and my heart skips over itself.

"Is this close enough?" His breath coasts over my skin.

"I-I'd say so."

When the pad of his thumb gently smooths over the area, I think I might pass out.

"Does that hurt?"

"A little," I lie. Pain? What pain? The only thing I'm aware off is the square inch of skin that burns beneath his thumb.

Suddenly, it's gone. Giorgio stands and turns away from me. "You'll be fine," he says gruffly. "If you want, I can get you some ice."

"Okay." I pull up my shorts and let my shirt fall back down. "Thanks."

He drags a palm over his face and then turns back to me, his expression guarded.

"I'm sorry for coming in," I offer, gesturing at the room. "I thought you'd left. I couldn't hear you moving around."

"I was shaving."

"Well, you're a very quiet shaver."

He gives me a look, as if to say, *Good one, Martina.* "I'll give you a pass since you're right, I should have told you about the dog."

With his fist keeping his towel in place, he brushes past me. I clamp down on my bottom lip when his smell hits me— soap and aftershave. I shouldn't, I know I shouldn't, but I glance over my shoulder and take in that glorious back one more time.

God was exceptionally kind to him.

"Can I have my room back to change?" he asks without looking at me.

"Oh! Yes, of course."

What is wrong with me? Heat crawls up my cheeks, and I hurry out of the room.

"Be downstairs for breakfast in fifteen minutes," he calls out just as I'm about to close the door.

"Okay."

Once the door is shut, I press my back against it and groan into my palms. That was mortifying. Did I really make him look at my damn tailbone?

With my heart still racing, I fly into the bathroom to take a cold shower—I need it.

CHAPTER 6

MARTINA

Ten minutes later, after I manage to freeze the mortification and adrenaline out of me, I get out, comb my hair, and slap on a little blush to make me look less like a cast member of *The Walking Dead*. My clothes are still packed in the suitcases, so I grab whatever is on top—a pair of bootcut jeans and a soft yellow T-shirt. It's not my cutest outfit, but it'll do.

As soon as I exit my room, I hear voices and the clattering of dishes.

The thought of going down there to meet the staff makes me halt. There's energy in the air, and it's...daunting. I really don't feel like socializing or making small talk with strangers.

For a moment, I consider disobeying Giorgio and hiding out in my room, but I don't want him to think I'm embarrassed about this morning. Even though I am. But he can't know that. I'd rather throw myself off that tower we drove past last night than reveal my crush on him. It's so dumb. He's a grown man, gorgeous, and infuriating, and I am not crazy enough to think he'd ever look at me that way. Even in my dreams, I wouldn't allow myself to be so bold as to entertain the idea that he might ever see me as anything more than his future don's little sister.

Plus, staying in my room won't help me find my phone, and I need to get that thing back quickly.

I take a steadying breath and force myself to descend the steps.

Since I didn't get more than a tiny glimpse of the castello last night, I can't recall which way anything is, but I let my nose act as my compass.

It leads me right to what appears to be the dining room.

Giorgio is already at the head of a table that's big enough to seat at least a dozen people. Standing beside him is a tiny, gray-haired woman, dressed in a dark, uniform-like dress.

"Tommaso was working on the bread since four am this morning," she says to Giorgio. "He said last time you were here, you told him you liked it very much, but as I recall, it was actually the pecorino rolls that you enjoyed. His memory isn't what it used to be. The man's nearly seventy, even if he refuses to admit it."

I halt in the entryway and observe them. Giorgio looks like he's only half-listening, his nose buried in a newspaper, but that doesn't seem to deter the woman.

"He still insists on going on a run with Polo every other Saturday, but I'm worried he's going to trip and break a leg one of these days. The forest floor is so uneven in some parts, and there are some really slippery roots. I've been meaning to ask Polo to—"

Giorgio's eyes suddenly flick from the newspaper to me. "Martina."

The woman quiets and follows his gaze. For a moment, she seems confused at the sight of me, then her expression melts, and her mouth forms a cheerful smile. "Hello! Our guest!" She patters to me in a succession of quick steps and unceremoniously places her hands on my cheeks. "What a pleasure it is to have you join us. Gio, look at her freckles. *Bellisima!* How charming."

"Hi," I insert between her two kisses. "I'm Martina."

"Of course you are, and I'm Allegra." Her eyes twinkle. "We are so happy to have you here. We haven't hosted any visitors since..."

Pressing her palm to her forehead, she whirls around. "*Dio mio*, has there been anyone since Polo? And he hardly counts, given he now works here."

"You know I don't like people," Giorgio says, already back at his newspaper.

Allegra's eyes widen, and she makes an awkward laugh. "He means he doesn't like people in his personal space, not in general."

"No, in general too," he deadpans.

She swats at him with a towel, then guides me to a seat to his right. "A strange sense of humor he has. Sit, sit. I'll bring you your breakfast, and then we'll all sit down. Polo is just a little late. It's been very dry this month, and the garden needs a lot of watering. Cappuccino?"

"Yes, thank you."

Allegra disappears down a hallway and leaves us on our own. I'm not quite sure I can look at Giorgio without blushing just yet, so I take in the room instead. Fine art, gold-plated candelabras, and furniture that appears to be well-maintained antiques. A stone fireplace acts as the centerpiece of the room, but since it's summer, it's not lit.

There's a snort, and then the tablecloth lifts to reveal a snout. Sophia places her head on my lap and offers me her best puppy eyes.

"Hi."

She licks my hand.

Out of the corner of my eye, I see Giorgio fold the newspaper and place it on the table. "Sophia likes to sleep in my room when I'm at the castello. If she keeps scratching at the door, I'll ask Tommaso to take her for the night."

"How old is she?"

"Four, although she still likes to act like she's a puppy."

"You leave her here when you're gone?"

He brings his coffee to his lips. "Yes. I'm not here often. Technically, she's Tommaso's dog, but she's developed an attachment to me I can't really explain. I haven't done anything to encourage it."

As if sensing the topic of conversation, Sophia leaves me and pads over to him.

"Sit."

She follows his command immediately and sticks out her tongue.

I'd miss it if I wasn't watching carefully, but something soft bleeds into Giorgio's expression as he drags his palm over the dog's head.

I'm not about to tell him this, but her attachment is really no mystery when he looks at her like *that*.

"Your ice is in that bucket, by the way."

Oh, right. I reach inside the metal container and take out a small ice pack before pressing it against my tailbone. "Thanks."

"I hope your grave injury doesn't bother you too much."

"I'll survive."

He glances at me, amusement dancing inside his eyes. "Have you decided what you'll be doing today?"

"You know what. I'm getting my phone back."

His lips twitch. "Hmm. It might be harder than you think. I doubt you'll accomplish it in a day."

"We'll see. I'm very determined."

Something satisfied settles over his expression. "I had an idea for another way you can channel that determination."

"I'm fine, thanks."

He chuckles. "You know, your brother described you to me once as a 'sweet little girl.' There was no mention of this attitude, though."

Ugh. Did Dem really say that to him? I hate when my brother talks about me like I'm still five. I love him more than anything, but I swear it's like he's in denial about the fact that I'm fully grown. Sometimes, he still treats me like I'm a child.

I'm not, though.

And the thought that Giorgio might think of me as one makes me bristle with indignation. "Yeah, I'm sweet to people who don't confiscate my stuff."

His eyes spark. "Hmm. Well, like I already told you, my house, my rules, so you're just going to have to put up with listening to my ideas whether you want to or not. Have you ever learned any self-defense?"

His question takes me by surprise. "No. Why would I? I've had bodyguards my entire life."

"And what happens when they're incapacitated or get separated from you?"

"I guess I'm screwed."

He adjusts his cufflinks. "You can't make a habit of relying on other people. You need to be able to take care of yourself if it comes down to it."

My eyes widen. I agree with him...but Dem would definitely not. One time, I asked my brother to show me how to use a gun, and he categorically refused. He said he'll always be there to protect me, so I don't need to worry about it.

But that's not how things have worked out.

"What do you think about giving it a try?" Giorgio asks.

"I don't know." If I knew some self-defense, could that have really helped me fight off Lazaro when he showed up in Ibiza? Maybe. Then again, he was so strong, his arm felt like it was made of solid steel when it was wrapped around me. I felt completely powerless. Vivid memories of that day surface back up.

"I just..." I sigh, dropping my gaze to my lap. "The man who attacked me was very strong."

"There are techniques that allow you to use your opponent's strength against them."

I shake my head, still staring at my lap. I'd probably suck at it and embarrass myself in front of Giorgio. Haven't I managed to do that enough already in the past twenty-four hours?

Something presses against the underside of my chin—his fingers. He makes me meet his gaze.

"I could teach you," he says, his voice so soft I barely hear it over the burn from his touch. There's a flutter in my belly. It multiplies when he says, "I have a feeling you'll learn quickly."

He searches my expression, and I wonder if he can read all the hesitation spelled out across my face.

"I'll think about it," I say.

He looks like he's ready to argue further, but then Allegra's voice streams back into the room, and quickly, he drops his hand.

When Allegra returns, she's not alone. Tommaso follows behind her, along with a younger man.

Tommaso greets me as warmly as the night before and then gestures at Allegra.

"We're married," he says, "although she's been threatening to divorce me for the past decade."

"Quiet, Toma," Allegra chastises as she hands me a cappuccino. "Martina has just arrived here. You can wait a few days before you air out all the dirty laundry in front of her."

"Thank you," I say, taking the drink from her.

While Tommaso takes his seat, I glance at the man who came with him.

Curly hazel hair, sharp features, and a youthful glow that seems to put him around my age. His lips quirk up into a mischievous smile. A strange feeling washes over me. There's something familiar about this guy, but I can't quite place it. We've never met before.

Giorgio puts his coffee down and stands to greet the newcomer. "Polo."

They stare at each other for a moment and then exchange a brusque embrace that hints at familiarity, yet it contains little warmth.

"We weren't sure if you were really coming," Polo says. "You usually give more notice."

"It was a spontaneous decision."

"Yes, you're known for those." The way Polo says it makes it clear he means the opposite. His attention flicks back to me. "And you brought a guest."

Giorgio nods as he lowers back into his chair. "This is Martina De Rossi, sister of one of my colleagues. She'll be staying here for a while."

"Nice to meet you," I say.

Polo scans me over with his gaze. "The pleasure is mine. As you've probably heard, we don't get a lot of guests. Are you sure you didn't kidnap her, Giorgio? Blink twice if you need help."

Allegra and Tommaso chuckle, but for me, his joke hits too close to home, and I can't even muster up a fake laugh. I look down at my plate.

An awkward silence descends until Giorgio says, "Have a seat, Polo. Martina is too tired from last night's journey for your jokes."

I glance at Giorgio from under my lashes, and he gives me a tiny nod. I appreciate him taking the spotlight off me. I guess it's still too soon for kidnapping jokes.

"Let's eat, the food's going to get cold." Allegra says, removing the covers from the plates. There are scrambled eggs, yogurt, freshly baked bread, cold cuts, and a platter of berries.

"These are from our garden," she says in reference to the latter. "They're as sweet as candy."

My appetite stirs at the sight of the food. The last time I ate was when I was still in Ibiza.

While we take turns heaping our plates, the conversation around the table starts up again.

"Martina, have you been given a tour of the property? It's easy to get lost here if you don't know your way around," Allegra says.

"No, I haven't."

She gives me a smile. "How about after breakfast? Polo can show you around the pro—"

"I'll take her," Giorgio interrupts as he spears a piece of tomato with his fork.

I'm relieved to hear him say it. I don't know why I'm feeling so antsy around new people, but the thought of forcing a conversation with Polo fills me with anxiety. At least with Giorgio, I know what to expect.

"Sounds good," I say. A tour will help me get oriented around here so that I can figure out where he could have hidden my phone.

"Why did your brother send you here?" Polo asks from across the table. "Strange place for a young girl to spend her summer all alone."

"She's not alone," Giorgio responds. "She's with me."

Um. Does he have to say it like that? I shoot him a look.

His eyes meet mine, and my mind is probably playing tricks on me, because for a second, I think something possessive flashes inside of them.

"And what are your plans while you're here?" Polo asks, flicking his gaze between Giorgio and I.

"Martina's here to reconnect with nature," Giorgio says.

I purse my lips in his direction. Reconnect with nature? *Seriously?*

"Wonderful," Allegra says. "You couldn't have picked a better place. You'll see, this property is truly something special."

CHAPTER 7

MARTINA

BREAKFAST WRAPS UP SHORTLY AFTER, and when I finish my cappuccino, Giorgio leads me out of the dining room to begin our tour.

"The staff know better than to ask a lot of questions, but it appears they've forgotten their manners due to their excitement," he says once we're out of everyone's earshot.

"Thanks for answering them," I say quietly. "I didn't really know what to say."

"When in doubt, say less," he advises as we enter the living room.

"Is that a life philosophy?"

His lips twitch. "Something like that."

We stop by an enormous arched window, where I'm treated to another spectacular view of the forest I saw from my bedroom this morning. The skies are gray, but here and there, sunlight peeks out and paints patches of gold across the treetops.

Out of the corner of my eye, I see Giorgio turn to me. "I should make one thing clear. You are not to leave the property under any circumstances."

I resist the urge to roll my eyes at his grave tone. I mean, where would I even go? On the drive here last night, this place seemed like it was in the middle of nowhere. From up here, I can see a smattering of homes up on the hills in the far distance, but they're on the other side of the forest. "Fine."

"Besides that, you're free to roam the property with the exception of the forest. It's easy to get lost in."

I send a frown in his direction. "Allegra said Tommaso and Polo go running there."

His expression narrows with warning. "They know the land. You don't."

I let it go, not in the mood to argue over a point that doesn't matter much to me. Hiking isn't in my plans.

Closer to the castello is a large, rectangular pool with a stone deck around it. A small bird with a bright-yellow beak bobs on the surface of the water.

"Do you like to swim?" Giorgio asks.

I glance at him. He's facing the window, his arms clasped behind his back.

"I've lived in Ibiza most of my life. Of course I like to swim. Do you?"

"Not particularly."

"Really? But you're from Naples, and it's right on the sea."

"My mother was afraid of water, so we rarely went when I was a kid."

"Why was she afraid of it?"

He's still looking out the window as he says, "She had a bad experience once. Nearly drowned. I must have picked up on her distaste subconsciously."

"Hmm. My mom was very afraid of bees. Dem told me it was because her cousin got stung and died. My brother's afraid of bees too, even though he won't ever admit it out loud."

Giorgio gives me an amused look, and something about it sends warmth spreading through my gut. "You shouldn't tell people that. Your brother's weaknesses are about to become extremely valuable information."

I pale. "Crap. Forget I said it?"

"I'm afraid I have an exceptionally good memory."

"Do you really?"

He nods. "It's almost photographic."

Oh, great. Well, there goes my hope that he'll forget all the stupid things I've said to him so far.

We leave the living room and pass through a few sitting areas before drawing to another stop.

"This is the gym," Giorgio says, holding the door for me to take a look.

I peer inside. "Wow, it's big."

"It's the biggest room on this floor, besides the living room. It used to be the master bedroom, but I converted it after I purchased the property. Now, all the bedrooms are on the second and third floors, but only the ones on the second floor are in use." He lets the door swing shut.

"There aren't that many bedrooms upstairs, are there? Where does the staff live?"

"There's a guesthouse in the east end of the property," Giorgio explains. "It's newer than the rest of the castello— only about seventy years old. We renovated it five years ago and made the interior more modern. Allegra prefers it that way."

The last room we visit on this floor is the library. Lots of wood shelves with elaborate molding, aged tomes with red and black spines, and a window made of stained glass. It depicts a swan floating on a lake, a large, round moon above it. When a ray of sun hits the window, the colors come to life.

It's achingly beautiful. Something eases inside my chest for a moment as I gaze upon the image. "Do you come here often?"

Out of the corner of my eye, I see Giorgio nod. "I like to read here in the evenings, although I rarely find the time."

My gaze falls on the two leather armchairs by a coffee table, and I can totally see Giorgio sitting in one of them, nursing a glass of...

"Do you drink whiskey?"

His attention moves to me. "Sometimes. But I prefer a good Negroni."

"Hmm. Too bitter for me. I like rosé."

"Aren't you too young to drink?"

I frown. Does he think I'm under sixteen? Surely, I don't look *that* young.

His lips curve, and I realize he's joking.

"I already told you yesterday, I'm nearly nineteen," I tell him haughtily. "My birthday is next week."

"I apologize," he says over a warm chuckle. "I'll make sure Tommaso keeps the fridge filled with rosé."

"Now you make me sound like an alcoholic," I grumble as I follow him out of the room, but for some reason, I'm smiling too.

We stop before the spiral staircase that leads to our rooms.

"Like I said, upstairs are the bedrooms, most of which you've already seen."

"That's all that's there?" I squint against the sunlight streaming through a window. "What's that door over there?"

"That's my office."

Bingo.

That's got to be where he's storing my phone. I need to get a closer look at the lock and see if it's easy to pick. Not that I have much experience picking locks, but desperate times and all... There has to be some way for me to sneak in.

We exchange a look. "You spend a lot of time in there too?" I ask innocently.

Of course, he sees right through it. "Lots."

"Huh." I'll get him out of there somehow.

We're taking our first steps outside when Giorgio halts and takes out his phone.

"*Cazzo*," he says under his breath as he reads whatever is on the screen. "I have to go take a look at something in my office." He gestures at a building across from the garage. "Polo should be over there. Are you all right if he finishes the tour?"

"That's fine. What's his deal, by the way?" I ask.

Giorgio cocks a brow. "What do you mean?"

"He's young. I didn't expect someone his age to work here."

A shadow passes over Giorgio's expression.

"Is he Allegra and Tommaso's son or something?"

"No. He's not related to them. I hired him a few years ago, and he's done good work around the castello."

What a non-answer. Just then, Polo steps out of the small building holding something in his hands. He doesn't notice us.

"How do you know each other? He talks to you very casually."

"Sometimes."

"Don't think my brother's employees would ever talk to him that way," I say, trying to needle him on purpose. "Dem knows how to keep people in line."

"Given how you turned out, I highly doubt it."

"How *did* I turn out?"

"Like trouble."

I whip my head around at the comment, but all I see is Giorgio's back as he steps inside the castello.

He's right, I am trouble. Or at least, trouble seems to follow me everywhere. And yet unlike Polo's joke from earlier, Giorgio's comment doesn't land badly. The way he said it was almost...playful. Was he teasing me again?

"Hey, Martina!"

Polo's voice snaps my head in his direction. He's walking over to me, his curls tossing in the wind, and when he gets close, he throws me a wooden basket.

"What's this?" I ask, catching the object.

He puts his hands on his hips. "We need to gather the tomatoes before they turn too ripe."

I frown at him, caught off guard. "And what does that have to do with me?"

He scans me with mischievous gray eyes and then smirks. "It's a fun experience."

"Fun experience? Sounds like free labor."

"Hey, city folk pay a lot to come to places just like these and pick berries or whatever is in season. You've never done it?"

"No. Back home, I get my vegetables at the store, like a normal person." I try to hand the basket back to him, but he won't take it.

"Where's home?"

"Ibiza."

He whistles. "Wow. Not bad. You live there with your brother?"

I give up and place the basket on the ground. "Yes."

"What's his name?"

I give him a weary look. Giorgio really could have given me more clear instructions about what I can and cannot say to people. But he already introduced me to everyone with my full name, so it's not a secret. If Polo really wanted to, he could just look me up and find out Dem's name.

"Damiano De Rossi."

Apparently satisfied with my answer, Polo nods and picks the basket back up. "Let's go. I'll show you the grounds and the garden, and then we'll get to work. You'll really be helping me out. There's a ton to do this week."

And that's how he gets me. I'd be an asshole to say no to helping him, right?

"All right."

Polo comes to my side and throws his arm around my shoulders. "I knew you'd come around. Now, soak it all in," he says, gesturing at the yard. "The landscaping, the water features, that great old hunk of a castello—isn't it glorious?"

I slip out from under this arm even as a smile tugs at my lips at his dramatic tone. He's an interesting character. "Very."

He laughs and places his palm against my lower back. "This way. We're going to take the long way around, so that I can point out all the sights. Giorgio will have my head if you end up lost somewhere."

We walk around the castello, with Polo pointing out the staff house, storage buildings, small gurgling wall fountains, and finally, the tower.

He stops ahead of it and shields his eyes from the sun with his palm. "We don't use the tower much, but you get the best view from up there. If you're interested, you can take the spiral stairs that lead up to the terrace. The place is a bit rickety, but it's safe."

I consider the old building. Unlike the castello, which is majestic and sprawling, the tower is narrow and prison-like. Tiny windows, gray brick facade. Not at all inviting.

"Maybe later," I offer. "Have you been up there?"

"A few times."

I turn to look at Polo, my curiosity about him stirring back up. "So when did you start working here?"

"When I was twenty-three. So two years ago."

I was right. He's not much older than me. "What brought you here?"

Polo flicks his gaze to me. "It's a boring story, to be honest. My mom knew Giorgio, and she arranged it with him. I'd graduated university, studying agriculture, but there was no work. So I took the only option I had available."

"How does your mom know Giorgio?"

"Knew. She died a few months after I started working here."

"Oh, I'm sorry."

Polo ignores my condolences. "My mom knew his mom. They used to live in the same neighborhood."

Strange. If this place is as big of a secret as Giorgio made it sound, how come he just hired Polo that easily? How did Polo earn his trust?

Our next stop is the greenhouse, which is just on the edge of the garden. Even from here, I can already spot the heaping tomato plants in the distance.

Polo holds the door of the greenhouse open for me. "Leave the basket here. I'll show you some of the plants we have and that will be it for our tour."

I enter the building and take it all in. The construction of a white frame closed in with plexiglass lets in abundant light and, as far as I can tell, the plants here are thriving. For a moment, I close my eyes, and inhale the earthy, wet smell. It sinks right to the bottom of my lungs, smooth and calming.

Polo comes to stand by my side. "There are a lot of herbs and leafy greens over here." He points to the section on the left. "Tommaso uses a lot of it in the kitchen."

I take a few steps closer and break off a piece of what looks like dill, bringing it to my nose and inhaling the distinctive scent.

"Many plants here are native to the region," Polo says, "but some are from places far away. This is a kava-kava plant." He points out a plant with big, heart-shaped leaves. "And

Mexican epazote. And here are the usual suspects: tarragon, rosemary, marjoram."

"Sage and mint," I finish.

He hikes a brow. "You know plants?"

I shrug. "I grew some herbs back home to use for cooking. Nothing special, just the basics."

"Well, if you ever feel like cooking dinner, I can guarantee you that Tommaso would appreciate the night off."

We wrap up the tour and head back outside, making our way to the tomato plants.

Polo gets his own basket, and after a quick demonstration, we both get to work. It's slow and monotonous, but it doesn't take me long to get into a mindless kind of flow. It's the same calming feeling I get when I work on a jigsaw puzzle. After a while, some pressure in my head eases, and my muscles relax.

It's surprisingly nice.

Polo doesn't say much while we work, but sometimes, I catch his eye.

"What?" I ask the next time I notice him glancing at me.

"It's just weird to have someone other than Tommaso and Allegra here. Giorgio never brings anyone."

"You ever feel like a third wheel?" I ask. I've felt that way before around Dem and Vale. Given how remote and secret this place is, does Polo even get a chance to leave now and then?

He chuckles under his breath, but it's humorless. "Oh, yeah. It's the worst when they fight. Doesn't happen often, but when it does, it's like being in the middle of a war zone."

I pluck off another tomato. "Do you get bored out here?"

"Like you wouldn't believe. Maybe it won't be so bad with you around," he says, nudging my arm lightly with his elbow.

Heat creeps up my cheeks. Is he flirting with me?

"Of course, I might not be here for much longer," he adds.

Scratching an itch in the center of my forehead, I look at him from under my hand. "Oh?"

He nods. "There might be another opportunity opening up for me. I just need to convince Giorgio to let me try my hand at it."

"What kind of an opportunity?"

Polo wipes his mouth with the back of his hand and places one more tomato inside his basket. "Can't tell you. I don't know how much you know about Giorgio, Martina De Rossi."

"Not much," I say, although I suspect Polo is alluding to Giorgio's affiliation with the clan. Still, there's no way I'll be the first one to broach that topic.

He appears to feel the same way, redirecting the conversation. "Nothing's been confirmed yet. I just have some ideas. This property is beautiful, but I don't want to spend the rest of my life taking care of it."

I glance back at the main building. "Why did he buy it?" The castello is enormous. If Giorgio wanted to have a safe house somewhere, I'm sure there are plenty of smaller places he could have bought that would be far easier to maintain.

"Giorgio had his reasons, but in truth, I think he hates this place."

My brows pinch together. "He does? Why?"

Polo stands and heaves his basket over his shoulder. He seems like he's about to say something, but then he gives his head a shake, and says, "You'll have to ask him yourself."

CHAPTER 8

GIORGIO

IMAGES MOVE across the dozen monitors attached to the wall of my office, their glow the only source of light in the room. The wooden shutters on the window haven't been opened in years, and that's just the way I like it. With the windows closed off, I can almost pretend I'm some place other than here.

My eyes scan the monitors, looking for any sign that key players in the clan are aware of the war on their doorsteps. It's those first few minutes and phone calls after the news drops that will reveal most of what we'll need. Fear and panic are powerful motivators. They cloud good judgment. They make people do revealing things.

I sink backwards in my leather chair and take a sip of coffee. One of the feeds is from a camera pointed at the main square in Casal di Principe. Some neighborhood kids run around the sputtering fountain in the plaza, oblivious to the four bulletproof cars parked in front of the church. The alert I got earlier came from the facial-recognition software I have running on this device when it detected Sal's arrival.

Another camera shows the church's interior. It's packed today for Sunday service, and Sal's in his usual spot in one of the front pews.

On Sal's left is his consiglieri, Calisto Lettiero, and on his right is his latest mistress. The two men are listening closely to the priest's sermon, a man Sal handpicked himself. In Casal, the mafia rules even in the house of God. Nothing escapes its reach.

The chair creaks beneath me as I shift my weight. I miss the setup I have back in my apartment on the outskirts of Naples. Double the monitors, a desk twice the size, and a chair that can comfortably hold my weight without any whining. When De Rossi called me about taking in Martina, I knew I'd be stuck here for longer than normal, and I briefly considered upgrading the equipment, but it felt too much like settling in.

The thought of doing that makes my skin crawl.

It had been a bad idea to buy this place, but I didn't realize it until it was too late. My mother lived here a long time ago. I thought I'd be honoring her memory. Instead, the first time I opened the door with my new key, I felt an overwhelming sense of intruding on something that wasn't meant for me.

There were other locations I could have taken Martina, but not on that short of a notice. The castello is the best place for her—secure, hidden, and comfortable. Big enough for both of us to have our own space during the day.

I didn't think she'd be so taken aback by our sleeping arrangements. After all, it made sense that I'd be close to her when she's asleep and most vulnerable. But after one night, I'm already starting to doubt the wisdom of putting her so near me.

First, that maddening "I sleep naked" comment. Then discovering her in just a flimsy pajama set in my room this morning—I could see the outline of her nipples clear as day.

And *then* that fucking bruise...

Just the memory of her smooth skin and the dip of her spine sends a jolt of lust to my dick. How her snooping around my room escalated to her pulling down her tiny shorts in front of me defies any kind of logical explanation.

I drag my palm over my mouth. Whatever the fuck that was can't happen again. I didn't need to touch her, but I just couldn't resist. I know better than to cross any kind of line with her. If she says a word of it to her brother, my plan is screwed. He needs to have full trust in me for all of the pieces to work, and whatever aspirations he has for his sister sure as fuck don't involve a man like me.

I freeze with my coffee mug halfway to my mouth when I see Calisto reach for his phone. Everyone knows not to call him during the sermon unless it's truly urgent, which means this might be the phone call I've been waiting for.

Calisto presses the device to his ear and listens.

I toggle to the camera located behind the priest so that I can see his reaction.

Slack expression. Wide eyes. His lips spit out a curse word.

This gets Sal's attention.

I read the don's lips. *"What?"* he asks.

Calisto hangs up and whispers something into Sal's ear.

The two men stand up and leave through the side door in a rush, a trickle of soldiers following after them. The rest of the audience exchanges worried looks. Everyone knows Sal never leaves Sunday service early unless something is really wrong.

Minutes later, the logs are bursting with frantic phone calls. I'm not omnipotent, but all my surveillance systems get me pretty damn close. I'll let the AI analyze the recordings for keywords, and when it's done, I'll send the relevant bits to Ras, Damiano's right-hand man. He'll have the unenviable task of listening through it all until he finds something useful for his boss.

My role in this war is pulling on certain strings from behind the scenes. If I announced I'm going to De Rossi's side now, there would be widespread panic. Probably good for De Rossi, but terrible for me. Even if he wins this war, as soon as it becomes common knowledge that I backed him from the start, I won't have a job left. I'll be seen as someone whose loyalty is easily swayed. None of the clan members will trust me again, and when it comes to giving someone priceless valuables to hide away, some trust is fucking necessary.

I have to play this carefully. I want De Rossi to win, but I can't fuck myself over in the process. If I make it seem like I switched sides only once the key players in the clan aligned themselves with De Rossi, I'll be seen as a neutral party simply following the lead of others.

The human version of Switzerland.

But sharing information is something I can do quietly, and it's a resource as valuable as money or ammo. I learned that lesson at fifteen when I managed to hack into encrypted police comms and sell that information to an area capo. The capo had been pressuring me for nearly a week to join his sorry gang of drug pushers in Secondigliano. If I'd kept brushing him off, the conversation would have turned to threats, so the next time he came to me, I handed him something far better than the cash he could have made off my back.

I'm doing the same for Damiano now. Lending him my particular skill set in exchange for freedom.

Or at least my version of it.

A knock sounds on the door. "It's Polo. Can we talk?"

Tossing back the rest of my coffee, I rise from the chair and step out into the hallway.

Sweat glistens on Polo's face, and his white T-shirt is marred with streaks of dirt. He must have just come back from the garden with Martina.

Something unpleasant twists inside my gut at the thought of them there together. I didn't like leaving her outside with him.

Especially after that comment she made about how young he was.

Yes, they aren't far in age, but so what? It's not something she should pay any mind to.

I meet Polo's gaze. "What is it?"

He presses his palm into the wall and puts his weight on it. "What is that girl really doing here?"

My lips tighten into a line. Polo and I have a thread connecting us that few people know about, and he thinks that gives him an excuse to push my boundaries. I let him get away with it more than I should because I know why he is the way he is.

I see much of myself in him.

"I already said everything I'm going to say on the matter."

"She's from Spain and she's here to reconnect with nature?" he mocks. "Since when are we running a wellness retreat?"

I ignore his snark. "Did you give her the tour?"

"Yeah, and I put her to work. She's still in the garden picking tomatoes."

When a frown appears on my face, he shows me his palms. "If that's not reconnecting with nature, what is?"

I massage the back of my neck with my hand. "How did she take it?"

"Grumbled a bit. Then did as she was told."

"She's not yours to command."

Polo sniffs, his eyes swimming with something that rubs me the wrong way. "Whose is she then?"

"No one's. She's a fucking guest, Polo. Treat her as such. No more garden duty unless she asks you for it."

Now, he doesn't bother trying to hide his scowl. "You're really not going to tell me what she's doing here?"

"It's none of your business," I grind out.

"Yeah, it never is."

"What is that supposed to mean?"

He volleys his gaze down the hall and then back to me. "Have you spoken to my father in the time you've been gone?"

Not. This. Again.

"Don't call him that," I bite out.

He whips his head around, anger contorting his features. Polo has a short fuse. He can be charming, but I've seen him at his worst, and that charm can turn right off at the flick of a switch.

"I can call him that if I want to."

"I've known you two years. How many more before you realize he'll never be that for you?" There was a time when I gentled my words, but not now. Not with everything that's going on.

"The letter—"

"Clearly, he didn't deem your letter worthy of a response."

Polo narrows his mistrustful eyes at me. "What if he never got it?"

A prickling feeling appears at the back of my neck. Can he know? No, this is just his desperation coming up with scenarios that would explain why his sperm donor never contacted him.

"Polo, he got it. It's time for you to move on."

Placing my hand on his shoulder, I give it a squeeze. His jaw tenses, and then he steps away from me, letting my hand drop.

I watch him retreat.

It's been two years since he came into my life. Two years since Signora Silvestri, his disabled mother, called me and begged me to take him in. She was dying, and he was her only son. As an only child myself, I knew exactly the lengths good women would go to ensure a decent future for their offspring. I couldn't say no.

She passed almost as soon as the arrangements were put in place, her soul finally free of burden and ready to let go.

Ever since, I've wondered if that's how my mother felt right before she died, or if the horrors of her past just became too much.

She struggled her entire life for me.

Because of me.

My "father" was useless. Even before I knew the truth about their marriage, I was repulsed by him. On occasion, he'd try to give me a hug when he was intoxicated enough to turn affectionate, but I'd never let him. It didn't take him long to give up.

Visiting him is something I loathe, but sometimes he has information no one else does. The most he attempts now is a handshake.

Polo never met his father, which has to be the reason why he's done nothing but romanticize the idea of him. One day, he'll have to let it go.

That day may be forced on him sooner than later.

I lock the office door behind me and make my way to the stairs. Through the window by the landing, there's a direct view of the edge of the garden, and I think I see a flash of Martina's golden hair.

A vise squeezes around my chest at seeing her all alone. At breakfast, she looked a little like a lost puppy when everyone was eating with us, but I don't blame her for being overwhelmed at being thrown into a new environment and meeting new people.

Allegra and Tommaso worked here even before I bought the property. It's their home far more than it is mine, even if I own it on paper. Still, I don't want them to be too much for Martina. Perhaps it's best if they take some meals separately from time to time. It'll give me a chance to better understand what's going on inside her head.

She already seems to be doing better. That hollow look in her eyes is gone. She's annoyed with me, but I can deal with her anger. While she's working on getting her phone back, she's focused on something other than her own thoughts, and anything is better than being stuck in your own head.

She'll heal one day at a time, and when I return her to De Rossi, he'll be even more indebted to me.

Before I know it, I'm outside, walking in the direction of the garden.

She's easy enough to spot kneeling amidst all the green. A full basket of tomatoes sits a few meters away from her, but now she's picking strawberries and she's so absorbed in the task she doesn't even notice my shadow falling over her.

I frown. She needs to learn how to be more aware of her

surroundings. I'm going to give her a few more days to think about the self-defense classes before I insist on giving them to her. The thought came to me last night while I was lying in bed. I put myself in her shoes and thought about how I'd feel if I was overpowered by someone the way she was by Lazaro.

Some confidence in her own ability to fight back if something like that ever happened again can't hurt.

I'm about to say something to get her attention, but then she picks out a fat strawberry and brings it to her lips. I watch her profile as she takes a bite, and blood rushes to my groin.

Fuck.

How many times do I have to remind myself she's a teenager? I know better than to fantasize about having those lips wrapped around my cock.

And yet I do.

Frequently.

I clear my throat.

She whips around, that plump mouth covered in pink juice before she laps it away with her tongue.

I bite on the inside of my mouth.

"What?" she says, startled. There's a smudge of dirt on her forehead.

"Everything all right down here?"

She flicks her gaze over me. "No."

Alarm ring inside my ears. "What's wrong?"

Clambering to her feet, she presses her small basket of berries into my chest. "Don't think I don't see what you're doing."

"What am I doing?"

"Trying to keep me distracted."

Oh. A smirk teases at my lips. "Seems like the distractions are working. Polo didn't ask you to do this bit, did he?"

She looks down at the strawberries. "They're a night away from being too ripe. It would be wasteful to let them spoil. I'm sure Tommaso has many uses for them."

"What about you?" I pass the basket back to her. "Your brother told me you also like to cook."

She shakes her head. "More attempts at distracting me? Trust me, Giorgio, my current interests start and end at finding my phone before I go completely insane out here."

Somewhere, a rooster emits a loud cry, as if to punctuate her last word.

Insane.

I've already gone insane here once. Or at least that's what it felt like.

My gaze sways to the forest, and I'm immediately transported right back to that night. Hours of digging. Earth, pink worms, and the smell of old, decomposing flesh. The rage I felt when I was once again forced to confront the circumstances that led to my mother's death was one of the most disturbing things I've ever experienced.

I succumbed to the anger. Let it take control of me. And when I finally snapped out of it, I found a trail of destruction.

Growing up, I always knew there was something sick inside of me. That night just served as a reminder that the sickness never left.

Cutting my trip down memory lane short, Martina attempts to shoulder past me, but I reach out and grab her by the forearm.

She looks at my hand, then at my face, her eyes wide and questioning.

Why am I touching her again? Because I can't seem *not* to, but I have to give a better reason than that. I look for an excuse and use the first one I find.

"You have dirt on your forehead."

She blinks and tries to wipe it off with a rough drag of her palm. "Did I get it?"

"No."

I lift my thumb to her skin.

Her mouth parts slightly. "You don't have to do that."

I know I don't. Gently, I wipe the dirt off. Her breath catches, and when I meet her gaze, a blush appears across her freckled cheeks.

The wide-eyed look she's giving me makes me think she's never been this close to another man. It's possible. De Rossi may have been lenient with her, but there's no way he'd let some random Spaniard touch his little sister. He knows her value. He knows he's going to have to make use of her innocence when it comes to forging the alliances that will cement his rule.

Martina is a virgin, that much is sure.

A wicked curiosity ignites inside of me. What would she do if I wrapped my hand around the back of her neck and forced her lips against mine? Would she fight against it? Stand there frozen in surprise?

Or would she turn pliant and let me taste the inside of her mouth?

You're never going to find out.

I drop my hand and step away. "It's gone."

She swallows. "Thanks."

I leave her and her strawberry-stained lips in that wretched dirt and make my way back to the castello.

CHAPTER 9

MARTINA

DESPITE BEING sure Giorgio's keeping my phone in his office, I spend the next two days trying and failing to come up with a way to break in.

Two. Long. Days.

Two. Long. Nights.

The lock on the door isn't one of those flimsy handle locks that you can pick with a bobby pin. I guess it was optimistic of me to hope that it would be, given it's Giorgio we're talking about. The keyhole is a strange shape. It looks like he has some fancy key for it, which he must keep on himself all the time.

On the third night, I request to take dinner in my bedroom and spend the evening trying to come up with some workable ideas, but I just end up giving myself a headache out of frustration.

I haven't been sleeping well, and I'm tired.

Polo has been inviting me to the garden every day to help him—yes, actually *inviting me* rather than commanding. At first, I thought he was doing it because Giorgio asked him, but yesterday, when Giorgio saw us leave the castello to go to the garden, he didn't seem too happy. He barked something at Polo in Neapolitan dialect that I didn't understand, and Polo gave him a curt reply before leading me outside. When I asked what that was all about, Polo brushed my question aside.

Maybe Polo's just taking advantage of me agreeing to help him, but in truth, I don't mind. I've warmed up to digging in the dirt and picking vegetables and berries.

Polo and I mostly work on opposite sides of the garden, so it's not like his company is a bother. He's alright. Besides an occasional flirtatious remark that makes my nape prickle uncomfortably, he hasn't been hard to get along with.

My problems begin when I come back to my room at the end of the day and there's nothing to do but sit with my thoughts. Ugly, painful thoughts. I need an outlet. Until now, I've always had Imogen.

That heavy-duty lock flashes again before my eyes. How do I get past it? *Can* I get past it? Or did Giorgio give me an impossible task?

Bouncing my head against the mattress, I release a loud sigh. The less I sleep, the more tired I am, and the more tired I am, the more I ruminate and keep myself awake. It's a vicious cycle.

Maybe it's time for plan B. There's got to be something else in this house that'll help me get to sleep.

My bags still need unpacking, so I occupy myself with the task until the clock ticks past midnight, and then when the house is quiet, I step out into the hallway. A light shines from under Giorgio's bedroom, and I imagine him reading one of those history books.

In my visual, he's topless in his bed.

I roll my eyes at myself. *That* incident hasn't been repeated, but I'd be lying if I said I haven't thought about it.

Often.

I bite down on my lip and eye his doorway. He's been busy with work, so I haven't seen much of him outside of breakfast and dinner. In the evenings, I hear him move on the other side of the wall, and just the knowledge of how close he is to me is enough to send a thrill down my spine.

His offer to teach me self-defense has stayed on my mind even though he hasn't brought it up again.

I'd be lying if I said I wasn't at least a little tempted to take him up on it. But when I examine *why* that is, the answer scares me.

It's not because I'm that eager to learn a new skill.

It's because I want to be around him.

There's something about his presence that draws me in. I have to keep reminding myself that he's the reason I'm miserable at the moment, but even that isn't enough to spoil his allure.

"Every object under my protection is of immense value, Martina. And you might just be the most valuable of them all."

My skin tingles at the memory. He said it like he meant it, and for a moment, I may have even believed him. But the truth is, I feel far from valuable. My name notwithstanding, I have nothing to offer to anyone. My brother's life would be a hell of a lot easier, and Imogen would still be alive if I were never born.

When the backs of my eyes start to prickle, I look at the ceiling and suck in a breath to stave off the tears. No, I refuse to cry out of self-pity.

Turning away from Giorgio's door, I move silently down the steps, through the living room, and into the kitchen.

Before I manage to find a switch on the wall, a light flicks on.

My heart drops.

"Jesus!"

It's Polo. He arches a brow. "What are you doing creeping around in the dark?"

"I didn't know where to turn on the light. What are you doing here?"

"Allegra asked me to get her some tea. We ran out of the one she likes in the staff house," he explains as he opens a cupboard and takes out a jar filled with dried herbs. "Fennel. It's good for digestion."

While my racing heart slows down, I walk over to him and peer inside. The cupboard is lined with shelves displaying glass jars of herbs and spices.

I hesitate for a moment before asking, "Do you have anything to help with sleep?"

Polo nods. "Sure. Valerian." He takes one of the jars and passes it to me. "Two teaspoons to a cup. Otherwise it's too strong."

I take it from him.

"We grow it in the greenhouse. All of these are from there actually," he says as he closes the cupboard. "Kettle should be on the counter."

"Thanks."

"You're welcome." His eyes drop to the neckline of my camisole, and when his gaze lingers, I get the sudden urge to cover up.

I wrap my arms around me, feeling exposed. I should have put on a sweater before I came down here.

He clears his throat and lifts his eyes back to my face. "Goodnight, Martina," he says with a tight smile.

"Night."

Once he's gone, I fill the kettle with water, put it on the stove, and find myself a mug. A sleeping pill would probably be more effective, but I'll give this a try.

Fifteen minutes after I finish the tea, I'm thinking Polo lied to me. I'm lying in bed in the dark, but nothing's happening. I should have used three teaspoons instead of two. Two teaspoons to a cup or it's too strong... Yeah, right. I close my eyes for just a moment.

~

The next time I blink, it's morning.

Propping myself up on my elbows, I glance at the clock on the wall.

Nine am.

My eyes widen. I slept for eight full hours? *How?*

Jesus. The tea. It worked!

I sit up and swing my legs over the side of the bed, but as soon as I do, I'm hit with a wave of lightheadedness.

Ugh. This is terrible. My head is *so* muddled.

I rub my fists over my eyes and glance around, trying to orient myself despite the brutal brain fog. I got to sleep all right, but I don't like how I feel right now. It feels like I was shaken awake halfway through a deep dream.

The fog clears after I take a long, cool shower, and when I come out, there's a plate of breakfast on my desk. I pick at it a bit while I try to formulate a plan for the day. I don't think I want to drink that tea again, so I'm back to square one. I really need to get my phone back.

I pace around the room. Stare out the window. When no great strategy comes to me, I venture out of the room.

A strange, rhythmic sound comes from somewhere downstairs.

I follow it until it leads me to the gym. The door is cracked open, and I peek inside to see Giorgio working on a punching bag.

My mouth goes dry as I take him in. I've never seen him in athletic clothes before. He's wearing a pair of dark-navy joggers and a fitted black shirt that molds to his athletic build. As he moves around the bag and throws punches, his back muscles flex, highlighting his sculpted physique.

A quiet sigh escapes past my lips. God, he's sexy. I could watch him move all day, and for a few minutes, that's exactly what I do. He seems oblivious to me, so I get bolder with my gaze, letting it drift over his back and down to his butt.

Firm.

Round.

Probably as hard as a rock.

Images of him on top of me and my nails digging into that butt assault my imagination. Heat swirls between my legs. I've never felt this kind of an attraction to a man before.

It's the hormones, remember? a weak voice says inside my head.

I clench my fists. Whatever it is, it's making me lightheaded again.

With considerable struggle, I manage to tear my gaze away from Giorgio. I'm about to walk away when something else catches my attention.

In the corner of the gym stands one of those wooden jump boxes, and laying on top of it is a set of keys.

The haze of my inappropriate arousal parts to make way for excitement.

I'd bet my left arm those are Giorgio's keys, and one of them leads to his office.

Suddenly, the punches cease. "Are you going to lurk in the doorway all day or are you finally here for our lessons?"

My attention snaps to Giorgio. He arches a brow in challenge and presses one gloved hand against the bag to keep it from swinging.

"Um..." I swallow, my mind still fixated on those keys. Given how crazy he is about security, I wouldn't be surprised if he only takes them out of his pocket here and in his bedroom. What if training with him is the best chance I'll have?

"Well?" He drops his arm from the bag and prowls toward me until he's only inches away. I resist the urge to take one step back. He's close enough for me to notice a single drop of sweat roll over his collarbone.

"I'll go easy on you," he says, the words rumbling inside his chest. When our eyes lock, he serves me one of his barely-there smirks. "At first."

I drag my damp palms over my thighs. Should I do it? It's the only semblance of a plan I have. I can't rely on that tea to sleep. It makes me feel too weird.

Decision made, I let out a breath. "Okay. I'll give it a try."

Satisfaction flashes across his expression. "Good. Go get changed."

"Right now?"

"You've already spent days humming and hawing. Let's go," he says roughly.

Looks like I need to brace myself for the worst. I get the distinct feeling Giorgio's going to be a tough instructor. "All right. Give me ten minutes."

"Five."

I shoot him a glare, but he doesn't notice, as he's already walking back to the bag.

When I return in my gym clothes, he's still throwing punches, so while I wait for him, I examine the gym a bit more closely.

Equipment lines the perimeter, and there's a big empty space in the middle with a padded mat. There's a lot of light, high ceilings, and the mirrors on the wall make the gym seem even bigger than it really is.

Giorgio catches my gaze in one of them as he takes off his boxing gloves.

"Ready?"

Not exactly. I anticipate I'm going to absolutely suck at this.

My tongue darts out to lick my dry lips. "Yep."

He nods. "Get on the mat then."

I shrug off my zip-up, letting it drop to the ground, and then meet him in the center of the mat.

His eyes scan my body, his gaze assessing but not entirely cold.

"Have you ever taught anyone before?" I ask, my heart bouncing against my ribs.

He cuts a circle around me. "No. But I had a good martial arts teacher many years ago, and I'm going to show you some of what he taught me."

I glance over my shoulder, following his movements. "I always thought made men learned this kind of stuff on the job."

He stops before me. "They do, but I wanted to have an edge. There's only so much you can learn from getting into brawls. We're going to jump right into practicing some escape skills. Those will be most useful, since for someone your size, the best strategy is to get away from the attacker and run. You want to avoid fighting at all costs, as chances are you'll lose," he says bluntly.

"Makes sense."

"Let's start with how you escape a wrist hold. Give me your wrists."

Snakes move inside my belly as I extend my arms. He's so intense. His big, warm palms engulf my wrists with a firm grip. "Try to escape."

I tug. And tug. And TUG.

"Ugh! I can't. You're too strong."

"Instead of pulling toward your chest, jerk your wrists up, as if you're trying to break through my thumb."

I do as he says, but his hold on me doesn't budge.

"Harder, Martina. Use all of your strength."

"I'm trying." His hand might as well be an iron shackle. "It's not working."

He readjusts his grip. "Pull downward first, and then quickly jerk your wrists up. You'll see, it'll help."

I'm skeptical, but I do as he says.

To my surprise, I manage to break free. My eyes widen. "How? You must've been holding me less firmly."

"I wasn't. Here, let's reverse. You'll see how effective the move is when you feel it yourself."

The tip of my thumb doesn't reach my index finger when I wrap my palms around his wrists, but I squeeze as hard as I can.

He uses the same technique on me, and suddenly, I understand. "It's like you're confusing me about which direction you're going to go in."

"Exactly. When I pull down, the thumb loosens."

"Let me try one more time."

He steps closer and takes me into his hands. While I run through the technique in my head, his right thumb slowly swipes over my wrist.

My gaze jolts up to his. The burst of adrenaline inside my veins from that tiny, barely-there movement can't be healthy. Why did he do that?

What does it mean?

Whatever answers I hope to find in his expression never appear. A shadow shifts over his face before he glances away. "Go ahead."

Down, then up.

The second I escape, he steps away.

We practice for another hour before Giorgio decides to call it a day. When we finish, he walks over to the wooden box, picks up his keys, and slides them into his pocket. "Same time tomorrow."

Brusque tone. Firm shoulders.

"Okay."

When he walks by me, all I get is a passing glance, and I'm left wondering if I imagined that light caress.

CHAPTER 10

MARTINA

As I step out of my bedroom dressed in my workout clothes, I'm met with the sound of heavy footsteps. My gaze lands on a pair of brown work boots thudding down the hardwood floor.

"Where were you yesterday?" Polo asks as he stops in front of me, his white shirt half-tucked inside a pair of well-worn jeans. "Bored of the work already?"

I give him a smile. "I was busy with something."

"Doubt it." His gaze skims over my shoulder before sliding back to me. To my surprise, he lifts his fingers up to my face and tucks a strand of hair behind my ear. "There really isn't much to be busy with around here."

"She was with me."

Giorgio's voice is like a distant roll of thunder, low and ominous. I whip my head around in time to see him step out of his room. He stops by my side, his biceps brushing against my shoulder.

Polo tips his chin up to look at Giorgio, his gaze sharpening and his lips curving into a smirk. "Ah. My apologies. I see you've taken responsibility for our guest's entertainment on yourself."

"He's not entertaining me," I clarify. "He's teaching me."

"Is he?"

"Yes. Self-defense."

Sarcasm soaks his voice as he says, "Oh, right. A critical skill to know while you're vacationing in a remote castello." He shifts his weight between his feet, linking his palms behind him. "I hope he's thoroughly *hands-on* with you, Martina. An engaged instructor is the best way to learn."

Embarrassment creeps up my chest. Is he insinuating there's something inappropriate about our lessons?

During the night, I managed to thoroughly convince myself that brush of his thumb along my wrist was a figment of my overactive imagination. At most, it might have been an absentminded twitch. If we're going to keep doing these lessons, I have to stop reading into things like that.

Giorgio takes a step forward, annoyance rolling off him in waves. "Indeed. The program I'm putting Martina through is intense, so she's unlikely to have the energy to help you in the garden. I know you're more than capable of handling it on your own."

Polo's jaw hardens. "Of course."

"Good."

They stare at each other for a long moment. Then, a palm wraps around my elbow and applies light pressure. "Come on, Mari. I have a hard stop at twelve."

Mari.

I somehow manage to mutter a goodbye to Polo despite all of my mental faculties zooming in on that one word.

Giorgio just called me Mari.

When did we get so familiar with each other?

My pulse pounds inside my ears even as the rational part of my brain says it's no big deal. But when I glance at Giorgio from under my lashes, his expression is tense, and he won't meet my eye, like he knows that nickname shouldn't have just slipped out like that.

He lets go off my elbow when my feet touch the padded mat, and he walks over to the box to dump his keys.

"We need to work on your strength and conditioning."

"Why—"

"Ten push-ups, twenty squats, thirty sit-ups. Five rounds. Go."

My brows scrunch up. "But why—"

His eyes flash with irritation. "Let's go, Martina! While you're with me, you do as I say, got it?"

The frustration in his tone snaps my spine straight. *Jesus.* What is his deal?

"Okay," I say, getting to the ground. "No need to shout."

He scowls. "I'll count it out."

What follows is twenty-five minutes of pure torture. Giorgio skips counting the reps I do with poor form, which is most of them, and after he demonstrates how to do it correctly, he forces me to do it all over again.

By the time I'm done with the five rounds, my body feels like jelly, and I can barely breathe. I fold over at my waist and anchor my palms on my knees. We haven't even started the actual lesson.

"What are we learning today?" I pant, peeking at him through the loose strands of hair hanging over my face.

He motions for me to come over to the center of the mat. "We're going to go over the same moves as yesterday."

Straightening back up, I walk over to him. "Really? I think I got it. Can we try something new?"

He considers me for a moment. "If you can break my hold on first try, we'll do something new."

A fire lights inside of me at the hint of skepticism in his voice. After the wringer he just put me through, I want to prove him wrong. "Fine."

Firm stance. His hands on my wrists. His grip tightens.

I don't waste a second before I execute the technique.

"Ha!" Hopping away, I raise my freed wrists above my head. "Told you."

The line between his brows softens. "Good work. You're a quick learner."

A smile tugs at my lips. "You're a good teacher—when you're not trying to kill me with drills, that is. Yesterday, you were much more patient."

He glances at me, his lips curving at the corners a tiny bit. "Patient? I must've finally acquired that quality in my old age."

My cheeks heat at the teasing tone of his voice. Is that a dig at me for calling him old on our way to the castello? "You know, I don't actually think you're old."

His gaze flickers with something dark. "Compared to you, I am."

I tilt my head to the side. "Let me guess. Thirty?"

"Thirty-three."

I suppose I can see it, but I have to admit I never thought thirty-three could look this damn good on a man. My eyes drag down his body, and something sparks in the air around us, like a current gone awry.

Giorgio clears his throat and casts a look at the wall. "Is there something particular you'd like to learn today?"

I rake through my brain, looking for an idea. I'm sure if I asked, he'd take the lead, but it feels like I *earned* this chance to direct the rest of the lesson. Might as well choose something that's interesting to me.

The obvious thing would be to try and reenact one of the situations with Lazaro, but the thought of attempting that makes my stomach hollow out. I'm nowhere close to ready.

Then it comes to me. A memory from before my life went to shit.

At my private school, there were rarely any fights, but in my third year, there was one fight that everyone talked about for weeks afterward. It broke out in the cafeteria—two guys discovered they were dating the same girl. One of them was the captain of the swim team. The other, an amateur boxer. They threw punches for a little bit, but then the bigger swim captain pinned the boxer to the wall, his hands around his throat. The size difference worked in his favor because the boxer couldn't reach him in that position. He was turning blue by the time security broke it up. Both of them ended up expelled.

I glance at Giorgio. "How would I get away if someone bigger than me pinned me to a wall?"

His eyes narrow, and his jaw hardens. "Has someone done that to you?" he asks, his voice razor edged.

I shake my head. "No. I just watched a fight once, and the guy who was pinned couldn't get away."

His shoulders lower. "That's what you want to learn?"

"Yeah."

"All right. Go stand by the wall."

When my back is pressed against the cold plaster and he stops a step away from me, my pulse picks up speed. Suddenly, I'm not so sure this is a good idea. With the wall behind me, there's nowhere for me to go. My insides flutter with nerves and vulnerability.

"In this fight, how was the guy held?"

"The other one put both hands around his neck."

Giorgio's expression grows very serious. Slowly, he brings up his big palms and wraps them lightly around my neck. "Like this?"

My eyes widen as the flutters travel downwards and settle in the place between my legs. An unexpected wave of arousal slams into me, soaking me through with heat, and leaving me hyperaware of how close we are.

I blink. Am I seriously turned on right now? Jesus. So that's what does it for me—the sensation of a gorgeous Camorrista's hands wrapped around my neck. No wonder I've never felt this way before. No one else in my life would dare touch me like this.

"Yes," I whisper.

Something licks at the edges of Giorgio's gaze. His grip tightens around my throat by a minuscule amount, and my skin begins to burn from the inside out. My nipples harden. Thank God, I wore my thickest work-out bra today.

"Grab my right wrist with your right hand," he instructs, his voice low. "Then use your left hand to grab one of my fingers."

I take his wrist and reach over my shoulder to slide one of his thick fingers, pressed against the side of my neck, into my palm.

"Now pull, as if you're trying to break it."

I swallow, making my throat roll against his palms. "Like this?" Gently, I bend his finger backward.

"Harder."

The thought of moving the appendage to an unnatural angle makes me wince. "I don't want to hurt you."

"I'll let go of you before you can."

I'm not sure I want you to let go of me.

"Okay." I do as he says, and he drops his hands, but he brings them right back up.

"Good. Again."

His big palms land on my exposed collarbones and then travel up until his thumb and index finger form a collar around my flesh. His forearms flex, making the tendons and the thick veins beneath his skin ripple. His hold on me is light, but if he wanted to, he'd have no problem crushing my windpipe in a second.

The implicit trust between us right now sends my stomach soaring. It's a cocktail of nerves, fear, anxiety, and something far more tender.

Our eyes clash, his dark and stormy, mine wide and aroused. *Shit*. Can he tell? Does he know?

His gaze falls to my lips. "Let's go, Martina."

We practice a few times. Each time he puts his hands back on my throat, my clit pulsates. Nervous sweat rolls down my back despite the fact we're hardly moving. I'm afraid he'll notice and wonder why, but then I realize his own forehead has a sheen to it. He's sweating too.

As if he's able to see that observation in my eyes, the next time I do the move, he steps back and lifts the hem of his shirt to wipe at his damp brow.

My eyes blow wide, and I think I stop breathing. His flat, chiseled abs move with each breath, their shape even more defined after the earlier crunches he did beside me. I let out a slow breath through my lips.

My God.

I shake my head, trying to focus on the task at hand. I'm supposed to be training, not ogling his body, but it's hard to ignore the way his abs glisten with sweat in the light of the gym. My gaze catches on a thin scar just above his belly button, a line of slightly raised skin that's a shade lighter than the rest.

"Where did you get that?" I ask before I think better of it.

He lets his shirt fall back down his body and looks at me. "What?"

"That scar above your belly button."

The moment the words leave my mouth, I realize I just admitted I was checking him out. I wonder if that's what injects that extra dose of intensity in his gaze, or if it's the memory of how he got the scar.

He drags an absentminded hand over his abdomen and saves me from marinating in my embarrassment by answering.

"I got it the year I got made."

Curiosity stirs beneath my skin. "How old were you?"

"Fifteen."

Wow. He's been made for as long as I've been alive. "Did you know how to fight back then?"

A hint of amusement flickers inside his eyes. "No. I got my ass kicked a lot in the beginning because I never had to deal on the streets. The others resented the fact that I got to sit behind computer screens all day. The first year was the worst. One night, I was coming back to my apartment, and three guys ambushed me. It was payday, so they wanted my envelope of cash, but they also wanted to prove a point. I fought them, badly. They had the upper hand within seconds. Things could have ended up way worse if it wasn't for my old boss putting a tail on me."

"Sal?"

"No, this was when I was still part of the Secondigliano Alliance. The area capo valued me, and he knew I had a target on my back, so he got one of his guys to keep an eye out. That's what saved me that night. I started learning martial arts soon after."

It amazes me that Giorgio knows what it's like to be over-powered. These days, I can't imagine him on the losing side of a fight.

"Let's go again," he says, but I shake my head.

"It's too easy. A bit contrived, don't you think? In a real attack, the person wouldn't patiently wait while I try to do all the steps."

He crosses his arms over his chest. "What are you saying?"

I blink a few times as I try to gather the courage to say my next sentence. "Do it like it's real. Move faster. Use more force."

I can tell the moment he decides it's a bad idea. There's a shuttering in his gaze. "This is only our second class."

"I just want to try it once. If you really want this to be helpful to me, the intensity needs to be on par with a real attack. Otherwise, I'll freeze."

A puff of air escapes past his lips, but he doesn't refuse once more like I'm half-expecting. He considers it, and then he drops his arms back to his sides and says, "Just once."

A shiver runs up my spine. I don't know why I want this, or what I'm hoping to get out of it, but this is the first time since New York that I've felt something that might qualify as real excitement.

Giorgio moves into position before me. "I'll count until three. Do whatever you need to get away, all right? Remember what I taught you."

"Got it."

He counts down, and when he reaches "three," he lunges at me, grabbing me by the neck, and pressing the length of his body against mine.

All air is pushed out of my lungs.

My adrenaline spikes, and for a moment, I'm just flailing blindly against him. All of my training is forgotten, and instinct takes over. I try to tear his hands off me, try to kick at his legs. When I land a kick to his shin, he grunts and slides a rock-hard thigh between my legs.

"Are you going to fight me or just annoy me?" he hisses in my ear.

What the— Is he *taunting* me?

It's enough to screw a few bolts back into place. I take his right wrist with my right hand. Grab one of his fingers.

Approval flashes in the depths of his eyes. "Good girl."

Those two words have an unexpected effect on me, but I don't let it distract me. I pull. *Hard.*

He drops one hand, but he doesn't back away like before. Instead, he moves his other palm to cover more of my neck, his body still pinning me to the wall.

Our eyes clash together.

The inches of space between us seem to shrink.

His gaze falls to my lips.

I've caught him doing that before a few times, and every time he does it, a steady pulse appears between my legs.

I wonder if he thinks about kissing me.

Probably not. I'd put the chance of that at 0.01%.

But even that tiny, *tiny* chance that he might be thinking about it makes me feel unbearably alive.

I use the same move on the remaining hand, and it works.

Yes.

He releases me and I hop away. "I did it!"

Giorgio smiles. Dear God, he *smiles*.

"Really good work." His warm hands land on the tops of my shoulders.

My heart pounds out an unsteady rhythm as I gape at him. How dare he just toss that smile at me like it's no big deal? Legally, it needs to come with a warning.

"Thank you," I manage to mutter.

He nods but keeps his hands on me. One second. Two seconds. Three.

He's...lingering. Isn't he?

"That's enough for today," he says finally, his voice low.

"O-okay," I stutter.

At last, he lets go.

I return to my room with my heart still pounding in my chest and the ghost of his touch still burning through my clothes.

CHAPTER 11

MARTINA

THAT NIGHT, I fall asleep quickly, my body exhausted from the day.

I dream of Giorgio.

We meet in a dark hallway somewhere inside the house, and he takes my hand, confidently lacing our fingers together as if he's done it a million times before. I glance down at where we're linked, and his tattoo, the crest of the Casalesi, winks at me. He's in a midnight-blue suit, I'm in a sheer nightgown. He leads me down the hall, our footsteps and the rustle of our clothing the only sounds in the air.

A door opens, and we step into the library. Giorgio leads me to a leather armchair and takes a seat in the one across. On the table between us is a book. He picks it up and starts reading to me.

Jane Eyre. The scene where Jane and Rochester kiss in front of Mrs. Fairfax after they're caught in the rain. Giorgio's voice is expressive. Hypnotic, even. I can almost hear the pattering of the rain against the windows of the library as he reads. The sound of the rain grows and grows in intensity until it's like a cascade of bullets, and I can no longer make out his voice.

Quiet, I whisper. *Quiet.*

But the rain won't listen, and Giorgio soon disappears like an apparition, leaving me alone amongst the bookshelves.

A chill drags over my skin.

I don't like rainstorms. I need to wake up.

Wake up. Wake up. Wake up.

My consciousness claws its way out of the dream. I blink into the darkness of my bedroom, but the rain persists.

The mattress squeaks as I sit up against the pillows, rubbing sleep out of my eyes. When my bleary gaze lands on the window, my heart sinks.

Rain pours down the glass in rivulets. The wind howls loudly, like a wild animal in heat.

Every muscle in my body goes rigid with fear, and I'm teleported right back to New York.

Glittering hotel lobby.

Imogen's red lipstick.

The rain coming down in sheets.

We marveled at the weather as we waited in the lobby for the car that was supposed to pick us up. Our umbrellas were comically inadequate. We giggled about it. There was a good chance they would fly right out of our hands as soon as we stepped outside, but we were desperate not to get wet before the main event of the trip. Lunch at Eleven Madison Park, the best restaurant in the world. I wanted to eat there so that I would understand what the pinnacle of culinary success looked like. I thought it would help me decide if it was what I wanted to do. It was the whole reason I convinced Imogen to come to New York.

When the car arrived, we lunged outside, screeching loudly as water slapped against our bodies. The back door swung open, and we slid inside.

A minute later, Imogen was dead, and all I could hear was rain pummeling against the car. The soundtrack to the worst moment of my life.

My chin bumps against my knees, and I claw at the sheets. Panic spreads through my lungs.

There was a man in the back seat of the limo. Lazaro.

We only noticed him after we already started moving, while we were wiping our wet hands on our clothes. He was sitting in the corner, his legs spread wide, his leather shoes shiny. Imogen stiffened beside me. Somehow, he noticed that minuscule movement. It made him smile and ask for our names.

Why did I answer him without thinking?

Naive.

Stupid.

I press my face into my palms and weep.

This is what happens whenever I allow myself to remember how quickly things can fall apart.

The rain drowns out my cries, relentless and uncaring about the misery it brings. What I wouldn't do to erase the past, to wipe it away like condensation on the bathroom mirror. But there is no trick for that.

Maybe the only way to get past the pain is through it. I haven't allowed myself to feel much of anything since Imogen died, and the feelings have been accumulating. The more I put them off, the stronger they'll grow. Even now, their power makes me cower. My chest shakes with sobs, and I fear it might cave in.

The side lamp turns on, and the bed dips.

I startle and shove myself into the corner of the bed as I meet a pair of azure eyes.

Giorgio observes me, a deep line etched between his thick brows. "I heard you crying."

I wipe my cheeks with the back of my hand, my gaze snapping to the window.

His own follows.

He stares at it for a while. "You don't like when it rains."

I give a small shake of my head. I should say something, offer an explanation, but I can't. Forcing my lips to move feels like the hardest thing in the world right now.

"Do you want to be alone?"

Our eyes clash, and I pray he can sense the words I can't say. *Please don't leave. It's not as loud with you here.*

After a moment, he nods.

Noticing the chatter of my teeth and the tremors coursing through my body, the frown on his face deepens. I feel pathetic. Who the hell is afraid of *rain*? It's not logical, but my body doesn't seem to care. The bedpost digs into my back as I press my curled-up form against it.

"Come here," he says gently, lifting the duvet and motioning for me to get back under it.

I gnaw on my lip. With some effort, my limbs manage to get unstuck, and I slide under the blanket, moving closer to Giorgio in the process. He tucks me in, brushes a strand of hair out of my face, and looks down at me.

The shadows dance around us.

"Why?" he asks.

I shut my eyes. Something inside of me urges me to confess, but when I try to speak, no sound comes out.

He blows out a slow breath, his gaze skating over my shivering form. "You're still cold." His palms drag over the outer online of my body, but the duvet is too thick for me to feel the heat of his touch.

The chill in my bones is so deep, I'm afraid even a boiling bath wouldn't be enough to get it out. "I-I'm freezing."

Giorgio rakes his fingers through his hair and looks conflicted for a moment, as if he's weighing a few options.

When a hard shiver runs through me, he appears to make up his mind.

He lifts the duvet and climbs under it, settling behind me.

What!?

The world tilts on its axis as my mind tries to make sense of what just happened.

Oh my God.

Silently, he turns me on my side, tugs me to his *bare* chest, and reaches over to turn off the bedside lamp. Then he tucks his heavy arm under the duvet and drapes it over the dip in my waist.

"What are you doing?" I choke out, finally regaining my voice.

"Getting you warm," he says gruffly, his chin bumping against the top of my head. His furnace-like chest is flush against my back, his hips lined up with my own.

My butt is practically in his lap.

He's engulfed me.

I take tiny breaths through my mouth as I try to calm down. He drags his palm up and down my arm, and it takes me a moment to realize he's still trying to warm me up.

I'm already warm. It's official. Giorgio is the world's most effective heater.

"Better?" he asks after some time passes.

"Yes."

He doesn't move away. Doesn't stop his gentle caresses along my arm. Eventually, my pulse starts to slow down, and I feel safe enough to close my eyes.

Giorgio adjusts his position, and I feel his next words drift over the back of my neck. "Tell me why."

I swallow. It's easier to talk when I'm not looking at his face. "It rained the day it happened. The day Imogen died."

The movement of his hand slows. "Your friend."

"Yes. Now, whenever it rains like this, I have a reaction. I can't control it."

"Flashbacks?"

"I see it like a movie inside my head. The sequence of events from the moment we stood in the lobby to the second she died. I think she knew something was wrong when she saw Lazaro in the car. She took my hand and held it firmly. Right before he shot her, she squeezed my fingers very hard, and then the pressure was just gone. Her death was tactile. One moment, she was so alive, and the next she was dead."

A low sob escapes me. Giorgio pulls me closer, like he wants to take me inside his body, and his lips brush against my nape. "Breathe. I've got you. It's all just ghosts. One day, they'll leave."

His chest expands and then contracts. I model the pace of my own breaths on the rhythm he sets, and soon we're moving in tandem. It's shocking how comforting it is to be held like this. I've dealt with all of my previous panic attacks on my own.

"Do you have ghosts?" I ask.

"Yes," he says.

"Have yours left?"

His voice drifts down my spine as he says, "Some. Some still come from time to time."

"Sometimes, I see Imogen in the shadows at night," I confess.

"What does she do?"

"Nothing. She just stares at me with a bullet wound in her head. I wish she'd say something, but she never does. I try talking to her, but all I get back is silence." A silence that rings with accusation.

I hear him release a long breath.

"You've killed men, haven't you?"

"I have."

"A lot?"

"I'm a Casalesi," he says by way of an answer, and I don't press him for specifics. It's all relative, I suppose.

"Are they your ghosts?"

"No. My conscience is clear with most of them. It's the ones that never should have died that haunt me."

"Me too. There was no reason for Imogen to die. It feels like a cruel fluke."

"It was. But sometimes life is reduced to just that."

When he drapes his arm back over my waist, I gather up some courage and drag my fingertips over his skin, feeling the coarse hairs on his arms. His body stiffens, but he doesn't stop me. If it were daylight, he would. I'm sure of it. But with the rain and the darkness wrapped around us, it's like we're suspended in time and space, floating in a universe with different rules.

His body molds to mine, and his breathing grows deeper. When I've nearly fallen asleep, the rains stops, and the noise quiets.

CHAPTER 12

GIORGIO

A᎐ᴍʙᴇʀ ʟɪǫᴜɪᴅ sᴡɪʀʟs inside my glass.

I'm not a whiskey drinker, but sometimes the circumstances demand it.

It's three a.m. I snuck out of her bed ten minutes ago when I was sure I'd lose whatever loose grip on reality I still had if I had to spend another minute with her scent taunting me.

I don't know what possessed me when I got into her bed. Madness? Pity?

No, something else. Something I'm incapable of naming, because how can you put a word on something you've never felt before?

That small body of hers pressed against mine felt like coming home. How fucked up is that?

I cross my feet on the coffee table in the library and drop my head back until I'm looking at the ceiling. There are no answers there. No manual for turning back time so that I can go back to the moment I picked her up in Ibiza and start over.

If she says a word of this to her brother, he'll demand I bring her back to him. A lowborn soldier in bed with his sister. We didn't do anything, but it won't matter. Damiano may respect my expertise, but not enough to risk putting her innocence into question.

Bad luck.

Bad fucking luck to want the one thing you can never have.

Martina isn't meant for me. Tradition dictates one day she'll belong to someone in the upper echelons of the Casalesi hierarchy, and De Rossi knows it. If he wants to be the new don, he knows better than to fuck with tradition.

Sitting up straight, I take another sip and eye the clock. I had work to do tonight, and none of it got done. My iPad lies forgotten on my bed. As soon as I heard her crying, nothing else mattered.

Martina's somehow strong and fragile at the same time. In class, when she pushes past her self-doubt, her eyes shine with fierce determination. But her past won't let go of her. One step forward, one step back. She's stuck, and for some reason, I feel it's my duty to get her unstuck.

For some reason...

I drag my palm down my cheek and toss back the rest of the whiskey. That reason *should* be getting into De Rossi's good graces, but I can't say he's been on my mind very much when it comes to the things I've done with her.

Buzz. Buzz. Buzz.

I grab my phone, check the caller ID, and pick up the call.

"Giorgio," Sal's voice filters through the speaker. "I'm not interrupting anything, am I?"

"Of course not, Don."

"Where are you right now?"

He can't track my location from my phone, so I answer easily. "I'm in my apartment in Rome. It's late. Is everything all right?"

"Yes, well, because of the nonsense with Damiano, I've had a lot of late nights recently. It's unfortunate he's made such a fatal error. It will cost him dearly."

"He's grown arrogant," I say, pandering to him.

"And now he's gathering fools for his court."

"More have joined his cause?"

"No one important," he quickly dismisses. "But yes, a few have miscalculated by going to his side, and I'm eager to put an end to this. It's a distraction for our business."

"It is."

"What of the girl? Have you found anything since we last spoke?"

Sal called me the day after the news of De Rossi's betrayal broke and gave me the expected instructions with regards to Martina. Find her and bring her to him. I wasn't the only clan member set to the task, but I'm not concerned about the rest. They'll never find this place.

"He's hidden her well. I've tracked her as far as a flight from Ibiza to Valencia, but her next steps have been hard to trace."

"How far have you gotten?"

"Someone saw a girl matching her description leaving in a Mercedes van from a car rental place outside the airport. The camera didn't capture the license plate." I planted evidence to corroborate this made-up story the day I picked up Martina, and now I'm simply sticking to the script.

"And then?"

"I'm still searching for the car."

There's a drawn-out pause on the other end of the line. "I expected more by now. It's been nearly a week."

"She could be anywhere in Europe. It takes time."

Time he doesn't have, but he'll never admit it to me.

"How have the other searches fared?" I ask.

"They've also tracked her to Valencia, and the trail goes cold there. I grow impatient, Giorgio. I need to get back to the business. The girl needs to be found, and I'm prepared to throw in whatever resources I need to get it done."

"Have you considered engaging outside help?"

"Yes, it's being done as we speak."

I frown. I didn't expect him to grow this desperate this quickly. He's already bringing in external contractors?

"Who have you contacted?"

"The Black Snakes and the Partnership."

Cazzo. Mercenaries, and they're the smart ones. Their combined manpower is the size of an army, which means they'll be able to scrutinize every digital record of anyone remotely resembling Martina.

Alarm fans through me. This could become a problem. I hope Damiano is in as much of a rush to get this finished as Sal is.

"They'll get you De Rossi's sister in no time," I say.

"That's the hope, and of course, I expect you to keep looking. You've done good work for me over the years, Giorgio, and I've rewarded you generously. I'm a fair man. Get me Martina, and you'll ascend to heights you never thought possible in my organization."

Biting on the inside of my cheek, I shake my head. Over the years, I've made Sal believe that my ambitions are large. That way, I've created the illusion he's in control. When you know what someone wants, you have power over them.

The truth is, I couldn't give a fuck about moving up in the clan. All I've ever cared about was getting myself to a place where I could orchestrate his downfall.

I got there. Now, I just have to stay there instead of chasing after Martina.

"Thank you, Don. Your words mean a lot."

"Goodnight, son."

Bile rises to my throat just as the line goes dead.

My next phone call is to De Rossi. He asked me to keep him appraised on anything to do with Martina, and he needs to know Sal has set the wolves on her.

The line connects. "Napoletano. How are things in— Ah, right, I don't have a clue where you are."

"I just got off the phone with Sal."

"And?"

I catch him up on what was discussed.

"Shit. I'm putting you on speaker, Ras is here with me."

There's a click of a button. The voice of De Rossi's right-hand man blares through my phone. "So instead of facing us head-on, Sal's going after an innocent girl." He scoffs. "Fucking one-trick pony."

"He didn't say it outright, but it's obvious he thinks Martina is the quickest way to end this."

"Should we be concerned?" Ras asks.

"No. She's safe here. But when they can't find her, they'll grow desperate. They'll start taking big risks. It's better for it not to come to that. What progress have you made?"

"My uncle Elio and Ras's father are with us. There are nine other key players in the clan," De Rossi says. "If we get them to turn, no one will dare oppose us. So far, we've made agreements with three—the traditionalists who worked closely with my father and who see Sal as a loose cannon. As I expected, they were outraged when I provided evidence of his attempted kidnapping of Martina when she was in New York. In their eyes, the fact that Sal didn't address his problems directly with me, one of his capos, and went after

132

Mari instead is a black mark on his character. They see it as a sign of weakness, and they won't support a weak don. I wish the rest would see it the same way, but they are proving more difficult."

"We'll get them," Ras says confidently. "But we need time to gather the necessary leverage, and we must be more careful. Yesterday, our car was attacked on the road to Casal. We got away, but it was a closer call than I would have liked. The driver was shot."

"Someone tipped Sal off?"

"We think it was a drone."

It's a wonder the two of them have made it this long. "You need to travel with a signal jammer. De Rossi, your security should be taken as seriously as Martina's."

"You worried about me, Napoletano?"

"Not particularly, but if you die, I won't be able to collect my favor. I'm not in the business of charity work."

Ras chuckles. "And you wonder why you don't have many friends."

"I assure you that's entirely intentional."

"How is Mari doing?" De Rossi cuts in.

"Fine."

Cazzo, I think I said that too quick.

"You sure? She was far from fine when she left a few days ago. Have you checked in on her at all?"

He's worried I've been ignoring her. I wish I fucking could.

133

"Yes, I see her regularly. Her condition has improved."

This would be the time to tell him about her nightmare, but I decide against it. He can't help her, and revealing this detail may invite questions I'd rather De Rossi not think about. Like how was I close enough to hear her. Or what did I do to calm her down.

"What does she do all day? We haven't had a chance to talk beyond that one call the day after she arrived."

"She's taken to the garden. And I've started teaching her self-defense, a skill you really should have equipped her with a long time ago."

"When did I tell you that you could do that?" De Rossi asks, his voice taking on a hard note.

"She should be prepared in case anything happens."

"You just told us she's safe. If you do your job, nothing will happen."

"Drop the ego, De Rossi. Just because I'm teaching her something you couldn't, doesn't mean it's not good for her. She's learning quickly. If you want to talk to her about it, you're always welcome to call."

There's a tense pause. "She's...enjoying these lessons?"

The memory of her delicate neck moving beneath my hands sends a jolt of lust to my cock.

"As far as I can tell," I say brusquely.

"Fine. As long as you're not putting any undue pressure on her."

"I'm not."

"She…" De Rossi clears his throat. "She'll have a role to play in all of this eventually."

A prickling feeling coats the back of my neck as I wait for him to continue.

"But I don't need to talk to her about it now. We have time."

It doesn't take a genius to piece it together. He's talking about marriage. "Who do you have in mind?"

"No one yet," De Rossi says.

"But the interest is there," Ras adds.

Of course it's fucking there. If De Rossi becomes don, Martina will be the most eligible woman in the clan. Her husband will take on a position of great power.

It doesn't hurt that she's beautiful and sweet and will likely make a perfect fucking wife.

"Tell Mari that Vale and I miss her."

"And if Sal calls you again, call us right away," Ras says.

"No, I'll send you a fucking pigeon. What else do you think I'll do?"

"Jesus, rela—"

I hang up.

Anger simmers beneath my skin. Why the hell am I helping this girl? So that she can be happy and perfect in time to marry some fucking asshole?

The glass of whiskey in my hand suddenly feels too empty. It's late, and I should get some sleep, but I'm not tired anymore.

Just pissed off.

Fuck it. I pour myself another glass.

My lowborn status has never bothered me. It hasn't stopped me from making money or doing my job well. Those used to be the only things I cared about. But one thing my status means is that I'll never be able to marry someone like Martina.

Not that I want to marry her, damn it. I just want *her*.

One time would do it. It would be enough to satisfy my curiosity. Every time I touch her in class, I can't help but wonder what she would look like naked on her hands and knees before me. Her ass up in the air. That silken hair coiled around my wrist. I can practically hear the gasp she'd make when I gave it a sharp tug.

My cock comes alive at the image.

She's too good for me. Too pure. If she knew about the poison inside of me, she'd recoil at my touch.

But how sweet would it feel to give in to my dark urges and claim that which can never be mine...

I drop my head against the chair and groan. *Cazzo.* I shouldn't even be thinking these kinds of things. It's the whiskey. I never drink this shit.

A soft knock on the door cuts through the night's silence.

My head snaps back up. "Who is it?"

"It's Martina." The door opens an inch. "Can I come in?"

I drag my palm over my face. "Yes."

136

She pads into the room, her hair messy, and her eyes bleary with sleep. Thank God, she threw a robe over her pajamas. The less skin I see, the better.

"I woke up and couldn't go back to sleep," she says.

"The rain's stopped."

She glances out the window. Crosses her bare feet at the ankles. "I know. I just... I didn't want to be alone."

I draw my attention back to my glass. A few sips left. I'll let her stay here until I'm done with this drink, and then I'll send her back to bed.

"Have a seat." I gesture at the chair across from me.

She takes it. "Why are you still up?"

"Had a few phone calls."

"Anyone interesting?"

"I spoke with Sal and your brother."

Excitement sparks in her eyes. "We haven't talked in a few days. How is he?"

This is not the best time to tell her De Rossi nearly died a few days ago, so I glaze over it. "Busy. He has a lot of people left to convince."

She nods, her delicate fingers curling around the armrest. "Why did you decide to take my brother's side?"

I shrug. "Like many others, I'm not happy with our current don."

"Why?"

"A long list of reasons. He's mismanaged the clan. The Casalesi have always run themselves like a business. We're more sophisticated than just about any other clan in the *sistema*, and we need a leader who's got a head for it. Sal doesn't."

Her brows pinch together, as if she doesn't quite believe my answer. "So it's all just logic? It's not personal?"

"Why would you think it's personal?"

"A difference in philosophy hardly seems like reason enough to betray your don. It's not like the clan is crumbling."

She's perceptive, and despite my earlier irritation, something about her inquisitive gaze makes me want to smile. "Your brother would probably argue it is, but you're right. I don't think the clan is crumbling. The Casalesi are formidable and have survived worse dons than Sal."

"So it *is* personal." There's a hint of triumph in her voice.

"Yes." I lean back in my seat and force myself not to stare at her legs. "We have something in common, you and I. My mother died because of Sal. Just like yours did."

Her lips part on an intake of breath. She was a baby when Sal murdered her father and took over as don. When Martina's mom discovered her husband was dead, her grief quickly turned into destruction. The woman killed herself, setting herself on fire in front of Sal's men. De Rossi saw it and had enough sense to grab his baby sister and run.

"He killed your mother?" Martina asks me.

If only it were that simple. But my mother's past with Sal is anything but that. She was a strong woman, even after Sal destroyed her. She lived with her pain for a long time...until one day, it became too much. "Sal didn't pull the trigger, but he's responsible for her death."

She opens her mouth as if to ask something, but then thinks better of it.

Good. I don't want to talk about this shit.

"You should go to bed."

Wide hazel eyes blink at me. "Okay. Before I go, I wanted to say thanks." Pink blooms across her cheeks. "For calming me down. I know it was probably...weird for you."

Climbing into your bed? Familiarizing myself with the smell of your skin? Using all of my willpower not to grind my stiff cock into your soft ass?

Sure. *Weird.*

"I've survived worse things," I say gruffly, my hand itching to pour myself another glass.

She recoils slightly at my words. Tugs her robe close around her. "I see. If it was that unpleasant, you really didn't need to do it."

My gaze pinballs to hers. Is she offended? What did she expect me to say in response to her thanks? *You know I'm happy to climb into your bed anytime, Mari?*

I hope to fucking God that's not the impression she's getting from me.

"Go to bed, Martina," I growl.

Her eyes narrow. When she stands up, the robe is tight around her chest, and I'm treated to an outline of her hard, small nipples.

I swallow down a groan. For the love of God, *leave already.*

Instead, she holds my gaze and mutters a, "Yes, *sir.*"

My cock stiffens immediately. *I should throw her over a knee and teach her what happens to girls who don't know how to obey orders.*

Before I have time to analyze that wild, intrusive thought, she turns around and waltzes out of the room.

CHAPTER 13

MARTINA

I WAKE UP MAD.

I've survived worse things. The sentence plays inside my head on repeat as I fling the duvet off me and stomp to the bathroom.

What a jerk. Did I ask him to get into my bed? No. Why did he do it if it was so disgusting for him to lie beside me?

Brushing my teeth, I look at myself in the mirror. My skin's lost some of its usual color since I stopped spending regular time at the beach, and the highlights in my hair could use a touch-up, but I don't look that terrible, do I? I spit out the toothpaste and sniff under my arm. I don't even stink!

My fingers wrap around the edge of the sink. Even if I did, he could have chosen not to be so rude. I get it, Giorgio doesn't find me attractive, but there's no need for him to throw it in my face like that.

It's late, and I missed breakfast, so I take my time getting dressed and then make my way to the gym.

As soon as I pass through the doors, my gaze jumps from Giorgio—he's throwing punches on the bag—to his discarded keys. They've been lying in my vicinity during each of our classes, but there's never a moment when he's not near me. Plus, I've been distracted.

By him.

By his touch.

By the way his hands feel on me.

But no more. It's time I get one up on him.

He throws his last punch and turns around. "Let's get started."

It quickly becomes obvious he's decided to pretend last night never happened. He makes me do some brutal conditioning before he starts teaching me a new skill.

It's awful.

Our conversation is stilted, and he won't meet my gaze. I get the sense he'd rather be anywhere but here.

And in turn, I can't seem to learn anything he's showing me.

"I don't get it," I exclaim after I fail to correctly do a sequence he's demonstrated three times.

"You're not listening," he snaps. "Where is your head at?"

His frustration leaves a sour taste in my mouth. I give him an are-you-kidding-me look. "I had a rough night. Apparently, you did too. Maybe we should end class early."

His eyes narrow at my suggestion. "You have something else to do?"

"Plenty."

A dry scoff. "Is this about your phone? Move on. If you could, you would have gotten it back by now."

"Oh, is that what you think?"

"I *know* it."

Fire licks the inside of my stomach. I'm definitely finding that damn thing today, just to prove him wrong.

"Whatever, Giorgio. I'd rather help Polo in the garden than do this with you right now."

Something dark flashes in his eyes. "Watch your tongue."

I bite down on the retort threatening to come out of my mouth as the air between us vibrates with tension. He's angry, and so am I, but somewhere in the back of my mind, I know that I need to keep a handle on myself.

What he said to me last night only hurts because I *like* him. If he sees how upset I am, he'll suspect it, and God, I don't think I'd be able to handle the humiliation.

I need to get out of here.

He appears to be of the same mind, because he blows out a breath and goes to get his keys. "We'll resume tomorrow."

"Thank you," I say to his back, and he nods without looking at me.

I go to my room, shower, and get a snack from the kitchen. Despite what I said to Giorgio, I decide against going outside. The ground is still wet from the rain, the sky is cloudy, and the prospect of digging around in the mud isn't all that appealing.

Instead, I settle inside the library, moving one of the heavy leather armchairs close to the window so I can enjoy a perfect view of rolling hills, yellow wildflowers, and pines spearing the sky. The forest that encircles the property looks somewhat ominous under the gray clouds, and I remember Giorgio's warning about not going there. Belligerence stirs beneath my skin. Maybe I should do it just to piss him off.

Shaking my head at myself, I tap my fingertips against the side of the armchair. I'm not usually this bratty. Maybe on occasion with Dem when he really manages to irritate me. But Giorgio seems to bring it out easily and often.

I'm watching an eagle soaring above the tree line when a hinge creaks nearby. I glance over my shoulder to see Sophia squeezing past the door. She pads over to me and rests her head on my lap.

"Hi, girl," I say softly, patting her bristly fur.

She blinks at me and then turns to the window, looking in the same direction as I was before.

"Do you go there often? Does someone take you on walks in the forest?"

She snorts and lies down on the floor at my feet, as if to say I should know better than to ask her questions she can't possibly answer.

I reach for a book lying on the windowsill.

The Herbal Alchemist—a guide to herbal medicine.

This must be Polo's. The table of contents is extensive, and I stop on a familiar word. Valerian. Huh. That's the herb Polo gave me in that tea. I wonder if this book was his inspiration for growing it.

I turn to the page, curious to see what it looks like, and find an illustration of a plant with lots of tiny pink flowers. The text below states it's a natural sleep aid that can reduce the amount of time it takes to go to sleep and improve its quality. That checks out. I can't recall the last time I slept that deeply. On the page next to the picture, there's some additional information written in tiny script. I bring the book closer to my face to make it out.

When mixed with kava-kava, it can induce powerful, hypnotic sleep. Fast acting.

The words stir inside my head. Wait...

I suck in a harsh breath.

Oh my God, *this is it*. This is how I get that key! I can use this recipe and make Giorgio fall asleep.

I hop out of the armchair and circle the room, a triumphant feeling flourishing inside my chest. Sophia makes a soft bark, eyeing me with a hint of suspicion.

Make the tea, give it to Giorgio, and wait until he falls asleep. I'll get the key from his pocket, get inside his office, and get my freaking phone. Oh my God. Can it be any more perfect?

The look on his face when he realizes how I've outsmarted him? Oh, I am going to be waiting with my camera, ready to take a picture.

A laugh bursts out of me.

Only there's one problem. How can I get him to drink this tea without making it obvious something is going on?

I halt in the center of the room and adjust the thick book under my arm. This is where I have to be really smart. He can't suspect foul play.

I spend the rest of the afternoon mulling the problem over. When I get called down for dinner, I still haven't come up with anything, and my head pulses with frustration as I make it down to the dining room.

I'm so distracted, I'm sure I won't be able to hold a single conversation at dinner, but when I enter the room, only Giorgio sits at the table.

"Where is everyone?"

His dark gaze lands on me. "I asked them to have their dinner in the staff house."

My brows pinch together. "Why?"

He rises from his seat and puts a hand on the back of the chair beside him. "I wanted to give you some space after the past few days. I know it can be a lot to be around new people every meal." He drags the chair out and motions for me to have a seat.

A tiny flutter appears in my belly. I ignore it and sit down beside him.

"It's fine. You didn't need to do that."

He pushes my chair in. "They don't mind."

When his hand accidentally brushes my shoulder, sparks crackle against my skin. We're about to have dinner, alone.

In an alternate universe, this could have been a date. I've been on a few dates before— Well, more like I thought we were just hanging out as friends, but the guys I was with clearly had something else in mind.

How the tables have turned.

Giorgio's changed into a simple button-up shirt with rolled-up sleeves. My eyes trace the thick veins that snake up his forearms, and I get a sudden urge to run my fingertips over them. Instead, I curl my hands into fists and press them into my lap.

The air around us grows heavy with silence.

He breaks it first. "I shouldn't have pushed you as hard as I did after last night," he says gruffly as he places a napkin over his lap.

Oh. I wasn't expecting that.

"It's fine."

He slides his palm over his chin. "Did you have a good time in the garden?"

"I didn't go. It was too wet. I stayed in the library."

"Ah." I think I see his lips give a small twitch before he reaches over and removes the domed lids off the plates in front of us.

Steak with what looks like fresh pesto over a bed of mashed potatoes with a side of roasted asparagus, carrots, and onions.

I suck in deep breath and sigh. "Smells incredible."

"Tommaso will be happy to hear that. He's worried you've been eating so little because you don't like his cooking."

"That's not true. He's a great cook." I pick up my cutlery.

"The trays he's sent to your room came back barely touched."

I spear a piece of the asparagus and narrow my eyes at him. "You've been checking how much I eat?"

"I have."

His response is delivered calmly, as if there's no problem with what he's just admitted to.

I lean my fork and knife against the edge my plate. "Giorgio, my eating patterns are none of your business."

A hint of amusement flashes over his lips. "You're my ward, Martina. Your health is very much my business."

His *ward*. Hearing that word makes me wrinkle my nose in distaste. I don't know why I hate it so much, but he'll throw it out randomly, and every time he does, it twists my insides.

"Don't call me that," I mutter as I cut into the steak.

"Why not? It's what you are."

"Didn't I tell you I'm turning nineteen next week?"

"You did," he says smoothly. "But a ward is—"

"A word used to describe a helpless little child."

"It's—"

"It's insulting, that's what it is. Especially after everything I've lived through. When you call me that, it feels like all of it meant nothing."

148

My outburst soaks the room like a bucket of ice-cold water.

There's a quaking deep beneath my ribs. A fault line triggered by my anger. Anger at what happened. At what it exposed in me.

I used to like myself, but I can't remember what that felt like. Now, all I feel is repulsion at my weaknesses. They seem to dominate the landscape of who I am. No wonder Giorgio was grossed out about lying next to me. He feels it too.

The backs of my eyes prickle, and all I can do is stare at my plate.

In my periphery, Giorgio places his cutlery down.

"It's a term we use in the clan to mean someone who's under the sworn protection of a made man," he says more gently than I thought him capable of.

Oh. I didn't know that.

"You're not a child to me, Martina. I apologize if I've made you feel like one. You've lived through some difficult things, and I'd never attempt to dismiss them. They're a part of you now."

My blood slows its trek.

"I know you've been struggling, but you're strong. I know you'll get through this."

At this, my suspicious gaze darts to him. Is he just saying what he thinks I want to hear? "If you think I'm strong—"

"I don't think it. I know it."

I shift in my seat. "You don't even know *me*."

His eyes tighten at the corners. "We've spent a good amount of time together over the last few days, don't you think? Do you want to know what I've seen?"

My pulse flutters. "What?"

"There are two types of people in this world—those who experience pain and let it consume them, and those who accept it as part of themselves, learn from it, and keep fighting. You're a fighter, Martina."

"Have you forgotten what I was like when you picked me up? I was practically catatonic."

"But you didn't stay that way for long. It's not in your nature to wallow in misery."

"That's because you didn't let me!"

His lips lift on one side. "I may have provoked you, but trust me, if you really wanted to continue drowning in your guilt, you would have. You responded to me. You went out to the garden. You came to the gym. I barely did anything. It was all you, *piccolina*."

Little one.

My eyes widen until they must take up my entire face. He takes in my expression and sucks in his cheeks before glancing away.

I finger the edge of the tablecloth, at a loss of what to say. How can his opinion of me be so different from how I feel about myself? Yes, I feel slightly better than when I first arrived. The classes have helped me gain some confidence, but the feeling is fleeting. When we're on the mat, I'm in the moment, and there's no time to question myself. But when we're off it, reality creeps back in.

I've failed so badly, and at such a high cost...

"I don't feel like a fighter," I say softly. "I wish I was different."

There's a pause. Unexpectedly and almost hesitantly, his big hand reaches across the table and clasps mine.

"I think you're perfect just the way you are."

I lift my chin, and our eyes lock. His expression is closed off, but some emotion crisscrosses over it. A flash of warmth he can't contain. It travels through the air and pierces through my chest.

Seconds later, he's pulling back his hand and picking up his cutlery. "Healing takes time, Martina. But you'll get there," he says, his voice gruffer now.

I pretend to get back to my food and move it around my plate.

Did he really just tell me he thinks I'm *perfect*?

I feel like I'm having a stroke.

My breathing is unsteady, and my heartbeat is a jumbled mess.

I force myself to take a bite, but my gaze keeps returning to his face.

Sharp cheekbones. Fine lines around his eyes. A well-defined jaw. He seems like such a hard man, so difficult to read, and yet this isn't the first time he's shown me softness.

Does he show it to anyone else but me?

"When I spoke to your brother last night, he asked me to tell you both him and Valentina are doing fine, and that they miss you," he says, and I get the feeling he's trying to change the direction of our conversation.

I swallow. "What else did he say?"

"Their days are filled with many meetings and negotiations."

"With the capos?"

"Yes, and other key players in the clan."

"Are things going well?"

"They've managed to secure a number of important alliances already, and more will be finalized in the coming days."

"That's good."

He cuts a piece of his steak. "I should tell you that he and Ras were attacked on the way to a meeting. They're both fine."

I drop my cutlery, and it rattles against the plate. "*What?* Why is this the first time I'm hearing about this?"

"It just happened. The only casualty was their driver."

My heart pounds. "Oh my God."

"These things are bound to happen."

I know what my brother is doing is dangerous, but to hear Giorgio mention it so casually freaks me out. "I can't believe he didn't say anything to me. We haven't been talking often enough."

"It's better that way. The less he calls, the smaller the probability your location gets somehow exposed."

"Don't you think he's overestimated how much danger I'm in? Is anyone even looking for me?"

At this, Giorgio's expression grows serious. "Oh, they're looking."

I swallow. "Sal?"

"And his army." He wipes his mouth with a napkin and leans back into his seat. "I'm not trying to scare you, but you need to understand that your value increases with each passing day of this war. If any of your brother's enemies get their hands on you, your brother will have a very difficult choice to make."

I drag my palms down my arms as the air in the room suddenly turns cold.

"He knows that too. He's known it from the moment he decided to start this war, which is why he entrusted you to me."

The implication is clear. He's the only one who can keep me safe.

I finish my dinner in silence as I process everything he's said.

"Tommaso was making preserves all day and didn't have time for dessert," Giorgio says as he folds his napkin and places it on the table. "It's a shame."

I arch brow at him. "You don't seem to me like someone with a sweet tooth."

"Why's that?"

Oh Lord. My cheeks heat. I can't tell him it's because his body makes it seem like he survives on chicken, potatoes, and broccoli. "Just...your vibe," I say awkwardly.

He drags his hand over his jaw. "I like dessert."

I could make him something. The kitchen's fully stocked, and I don't need a lot of time to whip up something simple.

Suddenly, my thoughts screech to a halt.

This is how I'm going to get him to drink that tea.

That's it. I just got the opportunity I've been waiting for.

CHAPTER 14

MARTINA

ALL OF THE pieces click into place.

Giorgio was the one who brought up dessert. My offer to make him something won't look at all suspicious. Neither will me serving it with some tea.

Plus, the staff are gone and won't be back for the night.

It's perfect.

Keeping my expression carefully guarded, I lift my gaze to him. "I can make something."

He cocks a thick brow. "You can?"

"Of course." I rise from my chair. "I used to do a lot of cooking and baking back home. It won't take me long."

"All right," he says easily, and I try my best not to seem too eager as I make my way to the kitchen.

As soon as I'm out of his line of sight, I increase my pace. I don't have the recipe for the tea, which means I'll have to improvise. The book didn't have any specific instructions, just that the two herbs brewed together would do exactly what I need them to do.

I fly toward the cupboard with the herbs and fling the doors open.

Valerian.

Kava.

My fingers freeze midair as I see what's in the second jar. It looks like...pieces of wood bark? What the hell? I was expecting dried leaves, not this. What am I supposed to do with this?

I whirl around, gnawing on my bottom lip, and just when I start to question if I'm going to be able to pull this off, my gaze catches on an iPad lying on the counter.

Hell yes!

It must be my lucky day, because it's charged and unlocked. I mutter a thank-you to Tommaso under my breath. He probably uses this when he's cooking. A few moments later, I'm looking up instructions on how to make kava tea.

*Grind the root into powder, pour it into a strainer, then pour hot water over it and let it sit for...*forty-five minutes!

Crap. I have to get this going right away or Giorgio will wonder what the hell I'm doing here.

I prep the kava and put aside the valerian. I'm going to brew the latter like a regular tea when everything is nearly done and mix it with the kava.

I decide to make *Torta Caprese*, a Neapolitan dessert Giorgio must have tried before. It's a rich chocolate cake made out of almond flour, eggs, butter, and plenty of dark chocolate. You'd have to be soulless not to enjoy it. All of the ingredients are easy to find, and in no time, I'm mixing up a bowl of batter.

Excitement builds inside of me—a premature and wicked satisfaction at outsmarting Giorgio. Yes, after the things he said to me at dinner, my anger's lost its edge, but that doesn't mean I'm going to backtrack or feel guilty about what I'm about to do.

It's just a bit of fun, right? I wonder what he'll say when he wakes up and realizes what happened. I think he might be impressed.

And it'll be nice to have my phone back.

The thought passes through me, but I discover it lacks the weight it had before. I'm actually managing better than I thought I would without it.

A small smile tugs at my lips as I pour the batter into a round dish.

When the cake is in the oven, I return to the dining room and find Giorgio standing by the fireplace. It was unlit when I left, but now a small fire crackles within, filling the space with warmth.

I eye the clock. It's five past nine, and I need to get the cake out in twenty minutes.

Giorgio angles his head to look at me. "All done?"

"It's in the oven," I say, moving until I stand in front of the fireplace beside him.

The flames lick at a few branches, illuminating old stonework. Small patterned tiles are embedded inside the bricks, but they've been darkened with soot over time. I sneak a glance at Giorgio and note the severe lines of his profile as he stares into the fire. Polo's words come back to me.

In truth, I think he hates this place.

Hate is a strong word. Would he really agree to stay here with me if he hated it?

"Does the castello have a name?"

He keeps his gaze on the fire as he answers. "Castello di Bosco. A long time ago, it was Castello di Fiero, but then there was a big fire that burned down the church that used to be on the property, and the owner at the time decided the name brought bad luck. He renamed it in 1782."

"This place is ancient."

Giorgio gives a small nod. "It has a lot of history."

"How did you find out about it in the first place?"

He drags his teeth over his bottom lip, and I get the sense that he's wrestling with how to answer.

Finally, he says, "My mother used to work here."

My jaw slackens. That was definitely not the answer I was expecting.

"Really? I thought she was from Naples?"

"She moved to Naples when she was eighteen, but she grew up here. My grandfather was the groundskeeper here, and my grandma was one of the cooks. This was a long time ago.

Tommaso and Allegra started working here a few years before my grandparents died."

I look around the room and see it with new eyes. Giorgio's entire family lived here at one time.

"And your mother? What did she do?"

"She gardened, like Polo. My grandfather homeschooled her. But like I said, she left when she was quite young. She was bored of this place and wanted to start a new life in Naples."

"That's amazing that you were able to buy it. Who were the previous owners?"

"A wealthy couple. The woman was a wine heiress, and her husband was an art collector. Old money. The castello was in their family for a long time until nearly all the relatives died out. It was never put up for sale. I told them a long time ago I would buy it if they ever decided to get rid of the place. About a decade ago, they called, and a few months later, it was mine."

"Huh. So why did Polo say—" I clamp my mouth shut.

He turns to me, a spark of suspicion inside his eyes. "Why did Polo say what?"

I glance to the side, suddenly feeling awkward without being sure why. Didn't Polo tell me to ask Giorgio about it? But this place is clearly very personal for him, and now it feels like maybe Polo shouldn't have said what he said.

"Tell me what he said, Martina."

"Um." I tuck a strand of hair behind my ear. "Well, he just mentioned you didn't really like this place," I say, softening Polo's real words.

"Did he?"

"Yes."

"He's wrong. I like this place just fine," he says in a clipped tone.

My face heats. There's definitely something he's not telling me.

"I must have misunderstood him."

"Hmm."

When the silence turns tense, I clear my throat. "Let me go check on the dessert."

I return to the kitchen and crack open the oven. When I stick a toothpick into the dough, a few wet crumbs come out. I wait another minute and take it out.

Well, here it is. Time to execute the plan.

My palms land on the cool marble counter, and my gaze volleys to the pot of kava on the counter. The valerian is steeping beside it.

To combine the liquids, I kind of have to guess the proportions, which makes me nervous. What if I make it too strong? Online, there weren't many warnings about overdoing it, but one website did say that some people respond to it more strongly than others.

Still, what's the worst that can happen? I'll get him to sit down on the couch so that when he falls asleep, he'll be comfy. He'll be awake before breakfast.

I place the slice of cake, dessert plates, forks, and two cups of tea on a tray and carry it over. The teas look nearly the same, but mine is just a mint and chamomile infusion.

Giorgio looks up from his phone as I enter and slips it into his pocket. The awkwardness that was there a few minutes earlier is now gone, and his lips twitch in a smile. "What's this?"

"Torta Caprese."

That smile grows. "One of my favorites."

I unload the tray and serve him his cup of tea. "It might be a bit bitter. That's on purpose to cut through the sweetness of the cake."

He takes the cup, not a hint of suspicion in his expression and takes a small sip.

I watch for any unusual reaction, anything that would suggest he's onto me, but there's nothing. I clamp down on my bottom lip to stifle a grin. He *has* to be impressed with me after this.

Giorgio pierces the cake with his fork and takes a bite. His eyes flutter shut. A low moan vibrates in his throat, and the room suddenly grows too warm.

He cracks his lids and pins me with a look that sends a shiver down my spine. "*Cazzo*, Martina. What did you put in this?"

I hide my smile behind the rim of my cup. "It's a secret."

He takes another bite, devouring half the slice in one go. "And this tea..." He lifts his cup. "An interesting flavor."

"I blended a few things from the cupboard."

While I eat my first slice, he inhales his second, and his enthusiasm fills me with satisfaction. This used to be one of my favorite things about cooking—seeing others enjoy my food.

When I see him finish his cup, I rise from my seat, worried he might notice the strange sediment at the bottom. "I'll bring these back to the kitchen."

To my dismay, he stands up too. "I'll do it."

"No, it's okay—"

He's already started loading up the tray.

I clamp my jaw shut and follow him into the kitchen even though I'm not carrying anything. Crap, I wanted to keep him seated until the tea worked. What if he falls and cracks his head open on these hard stone floors?

I bend my leg at the knee and tap my toe against the floor. This is literally the worst surface to fall on.

When I see him make a sudden movement, I don't think twice before I lunge to his side.

My hands grip his biceps, but he doesn't fall, just turns his head and gives me a befuddled look. "What are you doing?"

I swallow, my throat suddenly dry. "I thought you...tripped."

His gaze drops to my hand. "I'm fine."

I should let him go, but for some reason, my touch lingers on his muscular arms. My hand looks tiny in comparison, and something about that contrast makes my stomach tighten.

My breath comes out hot and shallow. "My mistake."

I drop my hand and move to back away, but he stops me, moving in front of me and caging me against the counter with his arms.

My eyes double in size. What is he doing?

His jaw ticks as he gazes down at me, his expression conflicted. In the small space between us, there's suddenly no oxygen, only the heady scent of his cologne and the awareness that this is bordering on inappropriate.

He should have let me move away. There's no reason for us to stand like this unless...

When he start to leans in, my skin becomes gooseflesh.

Oh my God. Is he...

Suddenly, he sways, and his eyelids droop.

"Giorgio?"

He gives me a few confused blinks. "What the..."

Oh God, the tea is working.

"Here, let's sit down." I lace my arm through his, but he shakes his head.

"Martina, go to my room," he mutters. "Something's happening. Lock the door and get the gun from my nightstand."

Guilt slices through me. He thinks this is some plot to get me. "No, Giorgio, it's okay. We just need to get you somewhere comfortable."

When he leans his weight on me, I nearly trip.

"Fuck." He slaps his free palm on the counter. "What the fuck is happening?"

The tea is working fast. We've taken two steps in the direction of the dining room, so at this point, I give up on that plan. "Trust me, you're okay. Just sit down on the floor."

To my surprise, he actually does it. Or maybe it's the fact that his knees are buckling, and our controlled slide against the counter turns into a barely controlled fall.

Oof.

We land on the floor, his body falling halfway onto mine. He's *so* heavy, he may as well be a marble statue. It's a struggle to maneuver him into a somewhat comfortable position, and by the time I accomplish it, my breaths are coming out in pants.

Holy crap. I actually did it.

I take an inventory of him. His chest rises with steady breaths, his lips are slightly parted, and the lines he always has between his brows have softened. He looks different asleep. More at ease.

My hand reaches out to brush a lock of hair from his forehead.

Am I crazy to think he was about to kiss me right before he started to feel the effects of the tea?

Yes, you are.

You're also an idiot to think Giorgio would ever look at you that way.

Don't read anything into the nice things he does or says. He's only doing this for your brother.

The usual thoughts are there, but for the first time, I don't fully believe them.

Fear and excitement skate through me. What if there really is something brewing between him and I?

Am I brave enough to do anything about it?

Dragging my palms down my cheeks, I decide I'm going to get back to that later. Despite the temptation to ruminate and appreciate Giorgio while he's this unguarded, I've got something I have to do.

Sliding my hand into the front pocket of his slacks, I feel for the key, but this pocket is empty. It must be on the other side.

When I reach into the other pocket, I'm acutely aware of the heat radiating from his skin. The pocket lining dips over his thigh, and as I push my hand all the way in, my fingers get dangerously close to the bulge in his pants.

What would he do if he woke up right now? Would he tear my hand off him? Or would he grab me by the wrist the way he's done so many times in class and move my palm to that bulge?

Heat blankets my cheeks at the image. I swallow, wrap my palm around the warm metal object, and quickly take it out. My heart hammers inside my chest as I stand.

As gently as I possibly can, I guide him onto his back, careful to protect his head with my palm, so that he doesn't fall sideways from a sitting position and hurt himself. When he makes a low sound at the back of his throat, I freeze, but it's nothing. He's still fast asleep.

With one last look at Giorgio, I leave the kitchen and hurry upstairs.

CHAPTER 15

MARTINA

THE KEY SLIPS SMOOTHLY into the lock, and with a soft click, the door swings open.

I'm greeted by a dim, eerie blue glow emanating from rows of screens hanging on the wall. The windows are shuttered, and the lights are off, adding to the unsettling atmosphere. I hesitate for a moment and then shut the door behind me, my palms resting against the cool surface as I try to take it all in.

This isn't an office.

This is a surveillance room.

We had one of these in our home in Ibiza, but it was half the size and not nearly this ominous.

A desk with a keyboard, trackpad, and notebook sits in front of the wall of screens, and there's a suit jacket haphazardly thrown over the back of the office chair. Across the room, a

167

tall metal shelving unit holds stacks of semi-clear plastic storage boxes

Unease drips through my veins. If I have to search all of those, I'm going to be here for a while.

Why are the windows boarded up? I cross the room and press my fingertips against the panels. Who wants to spend all day in a room with no sunlight? Is he a vampire? This is so strange.

My gaze drops back to the desk. I should search it thoroughly before I start looking elsewhere.

I glance behind the computer monitor and around the keyboard, but find nothing. For a moment, I consider taking a peek inside the notebook, but I decide against it. I'm not here to snoop on him, I'm just here for my phone.

Suddenly, my foot bumps against something.

It's one of those rolling filing cabinets.

I pull it out from under the desk and open the top drawer.

There, lying among the papers and folders, is my phone staring up at me.

"Yes!"

An excited smile pulls at my lips. I won Giorgio's silly little game, and I did it in a way he never could have expected. He's going to be impressed, I can feel it. The thought of his surprised look when he realizes what happened fills my chest with giddiness. There's no way he'll be mad at me about the tea. After all, this is what he wanted. He gave me a challenge, and I just crushed it.

As I'm about to shut the drawer, something catches my eye. A corner of a book peeking out from below a few loose sheets of paper.

My brows furrow. Is that...

I move the papers aside to get a better look. My heart picks up speed as I register the long scratch and frayed edges. When I open it up and see the first page, there's no doubt in my mind who it belongs to.

There, in the top corner, is the little sun I drew inside many months ago.

This is my copy of *Jane Eyre*.

Why does Giorgio have it?

Maybe it fell out of my backpack in the car, he found it, and simply forgot about it. No, that's impossible, because I remember exactly where I left the book after I finished with it. It was in our living room in Ibiza. I'd meant to return it to the library, but Vale told me she wanted to read it, so I left it lying on the coffee table for her.

Giorgio must have seen it when he came to pick me up.

And he decided to take it.

But why?

An outlandish fantasy grips me. It's crazy, but my body reacts to it nonetheless, a wave of electricity rolling from the top of my head all the way down to my toes. My belly bursts with butterflies.

What if Giorgio...has liked me all along?

Just formulating that thought feels like I'm hovering my foot off the edge of a sharp cliff. It's dangerous to entertain that kind of hope.

But what if it's true? What if my unrequited crush isn't so unrequited after all?

What if all those long looks, the lingering touches, the unexpectedly sweet things he's said to me weren't just because of his concern for my well-being or because of his duty to my brother? What if they were because of something *more*?

Something sparks to life inside of me. It pulses inside my chest, like an organ that's been dormant but has finally turned on.

I slide the book back into the drawer, close it shut, and slip out into the hall.

In the kitchen, Giorgio's lying in the same position I left him.

I approach him, my steps slowing the closer I get, while my pulse does the opposite. The adrenaline of getting one over him has faded, and nervous uncertainty ripples beneath my skin.

Did I take it too far?

Does he really like me?

What will he say when he wakes up? Will he remember what he almost did right before the tea took effect?

Running to the living room, I get him a pillow and a blanket and spend the next few minutes doing whatever I can to make him more comfortable. The fact that he doesn't even stir through the entire ordeal plants a seed of worry in the back of my head. What if he drank too much?

I eye the pot of remaining kava resting on the counter and press my fingertips to a thick vein in his neck. His pulse is steady, but his skin feels clammy and a little too warm despite the fact that he's lying on the cold floor.

I undo the top two buttons of his shirt and tug it open in an attempt to cool him down. My eyes drift over his muscular chest, and I count his slow, steady breaths.

One.

He didn't have to get involved with me when he brought me here.

Two.

He could have left me sulking alone in my room, but he didn't. He *saw* me. While I was trying so hard to avoid myself, he faced me head-on.

Three.

It was intentional. The phone. The lessons. The way he's paid attention to me. All of it designed to fix me.

Four.

The backs of my eyes sting. I slip my palm under his shirt and press it over his heart, absorbing his heat and wishing I could find some answers in the beat.

Suddenly, his peaceful expression morphs into a grimace. "No," he mutters.

I jerk my hand away as if I've been burned.

He shakes his head, his eyes still shut. "No, you can't leave her there. She doesn't belong there."

My brows furrow. I don't think he's talking to me. He's having a bad dream.

His expression grows more and more distressed, and anguish squeezes around my lungs. I brought this onto him.

Tucking my feet under me, I use all of my strength to lift the upper half of his body and move it so that his head can rest on my lap.

"Shhh. It's okay, Giorgio."

His brows scrunch together, as if he heard what I said and decided it was nonsense. "Why did you leave her? She wasn't well." He sighs a heavy breath. "She was crying in the morning. I asked you to watch her."

Who is he talking about? I drag my thumbs over the frown lines in his face, attempting to soothe him. "Shhh. Everything is okay."

It seems to work. He relaxes, his breathing slows.

"She deserved better," he mumbles. "Better than you and me."

"Giorgio, it's just a dream."

He quiets.

Questions bounce around my head. Is he talking about a real person? A woman in his life? There was real pain in his voice just now. Real regret.

When he doesn't say anything for a five-minute stretch, I let go of the tension I've been holding in my shoulders and release a long breath. I don't care how long he'll be asleep, I'm not leaving him. Even if there's a chance he'll be furious instead of impressed as soon as he wakes up.

Thick inky eyelashes fan out over his cheeks. I trace the shallow lines between his brows before moving the tip of my finger over the bridge of his nose. I've never touched a man like this, and it's intoxicating. To be this close to him. To see him at his most vulnerable.

A butterfly awakens in my stomach as I reach the corner of his lips. He has a wide mouth, and his bottom lip is slightly fuller than the top one. They look like they'd be soft to touch, but I hesitate.

No, that would be crossing a line. He's unconscious. I shouldn't be caressing him like this.

I fold my fingers into my palms and place my fists against the cold ground. My knees have started to ache from the position I'm in, and I decide to try to extricate myself from under him.

Cradling his shoulders and neck with my arms, I gently move him off me.

A hand shoots out and grabs me by the forearm.

I suck in a breath. Is he awake?

His eyes are still closed, but his grip on me is firm. When I try to pull away, he gives a sharp tug, and I fall right into his chest.

His body heat accosts me. As does the fist that appears inside my hair and tugs my head to the side. When he buries his nose in the crook of my neck and makes an appreciative *Mmm*, my head starts to spin.

"Giorgio?"

He answers with a hot, slow drag of his tongue against my throat, and then he sinks his teeth into my flesh.

I'm stunned.

Heat cascades down my body, like a chain of chemical reactions. I've never considered what it would be like to be *bitten* by a man, but I wouldn't have guessed I'd feel the ghost of it reaching right to my clit.

He drags his teeth over my flesh, the bulk of his body tensing beneath me, and then suddenly, he rolls us over, making me yelp.

My back hits the ground *hard*. His body crushes me from above, heavy enough to squeeze the air out of my lungs.

"Giorgio," I whimper. "You're too heavy."

He drags his nose over my cheek all the way up to my hair, takes a big inhale, and follows it with a deep groan that settles right between my legs.

My palms press against his abdomen, trying to lift him a few inches off me. Maybe I should be more worried about what's happening, but instead, there's an irrational excitement at having the freedom to touch him like this. His abs move, flexing beneath my touch, and I drag my palms all over them. Finally, he pushes himself up on his hands.

Is he awake? I try to catch his eye, but he immediately drops his face back into the crook of my neck.

The hot, wet kisses set off a full body shiver. Before I know it, my heel is trailing up his leg and pulling him closer, as if driven by some basic instinct. He hums against my ear and rolls his hips against mine.

I let out a moan. He's hard. And by the feel of it, *big*.

My core tightens with every pass of him against me, heat swelling inside. On the next pass, the pressure increases, and his length brushes right against my clit.

A loud noise fights its way out of my throat.

Holy shit. That felt *good*.

But it doesn't happen again. In fact, his body halts, and for a second, I consider the reality of the situation.

He's turned on, possibly completely out of it, and strong enough to do whatever he wants to me even if I resist.

What if he...

What if he takes me right here?

I swallow air as he rolls his hips again, more slowly this time, and my arousal starts to tangle with a thread of panic.

I'm a virgin.

I've never had sex.

And as wildly attracted as I am to Giorgio, I don't think I could handle the giant thing that's pressing against my pubic bone. Not like this.

"Giorgio, wait."

My hand goes to his chest, but he tears it off and presses it above my head. He does the same with the other. My vision turns hazy. This is the hottest thing that's ever been done to me. His hips buck against me, the movements more desperate now, and my weak attempt to wriggle out from under him is cut short when I feel his tongue drag a line against the neckline of my tank top.

My eyes flutter closed. God, that feels good. So good that when he moves his lips to kiss the outline of my nipple, I lose my train of thought.

His tongue sets off a slow burn beneath my flesh as he licks me through my shirt. *Pull it down.* The desire to feel that hot, wet heat directly against my pebbled flesh morphs into an irresistible need.

My eyes roll to the back of my head. "Giorgio..."

Maybe it won't be so bad.

His teeth scrape and tug.

Maybe it won't hurt.

He drops a hand to palm my breast.

Maybe it's exactly what I need.

"Giorgio. Take my shirt off, *please*."

The one-handed grip he has on my outstretched wrists eases and then disappears. He lifts his head, and for the first time since this started, blue meets hazel.

I swallow as I drink in the look on his face.

Eyes open but glazed over.

Hypnotic sleep.

He's not here. He doesn't know what he's doing.

Shit. Hollow disappointment solidifies inside my belly, even as he lowers his face to mine, and claims my lips with his.

I gasp into his mouth, and he swallows it up. The kiss is soft, lush, deliberate. His beard scrapes against my chin, his tongue darts out to taste my lips, and my body melts against his in response. Forgetting myself, I drag my palms up the planes of his muscular back and tangle my fingers in his hair.

I should stop this. I *need* to stop this.

But this is my first kiss, and he's already taken it without any hesitation, as if it was a given that it was his, so I tell myself I might as well enjoy it.

That hot tongue laps at my bottom lip, and I part my mouth to let him in. The moment he's inside of me for the first time, something catches inside my chest. I moan into his mouth, licking and sucking and trying to mimic him without any finesse. It's messy.

But he doesn't seem to mind.

I wonder if he's dreaming right now. In this dream, does he know he's kissing me?

Or is he dreaming of someone else?

The question hits me harder than I expect, making my emotions collide in a harsh bang.

Turmoil slams into desire and exhilaration, breaking them into a million little pieces.

Nameless, faceless women stream through my head. How many lovers has he had? How many meant something to him?

And how could I ever compare to the beautiful, elegant women a man like Giorgio would pick? Doubt slithers over my nape. I'm eighteen. Fucked up in the head. A virgin. Did I really allow myself to think for a moment he'd do this knowingly with me?

I turn my head to the side, breaking the feverish kiss. "Giorgio, stop."

A hand clutches my jaw and forcefully turns me back to him. His eyes are so damn empty. The usual spark is missing, as if his soul has left.

A tear rolls down my cheek.

He isn't seeing me.

For him, I'm not real.

He scrapes my tear away with his thumb. "Don't cry."

My mouth parts, surprise rippling down my spine. "Giorgio? Are you there?"

His voice is monotone, his eyes blank. He's on a hypnotic autopilot, and yet he repeats himself.

"Don't cry, Martina."

CHAPTER 16

GIORGIO

I SLAM the door of my childhood home and step out onto Via Cassano only to see Martina standing across the street.

What is she doing in Secondigliano? Her brother would lose his mind if he knew she's here.

Then I remember it's my job to protect her.

Fear engulfs me as I run across the street, trying to dodge the speeding cars. I'm afraid that when I get there, she'll already be gone.

But when the bus passes, she's still there, wearing a yellow sundress and a smile.

She laughs when I reach her and pulls me into an embrace. *"Giorgio, it's just a dream."*

In this dream, she's the same girl I've gotten to know over the past week, but she's different in a way I can't quite put a finger on. When I inhale the scent of her hair, my restraint evaporates in a flash. Arousal fills me, so strong and

179

demanding that my knees nearly buckle. When she makes a move to pull away, there isn't a single chance I'll let her.

All the times I've had to hold myself back from her flash before my eyes.

But this is just a dream.

And in this dream, she's *mine*.

I back Martina against the crumbling wall of the fabric store where my mother used to buy patterned silk for her dresses, and I begin working down a list of all the things I've wanted to do to her since that day by the pool. I can be honest with myself in a dream. Honest about the fact that since that moment, not a single hour has gone by without me thinking about how good it would feel to bury myself to the hilt inside of her.

She's tiny. My hands span the entirety of her waist, and my body engulfs her. Her sweet summer scent surrounds me and I press my nose to her throat where it's strongest. *Fuck.* I've never smelled anything better.

My lips part on a moan, and I press them again her flesh. She's soft and pliant, tilting her head to the side to give me the access I crave. I skim my lips down to her chest, dip my tongue into her neckline, squeeze her breasts. It's fucking heaven. My cock is desperate for more as I grind against her, lifting up her hands over her head, her skirt over her thighs. My fingertips skim over her panties.

"Giorgio, stop."

Tearing myself away from her is one of the hardest things I've ever done, but something in her voice gives me pause.

When I look at her, my heart sinks.

A wet track runs from her bottom eyelid down her cheek.

"Don't cry," I tell her even as a crack resounds inside my chest.

Even in a dream, I'm not good enough for her.

Even in a dream, it doesn't work.

"Don't cry, Martina."

I should step away, but the knowledge that this can never happen again keeps me frozen.

One last kiss, and then I'm done, I tell myself.

Wrapping my palm around the back of her delicate neck, I dip my head and press my mouth against her pink lips.

And the next time I blink, we aren't on Via Cassano anymore. We're lying on the kitchen floor in the castello.

Her eyes are wide and wet and *frightened* as she stares up at me, her hair a messy golden pool beneath her head.

I scramble off her, off the floor.

There is no air. Not a square centimeter of oxygen floating anywhere in this room.

My palms slam against the marble counter, and I put my weight on it, giving her a view of my back while my thoughts sprint over boulders and cracked earth to catch up with what just happened.

We were in the dining room, eating, and then...

What happened?

What the fuck happened to make me lose my head like that?

My heart beats so hard it feels like it might break through my ribs. I've never lost control like that, not since...

Nausea roils though me.

"Gio," she whispers, her voice broken and raw.

Did she scream for help? Did I *make* her scream?

"I'm sorry," she says.

She's closer now, but I still can't look at her. What have I done? Her apology floods a sour taste through my mouth. What the fuck is she apologizing for?

"It's my fault. The tea I gave you... It was meant to put you to sleep."

My eyes narrow at the jar of sugar sitting on a wooden shelf in front of me. "*What?*"

She swallows loud enough for me to hear it in the deathly silence of the room. "I found a book on herbs, and it said I could mix two specific herbs in a tea to make a sedative. I found them in the kitchen. I made the tea and gave it to you so that I could steal the key out of your pocket and get my phone from your office."

Quick, shallow breaths. She tricked me. I curl my hands into fists and press them into the counter until my joints whine in protest.

"I'm so sorry. I didn't mean for it to go this way."

I whirl around, and when she sees the look on my face, she backs away and bumps against the island.

"I'm so—"

"Don't say it." I point my finger at her. "Do not fucking say it."

Tears spill over the rims of her wide, red eyes.

I can't think.

As I prowl out of the kitchen, I hear her sob.

The sound ricochets between my ears even as I try to chase it away by slamming the door so hard it jerks on its hinges.

The dark colors of my bedroom swim before my eyes. What have I done?

I rake my fingers through my hair and review the sorry facts. She's cleverer than I gave her credit for. No one's ever managed to knock me out with a cup of tea before. The funny thing is that my little game to get her out of her funk worked. She got her win. I just never expected her to make a mess out of me in the process.

A vise wraps around my heart and squeezes it with a deathly grip. For days, she's been testing my will. I offered to be her teacher without a proper appreciation of what being in close quarters with her would do to me.

Being around her, touching her soft, warm skin for hours at a time, seeing those full lips part and speak and tremble... *Fuck me.*

Instead of obsessing over her every detail, I should have been thinking about how I could get out of the commitment I made to her.

But I convinced myself that my restraint would hold. And it did.

Until tonight, when she turned it into glass and shattered it at my feet.

Leaning my forehead against the wall, I thump my fists against it.

Life is irrational. I've always known this, but somehow, I've managed to navigate its irrationality for thirty-three years. Thirty-three years of schemes, plots, close calls, and tragedies.

And yet it seems my compass has finally broken.

The needle's stuck, and it's pointing in a single direction.

Martina.

The only woman in this world I categorically can't have, and yet it's her that I crave.

I never thought I'd be so drawn to innocence. That's what it is, isn't it? She bleeds it through her every pore—a cocktail of youth, inexperience, and strength that's fatal to a rotten man like me.

I push off the wall and drag my hand over my face. If Damiano ever finds out, I'm done. The favor won't materialize. And fuck, I need that favor. I need it because it will free me from the burden I've carried ever since I entered this world.

I have to be the one to kill Sal.

Damiano has to let me do it, even though it will put him at risk. If anyone finds out, his claim will be questioned, but no one will find out. I'll make sure of it. I don't want the fucking throne. I just need to be the one to squeeze the life out of that son of a bitch.

Resolve hardens my spine. I'm going to fix this. I'm going to get this situation back on track, just like I always do.

The remnants of the tea-induced fog clear from my mind, and with it comes a sinking sensation.

She was crying. I left her there *crying*.

The horror of what she's just experienced at my hands rams into me.

What was I thinking leaving her there like that?

Fuck!

I prowl toward the door, but before I have time to tear it open, a knock comes.

"Giorgio?" Her voice filters through.

It doesn't sound like she's crying anymore. The thought of her doing her best to calm down so that she could come and speak to me opens up a hole inside my chest.

I stop in front of the door and press my palms against the frame. "Yes."

"Can we talk?"

There's an inch of solid wood between us, and like a coward, I use it as a shield for a few more seconds.

What's the plan, Giorgio?

Make sure she's okay, apologize, then...lie. Use every excuse under the sun to make her believe the episode in the kitchen was nothing but the confused actions of a man under the influence. She can never suspect any of that was real.

When I finally set my eyes on her, her posture is slumped, and her face is pink and puffy. She averts her gaze to the floor before slowly dragging it back to me, as if struggling to do it.

"Martina." The word vibrates with feeling, no matter how I try to tamper it down.

She blinks at me, and she seems so small and dejected that it takes everything in me not to drag her into my arms.

"Did I hurt you?" I force out.

She sucks in a breath and shakes her head. "No."

"Where did I grab you? Was I...rough with you?"

I don't miss the absentminded drag of her teeth over her bottom lip. Did I bite her there? If I pull down that lip, will I see the marks from my teeth?

My cock presses against the zipper of my pants.

The fact that I have so little control over my body around her sends a pulse of frustration through my veins.

"You kissed me," she whispers.

I'm certain I did a fuck of a lot more than that.

Sensing my skepticism, she adds, "I'm fine. You didn't hurt me."

I feel a light brush of relief. "Good."

"I...I don't know what to say."

"What happened was a mistake."

She flinches and tries to hide it by brushing a lock of hair out of her face. "It's my fault. I had no idea how strong the tea would be. I take full responsibility."

I'm about to argue, but then I halt. This is good. She's already putting the blame on that fucking tea, and she clearly feels guilty for giving it to me. All I have to do is validate her understanding of what happened.

"You made it yourself?"

"Yes."

"Congratulations, you outwitted me."

She exhales through her mouth and shakes her head. "I thought you'd be impressed."

Despite the situation, a smile tugs at my lips. "I am. It was clever."

Her expression lightens a tiny bit. "After I got the phone, I came back to you and..."

Is she going to go into detail about what I did to her? I'm not sure I want to hear it.

She shifts her weight between her feet. "You were having a bad dream. That's why I was so close to you. I was trying to comfort you."

She was? The idea of her trying to help me pierces my chest. "How did you know I was dreaming?"

"You were talking in your sleep. Something about a woman. You said she deserved better."

The feeling that washes over me feels like being bathed in tar. Heavy and uncomfortable. How much of the conversa-

187

tion with my father did I say out loud? How much does she know?

"What else did I say?" I have to force the words past my dry throat.

"You said someone didn't watch her carefully. Who were you talking about?"

"No one. I was dreaming, but they were just dreams. Nonsense."

The way she holds my gaze for a second too long tells me she doesn't believe me.

She wraps her arms around her midsection and asks, "What did you dream about afterwards?"

Sundresses, lush lips, and soft, fragrant skin.

My hands curl into tight fists, my blunt nails digging into my palms. "Nothing."

"Nothing?"

"I didn't know what I was doing, Martina. Like I said, what happened with you was a mistake."

"You didn't know it was me you were kissing?"

"Of course not. I would have never done it otherwise."

Hurt flashes across her eyes. "You said my name."

"I did what?"

"You said my name when we were doing it. You said, 'Don't cry, Martina.'"

Panic spreads through my lungs. "You must have imagined it."

Her eyes narrow. "I didn't."

Why won't she let it go? "Maybe it was when I was already coming back around."

"But you kissed me again after you said it."

The silence that follows is tense. "Your brother would be very upset if he knew about this...misunderstanding."

Her expression clouds. "Ah, so that's what you're really worried about."

My jaw clenches. She doesn't know what's on the line for me, and it's likely she never will.

"He trusts me with you."

"Don't worry, I won't tell him about what happened." She takes a half-step forward, her gaze flashing with anger. "Or that I think you were kissing me in your dream as well."

My pulse races. "Even if I did, it must have been just my brain playing tricks. We had dinner right before it happened. It would make sense for my subconscious to latch on to the most recent person I've been with."

Her lips tighten into a thin line and then quirk up into a bitter smile. "I see."

I need to hammer the point home, because the last thing I can afford is her believing there's something here. "I'm a grown man, Martina. You're a teenager. I can fucking promise you I have no interest in teenagers whose primary concern in life is their damn phone. It was the tea, that's all."

She huffs a laugh. "Got it."

"Good."

"You know what's interesting, though?"

I wait for her to continue.

"My phone wasn't the only thing that I found in your office."

My muscles stiffen as something sparks inside her eyes.

"I hope you enjoy reading my book."

She brushes past me and slams the door behind her.

CHAPTER 17

MARTINA

AFTER THAT INTERACTION WITH GIORGIO, I climb into bed and spend long hours staring at the ceiling in the dark. My phone is charging on the nightstand beside me, but the itch to use it is strangely absent. I'm too wrapped up in replaying everything that Giorgio said to me inside my head.

The fact that there's only a wall between us makes everything worse. Twice, I throw off my duvet and march over to the door between our rooms, tempted to barge in and accuse him of being a liar, but both times, my bravado fails, and I crawl back under the duvet.

His cold denials hurt. His dismissal stings.

At first, I'm resolute that he's full of shit. He knew he was kissing me. Who does he take me for? A complete idiot?

But as the darkness in the sky depletes, so does my confidence.

Maybe it's true. After all, I have no way of knowing what was going through his head when he was on top of me.

He muttered my name, but was he thinking of me the entire time we were kissing or just when I told him to stop? And then there's the book. Could there be another explanation for why he took it besides him being into me?

The more I ruminate, the more uncomfortable I get. A sticky film of embarrassment coats my skin. Did I make it obvious that I *wanted* the kiss to be intentional on his part? Ugh, probably. And if he truly has no interest in me... Well, I think I may have exposed the fact I have a crush on him.

Now what?

I untangle my legs from between the sheets and pad over to the window to see the sun rise over the horizon. It's a new day.

I get dressed and head downstairs.

This early, only Tommaso is up. He's prepping something in the kitchen.

"Did you make that *Torta Caprese* last night?" he asks, pointing a flour-covered finger at the half-eaten cake I left on the counter.

"Yeah. Did you try it?"

He grins as he picks up a whisk. "Of course, I did. Couldn't resist how darn good it looked, and it tasted even better. Want to help me here? I'm making cornetti for breakfast. Prepped the dough yesterday."

I'm about to say no, but then I realize I'm not even sure what I was planning on doing when I came in here. My heart bounces in my chest, lost and aimless.

Might as well do something useful.

"I can help with the lamination."

Tommaso's eyes widen with surprise. "You've made them before?"

"I used to bake and cook quite a bit," I tell him. "At one point, I was actually thinking of going to culinary school."

Tommaso grins and hands me an apron. "Music to my ears."

We get to work, making envelopes of the dough around the cold butter and then rolling it out to triple the size. It doesn't take long for my arms to ache, but I don't mind it.

Tommaso hums in approval. "You're good. So what happened with the culinary school?"

"Um." I brush my hair out of my face with the back of my hand. "It just didn't work out."

"You don't sound upset about it."

The truth is, I'm not anymore. In the grand scheme of things I could be torn up about, my failed culinary ambition is a minor blip.

I shrug. "I guess I'm not sure what I want to do with my life anymore."

"I didn't either when I was your age," Tommaso says easily. "Changed my mind a half-dozen times before I got serious about cooking."

There was a time when I could see my future. Before New York, my life as a college student was something I'd visualize constantly. I saw myself experimenting in the kitchen of my small apartment, having friends over in the evenings for wine and cheese nights, going for long walks down tree-lined streets with music blasting in my ears.

One gunshot cleared away all of those images.

Ever since, there's only been darkness. One day at a time has become my mantra.

It dawns on me I haven't said it much since I arrived here.

I finish arranging the cornetti on a tray and lean against the counter. My gaze lands on the floor right where Giorgio kissed me, and for a moment, the darkness parts.

I see a small glimpse of the future I want.

And it involves him and me tangled on that floor again.

The realization softens my knees.

"I'm going to go for a walk," I tell Tommaso and make my way to the front door.

As soon as I step outside, the chilly morning air makes goosebumps appear across my arms. Instead of going back in for a sweater, I move my feet quicker and quicker until I break out into a full-on jog. I pass by the garden and keep going east, toward where the sun is suspended above the hills. With each step, my thoughts become a little more focused, my feelings clearer.

I like Giorgio.

Yes, I find him wildly attractive, but it's not just that anymore. There's a connection between us. A thread that's been pulling me to him from the moment we met, and no matter how he denies it, my gut tells me he feels it too.

My skin flushes with heat as I think back to the moment he pinned my wrist above my head and ground himself into me. Beneath the thick veil of my arousal, there was something even more tantalizing, and that's what calls to me now.

For a split second, I didn't feel like a broken, empty shell. To be wanted like that... It made me feel powerful.

And God, I haven't felt powerful in a long time.

My power was taken from me the night Imogen died. My confidence, my self-esteem, my self-worth—Lazaro took all of those things and left behind a crumbling husk.

Giorgio kissed me and made it right again.

He gave me a taste, and he expects me to just forget it?

The truth is, even if I wanted to forget, I don't know if I can. What awaits me on the other side if I do? More sleepless nights with shadows lurking in the corners of my bedroom? More endless hours of scrolling through posts of condolences and grief and pain?

I come to a stop at the edge of the forest, digging my heels into the ground and bending at the waist to catch my breath. My chest heaves.

I'm stuck here in this place with Giorgio for God knows how long, and I don't know how to turn off the feelings I have for him. They're so alive in my chest that my heart beats with them.

I want him.

I want his body and his touch.

I want to know what it feels like to have him naked and heavy on top of me, with his hands on my bare breasts and his length pushing inside of me.

And after last night, I think he might want the very same thing.

All he needs is a little push.

Am I brave enough to give it to him?

By the time I reach the foot of the tower, my jog has slowed to a walk. I'm sweaty and in desperate need of a shower, but I remember what Polo said about the view from the top and make a spontaneous decision to check it out.

There's a small door cut into a larger gate. I slip through it and use my phone's flashlight to illuminate the dark space. It's not hard to spot the spiral staircase, and after what feels like a century, I finally emerge at the top.

I don't know how tall the tower is, but it seems to me about the same height as a five-story building. Using my hand to shield my eyes from the sun, I spin around and take it all in.

Wow. The view is breathtaking.

I take in the vibrant green forest, the windy road at the bottom of the hill, and patches of purple and yellow wild-flowers. Leaves rustle in the distance. Birds sing, their songs overlapping and weaving together.

From up here, I can see what looks like a small settlement in a valley in the distance. Perugia is too far, probably hidden behind one of the hills.

I focus back on the forest, raking my gaze over the pines until I spot a gap in the foliage.

Is that a small house?

My chest presses against the top of the wall as I lean forward, trying to get a better look.

There it is. A sloped roof with a chimney. The lines aren't straight. I believe it's sagging in some parts.

Is that a part of the property? Why would someone build a tiny little house all the way over there? I don't see a road to it. It's got to be at least a twenty-minute hike from here.

My stomach growls. With one final look at the mysterious house, I turn and head back down.

I use the side door to get back into the kitchen and find Tommaso scrambling some eggs, humming a tune to himself.

"Isn't it still too early for breakfast?" I ask.

He glances at me over his shoulder. "Not at all. Giorgio is up already. Want me to make you a plate too?"

My heart cartwheels. Giorgio couldn't sleep either.

"Yes, please."

"Go ahead, I'll bring it out to the dining room."

I fix my ponytail and wipe a few damp strands from my face before I make my way over, my nerves ratcheting up with each step.

When I see him sitting at the head of the table, his broad back to me, I gulp down a steadying breath. His shoulders square, making me think he's sensed my presence.

"You're up early," I say as I round the table and take a seat to his right.

He moves his attention from his phone and gives me a once over, his eyes halting on the low neckline of my tank top. When they lift to my face, darkness swirls within them. "Good morning."

Messy hair. Plain black T-shirt. A pair of dark-navy jeans. Tiredness crisscrosses his face, but there are no other clues as to what's running through his head.

That is until I notice the way he's gripping his phone.

There's one thing I've realized about Giorgio over the past week—the man doesn't fidget. The most he'll do is run a hand over his tie or smooth his hair out of his face. Otherwise, his hands are as steady and controlled as a surgeon's.

But right now, his thumb is anxiously rubbing back and forth against the edge of his device.

Something wicked sparks inside of me. *Unsettled from last night?*

It's possible he's worried about me telling Damiano about the kiss, but by now, he has to know I wouldn't do that.

No. I'd bet anything the unease radiating from his stiff posture is there because he's worried he didn't fool me.

When he notices my gaze, his movements stop. He clears his throat and leans back into his seat. "You were at the gym?"

"No, I went running. To the edge of the forest and back. I also went to the top of the tower to check out the view. I thought I saw a small house in the woods? Do you know what that is?"

He flicks his hand dismissively. "Just an old ruin."

"A ruin?" It didn't look *that* bad.

Something tense passes over his expression. "There was a fire. The roof can collapse at any time. I've been meaning to get the thing torn down, but it's not bothering anyone over there."

We're interrupted by Tommaso bringing out two cappuccinos and a basket of the cornetti. When he retreats, Giorgio folds his hands on the table and pierces me with a serious gaze.

"How do you feel?"

I glance down at myself. "Sweaty. I need a shower."

"That's not what I mean."

"What do you mean then?"

His gaze darkens. "You know what. The incident last night."

Under the tablecloth, I press my fingernails into my palms.

This is it. Can I find it in myself to be brave? Enough to show him that I want him? Enough to push past his attempts to pretend like what happened last night wasn't real?

At worst, I'm totally wrong about him, and I'll embarrass myself. But haven't I already been doing that since I got here?

Really, I have nothing to lose besides my ego.

And who gives a crap about that?

I arch a brow at him. "You mean when you kissed me, and sucked on my neck, and dragged your mouth all over my breasts until I begged you to take off my shirt?"

He nearly chokes. "You did wha—"

"I begged you to take off my shirt."

He rakes his fingers through his hair, messing it up even more. "You were in shock."

"Maybe in the beginning, but I got up to speed pretty quickly."

"What I did was completely inappropriate. I apologize."

Nerves dancing inside my gut, I force my next words out. "No need." Our eyes clash together. "I liked the way you kissed me."

He hisses through his teeth and whips his head to look at the wall, as if he can't stand the sight of me.

The thick vein in his neck pulses.

"Do. Not. Say. That," he grinds out, his words underscored with exasperated warning. "It was a mistake."

"So you keep saying, but I don't believe you."

He still won't look at me.

Frustration coils inside of me, tight and ready to spring. I lean over the table into his space. "Did you take my book by mistake too?"

He presses his fist to his mouth. I think I hear him curse under his breath before he turns his head with a snap. Eyes blazing, he growls, "Do not push me, Martina. You're young. You don't know what happens when grown men are pushed past their limits."

My nipples tighten at the fire in his eyes and the implication behind his words.

A slow smile pulls at my lips. I was right. It's not just me. He wants this too, but he's fighting against it. If he wants to scare me off, he's going to have to do a lot more than that.

"You're right. I don't," I say, easing back into my chair. "Show me."

Giorgio bolts out of his seat. His hands are fisted, and they're...shaking.

A thrill runs down my spine. *Is that what I do to him?*

"I don't want to see you for the rest of the day," he barks in a tone that no one in their right mind would disobey.

And then he walks out of the room.

CHAPTER 18

GIORGIO

MY FIRST STOP after breakfast is the shower. I know I won't get anything done before I take care of the problem inside my pants. Water cascades down my back as I fist my cock to a visual of Martina begging me to suck her tits. Her name spills past my lips as I come all over the marble wall, the orgasm so powerful it nearly brings me to my knees.

This is turning into a complete disaster.

I've started to wonder if I've made a grave mistake trying to snap her out of her depression. I didn't expect her to go from barely talking to saying things that make me feel more like a crazed beast than a man.

She liked the way I kissed her.

I like the idea of her begging on her knees. It doesn't really matter what she's begging for—her clothes off, an orgasm, my cock in her mouth. I'm quite sure I'd give her whatever she asked of me in that position. Thank God, her provocations have been limited to words instead of actions.

For now.

I turn the water off, grab a towel, and dry myself.

This has to stop. *I* have to stop this, but I'm not fooling her with my denials, and it's a first. I'm a good liar. Excellent, even. Yet somehow, I'm not able to keep up my impenetrable mask around her.

When in the afternoon I get the summons from Sal, I feel a wave of relief. He wants to see me tomorrow and it's a fine excuse to leave the castello. To put some distance between Martina and me.

It's five am the following morning when I step out the front door. Sal wants to gather all of the capos and his inner circle together for a meeting. I don't fall into either category, but I got an invite as well. My guess is it's a sign he's growing irritated at my lack of progress when it comes to Martina, and he wants to remind me who's boss.

As if I could forget.

Sal's not known for being particularly clever, but he's paranoid, and after Damiano's betrayal, even more so. The fact that he's inviting me to this thing is a sign of desperation. I guess the mercenaries he's hired to look for Martina haven't gotten him the results that he's wanted.

After Sal's meeting, I'm going to see my father. That conversation won't take long unless he's in one of his rare sentimental moods. I need to know if Sal's been asking my father about me, and that's something that requires a face-to-face conversation. My father knows better than to say anything sensitive over the phone, especially when he might already know war is afoot. Not to mention, he might lie. It's a good thing I can see right through his lies.

The gravel crunches under my leather shoes as I walk toward the garage. Speed is my primary consideration for today, so I grab the key to my Ferrari from its hook on the wall and slip inside the car. The drive from Perugia to Naples takes about four hours, but I can make it in three by leaving this early. Unless there's bad traffic on the road, I should be back by midday.

When I pull out of the garage, I see Polo hurrying over. I wait for him to approach.

He places his palms on the hood of the car and meets my gaze. "Where are you going?"

"Casal and Naples. I'll be back later today."

"Take me with you."

"You know I can't."

"Are you meeting with him today?"

Irritation makes my nape prickle. "No."

Polo's eyes narrow. "I don't believe you."

"I'm going to see Nino."

"Isn't that nice? You can see your father whenever you want," he says, his voice tense with barely contained anger. "I should be able to do the same."

My hands tighten around the smooth leather of the wheel. "It's too early for this, Polo."

When he slaps the roof of the car with his palms, my patience runs out. I turn off the engine, get out, and stalk toward him until we're chest to chest. Fear flashes inside his eyes, but he doesn't back down. "I deserve to be a part of the clan as much as you do," he says angrily. "Do you think I want to be a fucking gardener for the rest of my life? I want to be *made*."

"It's never going to happen. I made a promise to your mother, and I don't intend on breaking it."

"My mother's dead. I can't live the rest of my life in accordance to the dying wishes of a sick woman. You think *your* mother would have wanted this for you?" He takes a step back and spreads his arms. "You're a fucking hypocrite, Gio. You're no different than me, remember? But you seem to take pleasure in keeping me a rung below you."

Does he really think this is about my fucking ego? I grab him by the collar of his shirt, my anger boiling over. "Watch your fucking tongue. I'm keeping you *alive*. Becoming a made man of the Casalesi is an early death sentence, especially for someone like you."

"Someone like me?" He makes a disbelieving scoff. "Just because I don't know computers or all of that security bullshit like you doesn't mean I can't be valuable."

"You'd be made a soldier, sent to the streets, and left to die."

His eyes darken. "You don't know that. You don't know what the don will say once he meets me."

The naive confidence in his gaze is so disappointing, I shove him away. "I know it's never going to be what you want to hear. I joined the clan because I didn't have a choice. You do, Polo."

His expression turns into a grimace, and he spits on the ground. "What choice? What fucking choice?" He points his finger at me. "*You've* made my decision."

I check my watch. "I don't have time for this."

"Yeah, you never do," he grits out.

My eyes scan him over. "While I'm gone, make sure Martina doesn't wander off anywhere. Keep an eye on her."

"You can't keep me here forever," he seethes. "I'm not your prisoner. One day, I'll walk out of this place, and you'll wish you helped me when I asked for it."

"I am helping you," I say as I get back inside the car. "You're just too blind to see it. Did you hear me? I said keep an eye on Mar—"

"I heard you. I'll take care of your pet while you're gone, don't worry."

My jaw clenches. I don't like his fucking tone. But I also need to get on the damn road if I want to get back here before nightfall.

I decide to let it go. Polo's angry, but he'll calm down. He always does. We have too much in common, him and I. When I was his age, I had the same restlessness inside my blood, but I put everything into my work, burying myself in projects. Polo doesn't have any place to channel it—something I suppose is on me to provide. I knew what I was signing up for when I took him on. Have I been neglecting my duty? I guess I always thought that working for Sal would be the last thing he'd want after what happened to his mother. It sure as fuck was the last thing *I* wanted, but at the time, it truly was the only way for me to survive.

I turn on the car. The more I let him entertain the idea of becoming a made man, the more invested he's become in the fucking fantasy. Has he forgotten what it's like on the streets of Secondigliano? Maybe his mother managed to somewhat insulate him from it growing up. She came from a wealthy family, and even after they'd kicked her out for getting pregnant out of wedlock, she had enough money to afford to live in one of the nicer buildings on the edge of the neighborhood. Polo has no fucking clue what clan business actually entails.

I should show him. Take him back there with me one time so that he can see what the life of a foot soldier looks like.

But I can't now. Not when I already have my hands full with Martina.

As I pull out of the yard, I register the furious expression on Polo's face in the rearview mirror, and it leaves a nagging feeling at the back of my head.

Everyone meets in Sal's office a few doors down from the main church in Casal. At least four icons hang around the room, Jesus's forlorn face gazing down at the twenty-something group of killers gathered in front of him.

The atmosphere is tense as we wait for Sal to appear. His consigliere, Calisto, stands by the desk and whispers something into Vito Pirozzi's ear. Vito's face is disfigured from a recent altercation with De Rossi involving a bowl of stew, and as he listens to Calisto, he itches the burn scar on his cheek. His younger brother, Nelo, isn't here, but he can't be far. The vultures are circling around the heart of Casal, waiting to see who'll prevail. Our piece of shit don, or his unproven contender.

At last, the doors part, and Sal walks in dressed in one of his best suits. He's impeccably groomed, a heavy watch shining on his wrist, his leather shoes so polished they gleam in the light.

Appearances matter more than most like to admit.

He's trying to project his power so as to cement his infallibility. Most here are smart enough to see through it, but not all.

Calisto pulls out Sal's chair, and everyone stands up a little bit straighter as they wait for the don to speak.

He surveys us with a slow and steady gaze, pausing on some faces longer than others. When he gets to me, he looks right into my eyes, as if they're two peepholes inside my mind. I keep my features neutral until he moves on, but that penetrating look raises the hairs on the back of my neck.

I've learned to trust my instincts.

Something's going on.

"Damiano De Rossi's futile rebellion has entered its second week," he begins. "I want to make it clear that agreeing to a meeting with him counts as betrayal in my books, and we all know how we punish traitors."

A few men nod around the room.

"While his attempt to gain more power is as likely as our Vito here winning a beauty contest—" some chuckles break out while Vito frowns "—he's managed to disrupt our business and anger our Algerian partners by denying them distribution in Ibiza." Sal twists his watch. "Not to mention, word of his rebellion has reached some of our enemies, namely the Mallardo clan. Since they don't have insight into the internal politics of the Casalesi, they think they'll gain something by backing him."

Of course they will. The only reason the Mallardos are our enemies is because Sal recently overstepped the decade-old borders between our territories to start building a factory on their side. He did it to show everyone how big his dick is. He got too arrogant to appreciate the Mallardos as valuable allies.

"This charade needs to end," he concludes.

"What's the plan, Don?" a capo standing beside me asks.

"De Rossi's plan relies on his ability to deceive others. Sources tell me his pitch is that he's capable of forging strong alliances and running this business better than I have for the past decade." Sal scoffs. "It just shows he has no idea what it takes to lead the Casalesi. Our collective business enterprise might rival that of Fortune 500 conglomerates, but at our core, we are just men who will do *whatever* it takes to maintain the clan's dominance. De Rossi is not one of us. Do any of you know why he never dared to challenge me before this?"

Vito crosses his arms over his chest. "His sister."

"She is his weakness," Sal says. "Now, he's also got a wife, but she's a less appealing target due to her connection to the Garzolo clan in New York. We don't need any Americans sniffing around our turf. As soon as we have Martina De Rossi, this war will be over."

"You really think he'll just give it all up for her?" someone asks.

"I know it. He hid that little bitch—"

My posture firms. What the fuck did he just call her?

"But it won't be long before I find her." He turns to me. "Giorgio is one of the many men I have working on tracking Martina. You all know how talented he is, so I have no doubt the search will be over very soon."

An image of me flexing my fists, flying across the room, and pummeling his face until all that's left is bloody pulp plays inside my head. But no hint of the fantasy makes it to the outside of my skull. I give him a relaxed smile. "I look forward to bringing her to you."

He nods and turns his attention to Calisto, whispering something into his ear.

After another fifteen minutes, the meeting wraps up. As I exit the building, I'm on high alert, so when I pull out of the parking lot, I notice the car following me immediately.

Cazzo.

Sal is suspicious of me.

I clench my jaw and spend the next ten minutes losing my tail before finally getting on the road to Naples.

As soon as I step onto the pavement of Secondigliano, the smells of the neighborhood slam into me like a shockwave.

The pizzeria on the first floor of the apartment building my father lives in has been producing pies since the seventies, when the complex was first built. The smells of grease, cheese, and tomato sauce work overtime to hide the smell of piss that soaks the sidewalks. There are two long benches right ahead of the main entrance of the building, and after eight p.m., they're crowded with junkies shooting up fentanyl they manage to score a few streets over. Civilians don't walk here afterhours unless they have a death wish or a sick kind of curiosity driving them to see how far human beings can fall.

The chef sees me through the window and gives me a curt nod. I respond with the same before I pass through the front door. The tempered glass has been cracked for the past few years, and no one seems too eager to get it fixed. What's the point? It'll only last a few days before someone breaks it again.

The apartment where I spent the first sixteen years of my life is located on the top floor.

Unit 404.

I knock.

There's the jingle of a chain. Then the click of a lock.

The door swings open to reveal Nino Girardi, and one look at his yellowish white dress shirt and sagging dress pants is enough to make me want to turn around and leave.

I might call the man my father, but I've never felt any familial affection for him.

He disgusts me.

For as long as I can remember, I've always told myself I'll never be like him.

"Gio," he says, his voice hoarse from cigarettes and age. "I was glad when you called. Come in."

I follow him inside the apartment, and it's like stepping back into a time machine. Nothing's changed since I left at sixteen, everything just grew older. I wonder what Martina would think of me if she saw the shithole I grew up in.

Maybe I should have brought her with me. That would be a sure way to kill whatever attraction she feels toward me.

Dim overhead light, peeling linoleum floor, textured wallpaper that's a few decades out of style, and bulky, worn furniture. Everything here seems to be in a state of decay, including my father.

There's a photo of me and Mama when I was around eight hanging above the TV with some plastic flowers pinned above it. It's the only photo in the entire apartment, and it feels like a shrine.

Nino talks about her now as if she was the love of his life, but when she was alive, he certainly didn't treat her like that. The ways he wronged her...

I swallow and clench my jaw.

He's had women since Mama passed. The man doesn't know how to take care of himself. The last one left without a note or explanation, and he complained to me about it until I told him I didn't give a fuck. Since then, he's hired a maid to come in and clean up his mess.

He offers me some water, which I refuse since I'm not planning on staying long, and we sit down in the living room. He groans as he settles on the couch.

"How are you, son?"

I ignore his question. "When was the last time you spoke to Sal?"

"It's been a while since you came by. I told you I'd like to see you more often, haven't I? The neighbors at the end of the hallway moved out, and now there's a family with three kids. Those brats never shut up. I've been meaning to go over and have a word with them. Maybe they don't know who I am, being new and all. The previous neighbors knew I liked my quiet, and they respected that, but this couple is young, and I don't like the way that husband looks at me, as if he's better than me or something."

He probably is, Father. It's not fucking hard.

"I don't have much time," I tell him. "Has the don contacted you in the last two weeks?"

He plants his hands on his knees. "Yeah. About a week ago."

"Why?"

"Your don values my opinion," he says, a self-satisfied smirk appearing on his face.

Jesus. He's as delusional as ever. My father is one of the clan's submarines—men tasked with delivering weekly stipends to the lowest level foot soldiers and their families in a given territory. The positions are cushy and usually reserved for men past their prime, but my father scored the job when he was still relatively young.

He wanted it so fucking bad he was willing to give up the single shred of honor he was born with for it.

"Nice of him to check in. He's a good man, that one. He pays me respect."

My eyes widen in genuine disbelief. Is he *fucking* serious?

It takes him a few seconds to register the expression on my face, but when he does, the smirk melts away, and he rubs his knees awkwardly. "He's changed, you know? He's not like he was back then."

Nino doesn't actually know Sal, so it's all bullshit. It's easy to get into my father's good graces. Treat him like he's someone important, and he'll eat right out of your hand. My father's pride has always been his most precious possession, and Sal cracked that puzzle three decades ago.

"What was he asking about?"

"Told me about the De Rossi kid." He scoffs. "They come and go, you know? Arrogant little fucks who think they know better than the man who gave them everything."

"Did he ask you any questions?"

He throws his hand up. "Sure, Gio. He asked me lots. How I was doing here, the word among the soldiers and their families..." He raises his shoulders. "I might not be in Casal, but I'm well connected here."

Sal couldn't give a fuck about these people. The bottom rung is irrelevant and replaceable.

"What else?"

"He asked about how you were doing. Too bad I couldn't tell him much since you never visit anymore." He has the audacity to give me an accusing look.

"What did he want to know about me exactly?"

"He asked if I knew where you spent your time these days. I told him his guess was as good as mine. You've got a place only thirty minutes away from me, and still you ignore your old man."

My small apartment on the outskirts of Naples is covered in cameras. No one could have gone in there without me knowing. But Sal could have put someone on surveillance, just to check if I'm ever around, and by now he knows I haven't been there. Has he done the same at my apartment in Rome? If he's trained his eye on me, he might already know I'm in none of my known residences, and with that tail he put on me...

My frown deepens. "That's all?"

"That's all, son. We talked some more about the word on the street. I told him his support is unwavering here, and then he got up to leave. He thanked me beautifully, Gio." He jerks his chin toward the floor. "Look."

Glancing over my shoulder, I see a crate of wine bottles. Probably from one of Sal's vineyards.

"Want to open one?" he asks.

I'd rather drink bleach. I stand and straighten out my suit jacket. "I have to go."

"Already?"

I'm tempted to just walk out of there, but something pulls me back to look at him. I drink in his aging body, fat and wrinkled all over. He's pushing seventy. Soon, he'll be dead.

We lock eyes, and he quickly grows uncomfortable beneath my stare. Shame creeps into his expression. He knows exactly what's on my mind whenever I look—really *look*—at him. Anger wraps around my heart and squeezes hard.

When I'm done making Sal pay for what he did to my mother, it'll be Nino's turn.

"Goodbye, Father."

I step outside, and shut the door behind me.

CHAPTER 19

MARTINA

YESTERDAY, after Giorgio told me he didn't want to see me for the rest of the day, I took it to mean our lesson was canceled. I spent a few hours bouncing around my room, my body buzzing with adrenaline. I couldn't believe the things I said to him. It felt like someone else had slid inside my body and started moving my mouth for me, spitting out bold, very un-Martina-like statements.

But it was working. I was getting through to him, and his struggle to keep himself from doing what he wants to do was addictive to watch. It filled me with a wicked sense of pleasure.

After a while, I got tired of pacing the floor of my bedroom and came down to the greenhouse. Polo was there. He seemed pleased to see me, and we worked together for a few hours during which he asked about my life back in Ibiza and shared funny stories about Allegra and Tommaso.

Today, he's far quieter. I barely get a hello when I arrive, and when I ask him if I should finish the project I was working on yesterday, he responds with a grunt.

I eye him curiously. There's a frown on his face, and his shoulders are slumped. Something must have happened.

An hour passes before I hear his voice. "Look over here," Polo calls, gesturing for me to come over. "The magnolias are in bloom."

I go over to his side and peer at the purple and blue flowers spilling out of a rectangular planter. "They're beautiful. Can I cut some for my room?"

"Sure." He walks over to a desk and extracts a pair of scissors from the drawer before handing them to me. "Here."

As I look for the perfect stem, I glance at him. "You okay?"

His frown returns. "Yeah. Why do you ask?"

"I don't know. You just seem upset."

He sniffs and looks down at the ground. "Nah, it's nothing."

Deciding not to push, I finish cutting the flowers. "You said something about planting more veggies the other day. Do you want to work on that today?"

"I won't have time. I've got an errand to run." He moves to the sink to wash his hands.

"Oh, okay. I guess I'll just hang around until it's time for Giorgio's lesson."

"He's gone. Didn't he tell you?"

I arch a brow. "Gone where?"

"Naples."

"What for?"

Polo's expression hardens. "He said he went to see his father, but who knows if he's telling the truth. Getting anything out of him is like pulling teeth."

The way he says it, his words short and clipped, makes it clear something happened between him and Giorgio. Did they get in an argument?

"Do you know when he'll be back?"

"He said this afternoon, but it's a long drive to Naples." Polo wipes his hands on a towel and nods at the cut flowers. "You should put those in some water. I need to get to the nursery before it closes."

I pick up the bouquet. "Where is that?"

"Near the closest town, and by town, I mean an intersection. It's a fifteen-minute drive or so."

"Can I come?" I ask, half-expecting him to say no. Giorgio doesn't want me leaving the property, but this is so close, it barely counts. Plus, there's nothing else to do, and I'm irritated he left without giving me a heads-up. We skipped our class yesterday, and now we're skipping it again today? He could have said something. He knows how important the classes have become to me.

Polo tosses the towel on the table. "I shouldn't—" He purses his lips. For a moment, he looks like he's wrestling with something, but then he blows out a breath and says, "Fuck it. We won't be going far. Go drop off your flowers, and I'll take you."

My eyes widen. *Hell yes!* "Okay, great."

I meet Polo in the courtyard a few minutes later, and we get into his truck. The back of my mind prickles with knowledge that Giorgio might not be happy if he finds out about this, but given how close we're going, we'll be back before he returns.

"I looked you up, you know," Polo says as he backs out of the gate. "Your brother is some big shot in Ibiza."

I pick some dirt from under my nails. "He owns a few businesses on the island."

"A few." Polo chuckles under his breath. "According to Forbes, his net worth is estimated to be close to half a billion."

Heat creeps up my cheeks. "My brother's done well for himself."

"How do him and Giorgio know each other?"

Ugh, what am I supposed to say to that? I still don't know if Polo is aware of Giorgio's involvement with the Casalesi, and I sure as hell am not going to be the one to bring it up.

"I'm not sure," I say dismissively. "Probably from their work."

"Yeah, their *work*." He shakes his head as he takes a turn. "Your brother isn't just a businessman, Martina, is he?"

The back of my nape prickles. "What do you mean?"

"I know what Giorgio does." His voice hardens. "He handles security matters for the Casalesi. Your brother must be a part of the clan, too. Why are you here, really?"

I meet his scrutinizing gaze in the mirror and wonder what I should say. So he knows some of it, but clearly Giorgio doesn't trust him enough to tell him why I'm here. Or maybe Giorgio just doesn't think it's relevant information. I school my expression into a neutral mask. "Giorgio already told you."

"I don't buy it. This isn't some kind of nature retreat. Like I said, Giorgio hates this fucking place. He comes often, but never for more than a few days. He wouldn't have agreed to stay here with you for this long if there wasn't something big in it for him."

I pull my lips into my mouth. There's nothing I can say to that. "Why do you keep saying he hates it here?"

"You won't tell me anything, but you expect me to tell you things?" He scoffs. "Forget it."

Something in how his face moves strikes me as familiar. I squint at him, trying to decipher who he reminds me of, but I come up blank.

We pass by an abandoned barn. "Polo, there's nothing to tell. My brother's busy this summer, and he thought I'd have a better time spending it out here."

"He sent you here over literally anywhere else in the world?" He adjusts his hands on the wheel. "You know what I think? I think your brother is the capo of Ibiza. And if he sent you all the way over here with Giorgio... You're being hidden away."

I don't react. He turns to look at me, dragging his gaze over my profile. When I don't say anything, he clicks his tongue. "Who are you hiding from, Martina?"

His proximity to the truth twists my nerves into tight coils. "What is it to you? It's my business."

"I'm tired of secrets." And then he mutters under his breath, "And I'm tired of being told how to live my own damn life."

Tension lingers inside the vehicle. After a while, Polo turns on the music, and I focus my eyes on the scenery outside window.

Unease swirls inside my stomach as we park in a dirt lot by the nurseries. Even though Polo's frustration is directed more at Giorgio than me, I don't like that he looked me or my brother up. Why does he care so much? Is he really just that bored, or is there something else behind it?

"I need to go talk to the owner about my order," Polo says, sparing me a look once we get out of the truck. "You can walk around while you wait."

"Okay. See you in a bit."

As he disappears behind the door of the office building, I spin around, taking it all in. The place is huge. The plant nursery is situated on a large, sprawling piece of land and is filled with rows upon rows of various plants and flowers. I can see a range of different species, from tall trees to short shrubs, and colorful blooms in every hue. My attention catches on the glass greenhouse a little farther away, and I decided to make my way over to it.

My conversation with Polo replays inside my head. I didn't say anything I shouldn't have, right? I didn't even confirm he was right about my brother being the capo of Ibiza. I'm probably overthinking it. Giorgio trusts him, and he must have a good reason for that trust.

As soon as I step through the door of the greenhouse, I'm

struck by warmth and humidity. The air is thick with the scent of soil and growing plants, and sunlight streams through the matted glass above my head. I suck in the earthy aroma and let out a sigh. It's gorgeous.

I walk over to a long wooden table stacked with potted plants and start to browse. Some of them we already have in the garden, but I find a few that will make great new additions.

Somewhere on the distance, a car door slams. Is Polo finished with the owner? I glance in the direction of the entry and then get back to my task. He knows I'm here. He'll come and get me before he leaves.

When I'm done sifting through the pots on the table, I crouch down to look at the ones on the ground.

A sound penetrates my ears. Heavy and sure footsteps.

Before I get a chance to rise, a pair of familiar leather shoes come into view. When I look up, I see they belong to a very angry Giorgio.

"Hel—"

He leans down, wraps his hand around my biceps, and hauls me to my feet. His hold on me is so rough, it's almost bruising.

I frown at him. "What's going on?"

"What the fuck are you doing here, Martina?"

The raw anger in his voice sends blood away from my face. His eyes are hard and dark with ire.

"I just came with Polo to get some air."

"You came here to get some air."

"Yes."

He jerks me closer. "Are you stupid?"

Hurt blooms inside my chest at his words. "No."

He flashes me his teeth. "You're living on ten acres of land. That wasn't enough fresh air for you?"

"We barely left the property. We—"

He shakes me, making my hair spill into my face. "Anyone could have seen you driving here!"

"No one saw us," I protest, jerking my arm out of his grip. "We drove straight here from the castello."

He grabs me again, wrapping both of his hands around my biceps and practically dragging me into him. "You *cannot* know that. Did any cars pass you?"

Did they? "I-I don't know. I wasn't paying attention."

"Of course you weren't," he growls.

Anger drips into my blood. "You're making a big deal out of nothing."

He snarls, turns me around, and pushes me out of the greenhouse. "There's a camera at the stoplight five minutes from here, which means it likely got a picture of you. Do you understand what that means?"

"Not really," I confess as we near what I presume to be his car.

"It means that unless I manage to erase any trace of it quickly, someone might use it to track you down to this precise location."

He jerks open the passenger door and stuffs me inside.

"Sal has an army looking for you," he continues as soon as he gets into the driver's seat, "and this is exactly the kind of idiotic slipup that might give him what he needs."

My stomach drops. *Shit.* As we back out of the lot, I notice Polo's truck. "Polo is still there."

The temperature in the car plummets. Giorgio's eyes are on the road, but I can't miss the grind of his jaw. "Polo should have known better," he says in an icy tone. "Now, he'll have to deal with the consequences."

"I was the one who asked him to take me," I say weakly.

"I'm doing everything I can to make sure no one knows you're with me, while you do the exact opposite. Do you know what Sal will do to you if he finds you?"

I swallow. "No."

"He'll use you to get Damiano to surrender. Sal knows how much your brother loves you, and he'll exploit that weakness to its maximum extent. Do you know the kind of man our don is? He doesn't have morals. There's nothing that's beyond the pale to him. He's a murder and a rapist, and he's ruined countless lives. If he gets his hands on you..." He slams his jaw closed and strangles the wheel with his hands.

He's worried about me.

Silence descends. When we take a turn into the property, I whisper, "I'm sorry. I wasn't thinking."

"That much is obvious."

"I'm trying to apologize."

"I don't need your apologies. I need your obedience, and for you to take your safety as seriously as I do."

A huff escapes my mouth. "Giorgio, I got it, all right? I won't leave the property from now on."

"That's not the only thing."

Tires squealing, we pull into the yard of the castello and come to a stop. Giorgio turns off the ignition but doesn't unlock the doors.

I have a feeling I know where this is going.

A beat passes. "I said it was a mistake," he says, his voice dropping low. "You need to let it go."

My eyes meet his. "Why should I, when I think you're lying? Do you think I haven't noticed how you touch me during class? How your hands linger, and how you stare at my lips? I might be young, but I'm not stupid, Giorgio. Your cold act... That's all it is, isn't it? An act."

Something wild and barely contained dances in his eyes. "You don't know what you're talking about. You're embarrassing yourself, Martina. Do you really think I'd be attracted to you?"

The air in the car turns heavy, pressing against my lungs. Just a few days ago, those words would crush me, but I see past them now.

I reach into the depths of myself and pull from that newfound confidence.

Undoing my seat belt, I lean over the center console and bring my lips close to his ear. The scent of his spicy cologne

226

washes over me, and his entire body tenses. "You don't fool me, Giorgio," I whisper, glancing down to see his hands curl into white-knuckled fists. "You can insult me all you want. It won't change the fact that you want me."

His breath hitches.

Slowly, *slowly*, he turns his head until his lips are a hair away from my cheek. His hot breath caresses my skin, fanning the fire licking inside of me. Anticipation wraps around my body, eager and impatient, every cell begging for him to claim my lips.

But he doesn't.

Instead, his hand shoots up and wraps around my neck. He pulls me away from him, his palm a tight collar around my flesh.

Our eyes meet for a brief moment before he shoves me back into my seat. The darkness and desire I catch in his gaze sends shivers over my skin.

"Get the fuck out of this car, Martina."

Some dormant survival instinct comes to life, and I decide maybe I've pushed him enough for today. Heart pounding, I reach for the door, but just before I open it, I cast one last glance at Giorgio.

Body tense, hands in fists, jaw as hard as granite.

And a bulge in his gray, Italian-wool slacks.

CHAPTER 20

MARTINA

My dinner is a lonely affair. The table is set for one, and when Allegra comes in to serve me roast chicken with fingerling potatoes and grilled asparagus, she doesn't chat the way she normally does. Instead, she shoots me a few apprehensive looks tinged with a hint of condemnation.

I lift my index finger to my lips and gnaw on a nail. By now, the entire household must know what happened earlier, and I'm getting the sense that going against Giorgio's wishes is kind of a big deal.

What did he do to Polo? I stood by the window all afternoon trying to catch a glimpse of him returning, but it happened the moment I stepped away to use the bathroom. When I returned, his truck was there, but I didn't see him.

"Stop eating yourself, *bella*. That's not going to help anything now."

I drop my hands and fold them on my lap, my gaze jumping to Allegra's.

She clicks her tongue and gives her head a shake. "That boy. He's gotten himself in a lot of trouble now."

"It was my fault as much as his."

Allegra rounds the table, putting a plate of sauce on the other side of my plate. "You shouldn't have left, but you wouldn't have been able to go anywhere if Polo didn't take you. I might not know the details of the things Giorgio is involved in, but I've never made the mistake of questioning his judgment. If he tells us you are not to leave the property, it means he's got a good reason for it."

I drag my teeth over my bottom lip. "What is Giorgio going to do to him?"

"I don't know," she says, widening her arms before dropping them back down to her sides. "But he's very angry. I only hope this will be a lesson for Polo not to do something this stupid again."

She leaves me to my dinner, but I barely taste the food. My mind is preoccupied with my role in this ordeal. I feel guilty for getting Polo into this mess, but I hardly had to convince him to take me.

It's almost like he wanted to piss Giorgio off.

The next day, in my eagerness for another self-defense lesson with Giorgio, I head down for our class a little early.

Okay, I'll admit it's not so much eagerness for the class as for the man himself. Our encounter in the car yesterday plays on repeat every time I shut my eyes, and with it comes the uncertain sensation of being close to getting what I want.

The truth is, I'm walking into completely unknown territory with him. I've never tried to seduce another man, if you can even call what I'm doing seduction. There's no rule book for me to follow, so I've been relying on instinct alone.

I could be making a fool of myself, like he keeps saying, but the words that come out of his mouth don't match the message I'm getting from his body. And the promise of what lies on the other side of his resistance is tantalizing enough for me to keep going.

While I stretch in the empty gym, I eye the clock. Our usual time comes and goes, and Giorgio doesn't arrive.

Fifteen minutes pass. Why isn't he here? At breakfast, Allegra told me he wasn't planning on leaving today, so he has to be somewhere in the castello.

Irritation bubbles beneath my skin. Is he just giving up on our classes then?

When the hand of the clock reaches the twenty-minute mark, I go looking for him.

My steps take me directly to the door of his office, and I give it three firm knocks.

The door jerks open to reveal Giorgio. Suit jacket and tie missing, he's in a crisp white dress shirt and dark-gray pants.

Clearly, he had no intention of training me when he got dressed this morning.

"These lessons were your idea, and now that I'm actually starting to enjoy them, you decide to flake out on me?"

Giorgio gives me a blank look before crossing his arms over his chest. "I'm busy right now."

"Are you? Or are you just avoiding me? And even if you are genuinely busy, have you ever heard of giving people a heads-up? Basic courtesy. Don't they teach you that in Naples?"

Something amused passes over his expression. "You're angry."

"I waited in the gym for you for twenty minutes."

"I'm sorry, did you have something more important to do?"

My mouth parts. Is he actually being this rude right now?

"Fine. If you don't want to work out with me anymore, I'll work out on my own."

"I didn't say that. I said I'm busy *right now*. We can resume tomorrow."

"What are you so busy with?"

He leans his shoulder against the doorjamb. "Erasing footage of you and Polo from all of the public cameras in the area."

Oh. My irritation eases a smidge. "Are there many?"

"More than you'd think."

"What did you do to Polo? I haven't seen him since yesterday."

Hi gaze darkens, like he's irritated with me for asking. "He and I had a conversation. I told him the next time he takes you off the property, he'll lose a finger."

Blood drains out of my face. "You did *not*."

"He disobeyed me," he says, his voice taking on an edge. "He knew there would be consequences, but it seems the two of you have the same problem. You don't know how to respect boundaries."

The nerve of him. He says it as if he wasn't the first one to trample right over my boundaries. Putting me in the room next to his. Climbing into my bed. Kissing me.

I don't even care anymore that he was still under the influence of that tea when he did it. The tea may have lowered his inhibitions, but he must have been thinking about it for a long time before then. It's the hypocrisy that grates on me.

I take a single, purposeful step toward him, my gaze never wavering, and slide my palms up his broad chest. It's firm and warm, and my palms look impossibly tiny in comparison. His gaze drops to where I'm touching him, and that small movement is enough to send tension rippling through the air.

His scent wraps around me, thickening my throat.

This close, there's no hiding the acceleration in his heartbeat. His body doesn't lie, even when his mouth does, and that knowledge makes me want to have my hands on him all the time. Then all of his secrets would be mine.

"Am I crossing another boundary right now?" I lean in an inch closer. "What are you going to do? Cut *my* finger off?"

The pissed-off heat of his gaze singes my face. He takes my wrists in his hands and tugs me off him, but he doesn't let go. "No. But if you try this again, I *will* punish you."

His tone is harsh, but my pulse leaps.

"Liar. You know you can't do anything to me or my brother will kill you. You're scared of him, aren't you? That's why you're so terrified I'll tell him what you did."

His eyes flash, and his grip on my wrists tightens until it's almost painful. "Careful, Martina," he breathes. "There are some ways I can punish you that you'd never dare share with your brother."

"Like what?"

He leans in, and my lungs stop moving. Lips brushing against me ear, he says, "Like bending you over my knee and making your ass so raw you won't be able to sit for a week."

My body grows perfectly still, even as my heart nearly leaps out of my chest. *What?* Did I hear him correctly?

He pulls back and takes in the stunned expression on my face. "Now, be a good girl and let me get back to cleaning up your mess. We'll resume our classes tomorrow."

I stare at him in shock as he closes the door in my face.

Did he really just...*threaten to spank me?*

My poor virgin brain can't take it.

I walk back to my bedroom in a trance and sit on the edge of the bed, staring at nothing in particular.

The thought of him doing that to me is terrifying. He's strong and could do some serious damage. But the way he said it... The heat in his eyes...

I squeeze my thighs together. *Shit.*

Burying my face into the duvet, I let out a groan. To be at his mercy like that is strangely arousing. It makes me think back to how heavy he felt lying on top of me, and the thrill I felt at the idea that I wouldn't be able to get away. Is that normal? Or is there something wrong with me?

Sitting up, I rub my eyes and replay our conversation. How can he say things like that to me while denying that the kiss meant anything? It's like he's addicted to gaslighting me. He probably doesn't even know what that term means, but that's exactly what he's doing.

Deciding to work my frustration out at the gym, I hop off the bed and walk past the closet when a flash of neon green catches my eyes.

My bikini hangs off a coat hanger.

Blistering sun streams through the window, and there wasn't a hint of a breeze when I was in the garden. It might be the warmest day since I arrived here. Perfect for a swim.

I contemplate the bikini for a few seconds, then I grab it off the hanger. After that encounter with Giorgio, I need to cool down, and the pool is the perfect solution.

I change out of my workout clothes into the bikini and grab a silk robe to cover up for my walk over. It's not far. There's a side door near the living room that opens right to a short path to the pool.

No one sees me as I slip out of the house. The deck around the pool is empty as always. The only person I've ever seen here is Allegra when she tidies it up once a week. I drop my towel on a lounger, then feel out the water temperature by dipping my toes.

It's nice and crisp. They must have stopped heating it.

The plants in the big pots scattered artfully around the area are blooming, the flowers attracting hummingbirds. A bee buzzes by my ear before landing on a marigold. I close my eyes and take a moment to listen to all the sounds around me, tuning in to the outside world to ground myself.

When I'm ready, I untie the belt of my robe and let it drop at my feet. I think I'll jump. Usually, I can't stand the shock of cold water slamming against my skin, but I'm feeling bold today.

I'm about to do it when the hairs on my nape stand straight, and I'm hit with a certainty that someone's watching me.

I whip my head around, looking back at the castello. In the window of the second floor, the one right at the landing, stands Giorgio.

His hands are pressed against either side of the window frame, and his serious gaze is trained on me.

A shiver runs down my spine. I'd do anything to know what he's thinking right now.

I glance down at myself, noticing the hard outline of my nipples. Is he enjoying the view? I'm not an expert, but spying on me while I'm in my bikini definitely feels like crossing a boundary.

When I look back at him again, he adjusts his stance, and it's obvious he's aware I've noticed him. And yet he doesn't look away.

Is that all he's ever going to be willing to give me? Heated looks from a distance?

I turn away from him and shake my head. Damn him and his boundaries. It's not fair what he's doing, how he's messing with my head.

I think it's time I give him a taste of his own medicine.

A nervous tremor works up my spine as I reach around my back to the knot of the bikini. My eyes are trained on the surface of the pool, but I'm hyper aware of Giorgio's gaze on my skin.

My fingers tangle with the strap, and I give the end a gentle tug, feeling it unravel.

The straps fall. I lift the bikini over my head and drop it to the ground.

I'm the only one here, but the air grows as hot and dense as it would in a room full of people. My thumbs hook on the sides of my bikini bottoms, and I ignore my heart palpitations and slowly drag them down my legs until they're pooled at my feet.

I'm tempted to look back at Giorgio one more time, curious about his reaction, but at the last moment, I chicken out. My chin hovers over my shoulder. No matter how brave I try to be, I can't move it another inch.

With a deep breath, I turn back toward the water and take two steps until my toes curl over the edge. My pulse thunders inside my ears. I clench my fists and jump in.

It's not like the bikini provided a ton of extra coverage, so it must be a mental thing, but *God*, the water is colder than I expected. I keep my head under as I swim to the other end of the pool. To swim back, I have to turn around.

I'm breathing hard as I gather the courage to finally do it.

But when my gaze lands on the big window, Giorgio's powerful silhouette is gone.

There's no one there.

He...left?

Disappointment and embarrassment pass through me. I really thought I did something there, didn't I?

I glance down through the water at my body's distorted shape and suddenly feel exceptionally ugly. I'm not vain. I've never spent much time thinking about my looks or the shape of my body, but I've always assumed it was acceptable. My brother called me cute my whole life, which I guess doesn't mean much. He's my brother. He'd be an asshole to say otherwise.

I spiral down memory lane, trying to dig up any evidence that I'm not absolutely hideous. Guys have flirted with me before, although not often. I always assumed people stayed away from me because Dem can be extremely intimidating when he wants to, but what if that's not it at all? What if the problem is with me?

God, I feel stupid.

I swim to the edge of the pool and climb out as quickly as I can, my confidence shredded into pieces. If Giorgio says something about this, I think I might cry. I can't get into the damn robe fast enough, and I don't even bother pulling the bikini back on. It drips in my hand, leaving a wet trail on the ground as I hurry inside.

What I need is a shower and another dinner taken in my room. No way I'm sitting down with everyone tonight.

I fly upstairs, scaling the steps two at a time. Thankfully, no one is around to see me. I don't know how I'd explain to Allegra why I look like I didn't even bother patting myself down with a towel. I slip inside my bedroom and shut the door behind me.

My gaze drops to my feet just in time to see a drop of water roll down my calf.

Suddenly, I feel like crying.

It's one thing to have the courage to go after what I want and another to accept humiliation after humiliation in the process. How much more can I take?

No, I'm not going to cry over him. I sniff and tip my chin up, forcing the tears back. So what if he just walked away? If he thinks I'm ugly? That's one man's opinion, and I—

A palm closes over my mouth.

My eyes blow wide. "Ungh!"

Before I can remember what I'm supposed to do in this situation from my lessons, soft lips press against my ear. "I warned you, Martina."

Giorgio. My body sags with relief.

But the feeling is short-lived, because the next thing I hear is the door clicking shut and the lock sliding into place.

CHAPTER 21

MARTINA

HE LOWERS his palm away from my mouth but keeps his other wrapped around my waist.

Excitement bleeds into my residual fear. "Why did you lock the door?"

"Because if anyone walks in on what I'm about to do to you, they won't be walking out alive."

My heart is in free-fall inside my chest. "Wha—"

"I'm going to teach you a lesson," he growls against my ear. "Did you think you'd get away with that scene by the pool without any punishment? Anyone could have seen you."

The dark possessiveness that slips into his tone makes the hairs on my nape stand. "No one was around." I swallow. "No one, except you."

He grips my shoulders, spins me around, and presses my back against the door. I get my first glimpse of his face since he grabbed me, and it sends a strange cocktail of fire and ice through my veins. His eyes are glazed over with heat and anger and something that looks completely out of control.

I gasp when he removes one hand from my shoulder and wraps it around my neck. It's not firm, but the warning is clear. He leans in close enough for his breath to fan against my skin. "Are you religious?"

What?

He gives me no time to be confused when he tightens his hold on my neck.

"Agnostic," I choke out.

"You might want to start believing in God, so you can pray no one saw you. I'd hate for Tommaso or Polo to lose an eye."

My mouth parts in shock as the situation finally sinks in.

He's *furious.*

I didn't just step cross a boundary this time. I leapt over it.

He lets go of my neck but doesn't move away an inch. I take a deep breath, my hard nipples brushing against his chest. He looks down, his expression thunderous.

I'm genuinely scared.

"What are you going to do to me?" I whisper.

"Exactly what I told you I would." His voice drags over that achy place between my legs. When his big hands wrap around my waist, it feels like he's touching bare skin. The thin robe is no match for the energy exchange between our bodies.

Before I have time to process what's going on, he throws me over his shoulder and steadies me with a hand on the back of my thigh.

"Giorgio!" I yelp. I'm completely naked under the robe, and if he moves his hand up just a few inches, he'll be touching my bare ass. If he looks over, he'll probably see... I swallow. I don't think he's realized I'm wearing nothing underneath.

He carries me through the doorway between our rooms and deposits me roughly on his bed. The belt of my robe is loose, and the entire thing nearly flies opens, but I manage to pull it tightly around me at the last second.

"I told you to drop it, didn't I?" He anchors his hands on the bracket of the four-poster bed and stares down at me. "Instead, you left my office and decided to tempt me."

I scramble onto my knees and edge up the bed to put some distance between us, but he's as fast as a tiger. He grabs me again, sits down on the edge of the bed, and throws me over his lap.

A puff of air escapes my lungs as my belly hits his thighs. "Giorgio, wait—"

The exact moment he realizes I'm bare is punctuated by a sharp hiss through his teeth. He grows deathly still, but his palm stays on my upper thigh, right at crease of my butt.

God, how I wish I could look at him right now. Instead, all I can do is stare at the floor.

A beat passes. Two more. Something hard pokes against my belly, and I realize it's his erection.

He's turned on by this.

By *me*.

The fact that he's growing hard while staring at my bare pussy sends a flood of heat through me. When I feel the pad of his thumb brush against my inner thigh, I shiver. He's so close to my lips, an inch higher, and he'll be touching me *there*.

"You're playing games with me, Martina," he rasps, that thumb moving back and forth, so, *so* close. "Dangerous games you can't win."

His touch feels so damn good. My breath starts coming out in shallow pants as his small, controlled movements send me flying higher and higher. Goosebumps cover my flesh. The anticipation—the thrill—of him closing that minuscule distance makes me tremble.

His other hand is pressing down on my lower back, keeping me in place, but I'm not completely immobile. When I can't take his stillness anymore, I rock over his thighs.

For a brief second, I feel pure bliss as his thumb brushes against the edge of my pussy, but then he tears his hand away, and next thing I know, my ass explodes in pain.

"Hey!"

He smacked me!

"What are you—"

SMACK.

I start to writhe on him, trying to get away, but the palm on my lower back is like a heavy iron.

SMACK.

"Ow! That hurts!"

"Good. How else will you learn?"

He lands three more hard smacks in a quick succession, the sound of them ringing in the air.

A tear leaks out of my eye. I'm speechless. He warned me, but I never expected him to actually do it. My ass burns, but it's not the only part of my body that's on fire. My pussy aches with heat. I don't know if it's the smacking or the fact that he can see *everything*, but I'm aroused like I've never been before.

He was right. There's zero chance I'll ever tell Damiano about this, or the kiss, or anything that happened before or after.

I wince when he places his palm back down over one cheek, thinking he's about to dish out some more of his punishment, but instead, he simply drags it over the tender flesh.

A tiny moan falls out of me. There's no indication he's ready to let me get off him, and to be honest, I'm not quite sure I want to either. His erection is still pressed against my belly, and his hand trails higher and higher up my inner thigh until finally...

"Jesus," he rasps. A finger traces my lips. "You're wet."

I swallow, unsure of how to respond. He exhales and delves deeper into my folds, making the uncertain words on my lips turn into more moans.

It's like his fingers are infused with electricity. Everywhere he touches me, sparks singe my skin with pleasure.

I start bucking against his hand, needed it deeper in the place that no one's ever touched before, but my reaction makes him curse. "You keep pressing that wet cunt against my hand, and you're not going to be a virgin for much longer."

Oh my God.

"How do you know I'm a virgin?" I whimper when he slides just the tip of his finger inside me.

"It's spelled out all over your face, *piccolina*. You've never been with a man before me."

"I've never been with you either."

He plunges his finger deep inside of me, making me gasp. He bends over me, lowering his lips to my ear. "The first time I saw you in the garden, I thought to myself, that girl has no sense of self-preservation. With every word out of your mouth, you prove me right."

I choke on my saliva, my mind reeling from the fact that he's inside me. I'm still provoking him, but I can't stop. I'm so turned on I'm sweating through my already damp robe. One finger becomes two, and he starts to thrust them in and out of me. My cheeks blaze from the wet sound that's produced. It's beyond lewd.

I pant as he picks up speed. "Gio... That feels...so good."

He groans, and without breaking his rhythm, moves his hand from my lower back to my neck, curling his fingers possessively around it. "You're so tight, I don't think I could fit another finger inside of you without hurting you. You'll never be able to take my cock."

244

My eyes slam shut as a pulse of pleasure crests through me. "Is that a challenge?"

"A warning," he snarls.

I try to turn my head to look at him, but he won't let me. He tightens his hold on my neck and holds me in place. "You're playing with fire, *piccolina*, and you don't even realize how close you are to being burned."

My moans are frantic now, his pace unrelenting. I'm so close, it nearly hurts, but I can't quite get there.

Suddenly, I'm empty once again, but before I can whine a protest, his wet fingers reach for my clit.

I jerk in his iron grip as he starts to rub in firm circles. My nails dig into his leg. "Oh my God, Gio..."

Every nerve ending in by body comes to life at the same time, buzzing, pulsing, and then everything bursts.

My orgasm hits me like a tidal wave, dragging me to a place I've never been before. A scream tears itself out of my throat, and he silences it by pressing his big palm over my mouth. I buck against him, riding the pleasure until it slowly starts to recede.

Then Giorgio's moving my body, pulling me upright so that my back is against his chest, and somewhere in the process, my robe slips down my shoulders.

When I lift my gaze, my reflection greets me.

The last time I looked into that mirror, he forced me to do it with a vicious grip on my chin. Now, he does the same, only this time his hold on me is gentle. He slips his knees under my thighs and spreads me open.

I gasp. Hot, thick embarrassment slips beneath my skin as I take in my twitching, dripping pussy. I've never looked at myself like this.

Never imagined I'd let a man see me like this.

"Gio—"

"Do you see that pretty cunt?" he rasps, meeting my gaze in the mirror.

I suck my lips into my mouth, unable to answer. I was brave today already. My reserves have run out.

His lips press against the shell of my ear. "This is what you're offering me, *piccolina*. It's not going to look this pretty when I'm done with you." His other hand falls over my inner thigh, and he brushes his knuckles against one side of my entrance. "It's going to look raw and well-fucked." He slides the tip of his finger inside of me. "And filled with my come."

Holy shit. His filthy, obscene words make me clench around his finger, and the dark gaze of his reflection once again flicks to mine.

He lets go of my chin and drags his hand down to my breast. The other presses against my lower abdomen. His hold on me is so tight, I can hardly breathe, but I don't care. Tilting my head backwards, I let my lips find the thick column of his throat, where I press messy, wet kisses. He mutters something as I do it, rubbing his hand over my tummy as I finish coming down from my high.

After a while, my orgasm fades away, and vulnerability rushes into the empty space it left behind. I need to see Giorgio's face. Gripping his arm, I adjust my position so that I'm straddling him.

His eyes are the color of deep ocean water. When I sink a little lower, the hardness inside his pants presses into my center.

Tentatively, I rock my hips against him.

He drops his hands to my hips and squeezes. "Stop."

"Why?" I whisper into his ear before moving my lips down to his. "I think your punishment backfired. I liked it too much."

My words are meant as encouragement, but he doesn't take them as such. He makes a tortured sound in the back of his throat like he knows he's losing but he's not ready to give up yet. He lifts me off him, places me on my feet, and stands up, raking his fingers through his hair.

Just when I think he'll put a stop to this, he whirls around and crowds me with his body, pressing me against one of the bedposts. He pinches my chin with his index finger and thumb. When he looks directly into my eyes this time around, it's like he's looking right into the depths of my soul.

"I've lived for a long time, *piccolina*," he rasps. "Nearly twice as long as you. Never in my life have I met anyone who hides so much wickedness behind an innocent face like yours. Your mind seduces me. Your body tempts me. A single glimpse of you, and I lose my train of thought. I become completely absorbed in your presence. You shouldn't have let me touch you like I just did, because now that I know how wet and warm you'd feel around me, I won't think about anything else for hours. Days. *Weeks*."

That confession reverberates through me like a clap of thunder, and then, everything stills.

He wants me. Badly. Desperately.

My daydreams are morphing into reality, and for the first time, I begin to question if I can handle it.

But there's no time to dig for an answer as his fingers tighten around my chin, and he hisses, "Damn you," before he crushes my mouth to his.

The kiss is chaos and fury. I press my body against his and wrap my hands around his neck, tugging him closer even though there isn't an inch of space left between us. He grinds into me. His bulge digs into my thigh as he works his own thigh between my legs.

Our tongues tangle, part, tangle again. He nips and licks at my lips, teaching me how to kiss by example, and I do my best to copy him. The world tilts. I lose myself in him.

When he grabs my ass and lifts me, I wrap my legs around him, my heels digging into his thighs. A sense of inevitability cascades through me.

Knock, knock. "Giorgio, you left your cell phone in the dining room," Allegra's voice filters through the door. "Someone's been ringing you."

He breaks our kiss only to mutter a muted curse and then dives back in again, his tongue lashing against my own, his hands learning the contours of my body.

When another knock comes, I whimper into his mouth, "Ignore it." I'm too far gone to stop now. His hand trails up my ribcage and palms a bare breast, squeezing it.

"Giorgio?"

"*Cazzo!*" He tears himself away from me, his eyes nearly black with arousal and his chest rising with rapid breaths. "One moment," he barks out.

For a moment, he seems conflicted between going and staying, but then he curses again, swipes a hand over my cheek, and moves to the door.

My heart bangs against my ribcage as I watch him leave. I wait for him to return, but he doesn't.

CHAPTER 22

MARTINA

My pulse still hasn't fully evened out when I make my way down to dinner hours later that evening.

I feel feverish. My stomach is in knots. There's even a persistent thrumming sensation in my clit. Is that healthy?

Jesus. My body isn't equipped to handle this emotional rollercoaster.

I sit down with Allegra and Tommaso and quickly learn from them that Giorgio has left the property. Something important came up, but Allegra doesn't know the details.

An anxious fear, potent and sudden, plows through my lingering arousal. What happened? Where is he? He's lying to Sal about me. What if the don found out? The thought of Giorgio being in danger is suddenly unbearable.

"He didn't say anything?" I ask, doing my best to keep my voice steady.

Allegra places a pork chop on her plate. "No, dear. Don't worry yourself about it. He'll be back before you know it."

The straight face I manage to hold through dinner costs me a year of my life, at least. I've never felt more jittery or anxious. I say no to the post-meal espresso Allegra offers me and retreat to my room. Sophia follows me upstairs. Maybe her doggy intuition senses that something is off with me, and she seems pleased when I allow her to jump up on the bed.

As I pet her short fur, I tune my ear to the room on the other side of the wall.

As expected, it's silent.

Maybe I should call Dem. He might know where Giorgio went. I fish my phone out of the nightstand and allow my finger to hover over his name for a few long seconds.

No, I better not. I don't want to disturb him if he's busy, and if I start asking about Giorgio right now, I'm not sure I'll be able to mask my concern. My brother knows me too well not to see through it.

It's been a few days since I last talked to Dem. He's been stingy with the details of how his plan is going. When we talk, he makes everything sound all right, but my brother is a master at controlling his emotions, and he's never shared much about clan business with me. I can only hope everything is fine with him and Vale.

I'm about to put my phone away when I notice the date.

My birthday is tomorrow. I'm turning nineteen.

I've spent every birthday with Dem until now. Ras is usually there too, and some years he'd bring his parents, who took

Dem and I in when our own parents died. The realization that tomorrow I won't see any of my family slams into me exceptionally hard.

I close my eyes against a surge of sadness that layers on top of worry, and the weight of the emotions press against my heart.

Will Giorgio remember it's my birthday? Not that it's important. The only gift I need is him coming back here safely.

Dem will call. Of that, I'm sure. Then I can ask him if he knows where Giorgio went.

The thought lifts my mood a tiny bit.

I turn off my phone and flick it under my pillow. Sophia hops off the bed as I settle under the heavy duvet and turn off the lights.

As the clock ticks, each second bringing me closer to midnight, my mind occupies itself with problems that suddenly seem urgent.

What am I going to do when Dem becomes the don?

For all of my complaints about Dem treating me like a child, I still rely on my brother a lot. That'll have to change. He has a wife now, and one day, he'll have his own family. He's mentioned to me before that he wants a lot of kids. If Vale is on board, I wouldn't be surprised if they start working on it soon. I'm not going to compete for his attention against my future nieces and nephews. They'll need him more than I do.

He's going to be even busier with work than before. Running a clan takes... Well, I'm not sure what it takes, but I don't imagine it's the kind of thing you check in and out from. He and Vale will probably move to Casal, where the rest of the powerful Casalesi families reside. Will they want me to go with them? Would I want to go?

I pull the blanket up to my chin and try to imagine it, but I draw a blank. Since we left Casal when I was very young, I don't remember it well. The place comes with negative associations. It's where my parents died in a house fire that destroyed our family's home. Dem told me the story when I was a kid, and it made me terrified of the town.

But if I don't go with Dem, where will I go? My culinary school dream faded after everything that happened over the last few months. I'm not sure what I want out of my future anymore.

I need to find my own place in the world. To carve a path out for myself.

The edges of my consciousness begin to blur with sleep.

I wonder what Giorgio will do when Dem wins. Will he return to Casal? Stay here?

The question that lingers, even as I drift off, is whether he will think about me when I'm gone...

When I wake up, there's already a long text message from my brother on my phone.

Happy birthday, Mari.

You're nineteen, and I feel old as fuck. How the hell did this happen? I still remember changing your stinky diapers that one time when Ras's mom wasn't around, and you had a blowout— scarred me for life.

I cringe at my phone. Dem's told me this story a dozen times by now. If he'd stop repeating it so often, maybe he'd manage to forget it.

Anyway, this is the first birthday we're apart, and I hate it. I wish I could take you out for a nice dinner like I always do. I told Vale about our gift tradition, and she loved it. Said she wants to participate next time.

A grin overtakes my face. Ras and Dem each bring an outlandish gift to my birthday dinner and make me guess who it's from. One year, Ras got me a talking parrot named Churro that screeched "Pretty girl! Pretty girl!" throughout the entire meal. When we walked out of the restaurant, Dem handed Ras the cage and said that under no circumstances would the parrot be allowed to go home with us.

So now Churro lives with Ras and I visit when I can. His vocabulary has been expanded into multiple languages to include "*stronzo,*" "*joder,*" and "fuck off." He says all exceptionally well.

When this is all over, we'll have a proper celebration, all right? I'm proud of you and the woman you've become, Mari. I'll call you soon.

I type out a quick response and then spring out of bed, my feet landing on the wood floor. The first thing I do is knock on Giorgio's door to see if he's there, and when no one comes, I press my ear against it.

Silence.

Disappointment flickers in me, but I put it out. He might be in his office or having breakfast. I shouldn't jump to conclusions.

Padding over to the window, I place my hands on the frame and give it a shove. The window creaks softly as it swings open, letting in a burst of fresh air and sunlight.

Birds chirp. Trees move gently in the breeze. A smattering of small, wispy clouds move across the sky.

For a few seconds, I stand there and take it all in, allowing the cool morning air to caress my skin.

I'm nineteen.

I get dressed in a pretty summer dress—yellow and sprinkled with tiny blue flowers. It hugs my chest and waist before opening into an A-line skirt that ends a few inches above my knees. I dab some blush onto my cheeks and put on a few swipes of mascara before I head downstairs.

Voices filter through the half-opened French doors of the dining room, and as soon as I pass through them, a sweet, heady scent envelops me.

My mouth falls open.

The dining room is laden with what seems to be an endless amount of flowers.

Bouquets of red roses, clusters of white tulips, heaping arrangements of peonies, and countless other flowers I don't know the names of. It looks like a dream—the kind of thing arranged for over-the-top proposals you can't help but gasp at on Instagram.

Actually walking into something like this feels like an out-of-body experience. My eyes don't know what to focus on, there's just too much beauty to take in.

"What's this?" I breathe.

Allegra stands, her head popping up from behind a bouquet on the dining table, and smiles. "Happy birthday, Martina."

"This is for me?"

"Giorgio wanted this day to be special," she says, a knowing spark in her eyes.

My insides perform a pirouette. He did this for my birthday?

"This was Giorgio's idea?" The question comes on a single breath.

Tommaso comes to Allegra's side and nods. "All him. He even told us what flowers he specifically wanted us to get."

My eyes bulge. Are we talking about the same Giorgio? The grumpy, curt, more-often-than-not rude made man that until yesterday wouldn't stop pushing me away thought of doing this?

A thrill zings up my spine.

I walk around the room, touching my fingertips to the velvety blooms and fighting against the delirious smile that threatens to overtake my face.

"Is he here?" I ask, taking a seat across from Tommaso and Allegra.

The latter shakes her head. "He's not back yet, unfortunately. He called us late last night and said he'd be back this evening."

I fight against my disappointment. At least he called, which means he's okay.

"So the two of you did all this?"

"We did," Tommaso says, his mustache lopsided from his grin. "Polo helped too."

My gaze travels to Polo's usual chair. It's empty. "Where is he?"

"He had to run an urgent errand in town," Tommaso says.

We dig into the food, and at the end of the meal, Tommaso brings out a freshly baked tart heaped with strawberries and blueberries and topped with a candle. They insist on singing me happy birthday in Italian, their enthusiastic rendition making me laugh, and then Tommaso serves everyone a slice of the tart.

My cell phone rings when I'm nearly finished with the dessert, and my brother's name pops up on the caller ID. I excuse myself and take the call from the library.

I'm smiling even before I pick up the phone. "Hi."

"Happy birthday, Mari. Vale's here too."

"Happy birthday!" my sister-in-law's voice streams in. "We miss you. I'm sad you're going to be celebrating without us. You are celebrating, right?"

I laugh. "Yes. I just had a birthday breakfast with Tommaso and Allegra. They work here. Tommaso made me a beautiful berry tart." I don't mention the flowers from Giorgio, even though their gorgeous scents have wafted through the entire house by now. I'm not sure how I could explain the big gesture without making Vale or my brother suspicious.

"That's lovely," Vale says. "Are you doing anything tonight?"

"I don't think so."

"Giorgio won't take you out for dinner?"

"I doubt there's a restaurant that'll meet his high security standards. Don't you know? I'm not allowed to leave the grounds."

"Good," Dem says. "Better to not take any chances."

"That's what Giorgio keeps saying."

"Wow. You must be bored out of you mind, Mari," Vale comments.

"I'm okay, actually. There's a lot to do here."

"Is there? Like what?"

"Well, I've been doing some gardening, and Giorgio's been teaching me some self-defense."

"Ah, yes, he's mentioned that," my brother says. "How have your classes been going?"

"I—" I clear my throat. "Well, I've been really enjoying learning from him."

"That's badass," Vale says. "Good for you! You'll have to show me what you've learned when we're all back together."

Sitting down on the edge of the armchair, I press the phone closer to my ear. "And when will that be?"

I'm not even sure what answer I want to hear. Of course I want Dem to finish doing whatever he needs to do so that he's no longer in danger, but selfishly, I don't want to leave here anytime soon.

I recognize my brother's sigh on the other end of the line. "It's hard to say, Mari. But everyone is interested in concluding this as soon as possible."

"Are we talking about days or weeks? Or longer?"

"Weeks. And actually, while I have you, I wanted to raise—"

Vale cuts him off, "Not now, Dem. Let Mari relax on her birthday."

My brows twitch toward each other. "What is it?"

"Ah, Vale's right. It's nothing that can't wait," Dem says. "Well, enjoy your—"

I still have to ask him about Giorgio. "Wait. Do you know where Giorgio is? He disappeared yesterday, and he's still not back. He doesn't usually leave me here alone for long, so I was just wondering if he's okay."

"Yes, we spoke just this morning. He's fine."

Some tension leaves my shoulders. "Oh, good."

"We'll talk soon, all right?" Dem says.

"Okay. Love you. Bye."

I languish around all day, keeping myself busy with some reading, but mostly keeping an eye on the clock as the hours tick by and it gets closer and closer to the evening. The desire to see Giorgio morphs into need.

Sophia comes to see me a few times during the day. When I hear her nails against the hardwood floor, I tear off a piece of ham from the half-eaten sandwich I had for lunch and offer it to her. She pads closer, her nose working overtime, as if she can't believe her luck.

"It's my birthday, girl. You get a birthday treat."

She snorts and swallows the entire thing in one go. I giggle. You'd think she was starving based on that move, but I see the big bowl of dog food Tommaso serves her twice a day.

She lets me pet her forehead for a little while before getting back up on her feet and trotting out of the room.

The sun's reduced to a bright sliver on the horizon. I watch the sunset and then leave the library.

Dinner's significantly less joyful than breakfast, despite all the flowers still looking beautiful. Tommaso and Allegra sit down, but Polo is missing.

As is Giorgio.

I know he's likely doing something important, but his absence has awakened my selfish streak today. I want to see him.

I want to finish what we started.

The meal concludes, and when Tommaso isn't looking, I steal a wine glass and bottle of rose from the fridge and take it to my room.

For the first time since I got my phone back, I pull up my messages with Imogen and start to type.

Do you remember how we celebrated my birthday last year, Imogen? We went to that beach club in Cala Nova with the others from our class. I lost my flip-flops in the water, and you guys wouldn't stop making fun of me. Then Seb tried to kiss me when we were getting beers at the bar inside. I felt bad for turning my head, but I didn't want to give him my first kiss. You know I never liked him like that. I never liked anyone like that until now. This birthday, I want someone else to kiss me, but he's not around.

After I send the message, I toss the phone aside and pour myself a glass of wine. I took a book from the library earlier, so I crack it open and start to read.

Three glasses later, and I'm struggling to follow the text. I'm not drunk, just a little tipsy. Tipsy enough to spill wine down my chin and onto my dress when I take the next sip.

"Shit."

Until now, some part of me still hoped Giorgio would return and see me in this dress, but this has to be a sign it's time to give up. I place the glass down on the night table and unzip the back. My chest glistens with the spilled wine. Better take a shower.

I rinse myself off and spend an extra long time just standing under the hot water. When my muscles start to feel like jelly from the heat, I turn the shower off, dry myself, and slip on my robe.

Just as I step into my bedroom, I hear a sound coming from outside. I run to the window to see what it is. Giorgio's Ferrari pulls into the courtyard, its bright lights illuminating the castello for a few seconds until he turns the car off.

My pulse accelerates as his suited form emerges out of the car. Maybe it's the wine lowering my inhibitions, but I don't think twice about hurrying out of my room and making my way downstairs to meet him.

The front door opens.

His azure eyes collide with mine, and I can see something shift inside of them.

He steps across the threshold, closes the door behind him, and lifts something out of his pocket.

It's a thin box.

He hands it to me. "Happy birthday," he says in a rough voice that drips into my bloodstream like a drug. My skin tingles under his gaze as I open the box and look at the object inside.

It's a pendant on a delicate chain. There's a big diamond in a setting that looks like a miniature gold wreath.

My breath catches. "It's exquisite." I drag my fingertip over the giant rock. "It's too much."

"Not for you."

Warmth spreads through my chest as I meet his thoughtful gaze. "Thank you." I extend the box to him. "Will you put it on?"

He's silent as he takes the chain out of the box and motions for me to turn around.

The pendant is as cold as ice against my flushed skin. When Giorgio's hands brush against the sides of my neck, a shiver rolls down my spine. He clips the chain and places his palms on my shoulders. "Look," he says softly.

I raise my gaze to the antique mirror hanging above the credenza.

The light in the foyer is dim, but the diamond soaks it in and sparkles on my neck like a beacon.

"It's beautiful," I whisper, smoothing the edges of my robe with my palms. "But it's not what I wanted for my birthday."

His eyes lock on mine in the reflection of the mirror. "What did you want, *piccolina*?"

Heat travels in a slow wave across my skin. The next word out of my mouth will be irrevocable. The step that sends me over the sharp edge of a cliff. It scares me, but choosing bravery over fear is what's gotten me to this point, and I'm not about to stop now.

Not when I'm so close to getting what I want.

"You."

CHAPTER 23

MARTINA

THE AIR THICKENS around us as pure desire takes control of my mind and body. I slide my hand over one of his and lean back against his chest.

His jaw ticks, and his mouth becomes a hard line. I can see the conflict play out in his eyes, and it fuels me. He told me I'm playing a game I can't win, but he's fighting a battle with himself, and it's a losing one.

"You didn't scare me yesterday, Gio. When you told me how you'd use me, it turned me on."

He exhales a long, shaky breath and slams his eyes shut. "Jesus."

I turn to face him. "I won't tell Damiano, you already know that. No one will ever know."

"It's so much more complicated than that."

"It's not."

Taking a step back, I grasp the ends of my satin belt.

His attention moves to my hands, and his eyes narrow. "Martina," he says, a clear warning in his voice.

I ignore it, undo the knot, and pull the belt out of its loops.

My body thrums with anticipation, heat, and desire, the trio fueling my bravery like a potent mix of gasoline. Darkness consumes his gaze as I slip the robe down my arms and let it pool at my feet.

His gaze drags over me, slow and sensual. He's older, obviously experienced, but the awe that slips into his expression as he takes me in makes me feel special.

Like I'm the first woman he's ever seen like this.

A vein in his neck pulses as he allows himself to linger on my breasts. The longer he stays silent, the more my rosé-fueled confidence starts to waver, but then his eyes climb back to mine, and I know I've won.

"Fuck," he rasps.

And then he's on me.

Moving as fast as a panther, be pushes his hand into my hair and tugs my face to his. Our lips crash together. The kiss escalates so quickly, it weakens my knees, but he slips his other arm around my waist and keeps me steady against his chest.

He untangles his fingers from my hair, drags a burning hot palm to cup my ass, and works the flesh for a few moments. We're so damn close to each other, you couldn't slip a sheet of paper between us, but it's not enough. Reading my mind, he lifts me, and growls into my ear, "Wrap your legs around me."

He walks us backward into the credenza, and the poor thing creaks loudly as my butt lands on its edge. Something drops, rolls loudly along a surface, then shatters.

"Shit," I breathe. "What was that?"

"I don't care," he mutters against my lips before moving down and pressing his mouth to my throat.

I suspect that even if every piece of china in this house broke right now, he wouldn't step away from me.

I tilt my head, giving him better access to my neck. He inhales deeply. "You smell like forbidden fruit. Too fucking sweet to be real." The gravel in his voice sends goosebumps spreading over my skin. His palms tighten on my thighs, and his hips roll against mine.

"Take a bite." I pant.

He lets out a chuckle and presses his teeth into my sensitive flesh. I moan. My body is a live wire beneath his touch. Digging my heels into the backs of his thighs, I tangle my fingers into his hair, lust carving a path through my lungs.

"I'm going to devour you," he growls as he pulls me away from the credenza and starts walking us toward the stairs. "You started this, Martina. Remember that when your body is tired and sore from me. Remember that when I insist on taking more."

Shivers erupt over my skin. He rounds the staircase, carrying me with complete ease, and just as he takes the first step, a flash of movement down the hallway catches my eye.

I squint through the near darkness of the house.

There's nothing. It must be just my eyes playing tricks on me.

Giorgio reaches the second-floor landing and pauses to press my bare back against the same window he watched me from yesterday.

The surface cools my hot, achy body down for a brief moment, but then he kisses me again, his mouth intent on eating me alive, and flames consume me once more.

I move my hips, my naked flesh rubbing against the fine fabric of his clothes. He moves one of his hands lower and brushes his fingers lightly against my center. "Are you wet for me already, *piccolina*?"

I'm pretty sure I'm leaving a big wet spot on his crotch. "Yes," I breathe as his fingers delve deeper. "I spent all day thinking about you. About this."

He makes an approving sound at the back of his throat and pulls me away from the window. "That's my girl."

He carries me inside his room, something primal flashing in his gaze, like he's a hunter and he just brought home a big prize. Closing the door behind him, he tosses me onto the bed. My back flattens against the soft duvet.

He begins to strip.

His jacket goes first, tossed carelessly onto the floor. Without breaking eye contact, he removes his platinum cufflinks, his tie, his belt. The buckle clanks against the floor in protest before it's swallowed up by his dress shirt and his pants.

Every molecule of air leaves my lungs as I take in his body. I've revisited the memory of him wrapped in a towel often, but it's true what people say. Memories are unreliable.

The real thing is so much more intense.

He's so hot it's unreal. My gaze licks up his powerful thighs, flat abdomen, and well-defined chest.

When he hooks his thumbs over the edge of his boxer briefs, I move to sit on my knees and claw my fingers into the sheets, so damn ready for what's next.

He tugs them off, and my eyes widen.

Never mind. I'm definitely not ready.

For the first time since we started this, fear scrapes against the back of my mind.

He's big. So big it seems like a mathematical impossibility for *that* to go inside of me.

I swallow. "Um..."

He smirks, reading my mind. "Don't worry, *piccolina*. We'll make it fit."

Wrapping his big palm around his length, he gives it two leisurely strokes. My mouth slackens.

Tentatively, I climb off the bed and approach him. Now that we're in his bedroom, he appears to be in no rush, and he waits patiently until I stop before him.

A nervous shiver tracks up my spine as I reach for him. He drops his hands to his sides, giving me access, and then says, "Wrap your hand around it."

I do, and dear Lord, my fingers barely touch. Giorgio sucks in a breath through his teeth. For a few seconds, I just hold him, allowing myself to get used to the strange contrast of soft and hard. Then I give it one shy stroke.

A hand shoots up and curls around my nape. "Keep going."

I do as he says, my eyes glued to his cock and the bead of liquid that appears at the tip. His abdomen tightens with every stroke, and when I get the courage to look up at him, I see that he's staring down at me.

Tightening his hold on my neck, he lifts his other hand and drags a thumb over my bottom lip.

"Do you—" I swallow. "Do you like it?"

A corner of his mouth lifts up. "What do you think?"

"I don't know," I say shakily. I want to please him.

"I like it a whole lot." He covers my hand with his. "So much that you're going to need to stop before I come all over your stomach." He takes a step forward, forcing me back toward the bed. "This is what you wanted for your birthday, isn't it?"

The backs of my knees bump against the bed frame. "Yes."

"You want me to fuck you."

Heat spreads over my cheeks. "Yes."

Giorgio gives me a push, forcing me to fall back onto the bed. "Then spread your legs, birthday girl." He slides his palms under my thighs and opens me up.

My entire body shivers. I've never felt more vulnerable, so completely exposed under his gaze.

He lowers to his knees and makes a satisfied sound. "Look at you. So wet. So perfect."

Without any warning, he makes a slow, thorough lick from ass to clit.

I gasp. "Giorgio."

He does it again. And again. And again. Until I stop counting and lose myself to the sensation.

I've touched myself a few times before, but it's never felt like *this*. My heartbeat patters around my ribcage as a tight, warm feeling grows inside my core.

Just when I think I've plateaued, he changes his technique, swiping his tongue in circles over my clit and taking turns sucking it into his mouth. My legs begin to tremble.

"Oh. Oh!"

He pushes my hips down, holding me in place while he feasts on me, making the occasional satisfied sound. I tangle my fingers into his hair, throw my head back, reaching, reaching...

"Ahhhh... Oh fuck!"

My world explodes.

The orgasm is a supernova, its brutal power swallowing me up. For a moment, I forget who I am. There's nothing beyond the pulses of pleasure that consume me.

It lasts a while. When I regain my senses, my body feels languid as if it's been wrung out. I blink at the ceiling and then push myself up on my elbows, greeted by the sight of Giorgio between my legs.

"Jesus," I mutter.

He doesn't grin, but his eyes spark with satisfaction. He wraps his palms around my shaky knees and then stretches his naked body over mine, letting me feel its weight. He braces his hands on either side of my head and traces my face with his eyes.

"Beautiful," he murmurs. "You're the most beautiful woman I've ever seen, *piccolina*."

The compliment becomes a million little flutters inside my body. I arch my back, dragging my hard nipples against his chest, and it's all the encouragement he needs to dip his head and draw one between his lips.

Sparks of electricity travel straight to my clit as he sucks and teases my breasts. My body seems to have forgotten it's already come, because my core aches for another release. It feels empty. Needy for him.

"Gio," I moan. "I want you."

His cock twitches against my thigh as he tears his mouth away and meets my gaze. "Not yet."

"I'm drenched."

He moves his hand between us and penetrates me with two of his fingers.

"Oh," I breathe, the sudden fullness tripping into discomfort.

"Take a deep breath."

In. Out.

The discomfort eases just in time for him to start moving his fingers in and out of me. The sounds produced make me blush.

"You're so tight," he mutters and slides another finger inside of me.

I choke on my next breath. "Ohmigod."

Our gazes latch on to each other. "Breathe, *piccolina*. I'm going to take care of you," he says, dragging his hand over my cheek in a comforting gesture that loosens something inside my chest. "But it will hurt a bit."

"I know. I don't care."

His eyes close for a surrendering blink. "Are you on the pill?"

"I have an implant."

Taking his fingers out, he settles once again over my body and gives me a long, thorough kiss. "Hang on to me."

My nails dig into his biceps. Nervousness tangles with anticipation and then turns into something far more vulnerable as the head of his cock presses against my opening.

He pushes in, just a bit, but it's enough to make the backs of my eyes sting. "Oh God."

"Fuck," he swears, dropping his forehead against mine.

We're close enough to exchange breaths, and I visualize the pain receding every time I inhale his. *I can do this.*

Moments pass before he drives in some more.

I gasp.

Body trembling with restraint, he lifts his head and meets my watery gaze. A softness creeps into his eyes. "You're in pain."

I squeeze him for dear life as silent tears stream out of my eyes, but the pain isn't enough for me to stop him. I want this so damn badly. I have to be brave.

My head moves back and forth. "I'm fine. Please...just do it."

He studies me for a moment, nods, and pushes all the way in.

A yelp tears its way out of my lungs, but he swallows it up with his mouth. The pain cuts through my center, sharp and stinging, but it lasts only a few seconds before it dulls.

Giorgio distracts me with his kiss, licking the inside of my mouth and nipping at my lips as I pant through the ache.

"You're doing so well, *piccolina*," he murmurs, skimming his lips over my cheek. "You've taken all of me."

His eyes brim with warmth and desire and vulnerability that matches my own. Maybe I'm imagining it. After all, sex makes some people emotional, doesn't it? It would make sense for a softie like me to get all loved up. But the longer I hold his gaze, the more I'm convinced I'm not just imagining it. Has he ever looked at any other women he's had the way he's looking at me?

Jealously runs through me. I won't ask, because I know the answer I want to hear, and it's not the answer he's likely to give me.

"Does it hurt?"

"Not as much anymore." It's true. The ache's receding to make way for an unusual kind of fullness.

When he makes a shallow thrust, tendrils of pleasure begin to unfurl. I moan into his ear. The sensation of him inside of me is surreal.

He does it again and groans. "Fuck. I need to see it."

Holding my hips, he pulls me along, keeping us connected as he sits up on his knees.

Gaze falling to where we're joined, his body shudders. He places his big palm over my mound and finds my clit with his thumb. "I'm going to play with you until you're begging me to fuck you."

The first strum makes me toss my head back. Everything down there is sensitive and charged, but somehow, he knows just how much pressure I can handle.

"That feels so good," I moan.

He pulls out of me a few inches before pushing back in. "This pussy is mine. All. Fucking. Mine."

His words coupled with the things he's doing to my clit make another orgasm appear at the edges of my awareness.

"Gio," I pant. "I need you."

His thrusts grow deeper, but it's not enough.

"Gi—"

"Beg for it, *piccolina*."

Our eyes lock. A hand skims up my chest and stops around my neck. I lick my lips and say the words, feeling them wash over my body like a wave of heat.

"Please, fuck me."

The sound that tears out of him doesn't sound entirely human, and when he starts to move, I finally understand just how much he was holding back.

He drives into me with the kind of intensity that could move mountains. My legs wrap around his waist, my arms around his neck. Thank fucking God I've adjusted, because if he'd fucked me like this five minutes earlier, he'd probably have split me in half.

"You're better than I imagined," he says roughly. "Better than a dream."

Pressure rises inside me, my core desperate for another release.

"Does your cunt like my cock?"

"Yes," I breathe.

"Good. It's the only one that'll ever be inside of it."

My eyes roll to the back of my head even as a tiny logical part of my brain latches on to his words and wonders, "*Huh?*" Must be his brand of dirty talk.

Removing his hand from my neck, he suddenly pulls out. I don't have time to do more than let out a whine, because he flips me over, pulls on my waist to get me on my hands and knees, and then drives back inside.

The new angle stuns me. "Oh my God." He hits a spot deep inside of me, over and over, until stars appear in front of my eyes. I'm close.

Gathering my hair with one hand, he coils it like a leash around his palm and tugs. When my back arches, a satisfied groan follows. "You were made to be fucked like this. I've never seen a more beautiful thing."

I begin to tremble again. My core tightens, Giorgio hisses, and then I'm falling. Literally. My body collapses, and he falls on top of me, catching his weight at the last moment. He pushes in one more time, *deep*, and then his body tenses with his own release.

As I shiver on the sheets, sandwiched between him and the bed, my body a puddle of pleasure, a realization comes.

There's nothing better than this.

Nothing.

CHAPTER 24

GIORGIO

A SMALL HAND rests on my lower abdomen. Silky blonde hair tickles the side of my neck. Martina's slow, deep breaths fan out across my chest.

I pull her closer to me, as if the feel of her body perfectly molded to mine will somehow make me forget about the consequences of my addiction to her.

Because that's what it is—an addiction.

An out-of-control need that's jeopardizing the entire reason she's here with me in the first place.

All day yesterday, I tried to get myself in check. I practically meditated on the fucking phrase. *You can't. You can't. You can't.*

All the good it did me.

I drag my hand down my face. Sal has me walking on a tightrope. Yesterday, Calisto called me on the don's behalf. Sal had something he wanted me to move for him. I raced to

Naples to pick up a small metal case filled with what I suspect is a few million worth of diamonds. I drove it to the closest secure vault in the area with one of Sal's men tailing me. After I dropped the case off, I picked something out of my own personal stash to give to Martina, and then drove back here in the most roundabout way possible to lose my tail and make sure no one else was following behind.

The whole exercise felt strange. Sal's drawing me out on purpose, clearly trying to track my movements. I need to check recent chatter on the recordings to see if he's doing it to others, or if I've become the principal target of his scrutiny.

What could have put him on my trail? Damiano's been careful not to mention my name to any of the men he's been meeting. No one outside of Ras and Valentina know I'm helping him, and their loyalty is without question.

I need to get to the bottom of it before this location is at risk of becoming compromised.

Martina jerks in her sleep, bringing my thoughts back to her. I drag a soothing palm over the smooth skin of her back, savoring the feel of it.

My resistance had crumbled even before she offered herself to me last night. I simply can't deny her, consequences be damned. Not when she's so willing to climb into my bed.

And fuck, last night was everything I wanted and more.

Innocence and sin. Inexperience and eagerness. Beneath that young face are layers and layers of dimensions, and I'm afraid I won't be satisfied until I've discovered them all.

I gaze down at her peaceful expression. Does she still dream of her friend, or have we managed to chase her ghosts away?

There's nothing of that empty girl I picked up from De Rossi's in her now. She's come alive. Flourished.

Come into her power.

And now she's ruthlessly exercising it over me.

I drag my palm over my jaw.

She said she'd never tell De Rossi about us, and I believe her, but what I'm concerned about is if this thing between us can run its course before she leaves. Neither of us know when this war will be over. Will we have enough time to work out our desire for each other?

Because that's what we have to do. We have to squeeze out every drop until there's nothing left and we can return to our lives.

Mine.

My stomach turns. Staking my claim on her last night gave me a high. In the back of my head, I knew the words coming out of my mouth were a fantasy, but I couldn't resist saying them.

They tasted so fucking good on my tongue.

Now, the thought of her with someone else makes me want to draw out the gun I keep in the nightstand and fire off a round into the ceiling.

Fuck.

One day, we'll look at each other and feel absolutely nothing. We will.

We *must*.

The only way I can keep her is to marry her. De Rossi already said a marriage proposal is in her future, but I'm the last fucking candidate he'd consider.

Martina purses her lips in her sleep, as if disapproving of my thoughts, and uncertainty fills my chest. Letting her go now would be impossible, but with time, I'll grow bored of her, as she will of me. And if it's not boredom that deals us the fatal blow, it will be truth. When I reveal my secret to De Rossi, he'll tell Martina. And when she knows who I really am, she'll look at me the way my mother did her whole life —with barely hidden disgust.

It will be hard to say goodbye, but it will be even harder to see *that* in her eyes.

Careful not to disturb her, I climb out of bed and walk over to the window. It's early dawn, the sky only starting to brighten. Bracing my palm against the window frame, I peer out toward the forest. I haven't gone in there since being back, but now it calls to me.

The pines sway in the wind as if beckoning me into their shadows.

I should visit her.

No one else does.

Instead, I stand frozen in place for a long while until Martina stirs behind me.

"Morning." Her voice is still hoarse with sleep.

"Morning, *piccolina*."

She climbs out of bed and comes to stand beside me. "I like it when you call me that."

I wrap my arm around her slim waist and draw her close to me.

"What are you looking at?" she asks.

"The sunrise, I suppose." It's beautiful. Pink and orange ribbons have unfurled across the sky, marbling against each other.

She gazes at the view and lets out a contented sigh. "I've been here for nearly two weeks now, and I'm still not over the beauty of this place."

It is sublime. I wish I'd given myself a chance to enjoy the castello in earnest before I spoiled it with bad memories.

"How are you feeling?" I ask, peering down at her. "Sore?"

She looks at me from under her lashes. "A little."

My hand tightens around her waist. "Let me make it better."

We forget about the sunrise, and she falls back on the bed, spreading her legs for me and showing me something even more beautiful.

I drag my tongue over her hot flesh, gorging on her taste and the sound of her timid moans, which soon morph into screams.

Her fingers skate through my hair, and when I bring her right to the edge, she gives it a firm tug. "Giorgio," she pants, her entire body trembling as her orgasm fights to take over her. "Oh my God."

I wrap my lips around her clit and suck hard on it, at last making her explode.

When she comes, I replace my mouth with my fingers and lift my head so that I can take all of her in.

Flushed skin, bitten lips, tangled hair. She blinks at me and gives me a lazy, satisfied smile that breaks something open inside my chest.

Fuck, she's so beautiful.

And she's mine.

For now.

I drag my palms up her thighs, her stomach, her breasts, and stop to cradle her cheeks. She gazes at me with bright, sparkling eyes, her mouth slightly parted. "You're going to get me addicted to this," she whispers.

Cazzo.

I press my lips to hers and taste the inside of her mouth while her hands drift low between our bodies. She wraps her palm around my aching cock and gives it an uncertain stroke. "Like that?" she asks.

A groan tumbles out of my lungs. "Just like that."

She works me with her hand, growing more and more sure with her movements. I lick around her breast and then tug on her rosy nipple with my teeth, making her hiss. Her grip grows tighter, and my orgasm starts to build right at the base of my spine.

My mouth makes it up to the side of her throat. "I'm going to come all over you, *piccolina*."

"I want you to," she whispers, keeping a steady rhythm.

I fist her hair, and when it hits me, as hard as a fucking truck, I bite her neck. God, she's making me see stars. My seed spills all over her belly and chest, and she keeps stroking me until there's nothing left.

I sit back on my heels and admire the view of her covered in my cum.

She glances down at herself, and a blush colors her cheeks. "Did that feel good?"

I drag my hand over my face. "Yeah, that felt fucking good."

She laughs as I take her in my arms and carry her into the shower. By the time I've got her clean, my cock is hard again, and she whispers in my ear that she's really not that sore, so I press her into the wall and take, take, take.

The morning passes in a blink, and while Mari returns to her room to finally get dressed, I go down to the dining room and have a cappuccino. I'm reading a newspaper—an old habit I doubt I'll ever give up—when Polo walks in.

He looks disheveled, as if he's running on only a few hours of sleep. According to Allegra, he's thrown himself into work since the debacle with Martina, busying himself with projects for the garden.

It's been a few days, but I'm still fucking furious with him for disobeying my direct orders and taking her off the property. His only saving grace is that I never told him what's at stake. He didn't understand the possible repercussions of his mutiny. Still, he works for me. I shouldn't need to explain anything. It's that damn temper of his that's getting out of control.

Polo halts a few steps away, waiting for me to give him my attention.

Slowly, I fold the newspaper and toss it on the table.

He meets my gaze, but only for a short moment. He's nervous.

As he damn well should be.

He licks his lips and says, "I want to apologize for my behavior. I was angry at you, and I took Martina with me out of spite."

I lean back in my seat and link my palms together. I've been too soft with him. All it took was one direct threat for him to finally understand I'm not playing around on the matter.

"I won't make that mistake again," he says, glancing at me.

I study him.

An apology is a good start. He seems genuinely remorseful, and that's something, given that he's young, impulsive, and maybe...too ambitious to stay here much longer.

I would never allow him to work for Sal, but Sal's reign is about to end. What about De Rossi? While he's in Casal, someone's going to have to run his business empire, and that person will need help. If Polo manages to get his attitude in check, he might make a good asset. He's eager to prove himself, and he'll be loyal to any don who'll give him that chance.

I could put in a word with De Rossi.

Polo waits expectantly for my response, so I give him a curt nod and reach for my cappuccino. "Good."

He visibly relaxes.

"But you still want to be made?"

Something flashes in his eyes. Longing, probably.

"Yes, but I won't bother you with it anymore. I'll wait until you think the time is right."

Finally. He's starting to fucking learn.

"It might come sooner than you think."

He blinks.

"I've had a lot of things on my mind lately, Polo, but I've heard you. I understand you don't want to spend the rest of your life here, and I can't blame you for that. If I was in your shoes, I'd probably feel the same." I prop my elbow on the edge of the table. "There's more you can do in life than join the clan. If you want to start a business, I'll be your first investor. If you want to study something new, I'll pay your way through school. But if being made is truly what you want... Well, I promised your mother I would keep you safe, but I also promised her I'd try to keep you happy. Think about it for a few weeks and tell me what you decide on."

His lips twitch. "I appreciate that, Giorgio. I'll consider all my options first."

"Good. Have a seat. We can eat together."

Polo sits down, and Allegra brings him a plate just as Martina comes down the stairs clad in a pretty black dress with a bold floral pattern. Her ponytail swings with each of her steps, and when she gives me a coquettish smile, my hand flexes with the desire to wrap those silky strands around my fist.

She sits down to my right. "Morning."

Polo glances up from his plate. "Good mo—" His greeting cuts off as his eyes fixate on something.

It takes me a moment to realize he's looking at Martina's neck.

Fuck.

There's a visible red mark from where I bit her last night.

"Wow, it smells delicious," she says obliviously and reaches for a freshly baked pastry from a basket on the table.

I tighten my fingers around my fork, watching as Polo takes a few seconds to put it together. Then his gaze narrows and darts to me.

My plan to introduce Polo to De Rossi grinds to a halt. Before I can do that, I'm going to have to ensure Polo doesn't speak a word about this to him.

Another complication.

Another fucking problem to deal with.

What was Martina thinking? Did I not make it clear no one can know about us?

"There's something on your neck, Martina," I say, keeping my anger out of my voice even if it pulses at the edges of my vision.

She turns to me, her expression crumbling when she realizes what I'm referring to. She slaps a palm against the mark. "I burned myself with a hair straightener," she says quickly.

Jesus Christ, Polo isn't an idiot.

He purses his lips, and a muscle flexes in his jaw. "Didn't know we had one."

"I brought one from home."

I pick up the newspaper. "You should be more careful next time."

"Yes, of course." She shoots me a worried look.

The anger settles in my gut and blurs the words in front of me, but it doesn't take me long to redirect to myself.

I knew what I was getting into.

I decided she was worth it.

And now? The consequences are mine to deal with.

CHAPTER 25

MARTINA

I CAN'T BELIEVE I didn't think about covering up the hickey. My skin burns for the duration of breakfast, and when I finally finish my food, I hurry upstairs and cover it up with some makeup. I keep waiting for Giorgio to storm into my room and tell me off for being so careless, but he never does.

Around eleven, I pull on my gardening clothes—leggings and a loose T-shirt—and decide to go outside. Hiding in here is just making me look guiltier.

When I reach the front door, I draw to a halt. Polo's sitting on the front steps, rubbing his ankle while Sophia whines anxiously beside him. He looks like he's in pain.

"Are you okay?" I ask.

He glances up at me. "Ugh, no. I was about to take Sophia for a run, but I twisted my damn ankle."

I move closer to get a look. "What? How?"

"Tripped over myself right here." He motions at the steps. "And it hurts like a bitch."

"Do you need to go get it looked at?"

He continues to rub his ankle. "No, but I'm going to get some ice. Sorry, girl," he says to Sophia. "You're going to have to do your business in the yard."

The dog barks, her tail wagging back and forth. She looks so excited to go for her walk that I say, "I can take her."

"You sure?"

I offer him a hand to help him up. "Yeah. I was just going to the garden, but I can walk her instead. Where do you usually go?"

Polo smiles. "Thanks, Martina. I take her into the woods. There's a trail that starts about thirty meters behind the greenhouse. It's marked by a red ribbon tied to one of the tree trunks, so you won't miss it."

A walk on the trail sounds nice, but Giorgio's warning sounds inside my head. I'm not about to break another one of his rules, especially after this morning. "Actually, Giorgio doesn't want me going there. I can take her around the property, though."

"Ah, that's right." Polo braces his palm against the wall to help him navigate the stairs. "Sure, just take her as far as you'd like."

"Should I keep her leashed the whole time?"

"She likes to run without it. She won't go far."

"Okay, sounds good. I hope your ankle isn't too bad."

"Thanks. I'll see you soon." He hobbles inside while Sophia totally loses her mind beside me.

"Don't worry, we're going," I tell her as we hurry in the direction of the greenhouse. "Just don't pee on the tomato plants, all right?"

We jog to the edge of the property where Sophia finally stops to sniff at some bushes, and I get a second to look around. The trail Polo mentioned should be somewhere here, but I don't see the marker. I wonder if the forest really is as easy to get lost in as Giorgio implied. The trees are dense but passable, and if there's a trail, shouldn't it be simple enough to stay on it? I suppose I can ask him to take me one day. He doesn't seem like the hiking type, but if I ask him nicely... I can even toss in a favor as a gesture of my thanks.

I'm sure Giorgio will have plenty of ideas of how I can thank him.

I giggle to myself. Last night was everything. My body can't help but heat a few degrees every time I think back to it.

And this morning... I didn't know it was possible to be so *ravenous* for another person. We both couldn't stop touching each other.

I'm still sore even though I told Giorgio in the shower that I wasn't. A little pain is nothing compared to the physical pleasure of being with him. I bite down on my lip at the memory of how he took his time to get me ready for him. How raw and unguarded he was while he was deep inside of me. How his eyes shone with fondness when I met his thrusts and told him how good he was making me feel.

I'm so lost in my own thoughts, I don't notice that Sophia is done with the bushes until she races past me.

My head whips around, and my eyes widen when I see her disappear into the tree line.

"Sophia!"

Shit.

I run after her, passing right past the red ribbon Polo mentioned.

"Please be close by," I mutter as the sky above me gets obscured with branches and leaves.

Ahead of me, there's an excited yelp, but I can't see her amongst the foliage. I halt, getting on my tiptoes to try to find her before I get too far.

"Sophia! Come back!"

The forest is alive with sounds. Crickets, birds, and rustling branches.

A dog barks. It's from farther away this time.

I glance down at my sneakers. I'm a decently fast runner, but Giorgio explicitly told me not to go into the woods.

Still, I can't just leave her.

"Wait up, Sophia!" I shout.

Sun streams through the foliage in bright patches as I jog down the narrow trail. It's clear it's not used very much. There are branches and tall grass growing right through it in some parts. I doubt anyone other than the inhabitants of the castello have ever used it.

I have to slow down when my breathing starts coming out in short puffs. "Sophia!"

There are two distant barks.

I wrinkle my forehead. She still sounds pretty far away.

I've got a stitch in my side, but I pick up my speed again, eager not to lose her.

The leaves blur around me as I follow the barely there path. Ugh, Giorgio will kill me if he finds out. At the back of my mind, a worry appears. What if I can't find my way back? Sophia will, though. She's been down here before. As long as I find her, she'll get me back home.

There's another bark, this time much closer. Suddenly, the trees ahead of me part, and I burst into a small clearing. In the center of the clearing stands an old cottage with a sagging roof, its walls covered in ivy. This is the house I saw a few days ago from the tower. My gaze drops to the steps leading to the front door, and when I see Sophia there, I release a relieved breath.

"There you are." Tall, uncut grass folds beneath my feet as I walk over to her and clip her onto the leash. She lets me pet her and then barks at the house.

Lifting my gaze back to the cottage, I recall what Giorgio said. It had been damaged in a fire...but where are the signs? I run my gaze over the wooden door. There's no soot. The windows are boarded up, but the frames are undamaged.

My brows scrunch together. Doesn't seem to me like there was a fire here. But why would Giorgio lie about it?

What is this place anyway?

There are spider webs all over the front door, displaying an assortment of decaying leaves and dead insects. It's pretty obvious no one's been inside for a very long time.

I glance down at Sophia. "Have you been here before?"

She snorts, hops off the stairs to run a circle around me, and then tugs on the leash like she wants me to follow her to the back of the house.

"Where are you going?"

This dog is acting like she hasn't been outside in weeks, even though that couldn't be farther from the truth.

We round the cottage, and she stops suddenly to sniff at a random patch of dirt. She whines and starts digging, sending dirt flying directly at me.

I jump to the side to avoid getting hit in the face. "What on earth are you doing?"

She digs for a while, but then stops and starts barking, glancing back at me as if she wants me to come take a look at what she's found.

"What's this?" I ask. "You found a...stone?"

She barks.

I suppose that's the kind of exciting stuff dogs live for.

"Good girl," I say, lowering down on my haunches beside her to take a closer look. "Oh wow, you got a big one." I swipe my hand over the flat gray surface, brushing some of the remaining dirt aside.

It's flat. Rectangular.

Hold on, is there's something carved into it?

I clear it some more, using both hands this time, until I finally realize it's a...grave.

Francisca Girardi

1970-2007

She will be avenged

The wheels turn. Girardi is Giorgio's last name.

Is this a relative? Someone who lived in the castello? But those dates are fairly recent.

Could this be the grave of his mother?

I frown. Why is she buried all the way out here?

And the lie about the fire... I glance back at the cottage.

Giorgio didn't want me to find this place. But why? Is it the grave he didn't want me to see? Or something inside the cottage?

Sophia settles at my feet and starts licking her paw.

I should respect Giorgio's wishes, right? I'm already going to be in trouble when he finds out I came all the way out here. If there's something personal inside, it's his right to keep it away from me.

But he knows so much about me, and I still know so little about him. I eye the web-covered door. The desire to understand him burns bright within me. What we have now likely won't last once I leave the castello and return to my brother, so is it really so wrong of me to want to gorge on everything Giorgio while I'm here?

I brush the dirt off my palms and stand back up. The door might be locked. I should probably check that before I waste more time thinking about whether or not I should go inside. If it is locked, I'll take it as a sign that I'm not meant to go in.

The wood steps creak beneath my feet, and a bird breaks into a song somewhere up in the trees. The rusted keyhole is covered with a web that I brush aside with a stick I find on the ground. There's a gap between the door and the door-jamb, and I can see that the deadbolt isn't even closed.

So it's just the big padlock keeping it in place. It looks pretty secure, but just to be sure, I reach over and give it a sharp tug.

The padlock falls open.

My brows rise up my forehead. Did whoever was here last forget to lock it, or is it just broken?

Well, no point in questioning my luck. I take the lock off and tug on the door. It's a bit stuck, so it takes me a while to inch it open, and while I do, Sophia starts to whine.

"I'm just going to peek inside," I tell her as I finally get the opening wide enough for me to squeeze in.

Sophia barges past my feet, and I follow her, careful not to get spider webs all over my hair.

Something crunches beneath my foot, but I have no idea what it is. It's dark inside. Since the windows are boarded up, the only light comes from the open door behind me. A chill runs down my spine as I inhale the cool, stale air. God, this is creepy. While I try to get the flashlight working on my phone, Sophia does her own examination of the space, her paws pattering loudly against wood floor.

Finally, I get the light on and point it at a wall.

My jaw drops.

Oh my God, this place is completely trashed.

It's as if someone has dropped a sledgehammer onto every surface, shattering windows, destroying the art hanging on the walls, and upturning furniture.

"Sophia, come here," I say urgently, pulling on her leash. The floor is littered with shards of glass and splintered wood. I don't want her paws to get cut.

She obeys me, coming close to my side.

We move cautiously through the room, trying to avoid the debris underfoot. The table and chairs in the center of the room are upturned and broken, and the sofa lining is spitting out feathers. The walls are pockmarked with holes and scratches, as if someone took a knife to them in a fit of rage.

Goosebumps erupt over every square inch of my skin as I take a step closer to one of the scratched-up walls. The scratches look like...

My eyes widen.

They're words.

I'm sorry.

My heart pounds out an uneven rhythm. Who wrote that, and what are they apologizing for? Is it for destroying this place?

Or for something else?

Fear wraps around me, making my blood run cold. I need to get out of this place. What if whoever did this is somewhere near?

If there was ever a time to listen to my instincts, it's now.

Pulling Sophia along with me, I make my way outside. With one final look at the cottage, I break out into a run.

We follow the trail back to the castello, the descending sun casting long finger-like shadows across the ground. The thick foliage scratches and whips at my arms, but I can barely feel it with all the adrenaline pumping through me.

After what feels like hours, we finally cross the edge of the forest, and the sky opens up.

I've never been so happy to see that tower.

Sophia and I don't stop running until I'm through the doors of the castello. I'm sweating, and the stitch in my side is unbearable. I practically collapse on the floor of the lobby, clutching my side and panting for breath. Sophia scurries around me, licking and sniffing at my body.

"Martina?"

I crane my neck and see Giorgio standing on the staircase, his expression drawn in concern. "Are you all right?"

"N-no." I wipe my sweaty forehead with my forearm and realize that I'm trembling. "I just came back from the woods."

He hurries down the steps and lowers down in front of me, placing his palms on my knees. "What happened?"

"I—" I swallow. "I was walking Sophia, and she ran into the forest. I followed her. I'm sorry, I know you said not to go there, but I was worried I'd lose her. I ran after her along the path and found her at the old cottage, the one I asked you about."

In an instant, his body grows tense, and his gaze narrows on mine.

I swallow. "I saw the grave."

Something dark flickers in his eyes and tangles with an accusation. This is why he didn't want me there.

"It's your mother's, right?" I ask, my voice dropping to a whisper.

"Yes."

"I was curious. I..."

"You what?"

"I went inside the cottage."

There's a drawn-out silence.

"You shouldn't have done that." His words settle like flakes of ice inside my lungs.

I want to stop talking. I want to, but I can't. Bracing myself for his next answer, I ask, "Who wrote on the walls?"

His palms tighten on my knees. "I did."

CHAPTER 26

MARTINA

THE GRAVE. The cottage. The words carved into the wall.

My hands clench by my sides, palms sweaty.

The apology was his.

Giorgio's.

The man who's always in control.

But people don't do things like *that* when they're in control.

My throat works. "Why?"

Pain stirs behind his eyes before his gaze darts down the hall. He stands and extends his palm. "Get up. I'll tell you, but not here."

He helps me to my feet and leads me upstairs, his hand clenched firmly around mine. My mind jumps to worse-case scenarios.

What was he apologizing for?

Something to do with his mother?

My stomach drops. Did Sal order Giorgio to kill his mom?

The idea is so terrible, and frankly *crazy*, that it makes me draw to a sharp stop.

Giorgio said he also had ghosts that haunted him. Is his mother one of them?

I draw in a shaky breath. Realizing I'm no longer moving, Giorgio looks over his shoulder, and his expression darkens when he sees how freaked out I am.

"I'll explain everything."

"Okay." My voice comes out like a croak.

No, Giorgio couldn't have killed his mom. There's no way. When he spoke about her, it sounded like she was really important to him.

He pulls me into his bedroom and locks the door. When he lets go off my hand, I shrink into the wall. "You're scaring me," I confess. "Tell me what's going on."

Giorgio stops in the center of the room, his broad chest rising and falling with steady, even breaths.

He rakes his fingers through his hair and says, "That cottage used to be the groundkeeper's. My mother lived there when she was a girl."

I wait for him to continue, my heart rapping against my ribs.

Walking over to the window, he links his hands behind his back. "When I was a child, she always told me she was happiest here. My mother regretted leaving her family behind to go to Naples. She married my father a year after she arrived in the city, had me another year later, and for the next decade and a half, she suffered from terrible depression because of what had happened to her."

"What happened?"

"My first memory of my mother is of her crying while she rocked me to sleep. She cried a lot during my childhood. My father hated when she did it in front of him, so she'd hold her tears back until we were alone."

My question hangs unanswered, but I don't dare interrupt him. The words drip out of him slowly, as if he has to work for each one.

"She killed herself when I was fifteen. Hung herself in her bedroom while my father was doing his deliveries around the neighborhood. I found her like that when I came home from school. That morning, I could tell she wasn't well, and I asked my father to wait at home until I got back so that someone would be there to keep an eye on her, but he didn't. He left, and she ended her life."

I cover my mouth with my hand. "Oh my God."

Giorgio shakes his head. "She never blamed me explicitly, and in some way, I think she loved me, but it was the kind of love that eventually tore her apart." His voice turns brittle.

I push myself off the wall and take a few tentative steps toward him. "Giorgio, I don't understand. Blame you for what?"

When he doesn't answer right away, I move closer and wrap my arms around his waist. I think he might push me away, but instead, after a moment, he drops one of his arms and places a palm to rest over mine. The fabric of his dress shirt brushes against my lips, and his familiar scent reaches my nose. I press deeper into him.

"She was violently raped."

My eyes widen in horror. "By who?"

"Sal."

He turns, and the movement forces me to drop my arms and take a step back. Late afternoon sun streams into the room from behind him, leaving his face cloaked in shadows.

"She was nineteen when it happened. She never fully recovered. My father knew she was unwell, but he didn't care. He spent many years telling her when she was at her lowest that she needed to move on. That it happened to so many women, friends of theirs. 'Look at them,' he'd say. 'They're fine. Why aren't you?'"

His face becomes a grimace. I realize then that Giorgio hates his father. Maybe as much as he hates Sal.

"I moved her body here after I bought the castello," he says in a somber voice. "She was first buried in a cemetery in Naples. My father owns the lot beside her. I couldn't stand the thought of him lying beside her one day, so I bribed someone to dig up the coffin, and I brought it here in secret. I wanted her to rest in the place she always considered to be her home.

"There's no good way to say it, Martina, so I'll be blunt. I didn't deal with it well... Moving her here. I...lost it in that cottage. I was so angry. I just wanted to destroy everything in my sight. I was ashamed of who I was and the pain I brought her."

My forehead crinkled. What pain? It sounds like Giorgio was the only one who cared about her.

"But—"

"I already told you I blame Sal for her death, but the truth is...I'm equally to blame." He drags a palm over his mouth. "My mother never told me the details, but—" He expels a harsh breath though his nose. "Based on some of the things she said, I know the rape was brutal and horrible. She had to go to the hospital afterwards. A few weeks later, she found out she was pregnant."

My heart stutters, and there's this feeling of a rapid descent.

"Wha-what did she do?"

He takes a slow, deep breath and then lifts his tortured eyes to meet mine. "She kept it. You're looking at the result."

My belly turns as the horror of what he just revealed sinks in.

"Sal is..." I force the words past the dryness in my throat.

Giorgio looks down at the ground, his skin turning sallow. "My biological father."

I open my mouth, but there are no words. No words to express even a fraction of what I'm feeling.

I'm frozen, glued to the ground as Giorgio gives me a bitter smile. "Now you know the truth about who I am. For my mother, I was a curse. A walking, breathing reminder of the worst thing that ever happened to her."

The pieces fall into place. The words on the walls... He blames himself for what happened.

"The fact that she managed to hold on for fifteen years is a miracle," Giorgio says, swiping a palm over the back of his head. "After what happened, Nino, the scumbag I call my father, did nothing to help my mother get justice. Instead, he accepted a bribe from Sal. He promised his silence in exchange for a promotion. We lived in the territory of the Secondigliano Alliance, but there was an intersection in the neighborhood controlled by the Casalesi. Nino is a vain man, Martina, and his vanity rendered him useless. He ran a tiny cigarette shop, barely scraping by, and he hated that lowly business with all his heart. When Sal offered to make him a submarine for the Casalesi, nothing could make Nino say no. Not even the knowledge that his wife was carrying another man's baby. After I was born, he pretended I was his, but my mother told me the truth when I was ten. For years, I'd ask her why she looked at me like—" he breaks off and purses his lips.

I press my nails into my palms. "Like what?"

"Like she was staring at a stranger instead of her son. I'd catch her doing it every few days, and it scared me. I'd tell her she was doing it again, and she'd usually snap out of it. One day, I made her angry, and she told me she never wanted me. That my father wasn't really my dad, and that the man who was, was an evil man. That I might turn out to be just like him."

My vision blurs. "She shouldn't have said those things, even when she was hurting. You were just a kid."

He dismisses my words with a wave of his hand. "My mother wasn't perfect, but I loved her. Finding out the truth didn't change that. If anything, it made me respect her even more for the sacrifice that she made, keeping me. She didn't live to see Sal get what he deserves, but when I found her cold, lifeless body, I made a promise to her that I *would* avenge her."

Everything makes sense now. "That's why you're backing Dem. You want to play a part in taking down Sal."

He averts his gaze. "Yes."

"Does Dem know Sal's your father?"

"No. None of the Casalesi are aware."

"But this is why Sal traded for you, isn't it?"

Giorgio scoffs. "He certainly wasn't driven by any kind of familial affection. Sal has many bastards scattered around Naples. I was a young hacker working for the Secondigliano Alliance and I helped the Alliance pull off a deal that Sal's men were also involved with. My skills caught Sal's attention and it didn't take him long to figure out who I was. When Sal told my old capo I was his son, the capo deemed me compromised. He'd probably have killed me if Sal hadn't made it clear he was happy to take me off his hands. Ten thousand euros and a medic—that's what Sal gave him in exchange. I didn't have much choice in the matter. I had to accept my new boss if I wanted to keep my life. And so I did. I put on a convincing face for a long time, but there hasn't been a day where I haven't cursed that man's existence."

He exhales and drags his palms over his face.

"Sal deserves to die. Maybe when it's done, I'll have it in me to burn that cottage down to the ground. I haven't returned to it since the day I buried my mother. It repulses me."

Of course it does. It's a physical manifestation of the guilt he's been carrying all his life.

"You wrote you're sorry, but you have nothing to apologize for—" I start, but he cuts me off.

"I do, Martina." His voice is firm. "I brought my mother terrible pain while she was still alive."

"You didn't choose to be born," I argue. "Yes, the circumstances were awful, but you were an innocent child. Your mother made the choice to keep you, to nurture you, despite what happened."

"And she regretted it for the rest of her life."

I step closer and take his hands into mine. "Even if she did, it's not your fault. You can't blame yourself for how she felt about her decision."

His eyes lock on mine, and a soft breath escapes past his lips. He lifts his fingertips to my cheek. "I didn't tell you this for you to pity me or to try to heal old wounds. I'm telling you so that you know exactly the kind of man I am."

It dawns on me then that he thinks there's something wrong with him. Because of the circumstances around his conception? Does he think I'll push him away now that I know the truth? True, his father is a terrible man. Sal's the reason my parents are dead. The reason Imogen is dead. But if anything, I feel closer to Giorgio now more than ever.

"And what kind of man is that?"

"Rotten," he says softly, dragging his knuckles over my cheekbone. "I'm broken, Martina. I don't know what it feels like to be whole."

I grip his wrist, holding him in place. "How do you think I felt when you first picked me up? Back then, I could have said those same words about me. I was so broken, I was still messaging Imogen's number even though it had been months since she died."

Surprise flickers in his eyes. "You were?"

"Yes. Seems crazy, doesn't it? That's why when you took my phone, I nearly lost my mind. Sending those messages used to be the only thing that would help me get to sleep."

"I'm sorry. I didn't realize..."

I let go of him. "I hated myself, Giorgio."

He clenches his jaw, clearly displeased at hearing that. "And now?"

"Now, I think even the most broken of things can be mended by the right pair of hands."

The vulnerability that bleeds into his expression takes my breath away. He stares at me like he's seeing me for the very first time, and that's when I decide I like that look more than anything. More than the kisses, or the sex, or the way his hands feel on me. In that look lies the suggestion of a future. A tantalizing hint at what this could be if my time here didn't have an expiration date.

"I crave you, Martina." He slides his fingers into my hair and pulls me closer to him. "I've craved you from the moment I saw you, and I promised myself I'd carve that craving out of me. But the deeper I cut, the deeper you burrow. I'm afraid that if I don't stop trying to rid myself of you, I'll end up cutting out my own heart."

"Then let go of the knife," I say, my lips close enough to brush against his, "and let me mend you."

He crushes his mouth to mine. His hands clutch me so tightly, it's nearly painful, but I wouldn't try to pull away in a million years.

A madness consumes us, erasing thoughts of consequences and complications. Nothing exists in the moment except for him and I. Everything else disappears.

He tugs my leggings over my ass and takes turns lifting my legs to finish stripping the material off without breaking the kiss. His tongue dances with mine, and his teeth graze against my bottom lip. When he bites down harder than usual, I jerk away and meet his eyes. "Is that punishment for not covering up that hickey earlier?"

Desire swirls in his wide pupils. "Not even close."

"You're the one who left it on me," I say breathlessly as he lifts me, his hands cupping my ass.

"That's because you are mine to mark." He runs his tongue over my neck, sending shivers scattering over my skin. "Mine to fuck. However and wherever I want."

Yes, please.

He presses my back against the wall, and I tighten my legs around his waist as he reaches around them to undo his belt.

When I feel his hard length pressing against my panties, I drop my head back, anticipation coiling inside of me. He grips my chin and forces my eyes back to his. "You will look at me while I fuck your tight, young pussy, *piccolina*." He nudges my underwear aside and pushes the tip of his cock inside, stretching my opening. "Do you understand? You look away just once, and I'll stop."

I nod frantically. "I understand."

He smirks. "Good fucking girl." And then he thrusts all the way in in one smooth stroke.

My body shivers from that delicious fullness. "Oh God."

He holds the backs of my thighs with an iron grip as he starts moving inside of me. He holds my gaze, and the force of his full attention reaches into the farthest corners of my mind, making the boundary between him and I blur. We become one.

My moans grow louder, more desperate.

He clenches his teeth and pumps faster, stretching me to my limits. My release starts to build, and as it does, my eyelids drift closed.

He rams into me once more and stops. "Look at me. I want to see your eyes as you fall apart."

My blunt nails dig into his shoulders. I follow his command, and when my pussy starts pulsing around his cock, I moan his name.

"Fuck," he groans. "Say it again, *piccolina*. I want you chanting my name as you come all over my cock."

I sob as my orgasm crests. "Gio!"

He helps me ride the wave with his steady thrusts, but soon his own release overtakes him, and he sinks all the way inside of me, pressing his forehead against mine. "*Cazzo*, this place between your legs, it's heaven."

I breathe in his scent and shudder as his cock twitches inside of me. His fingers are so tight on my thighs, I'm sure

I'll have bruises tomorrow, but right now, my body's oblivious to pain.

Around Giorgio, it sings with pleasure.

CHAPTER 27

GIORGIO

"Give Tommaso and Allegra the night off," Martina whispers in my ear once we're lying in bed and catching our breath. "I'll make dinner."

I press a kiss to her temple. "All right."

A moment later, she climbs over me and walks to the bathroom. A trail of my cum drips down her thigh, and I get the urge to drag her back into bed and shove it back inside of her.

The possessiveness I feel toward her is a recipe for fucking disaster, but I've decided that while she's here, I'll indulge it.

It crossed my mind more than a few times as I was telling her about my past that I should stop before I get too far. But then I thought, why hold any of it back? As the words left my mouth, I kept waiting for disgust to flash across her features. I was sure that when I saw it, it would put whatever we were doing here in a neat little box. A temporary fling between two people who couldn't be more unsuitable for each other.

But that's not what happened. She saw the real me and didn't even blink.

My lips curl into a bitter smile. She might think she can mend me, but she's so very young. I can tell she's an optimist at heart.

And me? I'm an old cynic.

I might find some peace when Sal is dead, but it won't absolve me of my original sin.

While Martina showers, I get dressed and seek out Allegra to relieve her and her husband of their duties. After I speak with her, I intend to search for Polo, but Allegra tells me he's gone into town and hasn't returned. Apparently, he twisted his ankle earlier, and it was bothering him enough that he wanted to get it looked at.

I spend the next hour reviewing recent phone calls I've recorded, but the exercise proves fruitless. My access to people in Sal's orbit has weakened over the last few weeks. The phone chatter has decreased. During times like these, conversations are had in person and in locations the don can be sure aren't bugged.

Fuck. I need to know why his attention is trained on me.

I pick up my phone and consider giving him a call, but I quickly decide against it. I never call him. Doing so now would only heighten his suspicion.

It'll show him that I'm nervous. I'm rarely nervous, because I'm always in control. But now, I feel the puppet string slipping through my fingers. I frown. Something is off, but I can't place my finger on what...

My thumb presses on a number, and three rings later, Damiano picks up.

"Did something happen?" he asks as soon as the line connects.

I lean back in my chair and prop my feet up on the desk. "No, everything is fine."

"Good. I was about to call you. We've had a few meetings fall through, and I was wondering if you know why."

"Who?"

"Carlo Moretti, Vittorio De Rosa, and the Esposito brothers."

With each name he lists, my gut grows tighter. "They were families I was sure we could rely on."

"So was I. Carlo and Vittorio are the ones who've suffered the most from Sal's strategic failure with the Mallardos, given that their territory is by the border. The Mallardos have already started doing raids in retaliation. Sal must have told them something to sway them, and I was hoping you could tell me what."

"I'll look into it. I don't have any ins with those two, but I have access to the cameras in Esposito's warehouse, since I'm the one who set up the system. The younger one, Allonso, spends a lot of time there. I can let you know if anyone from Sal's inner circle has paid them a visit. If they talked, there's a chance my cameras picked it up."

"Yes, fine." There's a long pause. "I don't like it, Napoletano. The meetings were easy to set up, but they cancelled abruptly. Only hours before we were supposed to meet."

"If they were definitely backing Sal, they wouldn't have cancelled. They would have just tipped Sal off on where to find you."

"I know. I still think they want to see me as don, but they got spooked. Sal's got something up his sleeve. Is there any chance he could have an idea about Mari's whereabouts?"

I tap my fingertips against the armrest. "He's been following me, but his tails aren't very good. I've lost them every time. I don't know if he's singling me out, or if he's doing the same to others."

"It's not just you," Damiano says. "He's more paranoid than he's ever been. Be careful."

"You know you don't need to tell me that."

"How is she?"

I drag my palm over my jaw. "She's doing well. Much better than before."

"Honestly?"

"Yes."

He exhales. "I'm glad to hear it. When I spoke to her on her birthday, she did sound better. I need to talk to her about something, but Vale tells me I shouldn't breach the topic until I'm confident she'll take it well."

"What topic?"

"The Grassis promised their support under the condition that she weds their eldest son."

My jaw clenches so hard I think I might shatter my teeth. "And you agreed?"

"I agreed to consider it," he says uneasily. "They are one of the oldest Casalesi families, and a closely knit tie with them would mean unfettered access to their militia. That manpower is valuable." He sighs. "I should have prepared her for this possibility, but we spent so long isolated on Ibiza that it was easier to pretend it would never come to this. In truth, I wasn't sure it ever would. I spent far too much time trying to decide if I should challenge Sal."

Liar. Deep inside, he knew De Rossi may have bided his time, but from the moment I met him, I knew one day he'd fight for what Sal took from him and his family.

It must be easier for him to pretend that the decision could have gone either way. How else could he justify allowing Martina to live in fantasy land?

That girl has no idea she's going to be traded away for an alliance. The question is, how will she react when she finds out?

She loves her brother, and she wants him to succeed. She might talk herself into making the sacrifice for his sake. That's exactly the kind of person she is.

My free hand tightens into a fist. "When will you tell her?"

"Not right away. I want to wait until I can see her in person."

"And if she says no?"

"I'll cross that bridge when I get there."

I run my tongue over the inside of my bottom lip. "I'll let you know if I find any useful recordings."

"Good. Let's stay in close contact on this."

I hang up and throw my phone across the desk.

Fuck him.

The whole practice is barbaric. Trading away young girls to men usually much older than them in what amounts to a business transaction.

And I'm no damn better, because the truth is, if De Rossi offered her to me, I'd already be driving her to the fucking chapel.

I spend another hour scrolling through tapes. When a knock sounds, I've managed to nearly forget about the marriage proposal, but as soon as Martina peeks inside the room, my anger spikes right back.

The eldest Grassi kid is a nobody. The only thing he has going for him is his fucking last name. What is he going to do with her? He won't be able to handle her. Martina might obey her brother, but that doesn't mean she'll fold to anyone else's whims.

I should fucking know.

She steps into the room, giving me a full view of her silky black dress. It molds to her body and reaches to her mid-thigh. "Dinner is ready," she says, giving me a bright smile.

I cross the office in two steps, push my fingers into her hair, and claim her mouth with a brutal kiss.

She makes a sound of surprise before melting right into me.

When I pull back, her eyes are wide. "What was that for?"

"Nothing," I say, knowing I can't tell her the truth. "Let's go."

The dining room is lit with soft candlelight, and the table is set. Martina urges me to sit down and then disappears into the kitchen to get our first course.

While I wait for her, I gaze at the fireplace. It's unlit, but she placed a few thick candles in the hearth, and their flames flicker inside.

I don't know why my mind takes me in that particular direction, but I begin to imagine what it could be like to truly be with her. To live here together and have dinner like this every night.

The vision comes far too easily. I see it in vivid detail, like a movie playing on a screen. The way she'd smile at me. The soft brush of her fingertips against my skin. The smell of her cooking and the soft murmur of our conversation. We'd eat dessert, and then I'd drag her out of her seat and onto my lap. She'd giggle at me putting my hands up her skirt and then moan when I made her come. I'd taste her on my fingers and tell her that no matter how much I love her cooking, she's still the best thing I'd ever taste.

Her voice snaps me out of my thoughts. "First course is rib eye with black peppercorn sauce."

I look at her and pretend like I didn't just imagine my ring flashing on her finger instead of some Grassi's.

There's a contented smile on her face, and as pleased as it makes me to see her happy, I can't stop thinking about the conversation with Damiano.

Soon, she'll be promised to another.

I knew it was coming, didn't I? I just didn't think it would happen this quickly.

"You haven't tried it," she says, gesturing at my plate as her smile dims.

Cazzo, I need to forget about that call.

I taste the meat, and fuck, it's good. She waits for my reaction and beams when I tell her as much.

Something bumps against my shin, and I look under the tablecloth to find Sophia looking at me with expectant eyes. "Tommaso already fed you," I tell her. She snorts and quickly abandons me for Martina, who doesn't even try to put up any resistance.

She cuts off a small piece of her meat and hands it to the dog, who swipes it immediately with her tongue. Martina smiles at Sophia. "I'm getting attached to you, you little cutie." She glances up at me. "She's tired. Probably from all the exercise she got today when she ran away from me."

Something occurs to me then. "Have you taken her on walks before?"

"No, this was the first time. I bumped into Polo after he hurt his ankle. Since he couldn't walk, I offered to take her in his stead."

I frown. "Did he tell you to go to the woods?"

"Yeah, I think he forgot you didn't want me going there, but I told him I couldn't. I was just going to take her behind the garden, but then she ran way." She drags her hand over Sophia's fur, and I follow the movement with my eyes.

Did Polo really forget, or was he trying to get her to go there on purpose?

I saw the way he looked at Martina the first day she arrived. Being stuck here, he must have been eager for a plaything, but I shut that down right away. I made it clear she was *my* guest.

Until she became so much more.

When he saw the mark on her neck, he couldn't hide his jealousy. Even though he'd just apologized to me and was clearly trying to keep a straight face, a flash of it had come through.

He knows about the cottage and the grave there. Did he think that by letting her discover that place, he'd push her away from me? Martina said the lock was rusted and easy to open. I haven't gone back to check it after I boarded the place up, but what if Polo tampered with it?

My suspicions seep like rot through my bones. I'll need to investigate, but for now, I won't let that boy's meddling distract me.

Whatever he may have attempted clearly failed.

I reach across the table and grasp Martina's hand. She meets my eyes. "Is everything all right?"

Instead of answering, I pull her out of her seat and into my lap. She'll be gone soon, but for now, she's here with me, and I'm selfish enough to take everything she's willing to give me and more.

She wraps her arms around my shoulder and burrows her face into my neck. "I love the smell of your cologne," she whispers into my ear. "It makes me crazy."

Widening my legs, I shift her over to the right one. She coils one arm around my neck and looks at me expectantly, waiting to see what I'll do. When I part her thighs and cup her pussy under her skirt, she lets out a gasp. "You're not done eating," she breathes.

"No, I'm not." I brush my lips over her cheek. "But I have a craving for something very particular."

I nudge her underwear aside and dip a finger inside of her. Her abundant wetness coats my skin, and her breathing grows ragged. "What are—"

I take the finger out and bring it to my mouth and suck it clean. Her taste makes my cock jerk. Fuck, she's so damn sweet. She watches me with hooded eyes, her expression growing hazy with lust.

We're interrupted by the sound of footsteps.

Martina hears it and tries to get off me, but I hold her in place. "Stay," I command. Allegra and Tommaso would know better than to come here after I gave them the night off. It can only be Polo.

Maybe he needs a reminder of who Martina belongs to.

He appears in the entryway moments later. His eyes take inventory of the scene before him, and then his gaze clashes with mine. He can't see my hand up Martina's skirt—the table's blocking it—but just the sight of her in my lap is enough to make his eyes narrow.

I tip my chin up, an arrogant smirk on my lips that's meant to remind him of his place. "I heard you sustained an injury today."

His lips twitch in a failed attempt at a smile. "An injury is too generous of a term. It's nearly back to normal now."

I trail my fingers up Martina's inner thigh. "I gave Allegra and Tommaso the night off."

"I heard."

And yet you're here.

Martina sucks in a harsh breath when my fingers slide into her underwear again. She drops her hand to my forearm and squeezes, signaling for me to stop, but instead, I inch inside of her wet heat.

"Can I help you with anything?" I ask.

Polo's nostrils flare. "I wanted to thank Martina for taking care of Sophia today."

"She was happy to do it." I insert another finger inside of her, and she digs her nails into me. "Isn't that right, *piccolina*?"

Her wide eyes stare at me, and her face is flushed with an embarrassed kind of arousal. "Yes," she chokes out.

I flick my gaze back to Polo just in time to see his jaw clench.

"Was there anything else, Polo?"

"No."

"Then we'll see you tomorrow. Be careful with that ankle."

His eyes darken for a brief moment before he turns around and leaves without another word.

"What was that?" Martina pants once he's gone. "Gio, do you think he saw?"

I curl my fingers and work a moan out of her. "No. All he saw is you sitting on my lap and looking very happy to be there."

Her head tips back as I roll my thumb over her clit, but she brings it back up. "You're crazy. He's never going to look at me the same after that little incident."

"I don't want him looking at you at all. I don't want *anyone* looking at you."

She groans and repeats, "Crazy."

I lick the shell of her ear as I fuck her with my hand. "You keep calling me that, and I'll show you real crazy. I'll bring you upstairs and tie you to my bed. Then, I'll paint your skin with my cum until you're covered in it. Until there's no doubt in anyone's mind who you belong to."

Her pussy clenches, and she comes apart all over my fingers. Body shuddering, she rocks over my thigh as her orgasm overtakes her, in the process brushing her leg against my aching cock. That small, unintentional movement makes me lose the last shred of control.

I send my plate flying and heave her onto the surface of the table, pressing her front against it. Her legs barely reach the floor. She's still shaking, and when I fling up her skirt, I'm met with the sight of her soaking pussy.

With a growl, I undo my belt, pull it off, and fold it into two.

Her nails claw at the table and she hisses when the warm leather brushes against the backs of her thighs. Grabbing her hair, I press my lips to her ear. "We never got to that punishment, did we?"

She trembles in my grip, her breaths coming out in little pants. "I thought that's what you were doing when you fingered me in front of Polo."

I tighten my hold on her hair. "I don't want to hear another man's name when I'm staring at your wet cunt." The belt caresses her supple skin, and after a few seconds, she relaxes into the sensation.

I lift the belt and whip her right where her ass meets her thigh.

She makes a sound that's a mix of a moan and a yelp, and it sends a pulse of blood rushing through my cock. "Careful, you're going to make me think you're enjoying it."

The next time I do it, she muffles the sounds coming out of her mouth by biting her forearm, but she can't make her cunt stop leaking.

I drag the belt over her pussy, leaving it glistening with her wetness. I show it to her. "This is what I do to your body, *piccolina*. Don't you ever fucking forget that."

Her skin flushes red.

The belt buckle clanks against the ground. I unzip my dress pants, take out my cock, and plunge into her tight hole.

She sobs from pleasure as I fuck her. "Gio, oh God, oh God, oh God."

If a fucking bomb went off, I wouldn't be able to stop being inside of her. All coherent thought is gone, leaving only chaos to brew inside my mind.

Fuck Sal. Fuck Damiano. Take her and run. You know none of them would ever be able to find you.

What do you want more? Her or revenge? The satisfaction of revenge is fleeting, but Martina...

Martina is forever.

My orgasm breaks through the surface, and I clench my eyes shut. I wrap my arms around her, cupping her small breasts, and she bucks against me, meeting my slowing thrusts.

She glances at me over her shoulder, her forehead glistening with sweat. For a moment, fear grips me. Did I hurt her? Did I go too hard with the belt?

But then she throws me a blissful smile, and it's an arrow through the heart.

Martina is forever, but there is no forever for a man like me.

CHAPTER 28

MARTINA

DAYS PASS, and we barely leave the house. Giorgio keeps me in bed. He's ravenous and insistent on getting his fill of my body.

The hours blur, as do the lines between us. I wonder if he regrets keeping me at an arm's length for so long now that he knows how it could have been during all those days he insisted kissing me was a mistake.

He doesn't say things like that anymore. No, now he showers me with praise. He tells me he's never kissed softer lips. Never touched more supple skin. Never fucked the way he's been fucking me.

With abandon and an utter disregard for consequences.

Last night, Giorgio taught me just the way he likes to be sucked off—deep and messy. I sat on my knees as he fed me his cock, coaxing my throat to open up for him. When I finally took the entire thing, he smoothed a palm over my wet cheek and said, "This is the only time I want to see tears on your face, *piccolina*." It turned me on so much, I had to touch myself while he fucked my mouth. We came at the same time, him down my throat, and me all over his floor.

I want to do that again. The memory makes me reach behind and cup Giorgio over his pajamas. He's still asleep but already at half-mast. I felt him prodding my behind all night long as he cradled me to his chest.

I don't think I'm going to fall back asleep. Early morning light streams through a gap in the drawn curtains, and I let out a silent yawn before I flip to the other side and look upon Giorgio's sleeping face.

Even when he sleeps, peace doesn't reach him. The line between his brows is softer, but it's still there, and there's tension in his jaw.

I know what his dreams are made of.

Revenge.

He's told me more about his mother during the quiet hours we've spent in bed. It's obvious he loved her, but I can't say I like her very much. I pity her for what she lived through, but at the same time, she seems cruel for making her son feel like a burden. What he must have felt like at ten to think he's responsible for why his mama cried every night? Her pain was too much for her, and she made him bear it. That boy grew into a man who still believes he's bad to his very core.

I let out a slow breath and carefully slip out of bed to use the restroom.

After I do my business and wash my hands, my gaze catches on my reflection in the large mirror.

My body's changed over the past few weeks from all the working out I've been doing. I look stronger, my posture's as good as it's ever been. Giorgio and I have resumed our classes, even though we often get distracted and end class with our clothes scattered all over the gym's floor.

When I return to the room, Giorgio is awake, and he beckons me to him. I climb over his legs and settle on his lap, but when I kiss him, he only gives me a peck.

"I have to leave for the day," he says, his voice still hoarse with sleep.

"It's so early. Where are you going?"

"Sal's sending me to Milan to retrieve something for him."

I wrap my fingers around the pendant at my neck. "Jewelry?"

"Yes. A lot of it."

"Why does he want you to get it for him?"

Giorgio raises one muscular shoulder before letting it fall. "I'd bet he's looking to sell it. His expenses have risen now that he's preparing for a war, and his income has fallen off a cliff."

Anxiety fans through me. "When are you leaving?"

He kisses me again and then gently lifts me off him. "Now. I'll likely be back tomorrow."

I watch him as he dresses—white shirt, navy slacks, and a pair of platinum cufflinks. He slips on his jacket and then puts on his watch.

The last piece of the ensemble is the gun he extracts from the dresser and slides inside his waistband.

And just like that, he goes from Gio to a man of the Casalesi.

In the darkness of this room, it's been easy to forget who we are in the outside world, but it's been a temporary reprieve. All of this will end, and I haven't been able to bring myself to really consider what will happen then.

Gio turns to me, and I sit up on my knees on the edge of the bed. He pulls my mouth to his and gives me a thorough kiss. Heat floods my core, and I'm about to beg him to stay for a little longer when his phone rings.

He glances at it and swears under his breath. "I've got to go."

"Please be careful."

He meets my gaze and gives me a soft smile. "I will be, *piccolina*. Stay out of trouble while I'm gone."

After he leaves, I can't fall back asleep, so I laze around for an hour and then head down for breakfast early. I decide to start roasting some potatoes, so that when Tommaso gets in, we can make a goat cheese and sun-dried tomato frittata, and we can serve it with the potatoes and a leafy salad.

When I get to the kitchen, Polo's already there.

"Up early?" I ask as I walk over to the espresso maker. I haven't seen much of him since the incident in the dining room—the memory of which still makes me break out in a sweat—so I awkwardly avoid looking him in the eyes.

"Yes. It's going to be a long day," he says, taking a sip of his cappuccino. "I wanted to get a head start."

"Well, Giorgio left for the day, so if you need any help, let me know." I grind the espresso, waiting for the noise to finish before I ask, "You've been out of the castello a lot lately, right? Something going on?"

He sniffs. "Just some stuff with my extended family. I've had to take care of some things, but it's all good now."

"I'm happy to hear that."

CRACK!

I whip around at the sound to see Polo's ceramic mug shattered all over the floor.

He curses under his breath and reaches for a towel, shooting me a strange look. He looks tired, dark bags under his eyes. "I'm jittery. Too much espresso." He sinks to the ground and starts wiping at the spilled coffee.

"Don't worry, it happens." I kneel down and help him get the mess cleaned up, but my movements slow when I notice how his hand is trembling.

"Are you all right?"

He finishes cleaning up the spill and hurries to the sink with the dirty towel. "I'm fine," he says, his back to me. When he's done washing his hands, he takes a clean towel to dry them, and then chucks it onto the counter.

I eye his back. He's so tense. I wonder why.

He turns, and one glance at his face tells me something is terribly wrong.

A drop of sweat rolls down his temple, and the way he's looking at me from beneath his brows makes an icy chill curl up my spine.

"Polo?"

He doesn't answer. There isn't a hint of humor in his expression.

"What's going on?" I ask, my pulse picking up.

He takes a step toward me. "You've been spending a lot of time with Giorgio lately. Have you realized by now he's a liar?"

I frown. "Polo, what are you talking about?"

"About a year ago, I wrote a letter and asked Giorgio to give it to my father. I never got a response."

I step back. His face is blank, but my alarm bells are ringing. Why is he telling me this? "I'm...sorry?"

"You see, I was sure my dad would want to write a few words back to me. I asked Giorgio if he was sure the letter got delivered, and he assured me that it did." Polo's lips curl into a bitter smile, and he takes another step in my direction. "He lied. He lied, Martina, but I won't lie to you. I'm telling the truth when I say you only have Giorgio to blame for what's about to happen next."

The backs of my thighs bump against something. I raise my palms ahead of me, fear coiling inside my gut. "Polo, stop. I'm sorry Giorgio lied, but what does that have to do with me?"

Darkness spills into his eyes. "Unfortunately, everything." He spreads his arms. "Look at this place. Look at what his money's gotten him." He keeps advancing. "And look at me, Martina." He plucks at his T-shirt. "I have nothing to my name. *Nothing*. Why do you think Giorgio's hidden me from my father all this time? It's not because he's trying to protect me. It's because he knows that given the same opportunities, I'd do far better than him. I wouldn't be a lone wolf acting on the sidelines. I'd be ruling the Casalesi right by Father's side."

A sour taste floods my mouth. My forehead wrinkles as my mind scrambles to piece it together. He can't be saying what I think he's saying. "Your father..."

He smirks, stopping so close I can smell the cocktail of sweat and faint cologne. "Yes. My father. *Our* father. Sal Gallo."

The pieces click, but there's no sense of satisfaction that typically follows solving a puzzle. Instead, there's just cold, hard fear.

Sal. That's who I saw in Polo. There's something about his eyes, his cheeks, the divot in his chin. No wonder I didn't make the connection. The similarities are so subtle they're barely there. In Giorgio, they're missing altogether, but in Polo, some of Sal's genes won out.

Goosebumps erupt across my skin, and in my head, someone is screaming *RUN*.

"We have the same story," Polo says, slapping his palms down against the table on either side of me. "Sal made both of our mothers pregnant."

"You mean he raped them?" I force past my dry throat.

Polo shrugs. "My mother never hated Sal the way Giorgio's did. She accepted that sometimes things just happen. She made her peace with it, and so did I."

"What the hell are you saying, Polo? Let me get this straight. You want to work for Sal? Whatever peace your mother made with what happened to her, I don't think she'd ever want her son to idolize the man who raped her!"

It happens so fast. One moment I'm shouting at him, and the next my cheek burns from his slap. It's more shocking than it is painful, but it tells me something that makes my blood run cold.

He has no qualms about hurting me.

Polo grips my chin, his fingers digging into my flesh, and leans in. "You have no idea what you're talking about, so shut the fuck up."

He tries to drag his nose over my cheek. I jerk away, and he snickers, finding my resistance amusing.

"When I realized Giorgio would never help me get in contact with my father, I took matters into my own hands. I found a way to reach Sal, and I told him all about who I was, how I ended up with Giorgio."

He lets go of me and drops his hand back down to the table. "It wasn't easy getting in contact with the don of the Casalesi. I sent letters to the church in Casal, hoping someone there would get my messages into the right hands. Eventually, someone did. I went to the post office whenever I could get away, and one day, a reply came. It was beautiful, Martina," he says, a sick smile playing on his lips. "My father wants to see me. He told me he's angry that Giorgio kept us apart, says he's never trusted Giorgio fully, and trust is important to him, especially now. Turns out my father is at war with your brother. I had a feeling Giorgio was doing something behind the don's back. I told Sal I might know where Martina De Rossi is hiding, and he was very interested to learn more. I'm going to do even better. I am going to earn Sal's trust by bringing you directly to him."

My stomach plummets. *Dem*. If Polo gives me to Sal, Dem will do everything he can to save me.

Everything, including giving up on his claim.

I can't let that happen.

"Polo, don't do this," I beg, clutching his shirt with my hands. "My brother will give you whatever you want."

But he's not listening. He takes my wrists into his hands and tugs me into him. "Giorgio has everything I've ever wanted, and it's clear he has no intention of sharing." His nostrils flare, and then his gaze lands on my necklace, the one Giorgio gave me. "So I'm going to just have to take it myself."

I have to get away.

Not wasting another second, I shove him as hard as I can, but all I manage is one step before he flings out his hand and wraps it around my wrist. He tugs me back, takes my other wrist, and holds me with an iron grip. Breath fanning against my face, he demands, "What do you see in him anyway? He's a sick man. I thought you'd understand that when you went inside the cottage."

A shaky breath leaves my lungs. That's why the lock on that door was broken. *Polo.*

"The only sick man here is you," I hiss.

Somewhat miraculously, I realize I know how to get out of my current position. Giorgio taught me. My training clicks into place, and I push my wrists deeper into Polo's chest before sharply jerking them back.

He doesn't expect it, and his hold on me breaks.

Not wasting a second, I run around the kitchen island, putting it between us.

His eyes flash with excitement. "Are you going to put up a fight, Mari? You'll only make it worse for yourself."

I sprint toward the door leading outside and make it halfway before he tackles me to the ground.

Shit!

My kneecaps connect with the hard floor, and pain shoots up my legs. I gasp as he rolls me onto my back, but just as he's about to straddle me, I pull my legs in, bending at the knees, and shove my feet against his chest.

He falls, grunting in pain.

RUN.

I do. I nearly make it to the door when he gets to me next, gripping my biceps and spinning me around.

My back collides against the door, and he wraps his hands around my neck.

Eyes wild and terrifying, he squeezes and says, "After I give you to Sal, he'll reward me generously. I'll ask him to make you my wife."

The spike of nausea is so sudden that for a second, I'm sure I'm going to throw up.

He presses me into the door and rocks his hips into me, his erection obvious. "I'm going to fuck Giorgio out of you. I'm going to make you forget you ever touched him."

The backs of my eyes prickle, and fear pounds against the back of my skull, but for the first time in my life, I'm able to push against it.

C'mon. I know this. We practiced this.

I take one of his fingers and bend it backwards. He screams in pain, let's go of me, and the rest is a blur. I think I manage to land a kick between his legs before I'm flying out the door and running toward the staff house.

"Allegra! Tommaso!" I shout at the top of my lungs. "Help!"

I think I hear footsteps behind me, but I don't dare look. The staff house is close, and Tommaso and Allegra will help me as soon as I get inside.

Thirty meters. Twenty. Five.

As my hand curls around the handle, I'm afraid it'll be locked, but thank God, it opens easily, and I tumble inside.

Sophia jumps on me while I lock the door and draw the chain, her yelps and barks reaching a fever pitch. She probably senses something is wrong. "Come with me!"

I race around the house, checking and locking all the windows and doors as quickly as I can. "Tommaso! Allegra!"

There's no response.

Where are they?

My stomach seizes. If they already went to the castello or are out at the greenhouse, it'll mean I'm on my own here. They won't hear me screaming from all the way out here.

I check to make sure I have my phone with me. As soon as I find them, we need to call Giorgio. He'll know what to do.

"Hello! Tommaso, are you here?"

Sophia won't stop barking. She comes up to me and then runs to the bottom of the stairs, looking back as if she wants me to go up there.

A horrible premonition washes over me.

"Fuck, fuck, fuck."

I run up the stairs, following the dog all the way to the bedrooms. I've never been up here before, but Sophia's barking at one specific door, so that's where I go.

My hands shake as I grip the handle.

When I open it, I immediately take a step backward.

A scream claws up my throat

My vision blurs.

Tommaso and Allegra are in bed, lying in pools of their own blood.

CHAPTER 29

MARTINA

No.

I blink a few times, but the image stays.

Crumpled white sheets soaked in vermillion. Dark gashes sliced into their necks. Closed eyes, and pale faces.

Their fingers are linked loosely together, and the thought of them using their last moments to reach for each other makes me choke on a sob.

Sophia jumps on the bed and starts prodding Tommaso's arm, trying to awaken her master.

"Get away from there," I cry out.

She must pick up on the desperation in my voice, because she listens. She hops back down and runs up to me. The poor dog. How long did she spend locked in here with them, confused about why Tommaso wasn't answering her?

My heart falls to pieces.

Polo spent two years with them at the castello, working side by side with them, sharing meals, laughter, stories. How could he do this? Did they see him right before he did it? Did their eyes flash with confusion when they saw him lift his knife?

Bile slicks the back of my throat, and I press my palm to my mouth, but I can't hold it back. I vomit in the corner.

Over the sound of my own retching, I hear something crash in the living room below, and it snaps me into action. I wipe my mouth with the back of my sleeve, slam the door to the bedroom shut, and push a heavy desk against it.

That will hold Polo, but not for long.

I need something to knock him out.

But there's nothing remotely resembling a weapon in this bedroom. I rush over to the closet and start digging through the shelves. Clothes, jewelry, more clothes. *Crap!*

Dropping to the ground, I pull out a random cardboard box just as Polo wiggles the doorknob.

"Come out of there, Martina," he shouts. "You're wasting time."

I throw the lid off the box, hoping this is exactly the kind of place Tommaso may have stashed a gun, but my chest falls when I see the contents. It's a set of new bathroom accessories—hooks, a small round mirror, and a long towel rack.

There's a loud thud and then a sharp squeal. Polo's moving the desk. I don't have time to look for anything else.

I grab the iron towel rack. It's heavy. I can swing it at him.

Getting into position at the side of the door, I wait while Polo continues trying to get inside. Let him exert himself.

It's the scariest few moments of my life.

My heart ricochets inside my chest as I count down the seconds. Sophia's not barking anymore, she's pressed up to my leg, hiding behind me. Tears spring to my eyes, but I wipe them off with my sleeve and keep my focus on the door.

Gio didn't teach me how to hurt people. He's only ever taught me how to defend myself.

But that's what I'm doing now, isn't it? I flick my gaze to the bodies on the bed and feel a sharp spike of anger.

How *dare* he?

I hold my breath as Polo finally starts squeezing through the crack in the door.

I lift the towel bar and swing.

The blow lands, but it doesn't have the effect I hoped it would. Instead of tumbling to the ground, he simply stumbles a few steps before whirling around and advancing on me. His eyes are so wide, I can see the entirety of his irises.

Blood drips down his forehead as he steps closer and closer. His mouth curves into a terrifying smile. "Got you," he whispers.

Then everything happens very quickly. There's a blur of fur, and a flash of sharp white teeth. Sophia bites into Polo's calf, and he lets out a bloodcurdling scream. He tries to kick her off, but I'm on him, pelting him with the towel bar. I don't stop until he falls to the ground.

"Sophia, let's go!"

I leap over Polo, tumble down the stairs, and sprint out of the house toward the yard. I manage to put some distance between us, and that's when I suddenly realize I have my phone in my back pocket. In my panic, I forgot it was there. *Stupid!* I take it out and dial Giorgio.

He picks up on the second ring. "What is it?"

The sound of his voice works an uncontrollable sob out of me. "Gio."

"*Piccolina*? What's going on?"

"Allegra and Tommaso are dead. Polo killed them. He managed to get in touch with Sal. He's going to bring me to him. He attacked me in the kitchen—"

"*Martina.*"

His sharp tone cuts through the blood rushing inside my ears. "Yes?"

"Are you hurt?"

My heart pounds. "I'm okay. A bit bruised."

"Where is Polo right now?"

"In the staff house. Sophia and I got away from him, but I don't know for how long."

"Mari, listen to me. You need to get off the property. Run to the garage and take one of my cars. The keys are hanging on the wall. Drive to the airfield where we landed, and I'll work on getting you out by plane."

"Okay, okay." I whip my gaze around. "Sophia!"

"Mari, you don't have time—"

"She saved my life. I'm not leaving her. If it wasn't for her, I wouldn't have been able to get away from Polo," I tell him as I run to the garage. My ears are peeled for sounds of footsteps, but there's nothing. I see the keys, grab the first ones I find, and press on the button.

A car beeps.

"That's the red Mercedes," Giorgio tells me. "Go, Mari."

My sneakers pound against the ground. I open the car, get Sophia into the back seat, and slide into the front. "Okay, I'm in."

"You're doing great," he says, not a hint of panic in his voice. "There's a remote clipped above you that will open the gate."

Pulling out of the garage, I scan the courtyard, but Polo is nowhere to be found. I jam my finger on the remote as I approach the gate, and it swings open at a glacial pace.

"Come on, come on, come on."

"What's happening?"

"The gate is slow."

"It'll be just a second. There's a camera right there. I can see you, Mari."

I take a deep breath. It's just a camera, but it gives me a bit of comfort knowing that he's watching over me.

Finally, the opening is big enough for the car to squeeze through, and I slam on the gas.

"Drive fast but be careful," he says. "Take a left when you reach the main road."

"Then what?"

"You'll see signs for the airfield. The exit is labeled clearly, you won't miss it."

I wish I'd seen it when we arrived here, but it was too dark. I keep my eyes peeled as I take the turn.

"I'm already in contact with your brother," Giorgio says. "The plane was in the air on its way to pick up De Rossi, but he's rerouted it to go to you instead. It will be landing at the airstrip in half an hour. It'll take you fifteen minutes to get there. Park as close as you can and *stay in the car*. If you see anyone approaching, you'll have to move."

"Okay, I got it." My clammy hands strangle the wheel as I race down the country road. The adrenaline pumping through me is like a mind-enhancing drug, and my vision tunnels on the strip of asphalt ahead. I've never driven as well or as fast as I am now. "I got it, Gio. I got it," I repeat as much to him as to myself.

"That's my girl. I'll stay on the line with you until you're on that plane, all right?"

Sophia whines from the seat behind me.

"Talk to me," I say.

"I don't want to distract you."

"Please. Hearing your voice helps. God, Gio, I can't believe he killed them."

"Are you certain Allegra and Tommaso are..."

I bite my lip to hold back a new slew of tears. Not now. I need to see the damn road. "Yes. He slit their throats."

"*Pezzo di merda.*"

"He told me he's your half-brother."

"Not anymore," Giorgio's voice is pure ice. "Soon, he'll be nothing but a pile of ash. That fucking boy killed two people who respected and loved him. And he did it all for a man who never will."

I pass a car. "Polo's mom asked you to take him in. She knew you were also Sal's son?"

Giorgio sucks in an audible breath. "Yes. Our mothers were friends. They lived in the same neighborhood in Naples. Sal would often come to the neighborhood to find his nightly entertainment. Usually, he stuck to hookers, but he didn't really care. If he saw something he wanted, he took it. To him, women were never more than objects to own and discard."

A tear escapes my eye. "Polo doesn't care that his father is a monster."

"He is his flesh and blood. That's always meant more to him than it ever did to me. I have another father, Mari, so I've seen just how useless they can be. After my childhood, I never craved that kind of figure in my life. But Polo's mom wasn't married when she became pregnant with him, and she stayed alone her entire life. Polo romanticized the notion of what a father is."

"He's fucked up. Tommaso and Allegra—" An ache moves down my throat. "I just left their bodies there."

"I'll take care of it. I'm already driving back."

"What?" I ask as I drive past a sign with an image of a plane on it. I must be getting close.

"I'll bury Tommaso and Allegra and then come straight to you and your brother."

I pull my lips into my mouth. The image of the two of them lying on their bed will forever be seared into my memory. I won't forget the kindness they showed me.

Kindness I repaid by bringing death to their doorstep.

"Two more lives lost on my account," I whisper as the realization cascades through me.

Oh God. I'm cursed. I must be.

"Stop it," Giorgio growls through the receiver. "If you want to place blame, place it on someone who deserves it—me. *Cazzo*, Mari. I should have known. There were signs, and I ignored them. I thought we were the same. Same history. Same original sin. Deep down, I was sure Polo would reject Sal the way I did, but it was wishful thinking. Turns out, we couldn't be more different."

I spot another sign for the airstrip, this one with an arrow. I take the next turn, and the airfield unfurls ahead of me. "I'm nearly there."

"Park behind the hangar so you can't be seen from the road," he instructs. "Do you see anyone following you?"

In the rearview mirror is an empty road. "No. There's no one."

"Did Polo say he told Sal you've been with me or give him any information about where you are?"

"I don't think he did. I think he wanted to be the hero and be the one who delivered me to the don."

"He wanted to get all the credit. We're lucky. It would be far worse if Sal's men were the ones looking for you. They would have been far more competent than Polo."

The hangar's bulky form grows closer and closer, and I veer off the paved road onto the grass behind it. After parking in the building's shadow, I turn off the ignition and reach behind to check on Sophia. She's lying curled up on the floor between the seats. What if she's hurt? I didn't have time to check her when we were running away.

"What's happening now?" Giorgio asks.

"I'm parked, but I need to take a look at Sophia. She may have gotten injured when Polo kicked at her." I run my hand over her fur.

"She bit him?"

"Yes. He tried to grab me, but I managed to fight him off. I used the moves you taught me."

"God, Mari. I'm so fucking proud of you."

"After I left the house, I hid in Tommaso and Allegra's bedroom, but Polo managed to break in. That's when Sophia and I took him down."

Warmth slips into his voice as he says, "That dog's going on a diet of prime meat for the rest of her life."

Sophia's back and belly seem fine, so I move onto checking her legs. When I touch one of the front ones, she jerks it back and whimpers.

"I think one of her legs is hurt," I tell Giorgio.

"I'll ask Damiano to have a vet ready for when you land. He's already called a doctor for you."

"I'm fine," I insist, giving Sophia a scratch behind her ear. She blinks at me with her big round eyes and then drops her head down to the ground. Her energy seems low, and worry swirls inside my gut.

"You're in shock. You might have injuries you're not even aware of," Giorgio says. "You need to see a doctor."

"I just want to see you. When will that be?" As the question leaves my mouth, I realize I don't even know where the plane will take me.

"Tonight. I promise."

A whirring sound reaches my ears, and I twist around, peering up at the sky through the windshield. "The plane's here!"

"Stay in the car until it comes to a stop. Can you see the number written on the side?"

"Yes."

"Read it to me."

I squint. "N707AM."

"That's it. Okay, put the phone in your pocket and get yourself and Sophia ready to run. Tell me when you get on."

Sophia barely perks up when I say her name, so I lift her out of the back seat and put her on my lap. "I'm going to have to carry you to the plane, girl," I whisper to her, praying I'll be able to make it all the way. She's far from tiny.

When the plane comes to a stop, I jump out of the car and book it. The pilot manages to get the stairs down just as I reach them, and he takes Sophia off my hands.

As soon as I'm inside the cabin, I pull my phone out of my pocket and press it to my ear. "I made it," I say breathlessly.

There's a long silence.

"Gio?"

"Thank *fucking* God." His voice shakes.

The raw anguish in those three words makes tears flood my eyes. Giorgio's been holding that back this entire time, staying calm so that I wouldn't freak out. "Mari, if anything happened to you, I would—" He makes a choked sound. "I'm so fucking glad you're all right."

The tears fall, dragging down my cheeks. "I got away. We did it."

"No, *you* did. Remember that."

I sniff and catch a glimpse of the pilot gesturing at me. "I have to go. We're about to take off."

"I—" He blows out a breath. "I'll see you soon."

After I hang up the phone, I finally break down and weep. Adrenaline seeps out of my body, and with it goes all of my energy. The past hour took everything out of me. God, what the hell just happened? I can't believe it. It feels like I watched a horror movie, like the events happened to someone other than me.

Sophia nudges her nose against my thigh, and I pet her while tears leak down my face and sobs ravage my chest.

The pilot tells me our destination over the PA system. We're going to be landing at an airstrip on the border of Campana and Lazio. It must be close to where my brother is staying at the moment. The prospect of seeing Dem so soon makes me cry even harder. He must be so worried about me.

My head pounds, and my entire body hurts, right down to my bones.

But I'm alive.

Hard to believe that only a few weeks ago, I wasn't sure if I even wanted to live. But that was before Giorgio.

He's changed everything, hasn't he?

The plane bursts through thick, white clouds, and through my tears, I see an endless blue sky.

CHAPTER 30

GIORGIO

By the time I reach the castello, hours have passed since Mari got on the plane, but my body is still threaded with electric anger, and my hands still shake when I recall the panic in her voice. Being inside this car is the closest I've ever come to knowing what a lion feels like caged.

I want to tear Polo apart with my own damn teeth for what he did.

The gate is open. It's the only obvious sign that something's wrong as I drive into the yard. The castello and the tower loom before me, their dramatic silhouette all the more ominous now that it's the scene of Polo's plot to betray me. I've always felt a hint of unease whenever I come back here, but it's different this time. There's something final about it.

After I'm done here today, I'm not sure I'll return.

Small rocks crunch beneath my leather shoes as I make my way to the staff house. I glance around, on high alert, but I don't expect Polo to be here. He would know to run far away after Martina got away. When I pass the garage, I look inside and see another car is missing—the black Ferrari he's always loved. Well, that's the confirmation that he's on his way to Sal to start his new life.

It'll be a short one.

The door to the staff house is cracked open, and when I step over the threshold, the air is still and quiet. A chair is knocked over near the center of the room. I swallow, imagining Mari knocking it over as she ran up the stairs looking for safety. She must have been terrified.

My *piccolina* is stronger than she'll ever know.

Inside the bedroom, I find Tommaso and Allegra.

The thought of Mari finding them like this makes me sick. The sight of their lifeless bodies crushes my chest, but I dig my nails into my palms and use the pain to dampen all other emotions. I don't have time to linger on this loss.

There's work to do.

Walking to the edge of the bed, I glance down at their blood-soaked bodies. On Allegra's chest lies the silver cross that Polo's always wore around his neck. He must have tossed it onto her body after he killed them. What for? Did he hope it would make God forgive him for his sins? He lived with the two of them for two fucking years. They were good people—kind, hard-working, modest. They didn't want anything other than to live a quiet life out here.

Something wet trails down my cheek. The moment I feel it, I look at the ceiling and suck in a harsh breath.

There's no forgiveness waiting for Polo at the end of this.

I pick up the cross and slide it in my pocket. Allegra's not getting buried with anything that belonged to that fucking snake.

The work that follows is difficult. I could have made it easier on myself by burying them by the castello, but I have it in my head that they should be laid to rest by my mother. So I get a wheelbarrow from the shed and move their bodies deep into the woods.

Then I begin to dig.

With each lift of the shovel, the reality of the situation sinks in deeper and deeper.

Polo was eight when my mother died. She knew about him, but she never told me. It wasn't until Polo's mother reached out to me that I found out I had a younger half-brother.

I remember when I first told Tommaso and Allegra about him.

They were happy to get a new face at the castello.

They got along with him.

And so did I. As soon as I met him, I projected myself onto him. I hadn't realized I was doing it, but I remember assuming he'd have the same need for vengeance against Sal as I did.

Then one night, he proved me wrong. It took us a while to even come to the topic, but eventually Polo's curiosity won out. He asked me if I knew our father personally, and when I said I did, his eyes lit up. He asked me lots of questions. I answered him honestly, explaining that our biological father was a despicable man.

I thought that was the end of it, but a few days later, he gave me a letter to send to Sal.

I said I would, but I never did.

And that lie was perhaps what started to shift the balance.

I'd forgotten that some young men long for a father. For them, knowing the substance of the man who brought them into this world is akin to a primal need. It overrides logic and reason.

I slam the shovel into the ground and squeeze my eyes shut.

How did I fuck up this badly with him?

How did I fail to recognize that his growing envy wouldn't just disappear one day?

How could I have been so careless and allowed this to happen?

Tommaso and Allegra were under my protection, and I failed them.

And Mari... At some point, my focus shifted from keeping her safe to keeping her in my bed.

I pop my eyes open and resume digging. As the pile of dirt grows with each lift of my shovel, so does my conviction.

Polo and Sal will die at my hands for what they did. I'll do whatever I have to in order to be the one to kill the don.

And Polo?

He'll watch me kill his precious fucking father, so that he knows exactly what's coming for him next.

~

I'm finished two hours and some minutes later. As I step onto the path that leads back to the house, I glance over my shoulder at the burning cottage.

The flames reach high up into the sky. Most of the stone foundation and walls will remain, but when the fire dies down, enough of this wretched place will be gone.

I always said this place was a reminder, but I don't need it anymore.

I know exactly what I have to do.

Polo's cross digs into my palm as I fist it inside my pocket.

When I get back to the car, I glance at the bag of diamond jewelry Sal had me retrieve and slam on the gas.

The bag slides on the seat and gets wedged between the cushions. I should probably be more careful with it, but I don't give a fuck. If there's one thing Damiano has, it's money. I'm half-tempted to toss it out the window.

After I got off the phone with Mari, I checked to make sure the diamonds were real, and they are. Clearly, Polo did a shit job coordinating his plan with the don. If Sal knew what Polo was planning to do today, there's no way he would have sent me on this retrieval. But now, the large amount of jewelry Sal wanted me to get makes more sense. Sal was trying to use me until he couldn't anymore. The pieces were in a vault only Sal and I can open, but he's not risking travel right now. So he sent me.

If Polo's expecting a warm welcome from his father, he's going to be disappointed. Not only is he going to show up empty-handed, he'll also be blamed for Sal losing the equivalent of ten million euros.

I scoff to myself. Polo was too eager to prove his worth, and instead, he showed everyone he's a fucking amateur.

Pathetic.

He must be panicking. He wanted to deliver Mari to Sal like an offering, and now all he has is the information she was with me and the location of an empty castle.

I drive to De Rossi's hideout in San Cesario like a madman, turning over my plans for Polo and Sal inside my head.

There's no time to play around anymore, which means the relationship between Mari and I has to come to an end. De Rossi can't suspect there was ever anything between us, because if he can't trust me with his sister, how the fuck is he ever going to trust me with a secret that could undermine his position as the new don? The fiasco with Polo is enough to put me on shaky ground as is, but I hope it's not enough for him to refuse to honor the favor he promised to me.

"Fuck." I blow out a breath and run my hand through my hair. Mari just survived an attack, and I'm about to push her away.

It'll devastate her.

But I'll be doing this for her too. She has to understand. She's a smart girl. Her and I were never meant to work outside the castello, because out here in the real world, I'm the last man her brother would pair her with.

No, I have nothing to offer her but vengeance.

The villa comes into view, its perimeter flanked by a tight ring of guards. I texted Ras a few minutes earlier to let him know I was almost there, and now De Rossi's right-hand man stands by the open gate, waving me forward.

I pull into the driveway, shut off the ignition, and climb out.

Ras walks over, and when he gets close enough, I throw the bag of jewelry at him. He catches it, weighs it in his hand, and smirks. "You come bearing gifts."

"Where is she?"

"Inside." He slaps me on the back. "You know, based on your reputation, I expected something better than this."

"Martina is alive, isn't she? I kept my end of the bargain."

He laughs. "Yeah, yeah. Well, I'm not sure if Damiano will see it that way, but you're welcome to make your case."

I clench my jaw. "How is she?"

Ras's smile melts, and his gaze turns contemplative. "She's shaken up, but she's fine. She got upset when Dem said you fucked up. You should have seen it. She shut him down real quick. Said she'd have never gotten away without you."

I don't like the knowing hint in his voice, so I shove past him and make my way inside the house.

As soon as I hear her, relief ripples through me. I halt in the foyer, just out of sight, and press my palm against the wall.

The desire to walk into the next room and take her into my arms is so strong it's nearly breaks me. I squeeze my eyes shut and just listen to her. She's talking about Sophia, telling De Rossi's wife about how the dog tackled her to the ground the first time they met. When she giggles, my chest constricts with longing. I want to record that sound and play it on repeat.

Get it together. You know what you have to do.

One breath in. One breath out.

Again and again.

When the reins of control are back in my hands, I run my palm over my mouth and step inside the room.

Martina doesn't see me right away. She's sitting beside Valentina on the sofa, De Rossi's standing near them, and they're absorbed in their conversation. He says something to her that makes her laugh.

I drink in her smile. I wonder if she'll ever smile at me like that again.

My expression fixed on neutral, I clear my throat.

Three pairs of eyes jump to me, but my gaze stays on her.

"Giorgio," she breathes.

My feet are glued to the ground. I should be happy she's not running to me. I don't know how I'd keep the emotion out of my face if she did. All I can think about is how fucking good it would feel to hold her again. To feel her soft, warm body molding to mine.

How long can I stay silent to prolong this moment?

The moment before I break her heart?

Cazzo. Not long enough.

"How are you feeling?" I let my voice cool, as if I'm speaking to a stranger. My hands are tight fists. If I let them relax just a bit, they'll shake. It's taking everything I have to put on this act.

Mari picks up on the change in me immediately, her brows furrowing at my tone. "I'm fine."

"Where's Sophia?"

She frowns. "She has a fracture in her paw. She's sleeping. The vet gave her a sedative."

"Good."

Her lips part, and her eyes are swimming with confusion.

I can't fucking take it. Breaking our eye contact, I turn to De Rossi. "We need to talk."

His jaw is hard. "I'm looking forward to hearing your explanation for how the fuck this happened. Come on."

We walk out of the room, and I resist the urge to look back at Mari, but I feel her gaze burning through my back.

CHAPTER 31

GIORGIO

De Rossi takes me to an office and shuts the door.

"Who the fuck is Polo?" De Rossi demands as soon as we sit down. "Martina wouldn't say anything until you got here."

I run my tongue over my teeth. *When in doubt, say less.*

"He's my half-brother."

De Rossi scowls. "And why would he want to betray you? Don't make me interrogate you, Napoletano. I want the full story. *Now.*"

I lean back against the chair and wrap my palms over the arm rests. "I'll tell you everything. I have no reason to hide this part of my history anymore. Polo and I have the same father."

"The submarine."

I give shake of my head. "Sal Gallo."

De Rossi's eyes widen, and a moment later, he's out of his seat and whipping out his gun. "You're Sal's kid?"

I stare down the barrel. "I am."

He disengages the safety. "You have thirty seconds to explain yourself before my bullet meets your skull."

There used to be a time when having a gun pointed at me would at least raise the hairs on the back of my neck, but that was a long time ago. I crack my neck. "Sal raped my mother. You're looking at the result."

De Rossi's forehead creases. "What the fuck."

"My mother kept me, and her husband—the man you know as my father—agreed to not make a fuss and claim me as his own in exchange for a promotion. That's how he became a submarine. That might have been the end of Sal's involvement in my life, but someone up there-" I point my finger to the ceiling, "-decided he wasn't done with me. Sal heard about a hacker working for the Secondigliano Alliance and discovered it was me—his kid."

Comprehension slowly crisscrosses over his face. "That's why they traded you to the Casalesi."

I nod. "Blood ties run deep in the *sistema*. Even though I'd never met Sal until then, he was my father, so in some way, I belonged to him."

De Rossi cocks his head. "Do you?"

"I've spent my entire life thinking about how I'm going to kill him."

He huffs out a sardonic breath and lowers the gun. "You should have done less thinking and more doing. And Polo?"

"Another bastard. He's never met Sal, but he's built him up in his head. He wants to join the clan and get a taste of the life of a made man. He betrayed me. He'll die for it." That cross in my pocket? I'm going to shove it down Polo's throat as he dies.

De Rossi takes a seat again and asks, "Why the fuck didn't you tell me this earlier?"

"You never would've trusted me if you knew."

"And I'm supposed to trust you now?"

"I did everything you asked of me."

"You allowed your half-brother to assault my sister. She barely got away," he snaps.

Yeah, I fucked up, but I can't admit it. I need to bluff so that he gives me what I want. "I helped Martina. Your sister was a shell of a person when I picked her up, but I snapped her out of it. She used the skills I taught her to defend herself against Polo. She's a brave woman. It was Polo this time, but it could have been anyone. At least now she's not a sitting duck. She needed someone to look out for her, and that's exactly what I did. Don't tell me you haven't noticed the difference already."

His chest rises and falls as he scowls at me, but when he doesn't answer right away, I know my point landed.

"She does seem better," he finally admits. "But I'm not happy, Napoletano. I want you here until this over. Sal knows you're on my side now, so there's no point in sending you away. This needs to end soon."

I meet his gaze. "First, I'd like to collect my favor."

"You don't waste any time."

"I want to be the one to kill Sal."

There's a long, drawn-out silence, and then he laughs, but it's humorless. "You either have a fucked-up sense of humor, or you're not as smart as everyone says you are. If you wanted to challenge me, the smart time to do it would've been when you still had my sister."

"I don't want to be don. I only want to be the one who ends him."

De Rossi shakes his head. "You know that's not how it works. I have to be the one who does it for my claim to be uncontested. We don't have time for a protracted struggle for the throne."

"We put you, me, and Sal in one room and lock the door. When the door opens, he's dead, and we tell everyone you killed him. No one will question it."

He scoffs. "You make it sound so easy. You've got it all figured out, huh? But it seems you've forgotten that Sal isn't just anyone to me either." His eyes darken. "He killed my father. Exiled me from my home. Repeatedly put Mari in danger. It's personal for me too, and there's no way in hell I'm going to give up the pleasure of choking that fat throat."

I realize then that he won't do it. "I thought you were a man of your word."

"You know what you're asking for is beyond unreasonable. If you wanted to kill him so badly, you should have done it by now. Why didn't you?"

"Like I said, I have no interest in running the clan."

361

"You could have killed him and left the clan behind. Let someone else deal with the consequences."

"I'm not the kind of man who makes a mess and expects someone to clean it for him. Enough people have already died because of Sal. If I'd killed him and left behind a power vacuum, a war far bloodier than the one you caused would break out."

De Rossi scoffs. "When did you become such a fucking humanitarian? Don't tell me you give a shit about the men we do business with."

"I don't. But I give a shit about people like Martina—innocent people who were born into this life. I don't want those deaths on my conscience, De Rossi. I waited for an opportunity that would allow me to do this cleanly, and reasonable or not, I'm getting what I want."

He looks at me like I've lost it. "I already said—"

I would push him harder on keeping his word, but it won't be enough. I need to add more to the bargain. "What's your plan? Have you gathered the support you need?"

He considers me with narrowed eyes and then stands up and walks over to a pour us some whiskey. "Not yet."

"I know now why Moretti and De Rosa backed out of the meetings. Sal told them he had a lead on Martina. This must have happened after Polo got in touch with him."

"Yeah, well, he's definitely not getting her now. But our progress has slowed, no matter how we try to push it along. There's hesitation."

I take a glass from him and take a sip. "You need me, De Rossi. Things aren't going the way you thought they would.

Sal's managing to hang onto his support because you haven't been a presence in Casal for many years. Sal's got a lot of flaws, but at least everyone knows what those flaws are. You, on the other hand, are a mystery. No one likes the unknown."

"That's why I'm negotiating with all of these people in person," he argues.

"Yes, but building a relationship takes time, and you're running out of it. You can't afford to play the diplomat any longer. This situation calls for a dictator."

He sits down across from me and scratches his chin, appearing to think it over. "Bend the knee or else... I didn't want to involve mercenaries in internal clan business, but I don't have enough firepower without them to make do on that kind of threat."

"You don't need to threaten their lives, just their money."

His eyes flash with intrigue. "What are you proposing?"

Something I told myself I'd never do.

I can reveal to him all of the secret stashes I've put in place for the families.

If I do this, my reputation is done.

No one will ever trust me again, but... Fuck. It's worth it. If I was willing to give Mari away for this, what's another sacrifice?

"Most of the families keep a large portion of their personal cash and valuables in secured storage facilities I designed. I know where they're located, and I've built backdoors into the security systems."

The slackening in De Rossi's expression tells me he understands the implications of this. "So you have access to the clan's riches," De Rossi mutters.

"Not everything, but a lot of it. Say the word, and I can lock it all down. There'll be panic, and it will be enough to turn the tide in your favor."

He sinks backward into his chair. "And all you want in exchange is…"

"To be the one to kill Sal."

He swirls his whiskey inside his glass, and then looks up and meets my eyes.

"Deal."

CHAPTER 32

MARTINA

VALE COMES out of the kitchen with two steaming cups of tea and hands me one. "You look pale, Mari. Are you sure you don't want to lie down? It might be the pain meds kicking in."

I bite down on my tongue. No, I don't want to lie down. I didn't even want the pain meds, but my sister-in-law insisted on me taking them after she saw me wince when she touched my wrist. Polo left a few bruises, but they're nothing that won't fade in a few days.

What I really want to do is storm into my brother's office and demand an explanation from Giorgio.

Yes, I expected him to act differently when he arrived, but I wasn't prepared for that perfect mask of indifference. Last night, Giorgio spent at least two hours with his mouth between my legs, and ten minutes ago, he looked at me like he didn't even *know* me.

Is this how it's going to be while he's here?

365

I nearly died, but clearly, his concern extends only so far. If the roles were reversed, I wouldn't care about anything other than being there for him. But he seems to care far more about what my brother thinks than giving me the support that I need.

Maybe it's the pain meds or the fact that I've had far too much adrenaline in my system in the past few hours, but the thought sets alight a blaze of fury inside my belly.

"I'm fine," I say, holding the tea tightly in my palms even though the cup is too hot. "I'll go to sleep soon."

Vale brushes a lock of hair out of my face, her gaze soft but concerned. "Now that Giorgio's talking to Dem, want to tell me what really happened? You've been scarce on the details."

Yeah, because I was trying to be loyal to Giorgio. I'm not sure how much my brother knows about Giorgio's family history, and I didn't want to be the one spilling his secrets.

Now, that loyalty leaves a sour taste inside my mouth.

Vale's gaze drops a few inches lower, and I become aware of the pendant Giorgio gave me—the one still hanging around my neck. My anger morphs into a prickling sense of doubt.

He never wanted Dem to find out, but *why*? What does he think my brother would do? Threaten to kill him for deflowering his sister? That's absurd. If I tell Dem I like Giorgio and want to keep seeing him, he wouldn't stop me. I'm sure of it.

So what if this was just a convenient excuse? What if Giorgio never saw me as anything but a temporary fling, and this is the end that he envisioned for us?

Was our connection really so one-sided?

"Mari?"

I glance at Vale, meeting her expectant gaze. "I'm sorry. What?"

"Are you going to tell me what happened?"

I open my mouth, but I can't get the words out. I know I don't owe Giorgio loyalty after he just completely blew me off, but something about spilling his business just feels wrong.

"I'm tired," I say by way of an excuse. "Dem can catch you up on the details when they're done in there."

She sighs and leans back into the couch before taking a sip of her tea. Her eyes volley to the clock before swinging back to me. "Who knows when that may be. It's nearly ten already. Good thing we ate before Giorgio arrived."

My shoulders relax. I know Vale must be dying from curiosity, so I appreciate her not pressing me any harder. "Do you think he'll stay here?"

She scrunches her nose. "Unless it's in a body bag, I don't see him leaving."

"*What?*"

Her eyes flash with amusement. "It's a joke. Trust me, if they were going to kill each other, they would have done it by now."

"I told Damiano that what happened with Polo wasn't Giorgio's fault."

367

"And I'm sure your words will count for something, but at the end of the day, the only one who can make that judgment is your brother," she says, her tone growing soft. "Don't worry, Mari. Everything will work out."

I peer down at my tea. "It's always going to be me, isn't it? I'm the weakest link in the De Rossi empire. Will there ever be a day when someone isn't trying to capture me or kill me?"

Vale makes a tight line with her lips, like she knows the answer won't please me.

I chuckle. "I need something stronger than this."

Taking the nearly finished tea out of my hands, she rises and makes her way to the bar in the corner of the room. She comes back a few moments later with two glasses of red wine. "Look, Mari, I respect you too much to treat you with kid gloves."

A jolt of surprise runs through me at her blunt tone.

Vale hands me one glass and keeps the second for herself. "Yes, you've been a target, and I'd be a liar if I said that's going to change when your brother becomes don of the Casalesi, but you're not the weakest link. Far from it. I grew up in this world, and I know from watching my own father rule his empire that a don's strength lies in the people he can trust unconditionally. Dem's circle is small, and he'll have to grow it if he wants his rule to last. You are an important part of that circle, and even though Dem still treats you like his little sister, I know he's starting to understand that you're no longer a child. You're smart, resilient, and brave."

When I knit my brows, she shakes her head.

"Don't even try to argue. Look around, Mari." She tips her head to the side. "You're in this room because you managed to fight off the man who attacked you. All. On. Your. Own. That fact won't be lost on your brother."

In the chaos of the day, I haven't really paused to process what had happened.

She's right. I stood up for myself, didn't I? Yes, I was terrified, but that didn't stop me from doing *something* this time around. The lessons Giorgio taught me paid off.

"As the don's sister, you'll have a lot of influence," she continues. "People will vie to be in your good graces. If you want to be a key asset in the organization, it's yours for the taking, but to start on that journey, you will need to stop thinking of yourself as the weakest link."

I chew on my lip. Is that what I want for myself? For a long time, I thought I wanted to escape this world.

What Vale is proposing would be doing the opposite.

I wanted to leave, didn't I? Go somewhere far away and throw myself into cooking? Do I still want that?

I'm not sure anymore.

Before what happened in New York, my life had been completely different. *I* had been completely different. When I remember that girl, I can hardly recognize her anymore. Maybe instead of anchoring myself to the past, I need to start thinking more about the future.

I finish off the wine with two large gulps and place the empty glass down on the coffee table. "You've given me a lot to think about."

Vale smiles. "I know. Take your time."

Yawning, I rub the heels of my palms over my eyes. "I think I better get some sleep. Can you show me to my room? I think I'll get lost if I try to find it on my own."

She leads me upstairs and points to a door. "It's this one. Sophia's still resting. We made her a makeshift bed with some pillows and blankets, but I'll get one of the guys to buy her a proper one tomorrow."

"Thanks," I say, leaning my head on her shoulder. "I know the circumstances are not ideal, but I'm happy to be back with you two."

She wraps an arm around my shoulders and gives me a squeeze. "Me too."

I'm halfway through the door when she says my name.

"Yeah?" I ask, glancing at her over my shoulder.

"I've put Giorgio in the bedroom down the hall. Dem and I are downstairs in case you wake up and need anything."

Our eyes lock, mine wide, hers glinting knowingly.

Heat blooms over my cheeks. "Okay, thanks."

I slip into the bedroom and press my back against the door. I can't shake off the feeling that she told me exactly where Giorgio will be on purpose, but how would she know? Either she has the world's best intuition, or my feelings are way too obvious.

Probably a bit of both.

I sit down on the floor beside Sophia and pet her bristly fur while she takes a well-deserved nap. This dog is a freaking hero.

My throat tightens. Her master might be gone, but I'm going to take good care of her while she's here. Tommaso would have been so proud of her for having my back.

I sniff and press the heels of my palms against my eyes.

Another cruel fluke of fate.

In the bathroom, I wash up, brush my teeth, and slip on my pajamas, but I know I won't be able to sleep. When the house quiets, I'm going to sneak out and talk to Giorgio, because I need to know what the hell is going on.

Maybe when it's just the two of us, everything will go back to the way it was. He owes me a damn apology for how he behaved earlier, but after everything that happened, I just crave to be in his arms again. I want the heat of his body and the comfort of his scent, and most of all, I want the peace I feel whenever I'm with him.

While I wait, I reach for my phone and pull up Imogen. My last message to her stares up at me. It's the one from the night of my birthday, when all I could think about was how badly I wanted Giorgio to kiss me. After he did, everything was different. I had him to talk to then, but I'm alone again now.

Im, I miss you. I hope you're having a good time wherever you are. Can you see the mess happening back here on Earth? It isn't pretty.

I slept with Giorgio. Did a lot more than that actually... I might have fallen in love with him, but I can't be sure because I've never done that before. You fell in love with someone once. Antonio, from math class. I remember how your eyes shone and you couldn't stop smiling when you told me about him. I wonder if I'd look like that if I got the chance to tell you about Giorgio.

I send off the message and start typing the next one.

Love or not, I'm scared he doesn't feel the same. He doesn't want Dem to know about us, so he's acting like I don't exist, even though I need him now more than ever. I'm angry, and yet I miss him more than anything. How strange is that? I've never felt these simultaneous extremes before I met him.

I know I can't make him love me if he doesn't, but at the very least, I want him to understand how horrible he made me feel. You'd probably tell me I'm crazy for chasing after a guy who doesn't want me with all of his heart, but I just can't leave it like this. I need to talk to him.

I read over the messages, then place my phone back on the nightstand and wait.

It's...not the same.

The usual sense of relief I've come to associate with sending these texts doesn't come. Anxiety simmers beneath my skin, insistent and uncomfortable.

Go find him.

Growling in frustration, I throw off the blanket and climb out of bed.

On the other side of the door to my room, the house appears to be quiet. I press my ear against its smooth surface just to be sure. When I don't hear anything, I slip outside.

The lights are off except for a small courtesy light near the landing and another one in the living room below. It's possible Dem's still working in his office, but he might be there for hours, and I'm not waiting that long.

The soles of my feet press gently against the floor as I make my way to the bedroom Vale pointed out. When I get there, a rapid clicking sound filters through the door.

Giorgio's working on his laptop.

Anger narrows my vision. I'm spending my evening thinking about him, and he's *working*?

Without bothering to knock, I step inside and pin my gaze on to the man himself.

Giorgio's at a desk, a glass of liquor by his laptop. He looks up, and when he realizes it's me, his azure eyes darken to a midnight blue. A weariness flickers through them, as if he knew I might show up but was hoping I wouldn't.

Too bad.

I lock the door behind me and try my best to dull the ache growing inside my chest. "We need to talk."

CHAPTER 33

MARTINA

His gaze slides down my body. Closing his laptop, he sinks deeper into his chair and takes a generous swig from the glass. "You shouldn't have come," he says, his voice a rasp.

"You're a fucking asshole."

He doesn't even try to defend himself. He just stares at me with a foreign expression, his lips drawn into a line, and his eyes dimmed.

"What the hell was that, Giorgio?" I demand, growing more and more irritated by his silence with each passing second. "I thought you sounded worried about me on the phone, but clearly, I must have been confused, what with being on the run for my life and all that. I can see now you don't give a damn."

His nostrils flare with an exhale. "You're angry right now, but don't you dare imply for one fucking second that I don't care about you. The first real breath I took since you called me was after I saw you sitting in that living room, alive and unhurt."

"Huh. So you decided to hurt me yourself, is that right? Did you look at me and think, 'she can take it'?"

He takes another sip of his drink. Another deep breath. "There was no other option. In a perfect world, we could say our goodbyes in private, but that's not the world we live in. What did you want me to do? Kiss you in front of your brother? Take you into my arms? You know I can't do that, Mari. There was no other choice."

I give my head an indignant shake. "Why are you so afraid of my brother finding out about us anyway? I know that when he asked you to take me, he probably didn't envision us sleeping with each other, but so what? Life happens. Shit happens. You didn't force me into anything. I wanted to be with you."

He huffs a laugh. "That is not how he'll see it."

I clench my fists. "You assume my brother thinks I can't make my own decisions."

His eyes narrow with frustration. "You're nineteen, Martina. I'm thirty-three and—"

"Who cares! We're the Casalesi, Giorgio! Look at any clan marriage in the past five decades, and you'd be hard pressed to find one where the age difference isn't that or worse."

"And what do you think your future husband will say when he finds out you're not a virgin?"

My jaw drops. "Nothing. The man I marry better not give a crap about things like that."

"Every time you open your mouth, you expose your naiveté." He tosses back the rest of his glass and stands.

"What naiveté?"

"Tell your brother you're not a virgin and see how he reacts."

"My brother isn't like that. He doesn't respect the old way of doing things, because he knows the old ways are broken."

For some reason, this makes him snarl. "You're blind, Martina, and you're in for a rude awakening." His eyes flick from my face down to my bare legs, and he grimaces like he knows it's the last thing he should be looking at. "De Rossi can't afford to disrespect the Casalesi traditions, his personal opinions notwithstanding. Do you even know what those traditions are? Or have you lived in total ignorance your whole life?"

When I don't answer right away, he scoffs.

"Let me enlighten you. The big families marry their sons and daughters into the other big families. The only exceptions that are accepted are those that cement powerful alliances outside the clan. De Rossi's wife happens to be one of those."

"I can guarantee you Dem wasn't thinking about that when he married Vale."

"Maybe not, but it sure as hell was a fortuitous coincidence."

"And what of your blood? You're the don's son."

His eyes narrow. "I will never claim him as my father. No, I'll die a Girardi, not a Gallo."

"Even if that last name is all you'd need to have me."

"Fuck. You still don't get it. It's not just the name, it's *everything*. Your brother would never give you to me. He'd get nothing in the deal. You are his only kin. Marrying you is the only way someone could become part of his family. Do you know how valuable you are to him?"

"Dem would never force me into a marriage I don't want."

"De Rossi will do whatever he needs to do to secure his power." He rakes his fingers through his hair. "Enough. This has gotten out of hand. We both knew this thing between us only existed inside the walls of the castello. No amount of arguing will change that."

"You act like I'm the only one who wanted this," I snap. "But it was *you* who stole my book. It was *you* who kissed me. It was *you* who kept me in your bed for days and told me how I'm perfect, and tempting, and fucking everything!"

He shoots out of his chair. "Of course, I wanted it. I don't regret a moment of what happened between us, but now that we're with your brother, it's done."

"You're scared. You're scared to admit to Dem how you really feel about me."

He advances on me, stopping only when our faces are mere inches apart. "I'm not the kind of man your brother would ever pair you with. De Rossi is giving me something I've wanted for more than half of my life. I won't do anything to jeopardize that."

A crack appears in my heart. "What is it that you want?" Clearly, it's not me.

"Sal."

My brows knit together. "Dem will kill Sal whether you want him to or not. He has to in order to become the don."

"I've asked your brother to let me be the one to do it."

My eyes widen. "But your precious tradition says the man who kills the sitting don becomes the next don."

"It will be done in secret. As far as everyone is concerned, it will be De Rossi who did it. Do you get it now? I've managed to secure your brother's trust. I'm not going to do anything to compromise that."

When the dots connect, air empties out of my lungs.

Giorgio's choosing revenge over me. Revenge for the woman who gave him life only to take parts of it away.

Revenge for a ghost.

His chest rises with heavy breaths. "I burned it, Mari. The cottage. After I buried Tommaso and Allegra, I burned it down. There's only one more thing left for me to do, and I'll be free. I'm doing this for my mother. And for you."

I swallow down a sob and meet his eyes. "You're *not* doing this for me. I don't fucking want your vengeance. And you're already free. You're just choosing not to see it."

His expression wavers. "Mari..."

I whirl around and walk out of that damned room.

When I wake up the following morning, getting out of bed feels like the hardest thing in the entire world, so I don't. I tell Vale I'm going to skip breakfast when she comes to collect Sophia for her walk, and then I fall back asleep.

It's my bladder that finally forces me to consider leaving my warm cocoon. My head slides out from under the duvet, and not a moment later, a wet tongue meets my cheek.

"Someone feels better," I say, giving Sophia a rub. She laps at my face, and I laugh. "Your breath smells, girl. I've got to get you some doggy toothpaste."

She cocks her head to the side, probably wondering what an earth I'm blabbering about.

The conversation with Giorgio last night scratches at the edges of my consciousness, but I don't want to think about it. What's the point? He's made himself clear.

I trudge to the bathroom. In the mirror, I examine my bruises. There are a few peppered over my legs and torso, but they're not painful unless I press on them. I wash my hair, blow-dry it, put some light makeup on, and venture downstairs.

I find Vale and Dem in the kitchen. They're standing by the island, but they're so absorbed with each other they don't hear me come in. My brother is holding his new wife in his arms, gazing lovingly at her face as she whispers something to him. He plants a soft kiss on her lips and smiles.

The sight of the two of them makes my chest warm, even if I feel like I'm intruding on a private moment. Was my brother this happy when we were all in Ibiza? Probably. I was just too out of it to notice. Even their wedding is a blur. A bitter kind of longing slips under my skin. It hurts to be alone after knowing what it's like to share yourself with someone.

Vale senses my presence and turns toward me. Her eyes

widen, and she lets out an awkward laugh and slips out of my brother's arms. "You're up!"

I grin at them. "Sorry for interrupting."

Vale gives me a quick hug. "Don't be ridiculous. We were just talking about how we were going to drag you down to hang out with us if you didn't come out soon."

Dem leans against the island, plucks a green apple from a big fruit bowl, and takes a crunchy bite. "Where is that pup of yours?"

"Resting in the bedroom. Also, she's Giorgio's, not mine."

Dem cracks a smile. "I think she likes you better."

I am a bit surprised Sophia hasn't tried to go to Giorgio, but maybe she senses I need her more than he does right now.

"So what's the plan for today?"

Finishing his apple, Dem tosses the core into the garbage and wipes his hands on a towel. "Actually, there's something I wanted to talk to you about, Mari."

Valentina's expression falls. "Give her time to settle in."

Their eyes lock, and they stare at each other for a beat, engaged in silent conversation.

A sense of foreboding spreads through my lungs.

"Better sooner than later," Dem says finally.

"What is it?" I ask, volleying my gaze between the two of them.

Dem places his palm on my back. "C'mon. We'll talk in my office."

Once we make it inside, I perch myself on the arm of a chair in front of his desk while he sits down across from me.

He doesn't appear to be in any rush to say what he's about to say, and his hesitation makes me nervous. My brother's a straight shooter, always has been.

He scratches his cheek. Bites on the corner of his lip.

"Dem, you're freaking me out," I confess. "Just say it."

He drops his palms on the desk and meets my gaze. "Do you recall meeting the Grassis?"

"Who?"

"They're a family in the clan. You met them when you were... Well, about five or so."

"Yeah, my memory isn't *that* good."

He releases a tense chuckle. "Right. Well, I probably could have done a better job keeping you up to date on the big players in the clan, but it didn't seem all that relevant while we were in Ibiza. The Grassis have grown into one of the most powerful Casalesi families over the last decade. Their cement business is booming due to the connections they've been able to establish with the local government, and they also control some of the most profitable factories in the area. They make perfect replicas of merchandise from some of the top fashion houses. Their exports to America have made them a fortune that almost rivals our own."

I listen attentively, knowing this is more than just a history lesson.

My brother picks up a pen and spins it between his fingers. "Most of the businesses are run by the patriarch, Emilio

Grassi, but he's started to slowly hand off various subdivisions to his eldest son, Matteo. I've met with the two of them a number of times over the past few weeks, and we see eye to eye. They're ready to support me if I can provide them with some kind of guarantee they will have an important place in the organization when I take over."

"Your word's not good enough?"

"As Giorgio recently pointed out, I appear to have a reputation problem," he says dryly. "I'm a man of my word, but they don't know me well enough to know that."

"So what are you going to offer them?"

He twirls the pen again. "They made a suggestion I want to run by you."

I snort. "I'm hardly qualified to advise you on these kinds of things. Vale would be far better at it."

"Oh, Vale's given me her opinion. I'm going against it by talking to you right now."

The notch between my brows deepens. "Okay... Well, what is it, Dem?"

"They suggested a marriage. Between you and Matteo."

My stomach hollows out.

Giorgio knew.

Last night, when I was telling him Dem would never force me into a marriage, he knew that's exactly what my brother was about to do.

"I don't have a choice, do I?" I breathe deeply as the room spins around me. "It's settled already."

His forehead creases. "What? No, of course not. I told him I'd consider his offer, but that the choice will be yours."

The spinning slows. "Is that true?"

"I wouldn't lie to you about this, Mari," he says, his voice softening. "You know that you and Vale are the most important things in my life, right?"

I swallow. "Yeah."

"If this path meant sacrificing your happiness, I wouldn't do it," he says, his voice ringing with conviction. "But I truly think our lives will be better once I'm in power. You will be safer. We won't be tormented by Sal anymore. We can live in Casal, our hometown, where our family has a deep and meaningful history. I'm doing this for the future of our family—one that I hope to grow with Vale one day. I don't want our kids to grow up with the constant threat that you and I had looming over us."

The thought of my future nieces and nephews getting kidnapped or seeing their friends get killed makes a heavy weight appear in my stomach. "I don't want that either."

Dem sighs. "I want to rule this clan because I believe I can lead it to greatness. This organization is already strong, but I can make it even stronger. Our father had a vision for the clan that he shared with me. He told me the Casalesi could be the fabric Italy is built on. We can thread through every organization of consequence in the country, from the lower-level federal agencies to the rooms that house members of our parliament. We can be ubiquitous. Our power unfettered. We can rule from the shadows, but we will be so rich and happy that we will have no desire to stand in the light. I want to honor him by bringing his vision to life."

His words move me. I don't have any memories of our parents. They died when I was too young. But Dem's told me stories, and when he speaks about them, it's obvious he loved and respected them very much.

"I know this marriage proposal is a lot to take in. This kind of an arrangement is common in the clan, but we've rarely talked about it," he says.

"All this time, we lived in a different world, didn't we?"

"In many ways, we did." He runs his fingers through his hair. "I despised the isolation, but there were benefits to it as well. You were able to live a relatively normal life on Ibiza. And now that's over." He gives a shake of his head.

The hint of regret in his voice makes me sit up straighter. I shouldn't have listened to Giorgio's cynical words. I know my brother better than he does.

Dem's always put me first.

He's leaving this choice to me.

"If you're feeling guilty, don't," I say. "You stayed on the sidelines for years to keep me safe. You've done everything for me, Dem. Now, I want to see you become don."

I mean it with all my heart. My brother deserves to win this war, and if there's anything I can do to help him, I have to consider it.

Smoothing my palms over my jeans, I meet his gaze. "Tell me a bit more about Matteo."

Dem clenches his jaw and then pulls open a drawer and takes a folio out of it. He hands it to me. "Here's his file."

I open it, and the first thing I see is Matteo's photo. He's younger than Giorgio, looks like he might be in his mid-twenties. Handsome in a forgettable kind of way. There's nothing about his face that stands out. Nothing that makes anything inside of me stir.

There isn't even a hint of what I feel when I look at Giorgio.

God, why am I thinking about him?

Giorgio knew about this. He knew my brother had a marriage proposal for me, and he made peace with it by all accounts.

He chose revenge over me.

Now, I need to make my own peace with everything too. There may never be another man who makes me feel like Giorgio does. What we had was special—a lightning strike to the heart. But I can't expect lightning to strike twice.

The backs of my eyes prickle as I turn to the next page—Matteo's biography. I scan it, forgetting what I read as soon as I get to the next word. It doesn't matter what's written there.

"What do you think of him?" I ask my brother.

"By all accounts, he seems like a fair and reasonable man. I had Ras talk to just about everyone who's ever dealt with him, and no one raised any red flags. There's nothing in his past that suggests he would mistreat you. And if he ever did, I would cut off his balls and stuff them down his throat."

I snap my gaze off the page. "Jesus."

Dem shrugs. "It's the truth. And you don't need to decide right away. I know it's a lot to think about."

Vale's words from yesterday come back to me. I could have a role to play in my brother's empire if I'm brave enough to take it.

Is that what I want?

My brother isn't a businessman, no matter how well he plays that role.

Dem is a criminal. And so was my father. And my mother. My grandparents. Most of my extended family as far back as anyone can remember.

On Ibiza, I thought I could be something else, but doing that would mean leaving Dem behind.

I don't want to leave my brother. Whoever he is, he's my only family, and I love him.

And if Dem's taught me anything, it's that love is sacrifice. He's made many sacrifices for me without a single complaint. Without ever making me feel like a burden.

It's my turn to do the same now.

I close the folder and put it down on his desk. Our eyes meet.

"I'll marry Matteo."

CHAPTER 34

MARTINA

I LEAVE my brother's office in a trance.

Dem told me he'll give it a few days before he tells the Grassis. I could tell my quick response caught him off guard. He's afraid I'll change my mind, but I know I won't.

It's done.

I'm about to be engaged.

In the kitchen, I chug a glass of cold water, then follow it with another. The cook is making dinner, and she shoots me a worried look. "Are you all right, signorina?"

"No."

She hands me a cannoli from a tray on the counter. "Here, you look pale."

"I don't think sugar's going to be enough."

She nods knowingly and splashes some vermouth into a thin glass. "Some *aperitivo* before dinner," she says as she passes it to me. "Signora De Rossi told me to have everything ready in fifteen minutes."

I thank her and head outside to the interior courtyard. There's a table with two chairs, and I take one of them as I sip my drink and nibble on the cannoli.

A fountain trills nearby, and the din of cicadas streams in from a nearby grove. It's far hotter in this region than back at the castello, and I wish I'd worn a lighter shirt. Closing my eyes, I meditate on the sounds, allowing them to pull me into the present moment. I don't want to think.

The door behind me opens. I recognize him from the sound of his footsteps, slow and steady and sure. He pulls a chair out and sits beside me, propping his forearm on the table, his fingers inches from my own. "How are you feeling?"

"You don't need to pretend to care."

"I do care, Mari."

I shake my head, refusing to look at him. "Enough. Like you said, it's over."

There's a pause. "You've come to terms with it then."

"Did you think I'd cry over you for days?" I flick my gaze to him. "I'll save my tears for far more worthy causes."

He recoils slightly, pain crisscrossing his face, but I don't care. I finish my vermouth and get up. "Dinner is about to start."

I hear him follow behind me, my awareness of his body still tuned to high.

I hope it won't last.

We sit down across the table from each other just as Ras, Vale, and Dem enter the room.

I reach for the bottle of wine and pour myself a big glass while everyone settles in. Is Giorgio going to join us for dinner every night from now on? God help me. I meant what I said. I'm done crying over him, but that doesn't mean it's easy being around him all the time like nothing's happened.

The food is served. Once the staff leave the room, Dem stands and picks up his glass, meaning to give a toast. "I have an important announcement to make." His gaze lands on me. "But first, I want to say how happy I am to have my sister back with us."

I smile.

"The last few months have been difficult for you," he continues. "You've lost someone important to you—Imogen. It was a senseless death. I have to admit that I spent many sleepless nights thinking about what I would do if you never returned to me. It is a hard thing to imagine. It's also the reason why I asked Napoletano to take you with him. I thought it was the best way to keep you safe, given his unique skillset." He turns to face Giorgio, who's looking at him with an unreadable expression. "It's a good thing you had the foresight to prepare Mari for the worst-case scenario, and of course, she was smart to listen to you. I want to thank you for ensuring that Mari got back to us in one piece."

We raise our glasses and take a sip. Vale shoots me a careful smile before turning back to Dem. My brother's clearly not done with his speech.

He swirls his glass, his expression pensive. "Mari, I can see that the time you've spent with Napoletano has had a positive effect on you."

Giorgio shoots me a look, and heat rises up my cheeks. If only Dem knew exactly how we spent some of that time.

"You'll always be my little sister," Dem says, his eyes warm, "but I have to come to terms that you're an adult now. Your decision earlier today confirmed that."

My eyes widen. Is he going to tell them now?

"Martina has agreed to marry Matteo Grassi."

The announcement is met with a momentary stunned silence before something shatters.

"I'm so sorry," Vale stammers, sliding out of her seat to pick up pieces of her glass. "I just...wasn't expecting that."

Dem rushes to her side. "Let me help you."

Across the table, Ras shoots me a grin, but Giorgio is frozen. Jaw clenched, he incinerates me with a glare so hot and furious it could rival hellfire.

As it burns all over my skin, I begin to doubt exactly what he knew about the proposed arrangement. Did he think I'd refuse? On his account?

I purse my lips and narrow my eyes. *Screw you.*

The thought travels. Something dangerous flashes across his expression, sending dread into the pit of my belly. While the cook comes out of the kitchen with a rag to help Vale mop up the wine, we stare each other down.

I want to scream at him. *Say something if you care so much.* But I don't, and then everyone is sitting back down.

"Last time I saw Matteo, he took me to his nona's bakery," Ras says. "The guy's a bit stiff, but that old lady was a riot. They're not a bad family to join, Mari."

"Thanks, Ras."

Vale reaches over and clasps my wrist. "Congratulations," she says, but her voice is laced with uncertainty. "When do you get to meet the groom?"

"I'm not sure." I look to Dem for help.

"I'll share the good news with Matteo's father during our next meeting in two days," he says, picking up his cutlery. "We'll arrange for you two to meet shortly after."

Now that Vale and Ras have congratulated me, the table's attention moves to Giorgio. He smooths his palm over his tie. Adjusts his cuff links. Finally, he says, "I would vet that boy carefully before you agree to their offer." His voice is as dry as bone.

"Ras already did," Dem says. "I'm confident he'll make a good match for Martina."

"I have access to sources you two don't. It would be a mistake to go through with this before I can talk to them."

Tension wraps around the table.

"Are you implying I did a sloppy job vetting the guy who wants to marry my sister?" Dem says sharply.

Giorgio shrugs, once again appearing fully composed. "Don't you want to cover all of your bases when it comes to her? Even if it's redundant, it can't hurt."

His conciliatory tone makes Dem back down. My brother shifts in his seat, his lips pursed, but then he gives Giorgio a nod. "Tell me what you manage to find."

Ras slaps Giorgio on the back. "You've gotten protective over Mari, huh? Your job's done, Napoletano. She's safe with us, and soon it'll be her husband's men watching her twenty-four seven."

Giorgio stiffens, and I halt mid-chew. Is Ras trying to get a rise out of him? My brother's right-hand man at times has a penchant for mischief, but I wish he'd drop it. I just want this conversation to end.

"Assuming Napoletano won't find anything damning on Matteo, securing this alliance should clear our path to Sal," Dem says.

Ras nods. "That asset seizure was an inspired move, Napoletano. Moretti and De Rosa are hours away from turning, I can feel it. With them, we have an in with every layer of Sal's protective detail except for his most inner circle."

"Calisto runs those men," Giorgio says. "And he's loyal to the bone."

"We might just have to brute force the last part," Damiano concludes.

Vale sends him an alarmed look. "I hope you're not planning on taking on an army by yourself."

"It'll be a dozen men at most," Dem says.

"Yeah, don't worry, Vale," Ras says. "When they see who's turned to our side, the smart ones will lay their weapons down. There will be less bloodshed than the time you sent me to ambush your psychotic sister."

Vale rolls her eyes. "You know, you bring up Gemma so often that if I didn't know you any better, I'd think you had a crush on her."

Ras laughs. "A crush? No, just a mild fascination at how someone can look so normal, yet be completely feral." He takes a slug of his wine. "How is she, by the way?"

"Still engaged," Vale says pointedly. "I guess we have a lot of weddings to look forward to after all of this is finished."

I cut into my steak. Does Vale know about their plan to let Giorgio kill Sal? Dem would tell her, I think. I wonder just how hard Giorgio had to argue to convince my brother to let him do it.

Anger spikes through me at the thought.

That's what he traded me away for.

My narrowed gaze lands on the man himself, and I notice he's not eating. His eyes are on me, but they're unfocused, like he's retreated deep inside his head.

What is he thinking about? Fantasizing about the moment he kills Sal?

Dem and Ras continue the discussion about their plans, but I don't care to listen anymore. I eat my food, finish my wine, and excuse myself from the table to go check on Sophia.

It takes me a few minutes to find her lying by the door that leads to the inner courtyard. She's looking longingly through the glass.

"Want to go out there?" I ask.

She perks up when I grab the handle of the door and trots outside once I get it open.

I sit down in the same chair I used earlier when Giorgio found me here before dinner and watch Sophia sniff around the bushes. She's limping, but her energy has returned.

My thoughts turn to my upcoming engagement. Whatever my husband will be like, I'll handle it. Dem was right at dinner. My time with Giorgio has changed me.

I fell in love for the first time.

Had my heart broken by a man for the first time.

I haven't quite figured out how to glue it back together, but I will.

Pulling out my phone, I tap on Imogen's name and write one last message.

I'll be married soon, my friend. My groom is someone I've never met before. You'd be horrified. You were always a romantic. But for someone like me, I think it's for the best. Turns out the one man that made me feel something doesn't want me, and something tells me I'll never find another one like him. So what does it matter who my husband is?

I tap send.

The message turns green. A second later, there's a red icon saying it's not delivered.

The number's been disconnected.

I hang my head. It was only a matter of time before this happened, but the red icon feels like one blow too many. A tear slides down my cheek just as the patio door squeaks open behind me.

The sound startles me. It's dark out now. I must have been out here for a while. I turn around, expecting to see Vale, but instead it's *him*.

He shuts the door behind him, slides his hands into the pockets of his slacks, and takes an unhurried step forward. His gaze falls to my cheek. "You're crying."

I use the back of my palm to wipe it away. "Trust me, it has nothing to do with you."

He looks down, shadows dancing over his face. "You read this guy's file?"

"Matteo's? Yeah."

"And?"

I tip my chin up. "I liked what I saw. After all, I agreed to marry him."

He grinds his jaw and then slowly lifts his gaze to meet mine. "Liar."

"You don't get to use that word in relation to anyone but yourself."

Something akin to a growl bursts out of his throat. "You will not marry him."

"This conversation is over." I make an attempt to brush by him, but his arm shoots out. He snatches me around the waist and pulls me against his chest.

"No, it's fucking not, Martina," he says, his mouth close to my ear.

I use all of my strength to shove him away. "What's the problem? You tossed me away like I was garbage, and now...

What is this? Are you jealous I'm going to give myself to Matteo? What did you expect me to do, become a nun?"

He advances on me. "You say his name one more time, and I swear the next time you utter it will be at his funeral."

A treacherous butterfly appears in my stomach even as I back away. "Get over yourself, Giorgio. You said it yourself. We're done." I glance over his shoulder. "You should move away. Dem might come out, and I know how scared you are of him. If he sees us here alone, he might get the wrong idea."

My back hits the wall, and he doesn't waste a second before closing me in with his arms. His chest heaves. "He's never going to be a good match for you."

"You weren't either, but we had fun together, didn't we? That's all you ever wanted from me."

He angles his head, as if he can't quite believe the words coming out of my mouth.

"Fun? What we had was madness," he whispers, his eyes wild. "Alchemy."

Electricity runs down my spine. "If it was madness, then I guess we've both finally regained our sanity."

"Not me."

Something softens inside my chest, something I desperately wish would stay as hard as stone. "You told me you don't want me."

"I never said that. I said that we're done, but I was wrong. I made a mistake. You're not something I can quit."

Don't listen to him. Don't listen to him. Don't—

But then his lips press against my throat, and my mantra disappears. He licks a trail from my collarbone to my ear, and I force the moan threatening to spill out back down my throat. "Stop it," I breathe.

"No."

My fingers tighten on his shirt. "We're done."

"Never." He moves to the other side of my neck, repeating the same movement with his hot tongue. It sets off a flurry of pulses inside my core.

When he pulls back, I meet his eyes. "What about your revenge?"

"I'll figure it out." He presses his lips to mine and then pulls back. "I'll have you both."

How? He really is insane, because this is lunacy. A desperate, reckless act. But no matter how I try to convince myself, I can't find the will to push him away. His scent envelops me. Our bodies connect, and it feels like coming home.

His tongue invades my mouth, sure and possessive. He drops one hand to cup my breast while the other cradles my nape. It's dark out in the courtyard because I didn't turn on the lights, but anyone can walk out here, and it wouldn't take them long to spot us.

"It doesn't work that way," I whisper as he drags a spaghetti strap down my arm and tugs my tank top to expose my strapless bra. "You have to let me go."

He makes an angry sound at the back of his throat and presses his forehead to mine. "I said I'll figure it out. There is no other choice."

Not waiting for my response, he presses his lips to the swell of my breast and then pushes my bra down. He darts out his tongue to my nipple. I moan, arching my back and giving him better access to the hard bud.

This is goodbye. We never got to say a proper one, so we have to do this now to put an end to our madness.

"You're mine, Martina. You will always be mine."

My eyes sting at his lies, but somehow, the heartbreak of this moment only heightens my pleasure. He moves to the other breast, lavishing it with the same attention, the same wanton desire.

Cupping my hand over his bulge, I rub him over his pants before I pull his zipper down and reach inside.

He groans, his erection twitching in my palm. When I swipe my finger over the tip, it's wet with precum.

"I will never stop wanting you," he says against my skin. "Never stop craving you. I was a fool to think otherwise."

You're still a fool. But I don't utter those words out loud, because I don't want him to stop. I want to feel him inside me one last time. I'll savor the pleasure of his cock and the way it's never failed to leave a delicious kind of ache. Tomorrow, that'll be my reminder of what we could have been.

He hikes up my skirt and rips my underwear, the sharp sound loud and clear in the quiet air of the patio. I drag my palms over his chest, his abs, his cock, trying to commit all the hard lines to memory before they become just that.

His lips find mine as he pushes inside of me. It's a good thing my legs are wrapped around his waist and he's holding on to them with a firm grip, because as he bottoms out, my body becomes jelly. My nerve endings buzz with pleasure.

He fucks me hard, as if he's trying to prove some kind of point. I know I'm right when he presses his cheek to mine and whispers, "He'll never fuck you like I do. Never make you moan like the world could be on fire and you still wouldn't tell me to stop."

I bite down on my bottom lip as my pussy trembles around him. He's right about that. I have nothing to compare Giorgio to, but somehow, I know deep inside my gut that no man will ever make me feel this good.

He reaches between us and finds my clit with his thumb. I press my face into his shoulder, muffling a groan with his shirt. The small circles he makes set off all the right sensations, as if I'm a game he figured out a long time ago.

"I'm close," I pant. "Don't stop."

"I don't plan on it, *piccolina*."

It's the nickname that does me in. I convulse against him as waves and waves of pleasure soak through me, right to the bone. He removes his hand, but only to move it to cup my ass. His thrusts speed up, and the cicadas are so loud they nearly drown out his groans. He buries his face into the crook of my neck. I gaze at the stars above us, and one falls just as he reaches his peak.

I should make a wish, but I don't know what to wish for. Maybe for time to rewind and take us back to the castle where this didn't feel so wrong.

If I expected this one last time to give me closure, I think I made a mistake. As Giorgio pulls out of me, I can't even meet his gaze. When he lets me down, I immediately clean myself up with my torn underwear, stuff it inside a pocket of my skirt, and move to leave. He zips himself up and then rushes to catch up to me. "Martina."

I shake off his hand, only for him to grab it again.

"Mari—"

"Leave me alone," I say, my voice shaking.

He doesn't. He pulls me into him, strong and unrelenting, and presses his lips to mine.

I'm so damn angry and *lost* that I don't hear the door behind me open until it's too late.

Someone sucks in a breath.

"Get your fucking hands off my sister."

CHAPTER 35

GIORGIO

DE ROSSI JERKS MARTINA away from me and whips out his gun.

I'm staring at a loaded barrel for the second time in as many days, and I have to admit, I deserve it this time.

I know how this looks.

I know what De Rossi will think.

"Did he force himself on you?" De Rossi grinds out from where he's standing a few paces in front of me.

Martina shakes her head, tears rolling down her cheeks. The sight of them makes my chest tighten with dismay. She said she wouldn't cry over me, but right now, there's no denying she's crying *because* of me.

It was selfish of me to take her like that, but I wasn't lying when I said I'd figure it out.

My mind's made up.

I'm not letting her marry that fucking Grassi.

"Dem, no. Put down the gun." She tries to take his forearm, but he swipes her arm away and pushes her behind him.

"What is this then?" De Rossi looks like he's half a wrong word away from putting a bullet in my head.

"We were..." Martina swallows. "We were putting something to rest."

Is that what she thinks we just did? No, that wasn't a goodbye.

When it comes to Martina, there will be no more goodbyes.

I made a terrible mistake yesterday. I was so angry at Polo and Sal for putting her in danger again that all I saw was red. The need to make them pay was all-consuming.

I wasn't thinking straight.

I was looking at the situation through matted glass, and it took De Rossi saying Martina was going to get married for the glass to shatter.

Suddenly, I could see everything clearly.

I've been pushing Mari away ever since I saw her, because the feelings she inspires inside of me are terrifying. I've never loved a woman before. How can someone who has never truly been loved know how to love another?

Maybe by learning from someone else.

I should have realized Mari was the one for me when she reacted to my story—this thing that's plagued me my whole life and made me feel so damn worthless. She listened and she reacted with kindness. With compassion. The man who killed her parents is a part of me. That should have been enough reason for her to recoil.

And yet she didn't.

Even the most broken of things can be mended by the right pair of hands.

Mari is mine. I might be lowborn. I might be too old. My name might not come with factories or an army attached to it. But I've spent my life solving impossible problems, and there's never been a more worthy prize than Martina.

Whatever I have to do to have her, I'll do it, because I know the truth now.

If she's not mine, nothing else matters.

"Is this what you've been doing with my sister the entire time the two of you have been away?" De Rossi asks, his voice low and deadly.

I run my tongue over my teeth. "Not the *entire* time."

He points the gun to the sky and fires off a shot. "*Fuck you*, Napoletano."

"Stop it!" Martina shouts. "Let's just go inside and talk."

He lowers the gun, moving his furious glare from me to his sister. "Go to your room."

"No, Dem, I can explain—"

"I said go to your fucking room, Mari."

Her eyes widen. I have a feeling he's never sworn at her before, and hearing him do it now momentarily stuns her. She swallows, her throat bobbing, then she lowers her eyes and nods. "Okay."

He watches her take the two steps to get to the door, and when she shoots me a look at the last moment, he snaps, "Do not look at him. Inside. *Now*."

The door slams shut, and then it's just the two of us. De Rossi assesses me, his jaw ticking. "This is why you were so insistent on checking Grassi yourself. Let me guess, you would have found something that disqualified him, whether it existed or not."

"Martina isn't marrying him."

"Like hell she isn't," De Rossi snaps. "You think it's up to you?"

"How do you think Grassi will react when I tell him his bride isn't a virgin?"

He throws a punch, and I let him land it on my cheekbone. Hurts like a bitch, but I earned it. Warm blood trickles down my face and drips onto my shirt. De Rossi moves to hit me again, but this time, I block it. "Enough."

"You won't be able to tell him anything if you're dead," he says, lifting his gun again.

"He won't give a fuck about the engagement in that case. Not if you've killed your best chance at winning this bid."

De Rossi laughs. "You think you've got a handle on everything, Napoletano. I thought maybe the situation with Polo would have humbled you, but it's clearly going to take more than that."

A cold sensation slithers down my spine.

"Calisto just called. Sal's so far gone that he lost it on his consiglieri. Insulted his family. Threatened to kill them all if

Calisto doesn't get him Martina. The kingdom is really imploding now, and Calisto is changing sides. Sal will be dead by the end of this week and it's going to be me who kills him."

My heart picks up speed. "The deal—"

"There is no more deal." He drops the gun but gets in my face. "Do you really think I'd trust you with something so delicate after what I just witnessed? You fucking lied to me. How long has this been going on for?"

"A few weeks."

He scoffs. "After you told me what you wanted with Sal, I thought I finally understood why you agreed to take Mari so quickly. But it looks like you had more than one motivation."

"I had no intention of anything happening when I agreed to take her."

"What the fuck happened then? You fell in love?"

I stare at him. It feels like a million worms are slithering under my skin, tight and uncomfortable. But I sit with the discomfort, and when it passes, something vulnerable appears.

This is what scared me all along. The feeling of wearing my heart on the outside of my chest, where everyone can see how it beats for her.

His eyes widen. "*Cazzo.*"

"So what if I did?" I ask quietly.

He whirls around, burying one of his hands in his hair. "No. No fucking way. You do not love my sister."

"She's not marrying Grassi," I say to his back.

He's shaking his head. "Jesus fucking Christ. I can't believe this."

"Damiano, wed her to me."

"Are you insane?"

"I know I'm not the man you envisioned for her. This won't be the alliance that secures your rule or increases your power. But if you truly love your sister, wed her to me. I will make her happier than anyone else. I promise you that." It's a bold statement given she just left in tears, and Damiano appears to have the same thought.

"You don't know anything about my sister."

"I know more than you think. We... We work well together."

"Then why the fuck did she agree to that marriage proposal, *stronzo*? She didn't have to think very hard about it either."

Because I fucked up.

"I pushed her away when I got here," I confess.

Damiano's lips curve into a bitter smirk. "Ah, now I see. You knew I'd be furious. You knew the deal you wanted would never happen if I found out. Did you tell Martina what you asked of me?"

"Yes."

"You chose getting revenge over her." He shakes his head. "My sister deserves better than that."

His words sting far more than the punch he landed on my face. "I didn't go about it right. If I could go back in time, I would handle it differently."

De Rossi's darken. "There's no need for time travel, Napole-tano. I'm giving you what most men never get—a second chance. You can make your choice again. I can let you kill Sal, or I can turn down Matteo's offer. What do you choose?"

"Turn down the offer and sign a contract promising Mari to me."

De Rossi makes a tight-lipped huff. "This isn't a negotiation. It's a binary choice. Whether my sister wants to marry you or not is up to her."

I grit my teeth. If I choose the latter, I could lose it all, Mari and Sal. But if I choose the first option, I'll lose Mari for certain.

And that's not an option.

I always thought I'd find peace when I avenged my mother, but now I realize I was wrong.

The only time I've ever felt peace was when I was with Mari.

I suck in a deep breath. "Kill the engagement."

Locking myself in the bathroom, I examine my cheek. There's a dried streak of blood that disappears beneath the collar of my shirt, but otherwise, De Rossi didn't do much damage.

I run cold water over a towel and use it to clean myself up, if only to not scare Martina when I talk to her.

The guilt I thought I might feel over my choice doesn't come. I felt far guiltier when I treated Mari coldly a few days ago than I do now.

Why was I so fixated on avenging my mother? I've never talked to a shrink, but one would probably tell me it has something to do with proving to her that I'm not as bad as she thought I was.

But she's dead. I have nothing left to prove to her.

I do have something to prove to Martina, though.

My eyes drift to my reflection in the mirror. Will she forgive me?

Something crashes in the distance, so I quickly dry my face and step out of the powder room.

Raised voices can be heard coming from De Rossi's office. It doesn't take me long to recognize Mari's.

"This was my choice to make!" she says, her voice muffled by the door.

I'm halfway to it when Valentina appears and blocks my way. "Don't go in there yet."

I peer at her over my nose. "Move out of my way."

She crosses her arms over her chest and doesn't budge. "You'll only make her angrier."

Since she's clearly been eavesdropping, I ask, "What has De Rossi told her?"

"That the engagement is off, and that you've asked for her hand."

"I should be there for this."

She shoots her hands out and wraps them around my wrist. "She said no."

"To what?"

"To your proposal," she says, like it should be obvious. "What did you think was going to happen? You told her you wanted nothing to do with her *yesterday*. Now you want to marry her?"

"What I said to her yesterday was a mistake."

"Uh-huh. And how does she know you won't change your mind again and say something else tomorrow?"

"Because I won't," I mutter, but in truth, I'm starting to see her point. "I'm trying to fix it."

"By going to her brother instead of telling *her* how you feel?"

"What would you have me do?"

She pokes my chest, making me back farther away from the office. "Give her space, for one. She survived another attack on her life, agreed to an engagement, had it cancelled, and now she has another proposal to consider? I know made men aren't strong on empathy, but can you imagine how she feels for one damn second? She's got whiplash from it all." She pokes me again. "Let. Her. Breathe."

Something else shatters in Damiano's office. Valentina glances over her shoulder and shakes her head. "Dem isn't any better than you at the moment. He was so angry about catching the two of you, he didn't think at all about how he should deliver the news, so he just dumped it on her."

Just then, the door bursts open. Mari flies out, giving me nothing but a glimpse at her tear-streaked face.

"Mar—"

She whirls around on me, her nostrils flaring, and her eyes throwing daggers. "*You*. How *dare* you? You told me it was over. You broke my fucking heart!" Her palms shove against my chest. "And you know what? I was dealing with it. I chose a new path. Maybe it wouldn't have given me a perfect life, but it would've given my life some meaning. Who gave *you* the right to take that away from me?"

Her anger makes the blood drain from my face. "Mari, you shouldn't need to compromise. You deserve a perfect life."

"And that's a life with you?" She throws her arms wide. "This? Does this seem perfect? Fuck you, Giorgio."

She whirls around and flies in the direction of her room.

I move to follow, but Valentina jumps in front of me.

"Don't," she hisses. "She doesn't want to talk to you right now."

I watch her hurry after Mari, and when they disappear, I glance over my shoulder at De Rossi.

He's staring at me with a mocking smirk, and I can practically read his thoughts.

You've lost control.

Now what?

CHAPTER 36

MARTINA

My SECOND MARRIAGE proposal is followed by some of the longest days of my life.

I don't leave my room.

I don't allow anyone except for Sophia and Vale inside it either.

My sister-in-law somehow knows exactly what I need. She doesn't force conversation or share information I have no interest in knowing.

Which includes everything to do with Giorgio.

We don't speak his name. We don't even allude to his existence.

But erasing him from our conversations is much easier that ridding him from my mind.

I do my best not to think about him, but it's a difficult task. How is it possible to destroy something that we built over the course of weeks in a matter of days?

He wanted me, then he didn't, then he did again. And Dem just let him toy with me like that?

What do they all think of me? That I'm just some game piece they can move around the board at will? A few months ago, I may have let them get away with it, but not now.

Not after what I lived through.

I don't feel numb anymore.

That terrifying emptiness inside my chest after Imogen's death? It's all filled in. Somehow, I've managed to pack it full of conviction and a desire to focus on the future.

I've healed. And I've sure as hell earned the right to decide my own fate.

Why do neither of them understand that?

This is day three since the incident in the courtyard. No, day four. I can't be sure. I'm curled up in an armchair with a book, although I haven't processed a single word I've read in the past fifteen minutes. Vale sits across from me, flipping through a magazine.

When I have to go back a page for the tenth time, I decide I'm just not in the mood to read.

"Has Dem done this to you too?" I ask.

Vale lifts her eyes off her magazine and arches a questioning brow.

"Made decisions for you," I explain.

She huffs a laugh. "He tries. He rarely succeeds."

"I guess I've always let him get away with it."

"He'll learn. In fact, I think you're well on your way to ensuring that he does."

Flipping through my book, I blow out a breath. "I'm just so annoyed with him. I thought I finally had a chance to help him by accepting the proposal, and it feels like he threw it back in my face. It couldn't have been all that important if he was so willing to call it off."

Vale folds her hands in her lap and gives me a gentle look. "It was important, Mari. But at the end of the day, your happiness is more important to him."

"Happiness? What does that have to do with anything? I'm sure I'd make it work with Matteo," I mutter even as my stomach clenches uncomfortably at the thought.

"I think Dem didn't want to risk tearing you away from someone who—" She clamps her mouth shut. "Someone who might be important to you."

"What were you about to say?"

"Nothing."

"Vale. What were you about to say?"

"I thought we agreed not to mention *him*."

I slam the book shut and toss it onto the coffee table. "It's been three days, and he's still living here. I can't pretend he doesn't exist forever. Tell me."

Vale drags her teeth over her bottom lip, as if carefully considering her next words. "It's not my place to say, but I know you won't drop it, so... The night everything happened, Giorgio told Dem he loves you."

Something tight and painful appears inside my chest. I don't want to believe it, because if I do and it turns out to be false... "Dem must have misheard him."

When Vale doesn't say anything, my eyes start to burn, and I whip my head around to hide my tears.

I said I wouldn't cry over him, but I already broke that promise. I cried when I left Dem and Giorgio on that patio and ran inside the house, my heart utterly broken. The way he took me against the wall—desperate and wild with grief— told me everything I needed to know. He wanted me, but *not bad enough.*

Not bad enough to choose me over his revenge.

When I talked to Dem next, he told me I was wrong. He detailed the new agreement they'd made. He explained how Giorgio was willing to walk away from Sal if it meant he had a chance with me. But Dem said that at the end of the day, the choice is mine.

I said no.

I understand now why some people actually prefer arranged marriages where feelings don't play a part. A marriage that's more of a business transaction than anything else is a much simpler endeavor than a union founded on love.

I don't know much about love, but given my recent experiences, it seems like a pretty shaky foundation for something that's supposed to last a lifetime. Giorgio walked away from me once. How do I know he won't do it again? How can I marry someone I don't trust?

"If he loved me, he wouldn't have treated me like he did."

Vale sighs. "Love is complicated. I mean, your brother tied me up in the basement and—" She coughs. "Well, no need to get into the details, but needless to say, it wasn't the kind of thing you'd expect at the beginning of a typical courtship."

"How did you move past it?"

"I... Well, it took me a while. When I watched you two interact and saw how much he loves you, I understood why he got so upset when he thought I may have been involved in your kidnapping. He didn't trust me. I didn't trust him either. But even after all that, we both felt a connection we couldn't ignore. So we opened up to each other and rebuilt that trust." She lifts her feet up to the edge of the chair and wraps her arms around her knees. "Do you feel a connection to Giorgio?"

Picking at my nails, I struggle with my answer. I want to say no, but then I'd be lying. Whatever I felt the first time I saw him is still there underneath the layers of hurt, rejection, and heartbreak. "Yeah. We spent a lot of time together when we were in his castello."

Vale gives me a sad smile. "Do you want to tell me about what happened there?"

I fold my lips over my teeth. Sigh.

And then I do. I tell her everything.

When I'm done, Vale hands me a tissue and takes one for herself, dabbing it under her eyes. "Wow. That's a lot, Mari. A whirlwind. It sounds like he tried really hard not to succumb to his feelings for you."

I blow my nose and toss the tissue into the trashcan. "He did."

"Why do you think that is?"

"He told me it was because he couldn't risk breaking Dem's trust. Otherwise, he'd never get Dem to agree to give him Sal." I huff out a breath. "He said other things too."

"Like what?" Vale asks.

"I think he never felt like he was a worthy match for me. He was sure Dem would never allow us to be together, that he'd want to marry me off to someone with a more powerful name."

Vale tsks at that. "Your brother is not marrying you off to anyone against your will, of that you can be sure. He'd never do that to you, and if he lost his mind and tried, I promise you I'd set him straight."

I give Vale a grateful look and reach over to squeeze her hand. The marriage Vale's parents forced her into was a living nightmare, and I know she wouldn't let anyone put me in a situation like that.

She squeezes back. "Well, I guess Giorgio's changed his mind, huh?"

"Looks like it."

"Based on what you told me about him, I think he's been very afraid."

My brows shoot up. "Giorgio? Afraid?"

"Yes. I think it was easier for him to push you away than to embrace the strong feelings he has for you and risk not being able to keep you because of things outside of his control. Do you see how that would really hurt him?"

I gnaw on my lip. Giorgio is a control freak, that much I know. "So this was his way to stay in control of the situation?"

She nods. "And when he found out you were going to get married to someone else, and that he was on the brink of losing you, he finally realized that he couldn't live with that outcome. He took a leap into the unknown. Look at what's happened since he went after you. Dem found out about you two, Giorgio lost his chance to kill Sal, and he messed everything up even more with you. He unleashed chaos on his life. He must be feeling extremely uncomfortable right now."

"As he should," I grumble, but her words settle over my skin like a cool breeze.

She's right. Giorgio put everything on the line to keep me. It might be the first time in his life that he's done anything like it.

"He's been leaving you letters," Vale says carefully.

This snaps me out of my thoughts. "Where?"

"Just outside the door."

"How many?"

"One each day. I wasn't sure if I should give them to you, since you said you didn't want to talk about him."

"Have you read them?"

She frowns. "Of course not. They're yours. I can give them to you if you want to read them." After a moment, she adds, "Or we can burn them in the fireplace."

I scoff and glance at the unlit hearth.

Would it hurt to take a peek at just one of them?

"I'll take them."

Vale nods and lifts out of the armchair. "Let me grab them from my room."

When she opens the door, Sophia trots in and curls into a ball at my feet. I bend down to scratch her behind the ear. Weird. She has a bow wrapped around her neck. And is that a new collar?

She used to have a black leather one, but this one is red, and there's a tag in the shape of a heart. My heart picks up speed when I read the inscription.

"Sophia De Rossi. If found, contact her owner, Martina De Rossi."

My eyes pop wide. Giorgio's giving Sophia to me?

I slide down to the ground beside her and reread the inscription a few times to make sure I'm not imagining it.

When the words stay the same, I wrap my arms around Sophia and peck her on her furry head. A traitorous butterfly flutters inside my belly before I will it to get on its way. This is a nice gesture, but Giorgio isn't going to be able to gift his way to forgiveness.

"If he changes his mind about this, I won't be giving you back," I tell Sophia.

She twists her neck and gives my nose a lick.

"I'll take good care of you," I promise her. "You won't even remember him after I give you the royal treatment for a few months."

Vale returns with the letters and places them on the bed.

I point at the bow on Sophia's neck. "Did you know about this?"

Her lips quirk up before she gets them under control. "I may have overheard something. I'm going to go check in with Dem. He wanted to talk to me. Are you two going to be okay here?"

"Yeah, of course."

"I'll come back with dinner," she says and shuts the door behind her.

One of Sophia's new toys—a mouse plushie—peeks out from beneath the armchair. I grab it and toss it across the room. It's her new favorite game. As expected, she perks up and runs to bring it back to me.

I rest my head against the edge of the armchair and throw the toy a few more times.

The next time I do it, Sophie ignores the toy and comes to sniff the letters lying on the edge of the bed.

She knocks them to my lap and sits down beside me, giving me an expectant look.

"Hey, you can't play both sides. You're on my team now, girl."

When my words have no apparent effect, I let out a sigh and glance down at the small stack of letters. They're bound by a black rubber band. My name peeks out from beneath it, written in Giorgio's handwriting.

It seems silly to just keep staring at them. Now that I have them, I know my curiosity won't let me leave them unopened. I take off the rubber band and open the envelope with the oldest date.

I haven't seen much of Giorgio's handwriting besides stumbling onto a few notes written in the margins of various tomes in his library. The script is elegant and has an unexpected flare.

Dear Martina,

I can't remember if I've even said I'm sorry. I am. I'm so fucking sorry. If we were having a conversation in person, I imagine you would ask me what I'm sorry for. The list of my wrongs is long, and writing them down will be painful, but it has to be done. I'll write them one day at a time.

I'm sorry I didn't give you the comfort you needed after Polo's attack. In truth, it was far easier for me to lose myself in fantasies of vengeance instead of being there for you. When you called me from the castello and told me what had happened, I learned the meaning of fear for the very first time. Knowing that you were in danger while I was hundreds of kilometers away and unable to physically help you was excruciating. I couldn't take a proper breath until I caught my first glimpse of you here, safe with your brother and sister-in-law, and when I did, I think some part of me rebelled at the thought of ever going through something like that again.

I told myself I was doing the right thing by pushing you away. The world will be a better place without Sal Gallo in it. But of course, Sal will be gone one way or another, and I understand now that I don't need to be the one to do it. Killing him won't fix my problems. No, I have to do something far more difficult to accomplish that. I have to look at the man I am and face the demons that have caused me to make so many mistakes when it comes to you.

Giorgio

I reread the letter twice before I carefully fold it and slide it back in the envelope. My heart is racing. I'm sweating. I get off the floor and wring my hands, unsure of what to do with myself.

That felt...honest.

Scarily so.

Giorgio's not good at talking through his emotions, but apparently, he's more than capable of explaining himself in writing.

The thought of his terror at knowing what was happening to me and being too far away to help softens me. Of course I knew he was worried. I heard it in his voice over the phone, but terror is an altogether different emotion. It's reserved for mere humans like myself, not someone like...

Ah, yes. I guess beneath that handsome face, fine suit, and facade of permanent control, he's made of the same stuff I am.

The stuff that makes us human.

And humans do stupid things when they're terrified. I know that better than most.

I eye the two other letters on the floor, equal parts curious and apprehensive. What else will he apologize for? How else will he soften the hurt?

Puffing out my cheeks, I blow out a breath and decide to wait before I read the next one. I don't think I can handle another one right now.

I take a bath, and when I come out, Vale is back in my room. She's sitting on the edge of the bed.

She flicks her gaze up to me from her phone, and I immediately know something's happened.

I hurry to her. "What is it?"

Her eyes are wide and worried. "They all just left. Dem, Ras, Giorgio."

My stomach falls. They left without saying goodbye.

"They—"

"They've gone to finish Sal."

Oh God. What if something happens? Dem will be well defended, but what about Giorgio?

Blood stalls inside my veins, turning my body icy cold. The idea of never seeing Giorgio again hits me like a truck, and it's unbearable.

He has to return.

I sink down on the bed beside Vale and bury my face in my palms.

CHAPTER 37

GIORGIO

THE TERRAIN IS rough in this part of Caserta. We drive for a long time over a bumpy dirt road before turning onto a highway dotted with potholes. We're about fifty kilometers from the location of one of Sal's safe houses. Calisto sent De Rossi a tip that Sal will be spending the weekend there with about thirty guards. With Calisto's help, I was able to hack into the cameras and determine their positions, so the two cars full of De Rossi's soldiers driving ahead of us will clear most of them before we even arrive.

I eye Ras's hands on the wheel of the Mercedes—hand actually. He's using his other one to type out a text, only half-paying attention to the road.

"Hands on the wheel or let me drive."

He flicks his gaze up to mine in the rearview mirror. "What are you? Our safety police?"

"Would be a shame if De Rossi died in a car accident on his way to Sal because you were too busy typing out a lame sext."

He rolls his eyes and tosses his phone down on the console. "I'll have you know the lucky few who've received my sexts called them erotic masterpieces. I'm thinking about publishing a book."

De Rossi chuckles. "Is that what you plan to do in retirement?"

"Sure." Ras smirks. "Not like that's happening anytime soon, so I have plenty of time to collect new material."

Retirement. A strange concept when it comes to men like us. Made men don't retire. We die. Some lucky few who get too old for the game are given a chance to disappear into obscurity, but it's rare.

I've never really thought that far into my future until recently.

For the last few days, I've noticed the strangest thing. When I think of what's to come after this business with De Rossi is done, the only thing I see is Martina's face. If I force myself to exclude her, I see nothing.

She's the only thing that matters now.

It's a shame it took me so long to see it.

I wanted to say goodbye to her before we left, but I decided not to at the last moment. She hasn't left her room since she screamed at me in front of her brother. I don't think she's read my letters either. She's still angry, and I want to give her space, even though it's killing me to be apart from her.

At least I have all the motivation I need to get back to De Rossi's in one piece.

I adjust my cufflinks and gaze out the window.

We're getting close now.

Our phones ping with status updates every few minutes from the cars ahead, and so far, everything's going smoothly.

Too smoothly if you ask me.

Calisto turning on Sal was something few would have ever predicted, but I have a feeling Sal's paranoia could have extended to his right-hand man, especially after their argument.

If Sal has set some kind of a trap, we'll know it soon.

After another ten kilometers, the side of the road turns dense with foliage.

De Rossi peers out toward the trees. The closer we get, the quieter he is. If there's anyone who hates Sal as much as me, it's Damiano, and I suspect his head is as heavy with memories as mine was a few days ago.

I've managed to let go of them since.

Now, all I seem to think about is Martina.

"I'm going to dance on that fucker's grave," De Rossi mutters, his elbow hanging out the window, and his fist pressed against his lips.

Ras pulls over and gives his guy a call. "Are you in position?"

I assume the answer he receives is yes, because the next word out of his mouth is, "Engage."

The first shots are fired.

Sal's not going to be the only person to die tonight. We're not taking any prisoners from his squad. Those men have been with him for a long time, and nothing good would come from keeping them alive.

As shots ring out in the distance, we climb out of the car and pop the trunk to get all the equipment. Bulletproof vests, knives, guns, ammo. I can't remember the last time I was armed to the teeth like this, but the occasion warrants it.

While De Rossi is going to be squeezing the life out of the don, Ras and I will need to make sure no one comes to the fucker's rescue.

When we're ready, we get back into the car and move much slower than before. Soon, we see bodies littering the driveway.

"I counted twelve," Ras says when the house is in sight. It's surprisingly modest by Sal's standards—the man likes to show off his money—but I suppose that's the kind of sacrifice you have to make when you're fighting for your life. A one-story concrete building, bulletproof windows, armored doors.

"Fourteen," I correct him. "You missed two lying by the trees."

"They're clearing the back of the property now. We should wait until we get the green light."

De Rossi shakes his head. "Let's go. If he's got an escape tunnel in there, I don't want to give him enough time to crawl through it."

We hop back out, our weapons pointed and ready. The crew did a good job here, so we reach the front door without getting into any scuffles.

Ras and De Rossi step aside for me to take a look at the mechanism on the door. I frown. We've got a problem on our hands.

"Get back. *Now*."

To their credit, they move without a word, trusting me to know what I'm doing. When we're a safe distance away, I turn to them. "Door is rigged with explosives. It'll blow if we tamper with it without disengaging the mechanism first."

"Tell me you know how to do that," Ras says.

"I know how to detect them, but I'm not an explosives expert. We need to look for another way in."

De Rossi nods. "I'll call Calisto. He might know of a weak point."

"I'm going to check the perimeter to see if there's anything I couldn't see on the camera feed." There has to be another way in.

I keep my gun close as I round the house and make it to the backyard. De Rossi's guys are all over it, but they're too busy with Sal's men to help. I press my back against the wall and take it all in. There's no back door, and the windows aren't big enough to squeeze through even if we could get through the glass.

That's when I see it. A patch of grass just ahead of me that's got a slightly different hue than the rest.

I run to it, get down on my haunches, and drag my hand around the perimeter. The handle is hidden, but the bite of its cold metal surface is impossible to miss. I jerk on it a few times until I feel it shift. On the next tug, it swings open.

Below is a dark tunnel that disappears into the ground.

I send a message to Ras and De Rossi, telling them where to go. Then I climb down into the shaft.

It's not deep, and my shoes hit what feels like packed dirt only moments later. The tunnel splits in two directions, and it's easy enough to work out which one leads to the house.

I move aside to let De Rossi and Ras descend the ladder. "If Sal ran as soon as he heard the shots, he would have passed this point by now," I say. "We should follow the tunnel out." I'm sure that's where he went. He doesn't want to die, even if he's rapidly running out of options.

"Let's go," De Rossi says.

We move as fast as we can, given this thing is fucking tiny and we all have to run crouched over. Thank God, it doesn't take too long for light to appear ahead. Judging by the length of the tunnel, its purpose is simply to get Sal to a vehicle hidden nearby, so that he can use it to escape.

When we burst out into the woods, my hunch is confirmed.

"He's there!"

Sal's barrel-shaped form is just ahead and he's running for his life. We book it after him, but fall back when a shot rings out.

"He can't have many men with him," Ras says from behind a tree. "Nearly all of his guys were back at the house."

"Fuck it," De Rossi snarls. "I'm ending this."

He runs low to the ground even as shots sound through the air. It's reckless, but I can imagine how he feels being so close to victory.

Ras and I follow.

There's shout. Another shot.

We burst into a clearing and finally find our target.

Sal is crouched behind a fallen tree trunk, peering at us with a gun in his hand. Beside him is another man.

Polo.

My vision bleeds red. So Sal took him in after all. Does Polo know he's cannon fodder?

Looks like I'll be getting a kill tonight after all.

"It's not too late to surrender, gentlemen," Sal calls out as we take positions behind some trees.

"Three against two," De Rossi says. "You're finished."

Sal laughs. "Odds can turn quickly. Giorgio, I have to thank you for the part you played getting me in touch with my son. We've spent a lot of time together over the last few days, and I have to say, Polo's impressed me with his ambition. I'm sure he learned it all from you. We've been talking about how we'll do things differently if we get a chance to really shake up the organization."

"You can handle this like a man," De Rossi shouts, "or you can die like a cunt. Choose quickly or I'll make the choice for you."

"Giorgio, son, don't forget we're family," Sal shouts. "Come to my side. It's not too late. Do me this favor, and we will rule the Casalesi together. Me and my boys."

"Your boys lie scattered all over the driveway to your house, and Polo will join them soon." There's no point in mincing my words. "You're both fucking dead."

"Gio! Don't do this!" that traitorous fuck dares to shout. His head pops up from behind the tree. "I'm sorry, I didn't mean for things to get so ugly with Martina. Forgive me, brother. We all make mistakes, don't we? Let's start over."

He's never called me brother before. Does he think that word means anything to me?

"Polo, you're a fucking piece of trash," I bite out. My gaze moves to Ras by my side. "We have to go around them, take them from the back."

He nods.

We move quickly, but Polo and Sal catch on. They abandon their positions and start running deeper into the woods.

"They're splitting up," I shout to Ras. "I'm going after Polo."

I hope he feels the terror Martina must have felt when he was chasing her. By now, he must realize there's no way he's making it out of here alive.

We exchange a few bullets and miss. The foliage is too thick. I see flashes of him between the branches up ahead, and since I don't want to risk losing him, I barrel through until he comes into full view.

He whirls around, points his gun at me, and shoots.

I jump aside, but it grazes my arm, spearing pain through it. When I return fire, I aim at his knee, and he goes right down.

"Fuck!" he shouts, his voice ravaged with pain.

I walk until I'm towering above him. Blood is dripping down my arm, staining the gun in my hand. I take in his shriveled form and feel a flash of disgust.

"I didn't mean for it to go this far." He pants, his panicked eyes fixed on my face.

I step on his hand, working a scream out of him. "Sucks being on the losing side, doesn't it? You know, before you betrayed me, I was considering putting a word in for you with Damiano. I was going to ask him to take you on."

That glance at a future he's never going to get now makes his expression twist with hatred. "You had everything I've ever wanted. If you'd shared willingly, I wouldn't have been forced to try and take it from you."

I crouch down and take him by the collar. "I had *nothing* but hatred and pain. Nothing until *her*. And you dared to try to harm her."

He chokes beneath my grip. "I'm sorry!"

"Sorry. How fucking sorry were you when you slit Tommaso's and Allegra's throats? Two years, they lived with you. Two years, they treated you like you were their own. And you killed them for a delusion." His eyes bulge as I tighten my hold on him with each word. "I don't think you're sorry at all for what you've done. You're only sorry for failing to accomplish what you tried to."

Polo jerks his arm, and a sharp pain shoots through my leg. I let go of him and look down to see a knife sticking out of my thigh.

He coughs, grabbing his throat with his hands and trying to get back up despite his bad knee.

I lift my gun and point it at his head.

His eyes meet mine.

"Gio—"

The gunshot echoes through the air.

CHAPTER 38

MARTINA

WE HOLD our vigil in the living room.

I'm bundled up under a blanket on the couch, while Vale sits straight-backed on a chair, her eyes glued to the dark screen of the phone lying on the coffee table.

"There should be news soon," she says as if to reassure herself.

"Dem will call you when it's done."

She sucks in her lips and shakes her head. "I should have gone with him."

"You know he'd never have let you."

"I'm just so stressed out. It feels like it's been days since they left, not hours."

I know exactly how she feels. Anxiety prickles beneath my skin as I worry about Giorgio. The moment Vale told me they left, some of my anger melted away.

Temporarily, remember?

Yeah, that's what I've been telling myself. He'll be on the hook again if he returns in one piece, but for now, I don't have enough space left in my heart for anger. It's filled with an anxious ache that won't ease until they're back.

I pat the spot on the couch beside me. "Come here."

Vale glances over at me. "I can't. I have too much nervous energy. I'm going to walk around." She takes the phone with her and heads outside.

I'm tempted to follow her, but I decide not to in case she wants a moment to herself. Glancing around the room, I exhale a heavy breath. Then I reach behind the pillow and pull out the remaining two letters.

My mind goes to the place I've been trying to avoid.

What if Giorgio gets hurt? What if he dies?

An unimaginable sorrow permeates my chest. Flashes of our last encounter on the patio stream through my memory, this time colored in an even harsher light.

We weren't good to each other that night.

It feels like a terrible end to something that was beautiful at one point.

He was my first kiss, my first love.

Was or is?

Even despite what happened, I can't lie to myself.

I want to see him again.

I take one of the envelopes and tear it open.

. . .

Dear Martina,

Today, I thought about the first time I kissed you in the kitchen back in the castello. When I snapped out of it and realized what I'd done, I was horrified, but for the wrong reasons. I was afraid I'd hurt you, yes, but I was also worried you'd reveal what happened to your brother and damage my relationship with him.

I was wrong about many things, including Damiano. We've had a chance to speak more these past few days, and he's made it clear that he'd never put his political aims above you. It's made me respect him more. It's also showed me that I projected my own insecurities onto you. I came up with all these external reasons why we could never work, but the real reason has always lived inside of me.

I didn't think I was good enough for you. I thought that once you knew my history and who I really was, you wouldn't want me anymore. And when you said you still did...I didn't believe it. I was sure it was a fluke, and that one day, you'd wake up and come to your senses.

I'm sorry.

That's why I pushed you away.

I let my fear guide me.

I promise you, I'll never let fear guide me again.

Giorgio

I pull my bottom lip over my teeth. Vale was right when she analyzed him earlier. He's starting to get it. He's seeing his mistakes.

435

But is it enough? Does he truly understand everything he's done wrong?

Well, there's no point in leaving the last letter unread.

Dear Martina,

The days that have passed have given me clarity. I was so angry when your brother announced you'd accepted Grassi's proposal. Furious at Damiano, at that fucker Matteo, at you, at myself. I was so lost in that desperate anger that I didn't consider you may've had your own reasons for agreeing to that marriage. My instinct was to assume you were doing it out of spite. I am a vengeful person, and I forget that you are not at all like me in that regard.

Now, I think I understand your motivations better. You love your brother, and you knew the marriage would help his cause. I think you wanted to make a sacrifice for him. A gesture of your love and commitment.

I'm sorry for taking that opportunity away from you, but I'm not sorry for breaking off your engagement. Matteo would never be good enough for you. He would have dimmed your light, and I couldn't allow that to happen. Not when I've seen how bright you can shine.

I love you, Martina. To call you my wife would be my life's greatest honor. But I shouldn't have tried to ensnare you by making a deal with your brother. I'm so sorry. You are not an item I can negotiate for, and I promise I'll never treat you again as such.

So I'm doing now what I should have done all along.

Marry me, piccolina. I'm asking you, only you.

The letter falls out of my hands just as Vale bursts into the room. "Mari! Dem just called!"

I rise off the couch, my heart in my throat. "What did he say?"

"Sal's dead. Dem and Ras are okay," she says, her eyes watering, but I can't tell if it's from sadness or relief.

I take a step forward. "And Giorgio?"

When she scrunches up her features, the floor falls from beneath me.

No. Please don't say he's—

"He's hurt."

A weakness unlike any I've ever felt before washes over me, and I crumble to the ground. Through my blurred vision, I see Vale run to me.

"Mari!" Her palms wrap around my shoulders. "He'll be okay. He's getting medical assistance now."

"What happened?" I can barely hear her over the sound of blood rushing inside my ears. I can't lose him.

"Polo was there. They fought. Giorgio...killed him."

I swallow. So Polo still went to Sal after he left the castello. He sealed his fate by doing that. Giorgio would never have let him live.

Not after what he did.

"It sounds like Giorgio was injured in the scuffle," Vale says.

"Injured where?"

"His leg, I think."

"How bad is it?"

"I'm not sure. Dem didn't give me too many details. But he didn't sound too worried."

Does that really mean anything? My brother has other things on his mind besides Giorgio. I want to scream. "Why didn't you ask more questions? Why didn't you give me the phone?"

Vale helps me up and pulls me into a tight hug. I think she's afraid I'll sink to the ground again, but the shock is already wearing off.

"I'm sorry. I should have asked. He was speaking so fast. I could barely get a word in, and then he had to run. He said he'll call me back."

A tear slips down my cheek as I clutch onto her. "Giorgio can't... He can't die."

"I know. He won't."

Marry me, piccolina. I'm asking you, only you.

It's not fair. I want to hear him say those words to me, and now he might never get the chance.

I pull away from Vale. "I want to go to them."

She shakes her head. "We can't. We have to wait here. Dem was explicit about it."

The phone in her hand rings, and when she lifts it, we both see my brother's name.

Vale picks it up. "Hello?"

"Ask him how Giorgio is!"

She nods. "Uh-huh. Okay, I understand. We'll be on the lookout. How's Giorgio doing?"

I watch her facial expressions as she listens to the response. When her skin grows paler, something breaks inside of me. I grab her biceps and start shaking her. "What is it?" My voice doesn't sound like my own.

"He got shot, but it's just a graze," she says.

Shot?

I let go of her and take a few steps back.

When you called me from the castello and told me what had happened, I learned the meaning of fear for the very first time.

And now it's my turn.

I thought I knew fear by now. We'd met on more than one occasion. But it's never been this cold, this desolate before.

Vale says goodbye to Dem and turns to me. "Mari—"

"I need to be alone."

She opens her mouth to argue, but I cut her off before she utters a word. "Just for a while. Please."

She bites down on her lip, then nods.

My feet carry me upstairs, all the way to Giorgio's room.

His bed is messy and unmade, just like it was back at the castello. I sit on the edge and press my face into his pillow, searching for his familiar scent.

It's there.

And it fills me with longing so profound that in that moment, I secretly forgive all the ways he's hurt me.

"Please live," I beg against the pillow, my tears staining the fabric wet. "Come back to me so that I can give you grief. So that I can tell you all the ways you need to make it up to me. So that I can tease you and tempt you until you can do nothing but give in."

I cry for a long time, my chest vibrating with anguished sobs. At some point, Sophia comes in and climbs onto the bed beside me, pressing her warm body against mine. She licks my face as if she knows I need to be comforted. I scratch her behind the ear and sit up against the pillows on Giorgio's bed.

My gaze catches on the book lying on the nightstand.

I reach for it even though I already know what it is from that raggedy cover.

My copy of *Jane Eyre*.

It's more worn than the last time I saw it, and when I imagine him reading it while lying here alone in bed, my eyes prickle. Did he think about me as he read the passages?

I flip through the pages and then press the book against my chest.

～

It's past three am when I hear cars pulling into the driveway. I rush over to the open window and look out at the three black SUVs.

My brother steps out first.

I make a little sigh of relief, but I already knew from Vale that he was fine.

It's Giorgio I need to see.

He doesn't keep me waiting long. Another door opens, and Ras helps him out of the car.

My breath catches at the sight of him. He's limping, and his arm and leg are bandaged up, but he's okay. Despite his injuries, he looks formidable. I catch a glimpse of his profile illuminated by the moonlight, and something clicks into place inside my chest.

His face is fixed into a stiff expression as he says something to Ras. Is he in pain?

I want to run down there, but I hold myself back. He just killed a man—his half-brother—he's injured, and he needs to rest. This isn't the time to have our confrontation. For hours, I've been telling myself that all I need is for him to get back safely. He's here.

The rest can wait.

I wait until I see him enter the house before I reluctantly return to bed, but sleep won't come, and eventually, I decide to read.

I pick up my copy of *Jane Eyre*—I took it back from his room —and open to somewhere near the middle of the book.

"I had not intended to love him; the reader knows I had wrought hard to extirpate from my soul the germs of love there detected; and now, at the first renewed view of him, they spontaneously revived, green and strong! He made me love him without looking at me."

A shiver runs through me.

Can it really be a coincidence that the first words I read match what's in my heart? Or is it a sign?

A sign to move forward and step into a new chapter of my life?

I nearly lost Giorgio tonight. During moments like that, forgiveness comes more easily, but it's not just that that's made me soften. It's his letters. His words and thoughts spoken openly and honestly.

He wants to be with me.

In the end, he chose *me*.

I close my eyes and let it all sink in.

Inside the nightstand, I find a pink highlighter and run it over the passage just as there's a knock on the door.

"Come in."

Giorgio steps in. His jacket is missing, his shirt stained and half-undone. My eyes fall to his pants. They're ripped and bloody.

And still, the sight of him makes warmth spread over my cheeks.

"Oh my God. You shouldn't be up." I jump off the bed. "You're hurt. Did anyone treat your wounds?"

He takes a hobbled step inside and closes the door behind him. "It's nothing, Mari. I needed to see you."

My arms link with his, and I lead him to sit down on the edge of the bed. He's warm to touch.

"You're running a fever." I press my palm against his forehead.

"They gave me something to bring it down."

"Gio, you need to rest. Lie down."

He follows my direction, his tired eyes glued to me. "Sit close to me."

I scooch over and sit cross-legged by his side. He places his palm over my knee, and his warmth seeps through my leggings.

It feels so damn right.

"How are you feeling?" I ask, covering his hand with mine.

"I've felt better," he says softly. "But I'll be fine in a day or two. It's just a few scratches."

I brush my fingers lightly over his leg, and a white bandage peeks out through the rip in his pants. It's stained with blood. "You're still bleeding. Did Polo do this?"

Darkness seeps into his gaze. "Yes. He tried to fight me, but at the end, he paid for what he did to Allegra, Tommaso, and you." His voice is hard, and it matches his expression.

"That couldn't have been easy," I say softly. "He was your brother."

"No, Mari. He was nothing to me after what he did. Killing him was justice." He glances away. "We are not defined by

443

whose blood runs through our veins. We're defined by our choices. His were exceptionally poor. I won't miss him." He closes his eyes.

I've never seen him look this tired. After a few minutes, I think he may have fallen asleep, but when I shift slightly, he cracks his eyes open.

"Don't leave. I know things aren't right between us, but just for tonight... Please, don't leave."

"I won't." I pick at my cuticle before I meet his gaze again. "I read your letters."

Surprise flashes across his expression. "You did?"

"Mm-hmm."

His jaw works. "What did you think?"

"You seemed apologetic," I say mildly.

It makes him crack a smile. "I'm glad that came through."

"And they explained a lot about what was going on in your head through it all."

His smile fades away. "I did wrong by you, Mari."

"Yeah, you did."

He swallows, like he's waiting to hear what else I have to say.

"But I guess I would be a hypocrite if I expected you to act perfectly in every situation life throws at you."

Something like hope flickers in his eyes.

"You hurt me, Giorgio, and those letters alone haven't fully erased that hurt. But after tonight, I realized just how much I still care for you. Knowing you were injured threw me into a fit. I couldn't imagine never seeing you again." My fingers twine with his. "I couldn't imagine never holding your hand again."

He makes a choked sound. *"Piccolina..."*

I take the book off my nightstand and hand it to him. "Open on the earmarked page."

He does, and his eyes scan the highlighted text. The tension in his face eases. "And now you teach me the meaning of true happiness," he says, his voice hoarse. He lifts himself onto his elbow and cups my cheek. "I love you so damn much, *piccolina*."

"I love you," I whisper. "And I'm willing to give us another chance. But let's take it slow. Let's be together and enjoy each other without any secrets or lies casting a shadow over us. Let's not jump into marriage just for the sake of it. After everything that's happened, let's take our time."

Understanding swims in his warm gaze. He drags his thumb over my bottom lip and nods. "However long you need. You are worth the wait."

He wraps his palm around my nape and gently pulls my face toward his. Our lips meet. The kiss is different—slow, steady, intentional. He slips his tongue into my mouth, and he makes a satisfied sound in the back of his throat, as if he's been waiting for this. The kiss spreads a familiar kind of warmth through me, and my body is soon buzzing with pleasure.

"Not a day will go by without me reminding you what you mean to me," he murmurs. "That's a promise."

I smile against his lips. "I'll hold you to it."

EPILOGUE

TWO MONTHS LATER

MARTINA

Reader, I married him.

We didn't do it right away, but it turned out I wasn't really interested in being patient once we were finally, officially, undoubtedly together.

After Sal's end, everything moved quickly. We left the safe house the day after and drove straight to Casal, where the capos pledged their loyalty to my brother. Not all of them, of course, but enough to cement his claim in stone. We settled down there for a few weeks while Dem handled negotiations, promotions, and the restructuring of the organization. It gave me the perfect chance to reconnect with the place where I was born.

Giorgio and I moved into a house next door to Vale and Dem's. It was a temporary arrangement. We didn't want to make any permanent decisions while everything was in flux, including where we would live. Of course, Dem made his preferences clear—he wanted me close to him—but when I told him I missed Ibiza, he pursed his lips and said he understood.

One evening, about three weeks after we arrived in Casal, my brother called me and invited me to come over. Said he wanted to talk to me about something. When I got to his house, the living room was full of fabric samples and papers etched with designs for a wedding dress.

"This will be Vale's?" I asked, picking up one of the sketches.

Dem stood leaning against a wall, his hands in the pocket of his slacks. "Yes. We want to have our proper wedding sometime next month. Her family is making their travel arrangements."

They were already married, but their first wedding was practically an elopement, with only Ras, Gemma, and I in attendance.

"Even her parents?"

He sniffed. "Yes, even them. I told her we didn't need to invite them, but she wanted to. She said she wants them to see how happy she is now that her life is in her own hands."

Vale's relationship with her parents is strained, but I get the sense that she doesn't want to cut them off completely. Maybe because of her concern for her younger sisters, or maybe because she believes they can mend things to some extent down the road. At the very least, I know she's developed some sympathy for her mother.

One night, after a few glasses of wine, Vale got a bit emotional and told me she felt sad that her mother had never known unconditional love. Maybe that's why she never showed it to her kids. It sounded like her mom had spent her life being devoted to her ruthless husband, doing whatever necessary to ensure his continued rule. Wiping away her tears, Vale said she was grateful that her and Dem's kids would know what it's like to have parents who love each other.

"Will you have the wedding here?" My eyes skated over the elegant design. The fabric looked light and breezy, perfect for a beach wedding. My eyes widened at the realization. "Hold on. Ibiza?!"

Dem smiled at me from across the room. "Yes. Initially, I wanted to do it at the basilica in Naples where our parents got married, but it turns out it's undergoing a restoration. We don't want to wait for it to be finished, so we're thinking of going back to Ibiza. Actually, that's why I called you. We want to get married at the cathedral, and we'll probably do the reception at one of my restaurants, but some of the smaller events will be at the house. Would that be alright with you? We don't want to trigger any bad memories."

I give him a smile. "It won't. We spent a long time in that house together, Dem. I have a lot of fond memories there, and one bad one. I have no intention of letting Lazaro's attack spoil the house for me. Is Vale okay with it?"

He nodded. "It was her idea."

I laughed at his crooked grin. "All right. Well, then it's settled."

That night, as I lay beside Giorgio, I couldn't sleep. In my mind, a movie of a wedding played out, but it wasn't Vale and Dem's.

I saw Giorgio and myself on the big lawn outside the house under a grandiose flower arch. Our hands were linked as a priest read out our vows against a backdrop of azure-blue water. I love that color. I spent my youth swimming inside of it, and it's also the color of Giorgio's eyes.

The movie kept playing, and at three am, I woke Giorgio up.

"What is it, *piccolina*?" he asked groggily.

"Let's get married."

That woke him up properly. He sat up, blinking sleep out of his eyes. "When?"

Right to the point. It made me laugh. "I don't know. But soon. And I want to do it in Ibiza."

"Your brother is also getting married in Ibiza."

His mind must have still been foggy with sleep. "I know. I was the one who told you that a few hours ago, remember?"

"You want a double wedding?" he asked, as if that wasn't a ridiculous question.

I hit him with a throw pillow. "Are you crazy? Of course not. I don't want to steal his and Vale's limelight."

Giorgio grabbed the pillow out of my hands and threw it to the floor. "It makes sense. Everyone is already flying down."

I frowned at him. "So we do it because of efficiency? How romantic."

Giorgio paled. "That came out badly. It's not what I meant."

My frown softened. He's treated me like a queen since we almost broke up, and I can see in his eyes that he loathes

449

upsetting me. "Don't worry about it. But no, I think we should wait. I want Vale and Dem to have their special day."

He did have a point, though. Everyone was coming down...

"What if we space it out by a few days?" Giorgio offered, his tone carefully neutral.

"You mean like we get married a few days apart?"

"Yes. A weeklong celebration. It would give us time to rest in between."

I brought my nail to my mouth. "That actually sounds...kind of fun."

"You'd be able to plan everything with Vale."

"I already told Dem I'd help with the planning," I said, running through the idea in my head. "I mean, I wouldn't mind, but I'm not sure Vale and Dem would be fine with it. Weddings are a big deal. They're individual. Special."

Giorgio folded his arm beneath his head. "Why don't you mind it then?"

"Because Dem and Vale are my closest family. Sharing the celebration with them would be special in its own way."

Giorgio smiled. "Why don't you ask them? See what they say?"

So I did.

And they loved the idea.

Vale squealed and dragged me into a hug. "So you and Giorgio are ready?"

"Truthfully, I think we've been ready for a while," I said once she let go of me and I was able to breathe again. "It all kind of fell into place quickly once we moved in."

"You seem happy," Dem said, his lips tugging into a smile.

"I am happy. Giorgio makes me happy."

Vale sighed. "This is the best news, Mari. Of course, we love the idea."

"Are you sure?" I asked as I carefully studied their expressions. "The thought is Giorgio and I get married at the house on Wednesday, and then you and Dem on the Friday as you were intending. The days in between will give everyone time to recover. But really, we won't be offended if you say no. We don't want to intrude."

"You couldn't even if you wanted to," Vale said, linking her hand with Dem as if to show me they're a united front. "I love it. When I was younger, Gemma and I would always fantasize about having a joint wedding. It seemed like double the fun."

I smiled. "Yes, I think it's going to be a lot of fun. A weeklong party."

Vale squealed again. "I'm going to see if my sisters can come for the entire week. This is going to be fantastic."

And so that's how we ended up on Ibiza a month later under that flower arch I imagined.

Giorgio slides a slim gold band onto my finger as I blink away a sudden wetness in my eyes. When it's my turn to do the same, I glance at him, and warmth spreads through my chest at the look in his eyes.

Adoring. Possessive. Reverent.

When the priest tells us we can kiss, Giorgio places his palm along the side of my neck and drags his thumb over my jaw as he pulls me closer. Our lips touch, and he whispers, "Mine."

A shiver runs through me. We kiss in front of everyone who matters. Everyone who has a say in this new world my brother has created. And as Giorgio's tongue slips inside my mouth, and he deepens the kiss, I know the message is clear.

I'm his.

And he's mine.

GIORGIO

I have a wife.

She's beautiful and clever and never fails to keep me on my toes. Sometimes, when I look at her, I have to blink a few times to convince myself she's real. Even in my dreams, I was never so bold as to imagine myself with someone like her.

Reality is an audacious thing.

The dinner starts shortly after the ceremony, and Martina and I are seated at a table with De Rossi, his wife, her siblings, Ras, and Ras's parents, who've seen Mari grow up.

I last fifteen minutes before I whisk Martina away, taking advantage of some idiotic sparring match that breaks out between Ras and Gemma, Valentina's sister. While everyone is distracted, I take Mari's hand and pull her out of the tent.

We stumble into the first bedroom we can find.

"Gio, they're going to notice," she says as I lick a trail up her neck.

"Let them." My hands sink into the silky fabric of her wedding dress, and I hike it up before lifting her into my arms.

She wraps her legs around me and kisses the side of my throat. "We're married," she says against my skin. "God, I can't believe we're married."

My fingers slide into her hair—it tumbles in soft curls down her back—and I pull back to meet her eyes. "My wife. Fuck, I need to be inside of you."

She blushes, her eyes growing hooded with lust. "I like it when you call me that."

"I'm going to call you that for the rest of your life."

I lower her onto the mattress before I get on my knees at the foot of the bed. When she realizes my intention, she tries to pull me up, but I catch her wrists and press them down at her sides.

"Gio, there's no time," she protests.

My teeth scrape over her thin lace panties. They're nearly transparent, and when my tongue brushes over her clit, she arches her back.

"Oh..."

I bite down on the fabric and rip them off her with my teeth.

She gasps and pushes up on her elbows. "Did you just...?"

Her earthy scent hits my nose, and I groan, pressing my face against her pussy. I feel starved for her. I always am.

Martina moans as my tongue disappears between her folds. "We need—oh God—we need to get back to the party."

I give her a long, slow lick and glance up. "They're having their appetizers. I'm having mine."

She giggles, but the sounds morphs into a desperate groan when I wrap my lips around her clit and suck. I alternate between sucking and teasing her clit in steady strokes, just the way she likes it. I've studied all her likes by now. All her wants. I don't think I'll ever get tired of seeing her surprised expression when I do something new that makes her toes curl.

"Oh fuck, okay, I'm going to—" Her fingers tug on my hair, and her thighs clamp around my head. "Ohhhh…"

I slip two fingers inside of her just as she explodes and feel how she flutters around me.

"Gio, I want you," she pants. "Come here."

My belt comes off. She sits up and helps me pull down my zipper, her hands frantic and desperate. When she looks up at me, meeting my gaze, I feel something shift inside my chest.

"I love you," she whispers as she wraps her arm around me and pulls me closer. "I love you."

We hold each other's gaze as I sink into her. Our hushed gasps layer on top of each other. "*Piccolina*, you are my world." My lips press to the upper swell of her breast. "You are everything."

Flesh on flesh. Soft, languid kisses. Her heels pressed into my thighs. When she comes for the second time, she mewls and throws her head back, her eyes squeezed shut.

She unravels me. My release roars through me moments afterward, and I collapse against her body, pressing my face into the crook of her neck.

When we untangle a few minutes later, she eyes the ripped panties and sends me a reproachful look. "You go. I'm going to get another pair from my room."

I kiss her temple. "Don't take too long."

She makes a show of peeking outside the door before slipping out, as if we'd get in trouble if we're caught.

As she disappears down the hall, I run my hand through my hair and discover it's a mess. I should probably fix it. Not that I care if everyone in attendance knows I just fucked my wife, but she might, and I don't want to embarrass my *piccolina*.

I dip inside a small bathroom I used the last time I was here and stand in front of the sink.

It seems like forever ago. Years, not months.

A lot has happened since I was here to pick Mari up, but in the last few weeks, everything has more or less settled. De Rossi is the don. Ras is his second in command, and I've been appointed as his senior advisor on matters of security.

There are a few loose ends. Nelo and Vito, the two idiot brothers, disappeared without a trace in the confusion after Sal's death. I told De Rossi not to worry. The two of them don't have enough braincells combined to evade our men for long. They must have gotten help from someone, though, because no matter how hard we've looked, we haven't found any hint as to where they went.

They evaporated.

Wiped blank.

A part of me suspects they were killed, but without their bodies, we can't be sure.

We decided to let it go for now, since there are more pressing concerns. Like smoothing things over with the Algerian suppliers that De Rossi cut out in the beginning of the war.

I finish adjusting my hair and put my thoughts about work on the back burner. Now that we're married, I'd much rather steal Mari away and spend the evening alone with her, but the party is important for *piccolina*, so I'll play along.

When I step out of the bathroom, I hear someone arguing.

Two voices talk over each other from a room down the hall, and my body moves closer out of habit.

"Look, all I'm trying to tell you is that you have a choice."

Valentina. I guess Mari and I weren't the only ones who snuck away during dinner.

"Vale, enough," Gemma, her sister, says. "You only make it worse by constantly bringing it up. I'm marrying Rafael. It's settled, and I'm fine with it."

"But you don't even know him."

"So what? This is what I've expected my whole life."

"That doesn't make it right or normal."

"We aren't normal. We sacrificed normal to be powerful."

"*We* didn't do anything. Our father did."

"You say that like you're making some kind of a point. We're a family. A fucked-up, messed-up family, but a family nonetheless. Papa's made it clear that my marriage is important for our family's survival."

Valentina makes a frustrated sound. "I don't understand. I thought that after you found out what they did to me by marrying me to Lazaro, you'd stop being so blindly loyal."

"What they did to you was a horrible mistake. They both acknowledge it now. You know that, right?"

"Father only acknowledges it because Damiano forced him to. His apology to me was said through gritted teeth."

"He's proud, but deep down, he knows what he did was wrong. And Mama cries in her bedroom at night. One time, I went to her, and she told me she'll never forgive herself for putting you in that situation."

"I don't believe her. She suspected what was happening, at least in broad strokes. She knew Lazaro wasn't right in the head. When I tried to give her the details, she wouldn't listen."

"You know she's never gone against Papa. She didn't know how to change anything."

"God, Gem! I'm not ever going to forgive them, all right? I feel sorry for Mama, I do, but it's not enough for me to excuse her for her role in all of this."

"Fine. I won't try to change your mind. Now, do me the same courtesy about my upcoming marriage."

Valentina sighs. "There was a time when you weren't okay with marrying a Messero."

"Maybe I've grown up since then. I was there when Tito, our cousin, died. You weren't. They brought him to our house while he was bleeding out, and I held his hand as he took his last few breaths. I've seen what perceived weakness can do to our family, how it makes our enemies foam at the mouth. My marriage to Rafael will ensure things like that won't happen again. So just stop it, okay? I'm fine with my decision. I don't need you to try to make me feel bad about it."

"That's not what I'm trying to do."

"It's what it feels like. Now can we please get back to dinner? Your husband will worry about you."

"Will yours?"

Gemma doesn't answer. I duck into the shadows as they pass right by me, and a few moments later, I follow behind them. Gemma turns into the kitchen, while Valentina continues outside.

I knew Valentina's father, Stefano Garzolo, was on shaky ground in New York, but the way Gemma spoke about it makes the situation seem far worse than I would have thought. I catalogue the conversation and make a note to bring it up to De Rossi after the end of the festivities.

When I step outside, the appetizers are being cleared away. Despite Mari's worrying, no one except De Rossi seems to have registered our absence. He shoots me a glare when I sit back down, and I arch a brow in response.

He has no ground to stand on. I'd bet my right arm he and Valentina will be disappearing throughout their wedding dinner as well.

When Mari slides into the chair beside me a few minutes later, she grasps my arm and leans into my ear.

"Oh my God, you won't believe what I just saw on my way back down from my room," she whispers conspiratorially.

"What?"

"I was thirsty, so I decided to pop into the kitchen for some water, but someone was already there. *Making out.*"

I huff a chuckle at her excited tone. "Okay...who?"

She moves closer until her lips brush against my ear. "Gemma and Ras."

My eyes widen.

Well, isn't that interesting.

~

BONUS SCENE

Giorgio teaches Mari a lesson ;)

Sign up here to receive it by email:
https://www.gabriellesands.com/thelesson/

ACKNOWLEDGMENTS

This book would not have been written if it wasn't for some amazing people in my life.

Number one is my husband, who is my rock, my biggest supporter, and the best person I know. Babe, you always encourage me to dream big. The process of writing this book was a bit of a rollercoaster and you were with me through all the ups and downs. Thanks you so much for being who you are.

Number two is my amazing critique partner and work wife Skyler Mason. You helped me make Giorgio into his delicious alpha self and made this book sparkle. Having you with me on this crazy journey has been one of the best parts of becoming an author. You inspire and motivate me. Never change!

And number three is my editor Heidi. Every time you edit for me, I become a better writer. I appreciate you and your expertise so much. Thank you for helping me wrangle the crazy stories in my head into something well structured and readable.

Also, a special shout out to my incredible designer Maria and my badass PA Lorna. You ladies are amazing and I'm so happy to have you on my team.

Last but not least, a huuuuge thanks to my incredible readers. Your excitement for When She Tempts completely blew me away. I hope this book was everything you were hoping it to be! Giorgio and Martina have a very special place in my heart. Thank you for reading and for supporting me!

Love,

Gabrielle